LADY IN DISGUISE

"Miss Beacham, do you know what lies east of Winestead, where you say you made your home?" he asked in the tone of someone about to spring a trap. She was looking at his face upside down as he lay in bed and could not discern his expression, which was just as well.

"Why, of course, Your Grace. I—"

"East of Winestead, my dear, is the North Sea!"

"Ohh!" she moaned.

"Methinks 'tis not a Lancashire lady at all that we have here, but a Scottish lass, whose name is undoubtedly *not* Rose Beacham!"

His voice had grown harsher and she jumped up, pushing the chair back. She turned to run but felt a strong, firm hand close about her left wrist and pull her back.

She squirmed, but he was too strong for her. He yanked her down until she fell forward and somehow found herself seated on the bed next to him. He did not let go of her wrist; she stared at his naked arm and that portion of his chest that was visible where the comforter had slipped down. She swallowed hard.

"Now," he said in a voice of deceptive softness. "You may begin by telling me who you are, where you come from, and what the *devil* you are doing at Milburne Hall!"

SCOTTISH ROSE

Janis Laden

ZEBRA BOOKS
KENSINGTON PUBLISHING CORP.

Also by Janis Laden:
   Sapphire Temptation
   A Noble Mistress
   Whisper of Scandal
   Bewitching Minx

ZEBRA BOOKS

are published by

Kensington Publishing Corp.
475 Park Avenue South
New York, NY 10016

Copyright © 1989 by Janis Laden

First printing: October, 1989

Printed in the United States of America

For Abigail,
my third daughter
and everyone's joy . . .

"The daintiest last, to make the end more sweet . . ."

—William Shakespeare
King Richard II

How fair yon English roses be,
Their honeyed scent doth beckon thee;
Gaze, lad, upon each petal soft
And hold each ripened bud aloft.
Thus, many flowers have I known,
Then left, to make my way alone.

Until one blossom didst me call
And held me in its fragrant thrall;
Beware the rose of Scotland, lad,
Whose nectar near to drove me mad,
Whose petals I but once caressed
And found myself fore'er possessed.
                    —Sir Issic Mariner

Chapter 1

Reginald Ayres, Duke of Milburne, handed the reins to his groom and descended easily from his elegant traveling coach. Before him stood the stately portico of Milburne Hall, his principal seat. It had taken him nearly two days to travel from London to this remote corner of northwest Devon, and he was glad to be home. He straightened his crisp white cravat as he marched up the gravel drive to the long flight of stone stairs, and flecked a bit of dust from his nearly immaculate coat of navy blue superfine.

He was always careful to maintain a sober, correct stance when he entered Milburne Hall, in the hope that by setting an example he might be able to instill some degree of decorum into his rather harum-scarum brood of siblings. There was, he knew, a new governess in residence. He hoped that at last his mother had found someone who could maintain order, and school his brothers and sisters appropriately.

When he'd left a month and a half ago, a Miss Pritchard had been shivering in her stout black shoes every time the ten-year-old twins, Timothy and

Thomas, had come within shouting distance. And before that there had been tiny little Miss Talwin, blind as a bat and unable to tell twelve-year-old Letty from seventeen-year-old Phoebe! The twins she'd not even attempted to distinguish! His mother, God bless her loving, trusting soul, was much too dotty to govern the children at all. And Phoebe was a hen-witted beauty in the tradition of her mother.

Whoever said the country was quiet? he wondered, already missing the hushed tones of White's and the measured, reasonable voices of his fellow botanists in London as they conferred on the formulation of the new periodical, *Journal of Botanical Research*. The duke still did not know how, at the age of twenty-nine, he'd come to be named editor of the *Journal,* but there it was. And much as he would have preferred to remain in London, or to go jaunting off to Iceland again to collect specimens, he had responsibilities here in Devon. And Reginald Ayres was never a man to shirk responsibilities.

And so he took a deep breath as he ascended the last step before the fluted Doric columns of the Hall and raised his hand to the knocker. Blast it all, why did he have to sound the knocker at all? Why hadn't the door swung open and Underwood announced his arrival at once? At the very least, a pair of footmen should have scurried to flank his ascent of the stairs. Really, this household of his was the outside of enough! How, he wondered, had his very proper father put up with it all?

Not a moment later the great carved mahogany doors swung open, whereupon His Grace the Duke of Milburn was greeted simultaneously by a smiling butler and a flying red ball. The duke groaned inwardly even as he ducked his head, narrowly escaping collision

8

with the whirling object. Well, nothing at all had changed in his absence, he noted, and watched in resignation as Timothy scrambled past Underwood in pursuit of the wayward ball.

So intent was the boy that he did not look up, nor notice to whom the spotless Hessians and fine buff-colored pantaloons belonged. His Grace merely shook his head and proceeded into the huge marble-floored entry lobby. Obviously, the new governess left something to be desired.

Underwood relaxed his proper, impassive countenance as he divested the duke of his hat, gloves, and cane. "It is good to have you with us again, Your Grace," the butler said, his smile reaching his dark eyes. His white moustache and thick white hair were carefully groomed, and he stood erect, his tall, lean frame undaunted by his years. But the duke heard more than mere pleasantry in Underwood's greeting. He heard the distinct note of relief.

He raised one blond eyebrow. "How goes it here, Underwood?"

The butler's countenance settled back into its impassive mask. "Everyone is . . . well, Your Grace," he said formally.

Reginald's lips twitched despite himself. "I was not inquiring as to anyone's health, Underwood, as I assume I should have heard had anyone taken ill, but rather as to the state of affairs at present. To wit, we do, do we not, have a new governess in residence?"

Underwood lifted his prominent chin a trifle higher. "Er, yes, Your Grace. As you say."

"And?" probed the duke.

"And, er, I am certain Your Grace will wish to repair to your rooms before greeting the duchess. And the, er, governess, of course," the butler responded in an uncharacteristic rush of words.

"What manner of woman is she, Underwood?"

"The, er, governess, Your Grace?"

"Never mind, Underwood," the duke replied, expelling a sigh. What hope, after all, could there be for a governess whose every mention must be preceeded by an "er"? He *would* proceed directly to his chambers to remove his travel dirt, and then seek an interview with his mother.

But as he strode through the lobby toward the wide circular staircase, he was distracted by a suspicious commotion coming from above. Perhaps from the drawing room, he thought. But who would be there at this time of day?

Steeling himself, he stalked across the marble floor and up the great staircase to the gallery above. The unmistakable sound of giggles and childish patter emanated from all the way down the gallery to his left, where the large circular drawing room stood looking down on the stately south lawns of Milburne Hall. Shaking his head, he turned and strode forward.

The drawing-room doors were open and the duke's eyes widened in shock at the sight before him. For in the center of the huge room, sprawled atop one priceless Jacobean chair and a large overstuffed powder blue sofa, were his ramshackle siblings. Or that is, most of them, Timothy having fled in pursuit of the ball. Thomas and Letty seemed to be on their knees on the sofa, their arms resting on its intricately carved frame as they leaned over its back and eagerly shouted words of encouragement to someone, or something, below. Phoebe, in the chair, joined in the rather agitated chorus that seemed to be shouting, "Come on, Desdemona!" Whatever was beneath the sofa was shielded from the duke's view by the ornate marble pedestal that held his mother's prize Derby vase.

Riveted momentarily to his spot, he let his eyes quickly scan the room. His lips tightened as he noted no less than three overturned chairs and a veneered Pembroke table leaning precariously against the eighteenth-century harp. He padded silently across the massive Oriental carpet to where he could see just what the attraction was underneath the sofa. And then he stopped short and blinked to clear his eyes and make sure he'd seen correctly.

For there, protruding from beneath the curved wooden frame at the back of the sofa, was a lovely, supple, well-rounded, female derriere. It certainly did not belong to his mother, and as it was clad in a fine midnight blue fabric, it could not belong to Cook or one of the housemaids. And it certainly could not belong to the housekeeper, Mrs. Longbotham, who undoubtedly had been born with a posterior quite a bit larger. And so the duke was forced to surmise that the lovely bottom belonged to none other than the new governess. The one who'd been hired to school his siblings in proper decorum.

Oh Lord, he thought, and in the next moment swallowed hard as that derriere wriggled further under the back of the sofa. He tore his eyes away just in time to see Letty slide down to the floor in front of the sofa. "Desdemona! You must come! You may not tear at the carpet that way! Oh, dear! Beachie, *do* something!" Letty squealed.

Whereupon the duke of Milburne, standing rigidly erect, finally cleared his throat.

"Oh, dear!" wailed Phoebe, turning pale as a ghost as

she saw him, and jumped up from the chair.

"Whatever—Lud! It's Reggie!" shrieked Thomas, slithering immediately from the sofa to stand beside Phoebe.

"I've got her!" exclaimed a deep, musical voice from under the sofa.

Phoebe had the grace to look stricken, but Thomas's attention was immediately diverted as, slowly, that lovely bottom made its way out from under the sofa. "You did it, Beachie! You're a Trojan!" he proclaimed, leaning once more over the back of the sofa as "Beachie," her back to the duke, slowly stood up. She was cradling something Reginald could not see in her arms.

"Naughty Desdemona!" Thomas scolded, reaching out to pet whatever Desdemona was. "Tearing at Mama's priceless antique carpet like that, and clawing at the draperies in the morning room. . . ."

"Beachie" murmured some flummery at the creature, and Letty joined Thomas at the sofa. Out of the corner of his eye, the duke saw Phoebe gesticulating to Beachie, but as soon as Reginald's eyes swung to her, Phoebe developed a sudden itch at the back of her neck.

"Ah, Beachie, ah, you . . ." Phoebe stammered, growing whiter by the minute.

"Ahem." Reginald, hands clasped behind his back, feet apart, cleared his throat again.

The room fell silent immediately and Beachie whirled round. A pair of large, midnight blue eyes widened in shock and dismay, but she did not, as he might have expected, drop the black and white bundle of mischief in her arms. Rather, her expression changed a moment later to one of barely suppressed merriment.

"You must be the duke," she said. "We were not—

Ugh! She scratched me!" she cried, whereupon Desdemona leapt from her arms and scampered off, Beachie, Letty, and Thomas in tow. Only Phoebe lingered long enough to cast an apologetic glance at the duke.

"Welcome home, Reggie," she said uncertainly, before she, too, joined the fray.

Desdemona led them all a merry chase round the enormous circular room, under and over countless chairs that lined the walls, behind the blue damask draperies, and atop the keys of the beautiful Broadwood grand pianoforte. Then the tiny feline, for so the duke was now able to identify that ball of fur, sprang onto the already teetering Pembroke table. Letty squealed, the table clattered against the harp, and the kitten fell back against the strings, creating a most disjointed chord as the harp itself wobbled precariously. At that point Beachie grabbed the harp, Thomas reached for the table, and Phoebe snatched up Desdemona.

And then they all suddenly became aware of the duke once more. He stood immobile, his face impassive, arms akimbo. Phoebe ventured a look at him and quickly lowered her eyes, cooing softly to the wayward kitten.

"Take her to the kitchens, Phoebe," Beachie said, and his seventeen-year-old sister scurried away without a backward glance.

It was at this point that Beachie stepped forward, the others having fallen silent. "Welcome home, Your Grace," she said in her rather deep, musical voice. She swept one graceful hand up to try to repair the disarray of her thick auburn hair, and he noted a smudge of dirt on her rather resolute chin. Why the devil was she so unconcerned? Why was she not trembling in her shoes, as a proper governess ought? "We weren't expecting you just yet," she added, a most irreverent twinkle in her eye.

"Obviously," he said dryly, torn between anger and a sudden urge to laugh aloud.

Suddenly she extended that same slender, graceful hand to him for all the world as if they'd just met in some elegant ballroom. "I am Rose Beacham, the new governess," she said graciously and for a moment he found himself staring at that hand.

It was beautiful, smooth, and white, its fingers long and slender. But a *hand,* after such a display? Not a curtsy, nor a bowing of the head, nor ... Suddenly remembering his manners, he took the hand in his, meaning to let it go perfunctorily.

But he didn't. For her hand was not at all what one expected of a governess's. Not, of course, that he had any notion what a governess's hand *ought* to feel like. For never had he had occasion to clasp the hand of the nearly blind Miss Talwin nor the highly strung Miss Pritchard. But surely a governess's hand ought not to feel quite so soft and delicate, nor so warm as to send a spurt of heat through his arm. ...

It was the look of confusion in her eyes that recalled him to himself. Abruptly he released her. "I see you are quite at home here already, Miss Beacham," he said with careful civility. "I think perhaps we had ought to have a little chat. Straightaway, if you please, in my study." He caught a flicker of apprehension in her eyes and thought it all to the good. Then he turned to Letty and Thomas.

"You will adjourn to the nursery. Now," he commanded quietly, and then strode from the room, only to collide headlong with Timothy, who was still chasing the red ball.

Susanna did not know where the duke had gone, for he was not in his study when she reached it. But the door was open and so she stepped a bit warily over the threshold. She had been here many times before, of course, searching for books for the children. It was a cozy room, with its comfortable furnishings, the obviously well-read tooled-leather volumes lining the walls, the smell of beeswax and lemon oil always lingering in the air. She had ofttimes wondered what sort of man inhabited this room, but now she was not so sure she wanted to know.

Susanna took a deep breath to compose herself. Pehaps he *was* a bit formidable, but she had expected no less from the children's descriptions of him. Perhaps he *was* a bit miffed at the minor brouhaha in the drawing room, but surely he could see that no harm had been done. Desdemona had simply become a bit too playful.

The duke's image rose in her mind. It was his eyes that she remembered most clearly from their brief encounter. They were clear and gray and piercing, the eyes of a man who would brook no nonsense. But she reminded herself that she had done nothing wrong; she would not act as if she had. She had the schoolroom well under control, which, she'd been told, it hadn't been for quite some time before her arrival.

Why then, did she feel so nervous? Why was she pacing the room? Stop it, Susanna! she chided herself. She was doing her job, one for which she was eminently qualified. If she had not come to it by the most

15

unexceptionable of means, well, what did that signify as long as the children were well taken care of? She halted her pacing and schooled her expression to one of calm. She must never give the duke reason to think she doubted her own right to be here. She must not show undue fear. She was Rose Beacham, governess, and she must act the part.

The duke's humor was none too improved as he made his way to his study. He'd given her enough time to precede him there. The door was ajar and he expected to see her standing before his desk, wringing her hands nervously.

He stopped short on the threshold. For what he beheld was not a cowering governess who'd just come very close to being turned off, but an elegant young woman perusing his bookshelves for all the world as if she were a guest given the run of his library!

"Miss Beacham!" he exclaimed, coming into the room.

She did not jump, or cringe in the slightest, but pivoted gracefully to face him. She stood to the right of his carved mahogany desk, he some five yards away, and for the first time he took a good look at her. Those large midnight blue eyes gazed back at him all too innocently, yet with a certain humor lurking in their depths that took him aback. A governess, as his father had told him countless times, ought to be sober and stern, a model of rectitude.

This governess had hair that was much too lush and thick, of a rich shade of auburn that hinted at a temper not at all appropriate. And for all the hair that had been pulled back into a respectable chignon, it was by now most *un*respectably disheveled. Her eyebrows, of the same shade as her hair, were finely arched high above her eyes, adding to her enchanting, wide-eyed look. Her long lashes, a tad darker than her brows, did not once sweep down modestly, and the lovely pink flush on her sculpted, high cheekbones seemed permanent, not at all the result of discomfiture. Her chin was held a trifle too high, and he squelched a sudden urge to wipe the smudge of dust it held.

Unwittingly he took a step forward, his eyes sweeping her length. She was tall, just a few inches shorter than he, with full high breasts and a small waist that emphasized the enticing swell of her hips. Her high-waisted blue jaconet muslin dress, though modest enough in design with its long sleeves and high neckline, hugged her curves in such a way as to lose all claims to modesty.

He forced himself to swallow. *This* was a governess? Good God! She was much too young, and beautiful, and well dressed, and—

"Your Grace." Her voice interrupted his reverie. "You have a marvelous Shakespearean collection, I am persuaded. The annotations are excellent," she commented.

"This is evidently not the first time you've been here," he said wryly.

"Why, no. I naturally assumed that as governess you would wish me to make use of *all* possible resources available here at the Hall." Before he could reply to that ridiculous assumption she added, "And, of course, I've brought the children in here. To look at the globe." Her graceful hand fluttered in the direction of the large globe that stood on the rosewood table beside the French doors.

"I believe there is a perfectly good globe above stairs in the schoolroom. I hardly think—"

"A very *pretty* globe, I grant you," she interrupted. She *interrupted him!* He could hardly credit it! "But sadly out of date, I fear. I do believe the map of Europe has been redrawn since the Congress of Vienna. Not to mention the problem of North America. The globe in the schoolroom shows the thirteen British colonies, but we fought a war over those, I am persuaded, and lost, if I do not mistake the matter. And then there was the purchase of the Louisiana Territory and—"

"Never mind, Miss Beacham," he interjected. It occurred to him fleetingly to wonder how she had made such headway with his siblings as to be concerned with any congresses or purchases at all; certainly no other governess in recent memory had. But he would not let himself be diverted from the matter at hand.

"Now then, Miss Beacham," he began sternly, "I believe this is all fair and far off. You will kindly tell me what you and the children were doing in the drawing room. I again call your attention to the perfectly adequate schoolroom on the—"

"Of course, Your Grace. I am aware of the schoolroom but—"

"Miss Beacham! That is the second time in less than five minutes that you have interrupted me. You will not do so again," he commanded, his voice cool.

He thought she blanched, if slightly, and something in her demeanor changed. "Yes, Your Grace, of course," she said quietly and then bobbed a curtsy. But such subservience was obviously not an accustomed pose for her, nor was the abject tone of voice, and he thought, perversely, that it did not suit her. "As to the drawing room," she went on, "I took the children there for a music lesson. After all, the pianoforte is—"

"We have a music room for that, ma'am," he

18

said curtly.

The abject posture left as quickly as it had come. "Indeed you have, Your Grace," she said with spirit, "but you will own that the harpsichord it houses is sadly out-of-date. There *is* the dulcimer, of course, but that is even older, I believe. And that lovely flute . . . but young ladies are not supposed to play the flute, you must know! Gives us wrinkles, you see." She puckered up her lips by way of demonstration and the duke found himself contemplating her rosebud lips.

He cleared his throat and began to pace the floor, hands clasped behind his back. "And I suppose that feline was also having a music lesson, ma'am?" he demanded.

"Well, no, actually," she replied. "She rather escaped the kitchens in pursuit of the red ball, with Thomas and Timothy, you see, and—"

"Spare me the gory details, Miss Beacham. You will, in future, confine your lessons to the schoolroom, the nursery, the gardens, and the music room. That ought to be sufficient, heaven knows. As to that cat, I hardly think the children need another pet, what with the dog and Horatio, et al. And that name, Desdemona. Whoever—"

"We named her together, the children and I. She *is* black and white, you must know, and we were studying Shakespeare, and the poor kitten is always getting blamed for mischief of which she is innocent and—"

"Miss Beacham!" he erupted. "Surely you did not tell the children what it is Desdemona was blamed for!" He had stopped in his pacing just two feet in front of her and his eyes blazed.

"Why, of course not, Your Grace," she protested, her hand gliding to her breast. "Whatever do you take me for?"

He peered at her through narrowed eyes. "I am not at all certain, Miss Beacham," he murmured. He did not take her for a governess, that was certain, nor a "Beachie." As to her given name, he'd known several comely tavern wenches and an upstairs maid named "Rose." But it was hardly a name for a lady. . . . "Where are you from, Miss Beacham?" he asked abruptly.

Why had he asked her that? she wondered, fighting down a sense of panic. She told herself it was a natural thing for an employer to ask. She must answer just as naturally, as if she hadn't anything to hide.

"I am from . . . Lancashire, Your Grace," she replied steadily.

He paced back and forth in front of her, eyeing her suspiciously. There was something about her voice—a certain lilt—that he could not quite place. But it did not sound like Lancashire. His old school friend Damon, marquis of Penderleigh, was from Lancashire and Reginald had visited him at Pender Castle several times in his youth. He remembered the native inflection, and he did not think Miss Rose Beacham had it.

"I see," was all he said in reply. Time enough to pursue that line of interrogation later. He stalked to the leather sofa and whirled round to face her. "I assume you came with references?"

"Yes, of course. I . . . I previously worked in the home of Lady Darnley in northwest Lancashire. Your mother has my letter."

He strode to her and regarded her pensively. "You are a long way from home, Miss Beacham," he said quietly. He could see the pulse beat rapidly at her throat and knew that she was nervous. And well she might be. She met his gaze but the twinkle was gone from those deep blue eyes. He found that he missed it, then chided himself sharply. His eyes swept over her; he watched the faint rise and fall of her full breasts and felt his own pulse accelerate.

He took a deliberate step backward, appalled at himself. He began to pace again. "How long did you work for Lady Darnley?" he asked brusquely.

"Six years, Your Grace."

Six years! Not unless she started in pigtails, he thought. "Just how old are you, Miss Beacham?"

Most women blushed at such a question. This one seemed to go a shade paler. "I am five and twenty, Your Grace."

Another clanker, he thought, coming to stand before her once more. He would give her twenty-one summers, at most. "Your family, Miss Beacham?" he snapped.

Keep calm, Susanna told herself. He is your employer. He has the right to ask all these questions. He has the right not to ask you to be seated. You knew it would be this way, for all neither his mama nor anyone else here treats you in the least like a servant.

Somehow she had to allay his suspicions. But it would be so much easier if he would not stand quite so close. Every time he came near her she had the strangest feeling in the pit of her stomach. It was not fear, although Heaven knew it ought to be, but something else. . . .

She swallowed hard and clasped her hands at her waist. Then she lowered her chin a trifle. "My father was a parson, in a small village in Lancashire. There . . . there never was much money, you must know, and . . . and I always knew I would have to make my own way."

21

Coming it a bit too brown, Reginald thought, almost laughing aloud. The submissive pose did not suit her at all. And as to this faradiddle about the poor parson's daughter, he'd like to know how that accounted for the dress she was wearing. One or two years out of fashion it might be, but it was of the first quality. The jaconet muslin was the finest, the dress cut to fit her beautifully, perfectly.

No she was *not* a governess, he reminded himself, and he meant to find out soon enough just what she was. "That will be all, Miss Beacham. For now," he said pointedly.

Oh, dear, she thought. She had not convinced him of anything. Whatever would she do if he turned her off? She felt a chill at the mere thought but then mentally shook herself. She simply could not let herself be cowed by him. She had learned long ago that such was not the way. . . .

Besides, she had the uncanny sense that he was not quite so stern as he appeared. Oh, he had a strong sense of his own consequence; she did not doubt that. And he was a very powerful man. He exuded power with his very stance, his every movement. And the set lines of his face bespoke great strength of character. But there was humor lurking in the depths of his gray eyes; she was certain of it.

He was staring at her piercingly now and standing rather too close. She took a step back and her lips parted ever so slightly as she regarded him.

It was not precisely a handsome face, she thought, for the light brows grew too close together, the nose was a bit too prominent, the jaw too square. But the gray eyes, hinting at some hidden depths, intrigued her, and the silver blond hair, combed forward in the

Brutus style, was thick and wavy. She wondered suddenly what he would look like when he smiled. And then her wayward eyes swept down his length, and she was most overset to note that he, having just emerged from his traveling coach, looked a great deal more presentable than she. His Hessians had only a trace of dust. The buff pantaloons, which hugged his powerful thighs with nary a crease, had none at all. And his coat of navy superfine might well have come straightaway from the press.

But it was neither the pantaloons nor the coat, she realized with chagrin, that held her in thrall. It was rather the figure beneath them. He was not the tallest of men, for he was just under six feet. But he was very broad, with square shoulders that seemed as if . . . as if they could carry a great deal of weight. For one wild moment she had the urge to fling herself into them and tell him the whole, but she scolded herself severely. She had done with schoolgirl fancies. No one could help her now, and there was no comfort to be found in a man's arms. Unwittingly she lowered her eyes to his tapered waist and well-muscled thighs. . . .

"Miss Beacham? That will be all." His voice startled her, and she looked up to see a faint look of amusement in his gray eyes. And why should she not scrutinize him? she wondered indignantly. Hadn't he done the same to her throughout this entire interview? A voice at the back of her head reminded her that *he* was the employer.

But she did not heed it, and, needing to get a bit of her own back, said airily, "Of course, Your Grace. I expect I shall see you at tea."

He raised one blond eyebrow. "Yes, Miss Beacham, I expect so," he said dryly. "Ah, but do comb your hair, my dear, and that, ah, smudge on your chin, just there . . ." He reached out and brushed her chin with his index finger. "You really must contrive to look more like a governess."

She flushed a beautiful shade of pink. No governess ought to blush so becomingly, he thought, or have skin half so soft. Or smell so good, of—what was it?—jasmine, he decided. He watched her take a deep breath. "Indeed, dear sir, an admirable idea," she said with what might almost be taken for hauteur. "And you, I collect, will wish to repair to your rooms to remove all of your travel dirt." And with that, she gathered up her skirts and marched from the room.

How dare she, he thought, then shook his head ruefully. Whatever could have possessed him to quiz her so, and to call her "my dear"? He sighed. His mama had done some addlepated things before, but this time she had gotten them into the devil of a coil. A very *pretty* coil, which made it all the more difficult.

And that very governess, her heart pounding as she hurried to her small apartment across from the nursery, berated herself for being ten times a fool. Why ever could she not contrive to remember her place? How could she have spoken to him in such manner? The duke held her very future, perhaps her life, in his hands! For if he should peruse her credentials at bit too closely . . .

Susanna closed the door to her small sitting room behind her and collapsed against it. She'd heard the children across the corridor with Annie, the nursery maid, and was grateful for a few minutes to compose herself.

She forced herself to take several deep breaths. It

was almost two months ago that she had run from her home in the middle of the night, a fugitive with blood on her hands. Only by the grace of God had she reached her own former governess, the real "Beachie," in safety, together they'd orchestrated the ruse that had allowed her to find her current position. She *must not* jeopardize it! But she knew herself well; she could not hold a meek pose for long.

Beachie had warned her that her wayward tongue might well prove her downfall at Milburne Hall. For while it had been the only way to survive in her father's house, the duke's household was another matter entirely. The *duke* was another matter entirely.

The very thought of him set Susanna's heart to pounding again. His image rose in her mind's eyes and she realized with a jolt that it was not merely his temper nor his displeasure that she feared. Suddenly she was not quite certain what discomposed her the most . . . the thought that the august duke of Milburne might turn her off, or that he might let her stay. For she recalled the wide set of his shoulders and the strength in his face. And she remembered the gentle touch of his finger on her chin, the warmth of his hand as it held hers. Unwittingly her thoughts flew to Duncan Mortimer, the last man to touch her. But Reginald Ayres was nothing like the blackguard Mortimer, and that, Susanna very much feared, was precisely the problem.

Chapter 2

The duke's rooms were at sixes and sevens, as he'd expected. The small, swarthy figure of Martinez stood in the midst of it all, gesticulating wildly to the footmen bearing the duke's various portmanteaux.

"*¡Ay! ¡Caramba! ¡No, muchachos! ¡Póngansela acá!*" exploded the Spaniard, his hands flying above his head as a very heavy trunk was deposited before the hearth in the duke's huge bedchamber.

"I really do not think you are making yourself understood, *amigo*," the duke said in an amused undertone.

Martinez threw him a dark look, then yelled, "Eeen the dresseen room, ju *idiotas!* And be queeck about eet!" As they moved to obey, he smiled his toothy grin at the duke. "I have jour bath ready, Don Reinaldo."

The duke merely smiled as he removed his coat and handed it into Martinez's outstretched arm. He preceded the valet into the dressing room, where a large steaming copper tub stood before the hearth. The water looked hot enough, but Martinez had a footman pour two more kettles of water from the fire into the tub. "I do not wish to tarry overlong," the duke said as his man divested him of his clothing. He ignored the footmen scurrying hither and yon with his luggage. "I needs must have an interview with my mother before teatime."

"Ah," Martinez said knowingly, draping the duke's white linen cravat over his arm.

"About the new governess," Reginald added, eyeing his valet expectantly.

"Ah, yes, the governess," Martinez echoed in his thick Spanish accent. The sides of his thin lips curled and he scratched his dapper black moustache. The footmen had disappeared, and the duke stood now in his natural state.

"Well, man, out with it!" Reginald demanded amiably, but Martinez merely advanced to the tub, testing the water and pronouncing it hot enough.

"The governess, Martinez. What have you heard?"

"Get in before it is cold as ice," Martinez said, "and then I will talk to you."

Reginald grinned and obeyed, savoring the freedom of nakedness and the soothing heat of the water.

Martinez handed him the soap and a sponge. "They say she is a little bit . . . lively, Don Reinaldo."

"An understatement, Martinez, I assure you. And?"

"And they are saying that there will be the devil to pay now that you are home."

"Another understatement, Martinez. But you can help me. I should like to find out as much as possible about our Miss Beacham's background. See what you can pick up in the servants' hall."

The amusement left his valet's face and the man said stiffly, "Forgive me, Don Reinaldo, but I do not think I will be spending much time in the servants' hall."

27

"Now, do come down off your high ropes, Martinez. I know this bit of intelligence work is not worthy of a man of your international experience, but still I—"

"It is not that, Don Reinaldo." Something in Martinez's tone, and the cold, faraway look in his eyes, caused the duke to sit up straight, oblivious to the soap bobbing in front of him.

"What is it, my friend?" Reginald asked quietly.

The valet walked over to the largest of the portmanteaux and unstrapped it. "Her Grace has a new maid."

"About time. I nearly had to carry that ancient relic she had up and down the stairs. But what has my mother's maid to say to the matter?"

"Her name is Angelique." Martinez pronounced the French name with contempt, for all he used the Spanish guttural "g."

The duke sighed. "I am sorry, Martinez. I have tried to prevent it before, but—"

"I know, Don Reinaldo. And she is such a pretty little thing. I am certain she never did anyone a harm, but one cannot help the way one feels, you know?"

"It was all a long time ago, Martinez," the duke offered softly.

"*Sí, amigo mío,* but not long enough."

Martinez fell silent after that, methodically removing shirts and cravats from the portmanteau, and took his leave shortly thereafter. He always left the duke to enjoy his bath alone, only to reappear magically the moment Reginald reached for the towel.

The duke sighed again and sank lower into the tub. He couldn't really blame his mother for hiring a French maid; the girl might well be an émigré with no great love for her native land. Still, had his mama thought it

28

through, she might have realized what a brouhaha it would cause once he returned with Martinez. But asking his dear peagoose of a mama to think something through was reaching for the moon; hence that woman who called herself governess.

Women, in Reginald's experience, came in two varieties. There were those like his mother and Phoebe—beautiful, biddable, without an ounce of guile or malice, and completely hen-witted. And then there were the clever ones; they might be beautiful as well, but they were also grasping, greedy little opportunists whose manipulative ploys would have been the envy of any general in His Majesty's army. It was one of the reasons he'd never married. For all he felt guilty about it, he did not want to wed a woman like his mother. His father had adored her, cossetted her and laughed with her, but in many ways Reginald knew his father had been a lonely man. There was so much of himself that he could not share with his duchess, who could never grasp the intricacies of estate business, or politics, or a new plant he was trying to cultivate.

And as to the clever ones, they pursued Reginald with a sly vengeance every time he set foot in Town. But when he looked into their eyes all he saw were pound notes. *His* pound notes, as they tried to tally his net worth and wondered how they would look with a coronet on their perfectly coiffed heads.

Even the other sort of female, the kind one didn't consider marrying, fell into the same two categories. Which was the reason he never had the same mistress in keeping for very long, and accounted for the fact that he had just given Lisette her congé. Warm and willing though she'd been, her maneuvering to try to get him to stay longer in London, and buy her a dashing new phaeton, had finally grated a bit too much.

Women, he thought in exasperation as he ducked his head to remove the soap from his hair, were always trouble. Which brought him back to the new governess. Just who was she, and what did she want?

Martinez, did he care to set his mind to it, could be very good at eliciting from his fellows information even *they* did not know they possessed. Reginald had suspected Martinez of having done intelligence work for the Spanish government, but of course the fellow would never say. Just as he would not speak of anything in his life prior to the day when Reginald pulled him out from under a mammoth stallion that had fallen in battle.

The year had been 1808, the first year of the Peninsular War. Reginald, at the age of twenty, had been seized with patriotic fervor and the longing for adventure. And his father, understanding as always, and knowing full well the responsiblities that eventually awaited him as heir to the dukedom, had felt it was best he have his adventures now in his youth. But it was not an adventure; it was a gruesome nightmare. And then in June of '09, he'd been at Talavera. The fighting was bitter, and then those raging fires had broken out. It was in the midst of that inferno that he'd found Martinez, although to this day he had no idea what he'd been doing there.

Reginald had dragged him out of there, seen to it that he had decent nursing, prevented the surgeon from sawing off his leg. And when he was whole again, Martinez had attached himself to "Capitán" Ayres, becoming his batman, messenger, and jack-of-all-trades. And when Reginald's English valet had begged to be sent home, Martinez had become that, too. And he had become Reginald's friend as well. He spoke English fairly well, even then. He seemed well read and had an opinion on everything. Reginald surmised that he was well born, perhaps even of a noble family fallen on hard times, but the Spaniard never said. He never spoke of his family at all.

He was a wily fellow and happily supplied Reginald and his company commander with information about French troop movements no one else seemed to know about. Martinez hated the French passionately.

Reginald had been in Spain just over a year when the terrible news had come from home. His father had suddenly been taken ill with pneumonia and died two days later. Not quite sixty years old, the father he had adored and revered above all others. His father, who'd been robust and in full health, was gone.

And now it was Martinez's turn to save the life of *el Capitán*. Reginald remembered nothing of the wretched journey home, only knew that he could not have made it without his friend. He had offered to send Martinez back once they reached Devon, but the Spaniard would not hear of it. Said he had nothing to go back to. And so Martinez had become his valet-cum-major domo and, always, friend. And Reginald had, at the premature age of twenty-one, become the duke of Milburne, possessor of numerous estates and one of the largest fortunes in all of England, and guardian to his four young siblings, the youngest of whom was still in swaddling clothes.

To Martinez *el Capitán* had become Don Reinaldo, since nothing could prevail upon him to use the duke's given name without a title. And *Su Gracia* or worse, *Su Excelencia* did not sit at all well with Reginald.

31

With a heavy heart the new duke had taken on his responsibilities. Martinez had understood his guilt over having been away, his feelings of being inadequate for all he had to do, his frustrations at having his own dreams crushed. Not dreams of war; he'd been cured of any illusions about that. But of making his mark as a botanist. His father had dabbled in horticulture, had built an excellent conservatory to the purpose. But Reginald saw the world as his laboratory; he wanted to study plants in their natural habitats.

It was Martinez who helped him see that he need not give up his dream, only postpone it for a while. And so he had, continuing his studies, and finally going on the Icelandic expedition, Martinez in tow. That had been the beginning of the realization of his dream.

But if Martinez harbored any dreams of his own, he never shared them. He merely went about his days with a cheerful equanimity that Reginald could only marvel at. For if the duke presented to the world a collected, calm exterior, inside he was not so sanguine. His repsonsibilities now, at the age of nine and twenty, years after he'd succeeded to his dignities, still weighed heavily on him. Even attending the endless balls and soirees of the Season took on the aura of duty, for he disliked most of them and he was sensible of the fact that he had ought to marry and secure the succession.

But, as he had reminded his mama before this latest trip, he had two brothers for that and he simply had no intention of leg-shackling himself in the foreseeable future. Women, he thought wryly, were an endless complication. Not that he disliked them. Quite the contrary. They were soft and warm and even amusing, for short periods of time at all events. And truly, one could not live without them. But living with them was the very devil, he thought, his mind going back to the French maid, who had come to cut up Martinez's peace, and the so-called governess, who had come to cut up his. The two newest additions to his harum-scarum household, if one didn't count Desdemona. Really, how could his mother imagine he could ever bring a wife home to all this?

On that thought he rose from the now-tepid water, only to see Martinez dash in, holding aloft a thick, heated towel. The duke of Milburne grinned and stepped out of the tub.

He presented himself in his mother's sitting room one hour before teatime, newly attired in cream-colored kerseymere breeches, charcoal gray waistcoat, and burgundy coat. His cravat was tied in the Mailcoach. It was not too high as to be uncomfortable, and its casual elegance was particularly suitable to the country. Reginald enjoyed elegance in his clothes, and of course the cut and fit was always of the first quality. But as to the first stare of fashion, he steadfastly refused to array himself in garments designed to produce acute discomfort and the most awkward of body movements. Hence his shirt points were never so high that he could not turn his head, nor his pantaloons so tight that he could not sit down. This tendency, plus a preference for more subdued colors than the prevailing mode, caused him to be the despair of Phoebe, who perused the fashion magazines with avidity and encouraged him to set more of a dash. And he supposed he was the despair of his mother as well; she harbored some strange idea that he would attract just the "right" sort of female if he but decked himself out as a Tulip of Fashion.

But Reginald, ever sensible of his responsibilities to his name and family, drew the line at his manner of dress. In this he pleased only himself.

The sitting room was done in varying shades of pink and mint green. A cheerful fire burned in the grate, for though it was near the end of June, the sun had not been seen at all this day, and a damp chill lingered in the air.

"Ah, Reggie dear, what a delightful surprise, although I've known of your arrival this hour and more. The house fairly buzzes with the news," she trilled, setting aside her book, a Nora Tillington novel, no doubt, and rising from her couch in a cloud of pale blue chiffon. She glided toward him, trailing wisps of gossamer fabric, and offered him her smooth cheek. He dutifully kissed her and then gave her an affectionate squeeze before leading her once more to the pink velvet chaise.

"You are in wonderful looks, Mama, as always," he said quite truthfully as he seated her and strolled to the window. Her face bore only a few lines to attest to her forty-eight years, and her blond hair was of a color so pale that the streaks of gray simply made it appear flaxen.

"Ooh, la, Reggie, save your flummery for the young ladies. *Eligible* ones," she said pointedly. "I do wish—"

"Now, Mama, do not let us descend into that boondoggle again, for I own I should not like it above half. You know perfectly well my feelings on the subject of matrimony and—"

"But surely you must have met *some* eligible females in London, my dear! You *did* make the rounds, did you not? Never say you spent the entire month with those

Friday-faced old men, poring over pieces of dead plants!" the duchess exclaimed.

Reginald's lips curled. "Those are specimens, Mother. And yes, I did do the pretty at three balls and some wretched breakfast that began at three in the afternoon and—"

"Did you go to Almack's?" she asked hopefully.

"Good God, I should say not! I was merely being sociable, mostly to please you, but I am not addlepated enough to set myself up as food for the matchmaking vultures. As I've no—"

"I own it is really too bad of you, Reggie, as well as being most unnatural for a duke of Milburne not to wish—"

"Enough, Mother. I did not come here to discuss me," he said firmly, drawing a chair that looked much too delicate up to the chaise.

"No, of course not, dear," she said in all seriousness. "I expect you've already had the news." Her lower lip protruded in a pout that he supposed his father had found adorable, but which he merely found exasperating. "Or perhaps you've met her? Then you *will* own that she is a sweet little thing—"

"I would hardly call her *little,* Mama," he said dryly. "As to sweet . . ."

"Yes, well, she is quite charming, and pleasant to have around, not to mention being a genius with hair, and a marvel with a needle."

"What has that to say to the matter?"

"Well, I realize we are not yet in London, but still one must keep up appearances. It simply would not do for—"

"Mother, what the *deuce* are you talking about?"

"Oh, dear. Now, I *have* got your dander up, and I

35

had so hoped to talk you round. Well, in truth, Reggie, what with you and Martinez being away, when my dear friend Lady Craddock suggested her to me, I own I did not even *think* of the difficulties. But perhaps they needn't see each other all that much, you know and—"

"*Who* needn't see each other? Mother, what the *devil* are you talking about?"

"Please, dear, your language," his mother scolded lightly, her eyes darting about the room as if expecting the very walls to have ears. "I am speaking, of course, of your man, Martinez, and—"

"Martinez! What does *he* have to do with it?"

"What does . . . well, my dear, surely *you* cannot object to her being French. I mean to say—"

"French! She's not—Oh, good God! You must be speaking of that new maid of yours. Well, I—"

"But, of course I am speaking of Angelique! Who else would set up Martinez's back in such a way?"

"Mother, please!" He put up his hand in protest. "I fear we are dealing at cross purposes, for it is not your maid I came to discuss. Although, now you mention it, I certainly *would* have wished you to think the matter through. But it is a bit late for that, and if you are truly attached to her—"

"Oh, I am, Reggie dear. And truly I could not turn her off, poor dear. She is an émigré, you must know, raised by a maiden aunt, for her parents were killed in the Terror when—"

"Yes, Mama. I've *said* you may keep her. I wish to discuss the new governess."

"Governess?" she asked, for all the world as if she could not recall even the need for one. Papa, he thought, however did you put up with it? "Oh, you must mean dear Beachie. Have you met her as well

36

as Angelique?"

"Yes, that is, I haven't met the maid, only the governess."

Her blue eyes narrowed. "Really? Did you make an appearance in the nursery already, then? How kind of you to—"

"No, Mother, I did *not* go up to the nursery. I encountered the governess and the children chasing some kitten round the drawing room."

"Desdemona! Isn't she a sweet little thing? Not but what I do not think Horatio is too pleased, but then, Horatio adopted us and not the other way about. I do wish Cook would become accustomed, but merely because Horatio is a *black* cat, she persists in flying into a pelter everytime he crosses her path. But as Desdemona is white as well as black, I do not think Mrs. Rackett will be too overset, do you?"

"Mother, I hardly think the children need another pet," he said dampeningly. "They have that basset hound and —"

"Of course, dear, but the dog really belongs to the boys, and it was Letty who found Desdemona. Nearly starved to death, she was, abandoned by her mother, and thank goodness she was old enough to lap, else Cook might have been obliged to soak a piece of linen in cream so Desdemona might suck, but even that mightn't answer, you know, and—"

"Mother, please!" Reginald jumped up abruptly and stalked to the chimney piece, but finding it too warm, went to lean against the window instead. "I do not care a farthing for how stray kittens are fed, nor for Mrs. Rackett's queer starts. Attend me, Mother. I wish to discuss the governess. Miss Beacham."

"Oh, yes, of course. You did say that. Oh, but what

can I be thinking? You must wish some refreshment. I—"

"No, Mother," he interrupted, before she lifted herself from the couch. "No refreshment. I merely wish information. Where did she come from?"

"Why, Lancashire, my dear. From a Lady Darnley, whose last child has finally left the schoolroom, you must know. And what a godsend Beachie has been, Reggie. I declare I was all to pieces when that poor Miss Pritchard left, what with you gone and Timothy and Thomas running amuck such that I feared Underwood would give notice!"

Her bejeweled hand went to her breast, and Reginald repressed the glimmer of a smile. This was hardly a laughing matter, after all. "From what I saw, Miss Beacham has done little to improve matters. The drawing room was at sixes and sevens."

"Yes, well, I daresay that was Desdemona's fault, not Beachie's. You may depend upon it that Beachie does keep the children in the schoolroom for part of the day. And Letty's been practicing on the pianoforte, and Thomas has become interested in the conservatory."

'The conservatory! Good God! What the deuce is she doing with my plants?"

At that the duchess rose from her couch, rather more quickly than was her wont, and glided to the window. "Reggie, dear, are you feeling quite the thing?" She raised her hand to his brow in a flutter of chiffon. "I vow, 'tis not at all like you to fly into a taking."

The duke sighed. "I am quite right, Mama, and not at all in a taking. I am merely overset at what I have seen today. I presume you have a letter from Lady Darnley?"

She nodded and strolled, at her usual leisurely pace,

to the delicate gold-leafed escritoire under the far window. The letter she handed him was written in a fine, neat hand, but the paper did not appear to be of the first quality. Certainly not the sort of writing paper one would expect of a woman beforehand enough with the world to keep a governess. His mouth tightened as he read the letter. It praised Miss Beacham to the skies, extolling her command of the classics, literature, geography, embroidery, pianoforte, mathematics— Mathematics, he thought! That was doing it a bit too brown! If a woman who looked like that could even do simple sums he would be much surprised.

Conspicuously absent was any mention of the duration of her employ, or the ages of the children in her charge. The letter was signed simply "Lady Darnley, Hapworth Manor, Lancashire."

"Mother, did you seriously consider this enough upon which to decide to engage Miss Beacham? Did you not check further?"

"Oh, but there was not time, Reggie dear. And it wasn't just the letter, you must know, but her address, so pleasing, isn't it? And the way the children took to her immediately. You cannot know what a relief it was when they virtually rallied round her and dragged her off to the nursery, instead of attempting to tie her up as they did poor Miss Pritchard."

The duke sighed and folded the letter, securing it in the pocket of his coat. "I see how 'tis, Mother, but pray tell me, do you not think her a trifle . . . young?"

The duchess glided to her couch once more and sank down gracefully. "I do not think so, dear. She *is* five and twenty, after all."

"That is what she *says,* Mother, but I own she looks no more than *one* and twenty."

A trill of laughter escaped the duchess. "Oh, dear Reggie, pray do not fly into a pelter over *that*. Why, I fancy it merely attests to her attention to her skin. I am persuaded she must use camomile for her eyes, and perhaps a mixture of honey, rosewater, and goose fat for her cheeks. I myself am most careful about—"

"Never mind, Mother. It is not her skin. It's rather that she is much too young and beautiful . . . and surely even you can see that her clothes are of excellent quality, not at all what one expects of a governess. Not to mention the fact that her manner is much too coming."

"Too coming?" She tilted her head to the side, her eyes narrowing. "I shouldn't think so. And it is her very manner that makes the children so devoted to her. Even Phoebe has taken to her, you must know, which I own is a good thing, especially now."

At that he frowned and came forward. "What do you mean, 'especially now'?"

"Oh, dear, I hadn't meant . . . not but what you were bound to find out soon enough . . ."

"Find what out?" he demanded ominously.

"Well, I am persuaded it is all a tempest in a pot of tea, but still I cannot like it. Oswald Hastings has come home."

"Oswald—you mean the baron's second son? What of it?"

"Well, he cuts rather a dash, you see, and I'm afraid he's been dangling after Phoebe."

"What? You cannot mean it! Why, she's merely a child!"

"Hardly, Reggie. She just turned seventeen."

"Of all the effrontery! The fellow has not a feather to fly with, besides being an inveterate gambler. You cannot mean to say he's turned Phoebe's head?"

The duchess sighed heavily. "I fear so, dear. She knows very few men, you see, and—Well, but perhaps Beachie will be able to talk her round. I do not think she lacks for common sense. Beachie, that is, whatever the cut of her clothes. Do contrive to get on with her, Reggie, for my sake?"

His mother fluttered her famous eyelashes, but the effect was entirely lost on her son. He took his leave shortly thereafter, promising to be perfectly civil to "Beachie" at tea.

Chapter 3

In the event, the duke came to regret that very rash promise. For when he ambled into the Blue Saloon at teatime, it was to see not only Phoebe, his mother, and "Beachie," as he'd expected, but Timothy, Thomas, and Letty as well. Not to mention that basset hound, Robin Hood, sprawled about the powder blue carpet, quite as if he owned the place. He shuddered to think where Desdemona might be lurking.

"And may I ask the occasion for this rather comfortable coze, Mother?" he asked with a raised brow after greeting everyone briefly.

"Ah, Reggie dear, do sit down, and I'll pour out. I collect you mean the children. Well, Beachie pointed out that if one wishes to instill in children some sense of how to go about in company, then one really ought to take them *into* company at times. So we lighted on the perfect solution of teatime! So much less formal than dinner, when of course one would not consider it. Lemon, dear?"

"I hardly consider this a solution to anything, Mother," he said, striding forward to take a seat across from the cream-colored sofa upon which his mother and Phoebe sat. Miss Beacham sat in a chair to his right. Letty sat to his left, trying to balance a plate piled high with biscuits on her lap, while the boys alternately wolfed down pastries and lemonade. "Henceforth I expect a civilized tea, without—"

"Your Grace, might I have a word with you?"

It was, of course, Miss Beacham. She rose before he had a chance to reply, obliging him to do the same, and before he knew what he was about, he had followed her out of the saloon into the corridor. She closed the door firmly behind them.

"Miss Beacham, you have a deplorable habit of interrupting me, and I will have it cease!"

"Good Heavens! I did do it again, didn't I? I do apologize, but you see I had to."

"Had to?" he queried, and then suddenly feeling they were in far too public a place for the set down he was determined to administer, he took her none too gently by the elbow and dragged her round the corner to a small alcove. "Now, then, you had to—"

"Yes, for I could not let you . . . that is, I knew you did not realize . . . what I mean to say, Your Grace, is that you were speaking of the children *as if they weren't there!*"

She stood with her back to the wall, he just a few feet in front of her. Her magnificent blue eyes sparkled and her cheeks were flushed. She wore the same midnight blue dress as before and he noted again the lush curves it hid. He deliberately put his hands behind his back but unwittingly took a step forward.

"Was I?" he asked, his voice rather softer than he intended. "That is undoubtedly because they ought not to *be* there."

"I apprehend you feel that way, but as you are desirous of instilling good manners in them, I am persuaded you would wish to set a good example."

Susanna saw something like amusement flicker in his gray eyes, but it was squelched quickly. "You go too far, ma'am! *I* am the arbiter of what is proper in this house and *I* alone set the rules!"

Remember your place, a little voice whispered to her. "Yes, of course," she said trying very hard to look contrite. Then she lowered her eyes and added a meek, "Your Grace."

He frowned suspiciously and took a half-step closer. She found herself wishing very much that he wouldn't. His proximity was unnerving. And he smelled good, she realized, of soap and leather and the out-of-doors. Not at all like her father, who stank of cheap perfume, or Duncan Mortimer, who reeked of whisky.

"The children are not permitted to dine with us, nor take tea anywhere but in the nursery. Phoebe, of course, is excepted," he said. "As for you—"

"Your Grace," she ventured, "may I offer a compromise?"

"You're interrupting again, Miss Beacham," he admonished, a trifle less sternly than before.

She wondered what his strong, grave face would look like if he actually smiled. "But do tell me of this compromise," he said.

"The . . . compromise," she said haltingly. "Aye, the compromise. I only thought, you see, that Timothy and Thomas might remain in the nursery with their maid, but that I might bring Letty to tea. Truly, I . . . I think she might contrive to behave."

It was ridiculous for him to consider such a thing, ridiculous for him to "compromise" with anyone under his own roof; of a certain his father never would have. But now he found himself distracted by the creamy smoothness of her cheeks and the pulse beating so rapidly at her white throat. And his eyes drifted lower still, and he swallowed hard. Take hold of yourself, old chap, he chided.

"Very well," he heard himself say. "We shall give Letty a se'nnight's trial."

She smiled, a beautiful smile that made her eyes crinkle at the corners. "I am persuaded ye'll not be disappointed, Your Grace. Thank you."

Something in her voice struck an odd note and for a moment he could not think what it was. And then he realized she'd said "Ye'll" instead of "You'll." And just a minute ago she'd said "aye," instead of "yes." People did not, in the duke's experience, speak that way in Lancashire, but rather farther north. North of the border, in fact, in Scotland.

"Your Grace, I . . . I think we had best—"

"Not so fast, Miss Beacham. We have unfinished business, as I recall," he said smoothly, and put his hand upon the wall, blocking her escape.

"Yes?"

"Where were you born, Miss Beacham?"

Her eyes darted about, as if looking for inspiration.

"Ah, in Lancashire, Your Grace."

"I see. Close to Lady Darnley was it?"

"Yes, but . . . farther north, you see."

"Ah. Farther north. And just where is Hapworth Manor? I own I've never heard of it."

"Why, it's just north of Preston, you must know," she said with much assurance.

"I see. And your father had the living farther north, then?"

"Ah, yes, and east," she said, trying frantically to think of a likely village.

"As far east as Winestead?" he asked nonchalantly.

Her mind raced. If he would but stand back a bit she could think more clearly. She must not let him pin her down too closely. "Yes, but still *farther* east, you must know."

Second mistake, my dear Miss Governess, he thought, torn between anger and amusement. For not only was Winestead in Yorkshire rather than Lancashire, but if one lived much farther east one would be residing in the North Sea! But he said not a word. Not yet. First he had a certain letter to write. And he needed a bit more information.

He was standing much too close to her, and yet he could not will himself to move. And she merely stood gazing at him, her breathing rapid, her color high. Slowly he brought the fingers of his right hand over to brush her cheek. Her skin was soft, flawless, rather heated. "You are a bit flushed, Miss Beacham. Are you feeling quite the thing?"

"I . . . yes, Your Grace. It is merely . . . a trifle warm, is it not?"

"Yes," he responded, feeling it too, despite the chill of the day. He suddenly could not remember the information he wanted. He was staring at her parted red lips, wondering what they would feel like under his. Good God! What was wrong with him, to even contemplate kissing the *governess!* An unprotected female living under his very own roof! It went against every tenet of a gentleman's code.

He lowered his hands and took a step back, clearing his throat. "Ah, Miss Beacham, I do think we had ought to rejoin the others."

"Yes, I . . . I daresay," she murmured, a bit unsteadily.

And then he recalled what else he'd wanted to ask. "Ah, tell me, Miss Beacham," he began, trying, and utterly failing, to regain his severe tone, "who was *your* governess?"

At this she smile fondly, "Why, Miss Sarah B-Bertram."

"Ah. Miss Bertram. And I suppose you called her 'Bertie'?" She nodded slowly. "Bertie and Beachie," he said with a mocking light in his eyes that made her very nervous. "How charming," he drawled.

He made her even more nervous still as he walked so closely beside her as they made their way to the Blue Saloon.

No one remarked upon their absence, thankfully, although Letty glanced questioningly at the duke for a moment. But Susanna found it very difficult to concentrate on the conversation around her as she sipped at her tea.

"Reggie dear, you're putting lemon in your tea!" the duchess exclaimed in horrified accents.

"And?"

"And you've already put in cream, dear, and you know you never—"

"Of course, Mother," he said soothingly. "Careless of me. In London I use the lemon, since our Devonshire cream quite spoils me for all others." She accepted that, but the governess threw him a curious look. And well she might. For it was not the trip from London that was causing his unaccustomed abstraction but the very recent and disturbing encounter in the corridor.

He almost welcomed the sudden cacophony of

voices outside the door.

"You cannot go rumbullioning in there, Cook, not while they are about havin' their *tea!*" bellowed Mrs. Longbotham in her gravelly voice.

"Well, it's sorry I am to be interruptin' Their Graces at tea, but if'n I don't there won't be no dinner, and that's a fact! Now, out o' my way, Mrs. L!"

Oh, Lord, Reginald thought, nothing has changed. He rose and sauntered to the door as Mrs. Longbotham began a scathing reply. As he opened the door the rather enormous housekeeper, who had apparently been leaning on it to block Mrs. Rackett's entrance, nearly toppled into the room. Reginald swiftly sidestepped her rather ample person.

The good housekeeper righted herself soon enough, wiping her hands on her black skirts and smiling at everyone ranged about the room. The diminutive Mrs. Rackett stormed in after her, hands on her hips, her small face screwed up in a scowl.

"Well now, that be better. Thank you, Your Grace. And beggin' pardon, Your Graces, Miss Beacham, I'm sure," she began. The duke wondered why she included the governess in her request for pardon, but he kept his council as she went on . "But as I tried to tell Mrs. L. here . . ." She gave the housekeeper a most indignant look, and Mrs. L. responded with some sort of nasal harrumph.

Cook lifted her nose farther into the air and advanced into the room, at which point the heretofore indifferent Robin Hood rose, gave himself a lazy shake, and lumbered over to her. Robin Hood began happily licking her right hand and then turned to licking the mess on Cook's apron.

"Oh, dear," said Mrs. Rackett. "It's the gooseberry

48

tarts, I reckon. But what I'm trying to say, Your Graces, Miss Beacham, is that gooseberry tart is about *all* will make it to the dinin' table this night. And 'tis all *her* fault." She pointed an accusatory finger at the housekeeper. "Deliberately openin' the door to the kitchen garden at exactly the time that evil cat is always lurkin' there, just awaitin' to plague me. And what does that cursed cat do, minute he claps eyes on me, but march across my path! And you all know very well once a black cat crosses my path there's nort for it but to run from the room. And as to cookin' anythin' further, well, you know I just couldn't! Black cats have been known to cast hexes, you must know, and what with the way that cat glared at me out of those evil yellow eyes, well, I'd not be surprised if the food be . . . poisoned! And I was agoin' to make the loveliest junket for Your Grace, not to mention the haunch of venison. And now I declare . . ." At this point Mrs. Rackett became all choked up and the duke looked meaningfully at his mother. Brangles between cook and housekeeper were, thankfully, not in his province. But his mother returned a look that was perfectly helpless.

At all events, it was Mrs. Longbotham who spoke. "And *I* declare, beggin' your pardons, Your Graces, Miss Beacham, that I wunt take much more. Everytime that cat Horatio comes near her, everytime Cook spies a couple of magpies, not to mention Cleopatra—why, she treats that fat old milk cow 'sif 'twer somethin' *holy*, 'stead of just 'nuther white cow!"

"Fat old—I'll not have you ballyraggin' me, Mrs. L., nor talking' 'bout things o' which you be ignorant! *Everyone* knows a white cow, especially one *so* unusual as to have a black brow—"

"Mrs. Rackett," the duke finally intervened, having despaired of his mother's doing so, "of course Mrs. L. does not mean to scold you." He cast a pointed look at the housekeeper, who folded her arms just under her huge bosom and grumbled into her chins, "But all the same, it is a bit difficult for her to see to the menus when she is never certain if you will cook, or whether Cleopatra will be milked. I can well understand that Horatio troubles you, for he *is* a great big cat, and black as night, but truly, I do not think the food—"

"Dear Mrs. Rackett," the musical voice of the governess interjected, Miss Beacham having jumped up suddenly and come to his side. Reginald was too grateful for any reinforcement to cavil at having been interrupted yet again. "How right you are to be concerned about Horatio. Where I come from we are very careful about black cats, I can assure you. And to have one cross your path—Oh, but do tell me, at what time did the unfortunate incident occur?"

"Well, I . . . I reckon I'm not quite sure, Miss Beacham," replied Cook, her scowl considerably lessened and her small, plump body beginning to relax.

"Was it just now, or"—here Miss Beacham lowered her voice most ominously—"or was it at the noon hour?"

"Why, 'twas just a bit ago. Not the noon hour 'tall."

Miss Beacham breathed a theatrical sigh of relief, and the duke began to enjoy himself hugely. "Oh, you do relieve my mind, Mrs. Rackett. Oh, but you do, ah, *know* about the shadow of the black cat, do you not?"

"Well, no, I—"

"How curious." Miss Beacham tilted her head. "Where I come from, *everyone* knows about it. You see, 'tis the *shadow* of the black cat, and not the cat itself, that is the danger."

"Never say so!" exclaimed Mrs. Rackett in wondering accents.

"Oh, yes," the governess continued. "One must take great care not to let the *shadow* of the black cat cross one's path. And, of course, there can only be a shadow out-of-doors, so indoors one is quite safe."

"Are you . . . are you certain, Miss Beacham?" Cook asked hesitantly.

"Oh, quite. No danger at all indoors. Except of course"—the musical voice grew lower again—"at the noon hour."

Cook swallowed hard. "The noon hour?"

"Yes, for you see, there *is* no shadow at the noon hour, the sun being directly overhead. Is that not correct, Your Grace?"

"Oh, yes. Indubitably," the duke returned gravely.

"So you see," continued Miss Beacham, "at the noon hour it is the cat itself who is dangerous. Indoors or out-of-doors, you must know. You *will* remember that, won't you, Mrs. Rackett?"

"Oh, yes, miss. 'Pon my word, I will. You're not to be worritin' your head 'bout that. As to the rest, I'll simply have one of the scullery maids to be gatherin' the herbs from the garden in the mornin', when there be shadows abroad."

"An excellent notion, Mrs. Rackett," the duke affirmed. Mrs. Longbotham's eyes boggled as they flitted between Miss Beacham and the duke, and out of the corner of his eye he noted his mother and Phoebe regarding them in no small confusion. The boys were well occupied with their pastries, but Letty was watching the scene with barely suppressed amusement. At least, he thought, there was hope for *one* of the females in this family.

"Your Grace," began Mrs. Longbotham, but the appearance of Underwood quite stopped her.

"Is there some difficulty, Your Grace?" the tall, dapper retainer asked.

"None at all," Reginald replied easily. "We were just, ah . . ."

"Discussing menus," put in Miss Beacham.

Underwood looked skeptical. Mrs. Longbotham turned to him, straightened her cap, and smiled. "How good of you to come to escort us back, to be sure, Mr. Underwood."

And Mrs. Rackett, not to be outdone, straightened her gooseberry-stained apron and said, as Underwood led both women out, "I was sayin' even now as how I be makin' my special junket for His Grace, and for you, Mr. Underwood, my potato pastries, with parsley and . . ."

The remaining company departed soon thereafter, but the duke detained Miss Beacham, closing the door once they were alone. "*Wherever* did you hear such a clanker about black cats and shadows, Miss Beacham?" he inquired, unable to keep the amusement from his voice.

Her great blue eyes danced as she stood just two feet before him. "That was rather a good turn, was it not? It just came to me, I must own, as she was going on about—"

"You just made that up?"

"Why, of course. You see, where I come from, superstition is quite rife, and it does absolutely no good to try to dispel any notions about bad luck and ill omens and the like. One must simply . . . change those notions a bit. Do you see, Your Grace?"

He was regarding her with a strange light in his eyes and then suddenly, for the first time since she'd met him, the duke of Milburne smiled. And it completely altered his countenance. The lines of determination about his mouth became laugh lines. The clear gray eyes twinkled most attractively and her breathing felt suddenly very shallow.

"Oh, yes, I see, Miss Beacham, and I am much obliged. I would not, as it happens, care for three courses' worth of gooseberry tart. Ah . . . just what do you mean to do about Cook's belief that if two magpies fly into the barn then the white milk cow must not be milked that day, lest she drop dead, or worse, give forth diseased milk?"

"I own I hadn't thought on't, but where I come—"

"Yes, where *do* you come from, my dear?" he asked softly as he folded his arms lazily across his chest and gazed down at her.

The question sent alarm bells ringing in her head, but the endearment, uttered in combination with that smile, nearly made her dizzy. Inwardly shaking herself for such foolishness, she replied, "Why, Lancashire, as I told ye."

"Ah, yes, now I recall. Near Winestead, was it not?"

"Aye. East of Winestead."

"Of course. Ah, do you swim, Miss Beacham?"

She blinked. "Why, yes, tolerably well."

"Oh, I'm glad, my dear. Very glad," he said, his eyes dancing. And then to her utter amazement, the duke of Milburne actually chuckled as he led her from the room.

But it was no laughing matter, he reminded himself,

closing the door to his study and sitting down at his desk. Her ingenious cajoling of Mrs. Rackett merely pointed out her devious little mind, the same mind that had helped her to bamboozle her way into his household at first stop.

That she was an engaging creature at times he could not help but admit. Perhaps she *could* hold the children's interest, and even command their obedience, although he rather doubted the latter, since her own sense of obedience was deplorably lacking. Still, he would reserve judgment on that score. That she had the entire household wrapped round her graceful fingers he did not doubt. But none of it signified in the least, not nearly so much as the questions which now plagued him. Why would a beautiful woman take a position which was obviously far beneath her and for which she was so patently ill-suited? Why would she come here, fabricate, in all likelihood, her name, previous employment, her very origins? *Who,* in fact, was she, and whatever did she want?

He saw no answers ready to hand, and the only possible avenues which seemed open to him at the moment were to catch her in more of her own lies, and to write that letter to his friend Damon, marquis of Penderleigh. Penderleigh's principal seat, Pender Castle, was in Lancashire, just south of Pendle Hill, and he might be prevailed upon to make some inquiries regarding one Lady Darnley of Hapworth manor. And Reginald would also ask him to look into a certain governess by the name, Reginald was nearly certain, of Sarah Beacham. He was beginning to have some idea of the way "Beachie's" mind worked, and he felt certain "Bertram" had been one of her spontaneous inventions. As to "Rose," he could not fathom where she'd got that. But he'd find out soon enough.

That his missive would find Penderleigh in residence he did not doubt. Just before he'd left for London he'd received a most amazing correspondence from his friend. The marquis of Penderleigh, hardened rakehell that he was, the man whose mistrust of the fairer sex was legend, had succumbed to the charms of a fiery redhead, niece of an old friend of his father's, and actually married her! "I have met my match, in more ways than one," Penderleigh had written, "and can only say I wish the same for you, my friend."

Reginald had hardly been able to credit the news, and in fact, would not have, had the missive not clearly been written by the marquis himself. Penderleigh and his new lady had been conspicuously absent from London for most of the Season, preferring to remain, as the on dits would have it, holed up in Pender Castle. The on dits would also have it that the new marchioness was quite a little handful, that they had been seen to quarrel quite loudly and publicly while in London at the beginning of the Season, before their rather hasty marriage in the wilds of Lancashire, and that the marquis was completely besotted with his bride. The duke shook his head, wondering, as he put pen to paper, whatever could have happened to a heretofore sensible, rational man.

The letter dispatched, he strolled up to his rooms, where Martinez was just finishing the unpacking.

Abstractedly, Reginald stripped off his coat and cravat. "Why, Martinez? Why would such a woman come here, insinuate herself so thoroughly into this household? My riding clothes, please."

"If you are speaking of the new governess, Don Reinaldo, I believe it was that she needed a position."

The valet took the coat and cravat and began setting out the duke's leather breeches, riding coat, and topboots.

"No, Martinez. There must be more. She is no more a governess than I am. What does she hope to gain?" the duke responded as his valet slipped him into his breeches.

"Why can you not simply believe she is what she says? I had the pleasure of meeting Señorita Beacham a few minutes ago. She is perfectly charming."

"A governess is not supposed to be charming, Martinez," Reginald said dryly.

Martinez smiled faintly. "Ah, Don Reinaldo, there she is now, with the boys."

Reginald sauntered to the window, where he espied the governess, Timothy, Thomas, Robin Hood, and that damned red ball fairly rolling on the south lawn together. "Oh, Lord," he grumbled. "She'll probably tell me it's a botany lesson." Martinez, his face quite impassive, held the duke's riding coat for him. As Reginald shrugged into it, he nonchalantly watched the scene below. His body stiffened as the group rolled perilously close to the beds of old roses and foxgloves. And then his eyes did a double take. For Miss Beacham threw the red ball far across the lawn, sending the dog yelping after it, whereupon she quickly shepherded the boys to a path between rosebeds. Then she led them down the rows of flowering bushes, pointing to this one and that, responding to whatever the boys said to her.

"A botany lesson, Don Reinaldo. You were right," said Martinez, his moustache twitching suspiciously.

Having overseen her young charges' dinner and

tucking them up for the night, Susanna hurried from the nursery to her own apartment. She threw open the doors of the wardrobe and felt a mounting nervousness as she tried to select a gown to wear down to dinner. The choice oughtn't to be that difficult; she hadn't very many with her.

But the problem was to find a gown which the duke would consider appropriate for a governess. She did now want to add to his already sufficient suspicions about her. It was plain he doubted her abilities, her reference, her origins, perhaps even her *name*. And she so disliked the position into which she'd been forced. Oh, not that of governess. She'd been rather content this month past, had been congratulating herself on securing such a place where the children were amiable and their mother all that was kind. Why, the duchess almost treated her like one of the family, insisting she dine with them and soliciting her opinion on any number of subjects.

No, the position she found odious was that of living a lie. It hadn't troubled her terribly until today, for no one had questioned her story and she hadn't needed to embellish it. But the duke was another matter. She'd already been obliged to invent a birthplace and who knew what else would come about?

But it was more than that, and as she struggled with the buttons at the back of the blue muslin she'd worn all day, she forced herself to examine her feelings. She'd become accustomed to everyone calling her "Beachie"; it had almost seemed a lark before today. And she had such fond memories of her own former governess that she'd rather enjoyed it. But she had been decidedly uncomfortable introducing herself as "Rose Beacham" today. And she'd grown more uncomfortable each time the duke addressed her as "Miss Beacham." And his questions about her own governess had quite unnerved her. He was all too shrewd; he might well tumble to the truth. Why, she'd almost given it away herself—Sarah Bertram, indeed. Oh, dear, she was such a poor liar.

But it wouldn't signify even if he did figure it out, she assured herself as she stepped out of her dress. Standing in her petticoat, she began removing the pins from her hair. Even if he tracked down a Miss Sarah Beacham in Lancashire, Beachie would cover for her. After all, it had been Beachie's idea that she take her name at first stop. "Rose" had been Beachie's idea, too. Beachie had been adamant when she'd protested that she wanted to keep her own given name, Susanna. It had such a musical quality to it; she'd always loved it and now felt bereft without it. But Beachie had insisted it was far too pretty a name for a governess and that changing it would help her "assume her character."

The problem was that she still felt like a "Susanna," not at all like a "Rose." She simply *must* remember to keep her place, especially round the duke. Perhaps after a time, when he saw how well she had the schoolroom under control, his suspicions might be allayed. And if he wrote to a Lady Darnley of Hapworth Hall, well, Beachie had assured Susanna there would be no trouble from that quarter. Of course, the duke might search in vain for a Reverend Beacham near Winestead, but she was certain she could talk her way round that. The only real danger would be if he were to learn her true identity. And that, of course, he could never do. She did not have so much as a monogrammed handkerchief with her.

There hadn't been time, that dreadful night when she'd fled her home, to take more than the most essential items. Besides, personal mementos might reveal too much. The only two she'd permitted herself were the miniature of her mother as a bride and her mother's pearls. The miniature was hidden in the bottom of the wardrobe, but she conjured the picture clearly in her mind. Her mother was seated in a lawn chair, the manor house behind her and the sweep of hills beyond.

Susanna sank down onto the bed, falling back on the coverlet as the memories assailed her. She had succeeded in stifling them for so long, but now they came rushing toward her. She threw one hand across her brow as she gave in to the onslaught.

Ballincraig. Her home in the Lowlands of Scotland. Ballincraig, where the lush glens gave way without warning to stark, barren moors. Where the mist could rise in the gloaming and drape the land in an eerie blanket, or glisten like so many jewels atop the flowers at daybreak.

The ancient stone manor house, nestled at the base of the hills, once echoed with laughter and the gaiety of constant visitors. Susanna could still see her mother's smile of welcome as yet another carriage drew up, could hear her infectious laughter. Susanna's handsome, dashing father, Laird of Ballincraig, had laughed then too, laughed more than he drank. She had known, even as a bairn, that her parents loved each other, despite what she thought of as the black times. Those would come unexpectedly, and she never knew exactly what happened. But Mama would be crying, and Papa would be begging forgiveness. Then invariably one of the maidservants would quietly disappear and Cook would mutter for days about the breeding habits of rabbits.

And soon Mama would laugh again and Susanna's world would be secure. And if Papa never had quite enough time for his only bairn, Susanna was not troubled, for she had Mama.

Susanna's childhood came to an abrupt end when she was ten years old. That was when the fever came and carried Mama off. Even now Susanna felt tears prick her eyelids as the sense of loss washed over her.

She'd been used to think her father had changed drastically after that, but her adult perspective told her that he'd simply followed his natural inclinations once her mother had gone. There was still laughter in the house, but it was quite different. It was coarse now, and very loud. There were visitors still, but the men were often in their cups and the women were not at all like Mama's friends. They wore flashy dresses and face paint, and MacFarlane, the butler, always tried to keep Susanna away from them.

There were times, in those first two years after her mother died, when it seemed as if MacFarlane was the only one in the household who looked after her. He would tuck her up at night, and hold her when she cried for her mother. Marta, the housekeeper, had never been her friend, and now she was dipping into the whisky as much as Papa, and giggling with him late into the night.

Of course, there *was* Aunt MacLaughlin, who tried to take an interest in her upbringing. But Aunt lived near to an hour away, and she had her own troubles, what with Jamie to raise and her husband long gone and those dreadful megrims that plagued her.

It fell to Susanna to check the linen inventory and the weekly menus, to fill in more and more when Marta was "feelin' poorly," as Cook would say. By the time she was twelve she was running the house; her father, if he was aware of it, never commented.

Her most joyous times were spent riding the hills, alone or with her cousin Jamie, her one playmate. She would set her favorite stallion to a gallop, her hair flying about her in the wind, and Jamie would follow as best he might. She'd been alone the day she'd encountered Dermot MacLeod, her father's solicitor, riding in his carriage. He'd always had a smile for her and so she'd reined in to talk to him. He was kind and he made her laugh, but he was rather overset to learn that she'd had not formal lessons since her mother had died.

The result of that chance conversation had been the arrival of Beachie. Susanna never knew how MacLeod had convinced her father that she was in need of a governess; Aunt MacLaughlin had tried several times and failed. Susanna shuddered even now to think what might have become of her without Beachie. Beachie was her friend and teacher and mentor. Beachie opened up the world of the mind to Susanna, the world her mother had begun showing her years before. Beachie taught her to speak and dress and act like a lady, like her mother And Beachie taught her that not all men were like her father and his friends. One of his friends in particular Susanna did not like. Duncan Mortimer. From the time she was fourteen, he'd had a way of looking at her that made her shiver with distaste.

When she was sixteen her father bade her put her hair up and become his hostess. She had no wish to do so, but he would not be gainsaid. Nor did her tears move him when he decided soon after that Beachie's services were no longer required. And so, except for

Beachie's letters, Susanna was on her own. She continued to read the books Beachie suggested, nourishing her love of fine literature. But most of her energy went into running Ballincraig, with a much firmer hand that before. Such was needed, for her father took less and less interest, Marta was near to useless, and it was increasingly born home to Susanna that funds were dwindling.

She husbanded what resources they had and learned to cajole her father into spending money where it was most sorely needed. She learned to soothe the butcher when a bill was overdue and maintain her equanimity when yet another village girl came weeping to her about being in the family way after that night with the laird.

She even learned to ignore the suggestive remarks of her father's friends at dinner. She would smile and bat her eyelashes and act the perfect hostess, all the while maintaining her distance. She supposed she was bonny, for she'd been told so often enough. But at times it seemed a disadvantage, especially when Duncan Mortimer would look her up and down in that way of his. And then there were the times he would contrive to brush up against her, or take her hand and hold it too long, and she would feel a wave of nausea.

Sometimes she would catch her father's eyes lingering on her speculatively. She never understood the look, until that day—she could not have been more than seventeen—when he'd called her into his study. Duncan Mortimer wished her hand in marriage. She'd been horrified. Mortimer was of an age with her father, and his very touch filled her with revulsion. Her father had raged. Mortimer was a very rich man and would make a fine husband, he'd said. But her tears had prevailed. He had not pressed the issue. Until the next year, and the next. Duncan Mortimer was very determined, and her father was edging closer and closer to dun territory.

She held Mortimer off for six years. Until the end, when Mortimer had run out of patience and her father had run out of funds . . .

Susanna's head was pounding, and she ruthlessly dammed the flood of memories. She did not want to remember that last night. She *would* not think of it! It was over. All over.

She forced herself to rise, and she washed her face with the cold water in the ewer. She would have to hurry about her dressing if she was to be on time for dinner. She selected a russet satin round dress, it having the highest neckline of any of her evening dresses. She twisted into it, reminding herself that learning to dress without a maid was one of the skills required of Miss Rose Beacham. And she must accept the fact that Susanna Fergusson was gone, possibly forever. She'd disappeared that rainy night nearly two months ago in the rolling hills of the Scottish Lowlands. And Rose Beacham had come forth to take her place.

Chapter 4

Reginald's eyes widened when the new governess strolled into the Blue Saloon before dinner. She graciously accepted a glass of sherry from a footman, smiled at his mother and Phoebe, and then slowly came toward him.

The gown she wore was cut outrageously low, not, he admitted, for a lady of fashion, but certainly for a governess! Why, her breasts swelled beneath the tiny corsage of the gown, and the little puffed sleeves fell off her creamy shoulders in the most tantalizing way. How could he simply sit across from her at table night after night and not . . .

Not what? He demanded of himself. She was the governess, dammit! Little more than an upper servant. Then what was she doing taking sherry in the Blue Saloon like a member of the family? But that he knew was his mother's doing; she'd always invited the governesses to take dinner with the family after the children were fed. Well, most of them. Poor Miss Pritchard even Mama could not abide at table, her manner was so overly deferential and her conversation so sadly lacking.

Miss Beacham, however, would do well to cultivate a bit of deference, and as for conversation, she certainly never seemed at a loss. Answers, truthful or not, fairly tripped off her tongue. She greeted him pleasantly, but with perhaps a bit more reserve than before; she did not extend her hand.

"Good evening, Miss Beacham," he returned, and found himself staring at her rich auburn hair. She had twisted it back ruthlessly into a sort of chignon, but some of it fell into soft waves about her face. The satin gown, almost the same color, gave her skin a luminous, creamy sheen. He took a long sip of his sherry.

"Did the boys enjoy their, ah, lesson in the garden this afternoon?" the duke asked after a moment, a glint in his eye.

Susanna met his gaze steadily. She had done nothing wrong, she reassured herself. "Why, yes, Your Grace, to be sure. Although in truth it is Thomas who is most interested in the varieties of flowers. Timothy was more concerned with which rosebushes grow the largest thorns, and could one dip them in poison and use them in battle."

"Yes, Timothy has always been rather military minded," he returned, trying, she thought, to hide his amusement.

"And horse-mad," she put in.

"That too," he concurred. "But as to Thomas, I was not aware that he had any particular affinity for flowers, or plants of any kind."

She cocked her head. "Thomas holds you in a great deal of . . . awe, Your Grace. Oh, they all do, the duchess included." He raised a brow and she could not help smiling. "But Thomas more than the others," she

65

went on, and then, more seriously, added, "I think he might be . . . hesitant to speak to you of his fledgling interest in a subject in which you have become one of the greatest authorities."

"He has spoken to you of this . . . interest of his?"

"Yes, although I do think his bent may run more to horticulture than botany. He has spend considerable time recently poring over your father's journals. He was the horticulturalist in the family, was he not?"

The duke's eyebrows snapped together. "How the devil did he get to those journals?" he demanded.

Susanna's cheeks reddened. Oh dear, she thought, just when things seemed to be going so well. "Why, he asked me for them, and I found them in the library. I felt it would not be amiss of me to avail myself of the library—for the children's lessons, of course."

After a moment, the duke relaxed, and Susanna felt relieved. "You have made your point, Miss Beacham. See that he treats those journals with care. They are irreplaceable."

"I've made certain he either reads them in the library or takes them into the conservatory."

"The conservatory! Now, see here, Miss Beacham—"

"Reggie, dear," the duchess interrupted, drifting over with Phoebe in tow, "Phoebe and I have been in a spate of curiosity ever since we received the last issue of *La Belle Assemblée*. Do tell us what you saw in London. Are the ladies really wearing bonnets with crowns so high they look like chimneys? I own I could not credit the pictures I saw, but my dear friend Lady Craddock insists that it is so!"

Unwittingly, Reginald's eyes darted to Miss Beacham, whose eyes held a suspicious gleam. "Yes, do tell, Your Grace," she said, and he groaned inwardly.

Life was becoming more complicated by the minute.

The duke rode out early the next morning, as was his custom, and once home breakfasted in blissful solitude as he read the morning paper. He was strolling jauntily toward his study, where his estate manager awaited him. No doubt there was quite an accumulation of work needing his attention after his absence. He stopped in the corridor outside the morning room, his attention arrested by the sound of a woman humming. Humming? His mother didn't hum, nor did Phoebe. Of a certain the servants wouldn't dare. Then who . . . Of course, he knew exactly who. He advanced closer, his boots silent on the carpeted floor. It was a beautiful sound really, even if it *was* unprecedented. It was deep, melodious, infinitely sweet, like her speaking voice.

The door was ajar. Today she wore a dress of lime green sarcenet. Her back was to him as she bent over a table, and he could not yet see what she was doing. Silently, he pushed the door open farther and walked into the room.

"Good morning, Your Grace," she said without turning round.

How did she . . . ?

"Good morning, Miss Beacham," he heard himself responding, and then he peered over her shoulder. "Miss Beacham! Just what do you think you are doing? Who gave you permission to cut these flowers?"

Susanna's busy hands came to a halt. "Permission?" she repeated. Rather stupidly, she thought.

"Miss Beacham," he said crisply, "flowers at Milburne Hall exist for the purpose of beautifying the garden, *not* the house. It is a tradition that goes back to my father, who, as you know, was a renowned horticulturist. Flowers belong in the *ground,* ma'am, not in some chinoiserie vase!"

Susanna blinked. Surely he could not be serious. But it seemed that he was, and she knew that she had ought to tread carefully. "I apprehend, Your Grace, that the gardens here at Milburne are very beautiful. But flowers do rather beautify a house as well, you must know. Perhaps we might—"

"Miss Beach—Oh! Your Grace, beggin' your pardon!" Mrs. Longbotham's gravelly voice boomed into the room as she appeared on the threshold.

The governess's gaze flew to the door. "I'll be with you straightaway, Mrs. L. Have you the books?"

"That I do, miss. Not but what some of the pages be missin' and we'll have to be doin' a mort o' guesswork. Some of the linens—tableclothes, especially—may be in the attics, I'm afeared, for the butler's pantry surely cannot hold them all, nor the linen room." She finally stopped, seeing Reginald's increasingly furious frown, and bobbed a curtsy. "I'll await you in the linen room, miss."

The minute she'd gone, closing the door behind her, he stepped round the table to where the governess stood. He took her by the arm. "Did I hear correctly? Are *you* doing the linen inventory? The one that is three years out of date at the least?"

Susanna knew he was trying to control his anger. His touch was firm and his jaw muscles looked clenched. She ought to be afraid of him; could he not hurt her the way Duncan Mortimer had? A ripple of fear went through her as she thought of Morimer and of her father and his friends. Did they not seduce maidservants, sometimes bruising them, if not outright beating them, at will? But not all men were like that, she reminded herself. Why, Cousin Jamie, who'd been nineteen when he'd left home three years ago, had always been gentle. Then there were MacFarlane and Dermot MacLeod, good and kind men.

And now there was Reginald Ayres. She was here, alone in a room with him, knowing that as her employer he had complete power over her. Yet she was not afraid. Oh, she knew he could turn her off at anytime, and that she did fear. But not his proximity, or his touch. His hand was making her arm feel decidedly warm, and it was not in the least unpleasant.

You ought to be properly cowed and meek and remember your place, a warning voice told her. But though she had gone against the very code of her upbringing by running away and then taking this position, she could not go against her very *nature*. And meekness did not come naturally to her. Without quite realizing it, she lifted her resolute chin.

Even before she spoke, Reginald could feel his anger slipping away. He'd watched emotions play across her face, seen the momentary fear in her eyes. It troubled him in ways he did not care to contemplate.

"Aye," she replied at length, "Yer mama asked me to do the linens, for the poor dear is quite busy as 'tis, what with her correspondence and the menus, and then the dressmaker was here—"

"Miss Beacham," he interrupted bemusedly, his mind registering two more Scottish words, "May I ask where the children are?"

"Oh, certainly, Your Grace," she replied graciously. "Thomas is in the library, reading one of the journals, you must know. Letty is in the music room, practicing her scales on the harpsichord. And Timothy is in the

69

tack room with—"

"Miss Beacham," he interrupted again, torn between exasperation and amusement, "would it be too much to ask that you spend *part* of each day in the schoolroom?"

She flashed him a lovely smile. "Why, of course not, Your Grace. We shall be there this afternoon. And you are most welcome at any time." She gathered her skirts with her free hand and took a step to the side. "Now if you will excuse—"

"Not so fast!" He pulled her right back, his hand on her forearm.

"Oh, of course. I quite forgot. In the matter of the flowers, I thought we might . . . ah . . . compromise, you must know." He arched his brow and she went on. "Perhaps you might permit me to use one small section of the gardens for my floral bouquets. And I thought I might instruct Phoebe in the art of flower arrangement." He noted that her beautiful face was most expressive when she was trying to be persuasive. And he noted that her lime green dress set off the highlights in her lustrous auburn hair and that her arm felt decidedly warm under his hand. And then he admonished himself severely, for none of those things mattered a whit.

He lowered his hand abruptly. "You would be better served to instruct Phoebe in how to inventory the linens. That, at the least, is something useful, and does not involve the destruction of vegetation!" he exclaimed. "Allow me to escort you to the linen room, ma'am," he added, and wondered whatever could have possessed him. One did not escort governesses anywhere.

But he did, and enjoyed the feel of her elbow beneath his hand and the faint scent of campanulas and foxgloves that clung to her. Enjoyed them all too well.

Martinez marched along the corridor to the master's chambers, intent on solving the problem of dinner. He always took his meals in the butler's pantry with the other upper servants. Of course, the little French maid would be there, would sit across from him at table. And while she was a much prettier sight than the duchess's ancient hatchet-faced former maid, still Martinez could not consider breaking bread with one of *them*. It was because of them he had no family, no home of his own. Though he loved Don Reinaldo like a brother, this was not his home, and his own brother was buried deep in the ground.

Last night Martinez had used the excuse of having much work to do, what with unpacking all of His Grace's things. And so he had simply filched some cold glazed ham from the kitchens. But he could not keep doing that. No one below stairs had any authority over him, but word would eventually reach Don Reinaldo, and Martinez did not want to involve him. This was Martinez's problem, and he alone would solve it.

And so it was a great shock to enter the duke's dressing room and see two drawers ajar. An even greater one to see none other than the French maid rifling through a third. "Señorita! Is there something I can do for you?" he demanded coldly.

She jumped nearly three feet. "Oh, monsieur!" she cried in a tiny voice. "You startled me. I . . . I am so sorry to intrude, but Her Grace asked me to . . . to see if His Grace had been given some of her handkerchiefs by mistake. She is missing quite a few, you see, and I did not wish to disturb you, so I . . . I came when . . .

no one was about."

Her voice grew weaker as his frown deepened, and when he advanced into the room she grabbed onto a chair and seemed to cringe. He stopped short. She was shaking like a leaf. What is wrong with you, Martinez, he asked himself, to so frighten a woman? Even one of *them*.

But he could not bring himself to smile, and so he stayed where he was and said, "I have not seen any ladies' handkerchiefs among His Grace's things, señorita. If I do I will send them along. You had only to ask me. There was no need for you to search the drawers."

"Very well. I . . . I am so sorry, monsieur. I did not mean to . . ." She did not finish her sentence, but sidled past him as quickly as possible and bolted from the room. And then Martinez indulged in a long, satisfying stream of Spanish invective. For the señorita was very pretty and very sweet, and he would not, could not, go near her.

Reginald decided it might well be prudent to look in on the schoolroom and so made his way to the third floor straightaway after luncheon. He stood on the threshold of the schoolroom and blinked, certain his eyes deceived him. For two footmen moved laboriously up the aisle to the large desk in front. They were struggling under the weight of a large globe, *his globe!*

"Excellent. Put it just here," the governess said, "and take this old one away. You can put it in His Grace's study. I am persuaded he would appreciate it." I'm going to wring her neck, Reginald thought. But not yet. He ducked out of sight as the footman left with the discarded globe. And then he stood once more at the threshold, unseen by anyone.

Letty stood under the windows, a book in her outstretched hand, her face tilted up as she recited,

"Spread thy close curtain, love-performing night!
That rude day's eyes may wink, and Romeo
Leap to these arms untalked of and unseen.
Lovers can see to do their amorous rites . . ."

Good God, Reginald thought. Suddenly Letty lowered the book. "What does 'amorous' mean, Beachie?"

"Ah, well, dear, it means . . . having to do with love."

"Oh. Well, what does this line mean, about losing a 'winning match, play'd for a pair of stainless maidenhoods'?" Reginald had all he could do to keep from bursting in at that moment. Not yet, he told himself. Give her more rope to hang herself.

"It's my turn, Beachie!" Timothy exclaimed, jumping up from his seat. "Now we've got the globe, you promised to show me where the navy was, and the army, when we licked old Boney."

"Of course, Timothy. Come here and we'll see about it. Letty, dear, keep reading, and I'll answer your questions a bit later. You must remember to read for the general notion, dear. 'Tisn't necessary to comprehend each word."

Letty went back to her book, and Reginald's eyes fell on Thomas for the first time. He was bent over a desk to the far right, his hands seemingly engaged upon some delicate operation. Suddenly his head came up. "Beachie, I do need your help. I've found the pistil and the stamen, I'm certain, but I cannot locate the stigma."

What the devil! Reginald strode into the room, straight to Thomas's desk. What looked like a mangled rose lay in pieces on the desk top, a text of Linnaeus's work beside it.

"Reggie!" Thomas stood up immediately, trying to cover the plant fragments with the book. Letty stopped her recital midsentence, and Timothy whirled around. Only Miss Beacham resolutely stood her ground.

"Your Grace," she managed. "You did come. Please do sit down."

"No thank you, Miss Beacham. I would have a word with you. Outside. Now!"

"But, Your Grace, the children—"

"Yes. The children. Do they not have a spelling book, Miss Beacham?" he demanded.

She blinked as if she'd never heard of such a thing. "Carry on, children," she said.

He followed her out. Just as he closed the door behind them, he heard Thomas shout, "No, Desdemona! You can't have that. Catch her, Letty! She's got the stamen! I haven't finished with it yet!" He heard the unmistakable sounds of a scuffle, and then Robin Hood barked.

He pulled the governess by the hand down the corridor and into an alcove under the eaves. Then he dropped her hand and rounded on her, intent on strangulation. "What the *devil* do you mean by this display?"

"Display, Your Grace?" The alcove was narrow, and she took a step back into the corridor.

"Don't play the innocent with me, ma'am! How could you let Letty read such things?"

"Read such—Why that's *Romeo and Juliet,* Your

Grace. It's by—"

"I *know* who wrote it, Miss Beacham! And it is completely inappropriate for a young girl at such a tender age. Why, to even repeat such words—She cannot possibly understand what she is reading. Unless . . ."

"But that is just the point, Your Grace. It is a beautiful love story, and *that* she can understand. As to the so-called inappropriate parts, why, if she does not comprehend them, pray tell me how they can possibly be objectionable! Truly, Your Grace, the study of Shakespeare is perfectly admirable. Why, I began at just her age. She did want to read *Othello,* because of Desdemona, you must know, but I felt it too complex. Do you not agree?"

"Miss Beacham!" he exclaimed, grabbing her upper arms and pulling her just a bit closer. "If you let her near *Othello* I shall wring your pretty little neck!"

"Oh!" she exclaimed, blushing, her eyes regarding him in complete confusion.

"And as to Thomas, could you not teach him about plant nutrition, or respiration? Why the devil must it be, er, reproduction?" His eyes swept over her and she felt suddenly warm.

She swallowed. "Well, you see, Your Grace, I'm not precisely teaching him, for I own I know very little about . . . about, er, about plants. He discovered it all himself, you see, and *he's* teaching *me.* Why, I had no idea that according to a man named Linnaeus, plants have male and female—well, I mean to say, is it possible, Your Grace, that they, ah . . ." Mortified, she ground to a halt.

"I say, Beachie! Where are you?" Thomas called, bursting out of the schoolroom. Reginald knew he

75

could only see Miss Beacham, and he didn't move. "Oh, there you are! Why don't you come back? Reggie didn't give you a trimming, did he? You mustn't be too distressed. He's very high in the instep, but I expect that's only because he's the duke. He really is a right one, you know."

"Thomas, I think you ought to go back inside," she called back.

"I shall have to start with another rose," Thomas said, advancing toward them. "Desdemona's eaten the stamen. Oh! Reggie!" he exclaimed, seeing the duke for the first time. "I, uh, I'll see about my spelling now." Thomas beat a hasty retreat.

An unholy gleam rose in the governess's eye.

"There is nothing in the least funny about any of this," Reginald said severely.

"No, of course not."

"And one more thing, Miss Beacham. How dare you take the globe from my study without permission?"

Oh dear, Susanna thought. She supposed she *had* overstepped herself. "I do apologize, Your Grace. I truly did not wish to trouble you. I knew you understood the inadequacy of the schoolroom globe. And as you'd already said we might not use your globe in your study, I thought it would be simplest if we moved it here." The duke frowned prodigiously. "May we, ah, keep it here, Your Grace? 'Tis for the children, after all."

He was not at all certain he trusted her meek tone. But he was not proof against the contrite look in those magnificent blue eyes. Hellfire, he thought and acquiesced graciously, telling himself it was, after all, for the children.

Chapter 5

It was in the Blue Saloon before dinner that evening that the duke received the rather disturbing news that Oswald Hastings had come to call. "'Tis a great pity that I was having my nap at the time, Reggie," his mother said in an undertone. "And you were closetted with your agent in your study. But you mustn't trouble yourself, for Miss Beacham sat with them as chaperone."

"And where, pray tell, were the children?" Reginald asked in the voice of one goaded nearly beyond endurance.

"Well, I own I don't quite know, dear, but I'm sure Miss Beacham does. Shall we ask her?"

"No, Mother, let us not," he said firmly, but too late. Miss Beacham had entered the room looking all too enchanting in an evening dress of coral net over satin. He sipped his sherry slowly, watching as she came toward them. "I could not help overhearing, Your Grace," she said, "but you may set your mind at rest. We had just finished our afternoon lessons, you must know, and Timothy went to watch Perkins work that new stallion you bought—"

"Hercules arrived? When?"

"Why, he arrived sometime today, Your Grace."

He wondered how it was that she seemed to know more about his household than he did but forebore commenting. Miss Beacham accepted a glass of sherry from a footman and Reginald noted that his Mama and Phoebe had drifted off to the side. He forced himself back to the matter at hand. "So, you allowed Timothy to go to the stables again. Let us hope he can spell the word *horse*," he murmured. "And what of the others?"

"Thomas volunteered to pick vegetables for Mrs. Rackett."

"Pick vegetables? How extraordinary! Why the devil can she not have the undercook do it, or pick them herself if it comes to that?"

"The undercook, Stella, has a touch of the influenza. And Mrs. Rackett will not venture outside."

He raised a brow.

"Because of Horatio's shadow."

"Oh, Lord," he groaned, more to himself. "I've surely descended into bedlam." Then in a louder voice he added, "But I'm positively agog with curiosity as to the whereabouts of Letty at the time, Miss Beacham. Pray enlighten me."

"Letty was in the dairy with Eliza and Cleopatra."

"Er, *Eliza?*"

"The dairymaid. And Cleopatra is the white milk cow."

"I see. Dare I ask what Letty was doing in the dairy?" Reginald's voice was ominously calm.

"She wanted to watch Cleopatra being milked."

"But of course. I should have guessed," he drawled. "And may I ask why you feel it necessary to include ani-

78

mal husbandry in my sister's education, Miss Beacham?"

"It seemed the best way to answer her questions about the purpose of a wet nurse."

Reginald choked on his sherry. When he had recovered he glowered at the governess.

"Miss Beacham, I consider such conversations with Letty to be highly inappropriate. You will heretofore confine yourself to the subject matter contained in the schoolroom texts."

"But surely, Your Grace, 'tis only natural curiosity. And 'tis not as though she asked how babes are *made,* merely how they are fed."

"Miss Beacham! Natural curiosity is all well and good at the appropriate time and place. Letty, I might remind you, is twelve years old!"

"I realize that, Your Grace. She only asked, you see, because we visited one of your tenants, Mrs. Scranton, last week. She just birthed her fifth bairn a fortnight ago, you must know, and she was giving suck to the child just as we entered the cottage."

"Miss Beacham! Before you came the children spent their days in the schoolroom, my mother paid her own duty calls, Mrs. Rackett even picked her own vegetables!"

"Och, what a great deal of blether!"

"Blether?" he asked.

Susanna sucked in her breath. How could she have let that slip? And she knew it was not the first time she had lapsed into Scots. It hadn't happened often with the others, before he arrived, but somehow with the duke it was much harder to control her tongue. How ironic, when it was with him that she need be most careful. His gaze did not waver, and she forced herself to reply.

"Yes, blether. 'Tis a . . . a Lancashire expression. It

means a . . . a farrago of nonsense. Before I came the children were running wild."

"Miss Beacham—"

"Nae, Your Grace, I will have my say. Why, no one even noticed before that Thomas simply wanted to emulate his big brother in his studies." Reginald felt himself flush at that and was annoyed with himself, and her. "And as to Phoebe, Your Grace, it was *I* who pointed out to the duchess that the baron's second son was becoming much too particular in his attentions."

"You? What do you know of it?"

"I happened upon Phoebe meeting Oswald Hastings down by the burn that separates the two properties."

He did not trouble to point out that *burn* was the Scottish word for stream; she would undoubtedly claim it as pure Lancashire broad. "Go on," he prompted.

"Well, I naturally brought her back with the children and me, and I apprehended from our conversation that such was not the first supposedly chance meeting. You may be sure I impressed upon her the impropriety of such meetings and suggested to her that she encourage him to call at the Hall."

"What? How dare you do such a thing! You know nothing of—"

"I know that I wouldn't trust that young man a stone's throw. And I also know, Your Grace, that it is far better for her to meet him in the morning room, under supervision, than off in the woods. But I must own I agree completely with your mama's idea of bringing Phoebe out in the Little Season."

"What?" he exploded.

"Oh, dear. Has she not told you?"

"No, blast it, and I—"

80

"Dinner is served, Your Graces," came the stentorian voice of Underwood. Reginald glared at Miss Beacham.

"Ah, and just in time, is it not, Reggie dear?" his mother chimed in, gliding over and causing him to shift his glare to her. "For I declare I'm positively famished. Come, Reggie, do take my arm. Beachie can follow with Phoebe." She smiled charmingly at the governess, but Reginald cast Miss Beacham a look that promised their conversation was far from over.

"Reggie dear," the duchess said as they walked ahead toward the dining room, "I'm very pleased that you are attempting to get to know Beachie a bit. I am persuaded that the more you know her, the fewer doubts about her you will have." Reginald raised an eyebrow. "Oh, by the by," his mama went on, "did I tell you—no I don't suppose I did, for you *were* occupied with your agent the better part of the afternoon, were you not? Yes, well, we have all been invited to dine at Beverwil on Thursday night."

"At the baron's? Good God! I hope you declined, Mother!"

"Of course not, Reggie. They are our nearest neighbors. Oh, I own the baron is a bit prosaic—"

"He is an oaf and a bore, Mother, and that sister of his is a shrew. As to his son, I thought the idea was to keep Phoebe away from him."

"Of course it is, dear, but as Beachie pointed out, the best way to do that is to allow Phoebe to get to know him better. That way she can see for herself that he is not at all the thing."

"Beachie" and her damned fool notions again, he thought.

"Oh, and they've invited Beachie as well," the

duchess added. "And I do think she ought to get about more, do you not agree, Reggie?"

"No, I do not, Mother! Beachie, er, Miss Beacham is the *governess,* you may recall, not a house guest."

"Ah, here we are. I do hope you won't cavil about Thursday night, dear, for I've already accepted. It's been rather quiet since you've been away, and I own I should welcome a bit of diversion. Emily Hastings may be a bit sharp-tongued, sad to say, but she always has some new recipe for me to pass on to Cook, and the latest on dits from Upper Milburne and—"

"Very well, Mother. We shall go." He capitulated and then bowed the ladies into the room.

There was no opportunity for private discourse at table, and Reginald did not enjoy the poached salmon with lobster sauce. For he could not take his mind off his aborted conversation with Miss Beacham. He wanted to know who to credit for that hubble-bubble notion to take Phoebe to London in the autumn. As if he didn't already suspect she'd put the idea straight into his mama's rather addlepated head. But he would ask the governess first, give her enough rope, as it were, and then he would have a word to say to his mother. For he had absolutely no intention of escorting his mother and sister to an endless round of soirees and balls. Why Phoebe was barely out of the schoolroom! They might well scotch any such notion straightaway!

Reginald did not enjoy the truffled chickens with braised root vegetables, for he could not keep his gaze from Miss Beacham, whose eyes sparkled in the candlelight and whose dress fit her in a way that no governess's ought.

And he did not enjoy the junket that Mrs. Rackett made to perfection, dousing it with the finest of

Devonshire cream, for he could not help wondering when he would receive an answering letter from his friend Penderleigh, and what it would say. And if the answer was as he suspected, what then? Armed with that, and the evidence of her own tongue betraying her Scottish origins, he could press her for the truth. And then he could turn her off. Which was exactly what she deserved, he assured himself, for impersonating a governess, insinuating herself into this household, and comporting herself without the least notion of propriety!

Suddenly he felt one of his rare and dreadful headaches coming on, and reached for the madeira, which was, of course, the worst thing he could do.

He did not linger long over his port once the ladies had departed, for he meant to pursue his discussion with the governess. But she was gone by the time he reached the Blue Saloon, having pleaded, Phoebe informed him, a headache. He felt a pang of disappointment at her absence and quickly replaced it with very justifiable vexation. The spurious, ubiquitous female headache, he thought disparagingly, and felt his own very real headache begin to pound on the left side of his head. Blast! This was about all he needed just now. And he supposed the alleged governess would have just the cure! Well, she would learn her place in the next few days, even if that place was *not* Milburne Hall!

Susanna could not recall the last time she had fabricated a headache to escape from company. Even in her father's house, she had fulfilled her role as hostess, enduring the crude company he kept, the snide remarks and suggestive glances, until she could politely leave. For it had not been her way to play the coward and flee. Not until that last night, when there had been no choice.

Why, then, had she departed the Blue Saloon so precipitously this night? She had not quite planned to plead that headache; the words had merely tumbled out. But she knew very well why. It had to do with Reginald Ayres, with the way his eyes kept finding their way to her, and the intensity with which they burned when they did. His gaze was nothing like Duncan Mortimer's cold, calculating leer, which used to make her shiver with revulsion. On the contrary, the duke's gaze had more than once caused a warm ripple to course through her. It was not at all unpleasant, and it troubled her not a little.

She had just reached the landing leading to the third floor when she heard the sound. It was the soft but unmistakable sound of weeping. But who? Surely Letty could not still be awake, and she'd just left Phoebe with the duchess, taking coffee downstairs. One of the servants then, she realized, and padded silently down the second-floor corridor toward the end of the east wing. And there, curled up on a small window seat, head in her hands, sat Her Grace's petite maid.

She put her arm on the young woman's shoulders. "Angelique, what is it? May I help you?" she asked softly.

Slowly the maid's dark head came up. "Oh, mademoiselle, forgive me. I should not be here."

"Blether! I should imagine you can sit here whenever you like. But, my dear, what is it that troubles you?" Susanna spoke soothingly, and the maid regarded her with the trusting eyes of a child. Yet she knew

Angelique must be a few years older than her own two and twenty. For the duchess had told her that Angelique had been the merest child during the Terror in France, when her parents were killed.

"He ate in the servants' hall! He will not eat with us in the butler's pantry, be-because of me. He . . . he cannot bear the sight of me, because I am French," Angelique said between quiet sobs.

"Who, Angelique?"

"The duke's man. M-Martinez. And he . . . he is a very kind man, you must know, but he suffered terribly in the War. Everyone says so. And he is so very handsome, although he frightens me so. . . . He has the temper, you see. But I—I would not for all the world cause him distress, nor . . . nor take his place at table. It is much more *his* place than mine. He has been with His Grace for years and years!"

Susanna sank down on the seat next to Angelique. Her heart went out to the little maid, who seemed to have the gentlest nature. Susanna patted Angelique's hand as her mind raced furiously. She considered presenting the problem to the duke but dismissed that notion out of hand. She suspected both Martinez and Angelique would be mortified should she involve His Grace. And His Grace would ring a peal over her for meddling. And, of course, the duchess, well-meaning though she might be, would be no help at all. As to Martinez, Susanna could not imagine what she could possibly say to him. Everyone knew how he felt about the French. Everyone at the Hall from Letty down to the lowest undergroom had known what would happen when Martinez returned. Everyone, that is, except the duchess. And Phoebe, whose head was unfortunately in a cloud over that wastrel Oswald Hastings.

Perhaps, Susanna mused, there was another way. She had met Martinez yesterday. He *was* handsome in a dark sort of way, and he had been most gallant. She had been carrying a pile of books from the library, and he had insisted on helping her. But to her chagrin he had read the titles. "Ah. The children are to study the works of Shakespeare, And Linnaeus. A most . . . unusual combination, Señorita Beacham."

She had felt compelled to defend herself. "Yes, well, the children have such varied interests, you see, and—"

"I quite understand, señorita," he forestalled her. "It will all be very . . . interesting, I am certain." He had chuckled to himself but refused to say more, and Susanna had sensed that he did not intend to say anything to the duke.

He *is* kind, she thought now, just as Angelique had said. But he must also be lonely. . . .

The Duke would flay her if he could read her mind. "Angelique, I have a notion," she said, before she could think better of it. *"You* must decline to eat in the butler's pantry as well."

"But how . . ."

"I shall speak to Cook and insure that she will allow you to take your meals in the kitchen. You will not mind terribly, will you? I am persuaded it will only be for a few days."

"Very well. But I . . . I do not understand. Why only a few days?"

"You must leave that to me, my dear. Oh, and if anyone should ask you why you have not taken your meals in the usual place, you must simply tell the truth." Angelique's dark eyes widened. "Yes. Simply say that you did not wish to discompose Mr. Martinez, who, after all, has been here for so long."

Angelique finally nodded and dried her tears with a handkerchief. And Susanna left her, resolving to have a word with Mrs. Rackett first thing in the morning. And she prayed that the woman could keep a still tongue in her head.

The duke slept poorly. The headache that had begun earlier only worsened as the night wore on. What little sleep he did contrive to snatch was disturbed by snippets of dreams. Dreams of big blue eyes and graceful, slender hands and lovely hips encased in lime green silk. The hands kept reaching out to touch him, but the eyes narrowed in fear, until they closed and disappeared.

He rose in the morning at his usual hour, knowing he would be violently ill before nightfall, but refusing to succumb to the pain and nausea a moment before he had to. He despised this weakness in himself and could not understand it. Megrims were for crotchedly old women and missish girls, not peers of the realm. They struck him only several times a year, but he was powerless before them. Still, he had at the least several good hours left to him, and he meant to use them to advantage. The day before, he had finally prevailed upon his aging steward, Carleton, to review for him the various repairs needed on some of the tenant cottages. He meant to visit several of his tenants this morning, and he had a backlog of specimens to catalogue in the herbarium.

The fresh air and the exhilaration of the ride out over his lands seemed to suspend the pain for a while, but once back at the Hall he found he had very little appetite for breakfast. He contented himself with black coffee and dry toast, and then made his way toward the herbarium. This was a large, locked room beyond his study. It was lined nearly floor to ceiling with specimen cabinets which one day soon would all be filled. He supposed he was never happier than when closeted there, and knew that the peace and quiet of his work was precisely what he needed just now. He would not be interrupted; the only member of the household who was allowed to enter that room was Martinez. For he had accompanied Reginald on the Icelandic expedition and other more local explorations. He knew how to care for the specimens and, Reginald suspected, knew the names and characteristics of as many as his master.

Visiting naturalists from all over Europe came to Devon from time to time to view the collection. Someday, when the children were older, Reginald would mount another expedition. In the meantime, there was a great deal of cataloguing to do, three papers must be written, and his work on Devonian ferns had to be continued.

At least, he mused as he rounded the corner nearest his study, the audacious governess had not attempted to gain admission to the herbarium. Unless, he reflected grimly, that was simply because she hadn't yet divined what lay beyond the locked door in the far corner of his study.

The duke did not, however, reach his study, for the sound of a male voice coming from the morning room caused him to frown and march in that direction instead. The door to the morning room was ajar and he squelched the urge to storm right in. Phoebe was seated on the plush gray and pink damask sofa. She looked a picture in a dress of pink muslin, her blond hair caught in ringlets and her blue eyes almost dewy as she gazed at—at Oswald Hastings! Hastings had drawn a chair up so close to the sofa that their knees almost touched. He seemed to be reciting some nonsensical poetry to Phoebe, and he looked a veritable coxcomb in an obviously padded lemon yellow coat and a green and gold brocade waistcoat. Reginald quickly scanned the room. Where the devil was his mother? Or even the governess, for heaven's sake? He pushed the door open farther and there, in a Hepplewhite chair by the window, sat Letty. Letty? What kind of chaperone was *she?* In that moment Letty picked her head up from her book and caught his eyes. She shook her head and brought her index finger to her lips to caution him to silence. Then she rose and tiptoed toward him.

"You mustn't interrupt him now, Reggie," she whispered as soon as she reached him. "He's calling her hair spun gold and her eyes blue aquamarines."

"Letty!"

"Dreadful, isn't it? Oswald is not very poetic, you must know. He really had ought to reread his Shakespeare. 'Oh, she doth teach the torches to burn bright,'" she quoted, and when he glared at her, added, "Well, at all events, I know he is but giving her Spanish coin, but Phoebe loves it, and I do too, actually. For I am sure no man will ever say any such to me."

She said this last with no regret, just simple acceptance, and Reginald was shocked. He quietly closed the door and asked gently, "Why ever not, Letty? Of a certain you will grow into a great beauty when—"

Letty giggled. "Now *you* are offering Spanish coin, Reggie, for you must own I will do no such thing. Why, I am far too plump, my nose is too wide, and my hair is a most insipid brown. But it doesn't signify, for I shall become a bluestocking!"

"A bluest—Who put such an odious notion into your head? Miss Beacham, I suppose?"

"Of course not, Reggie! And do keep your voice down. Beachie could never be a bluestocking. Why, she's the most beautiful creature I've ever seen! Do you not think so?"

Her ingenuous question caught him off guard and he smiled. "Yes, poppet, I think she is very . . . lovely. But I'll wager 'twasn't always so. She might once have been plump too, with dreadful pigtails and freckles on her nose." He tapped her pug nose with his finger and she laughed. He made a mental note to tell Miss Beacham about her freckles and pigtails before Letty got to her. "There, that's better. Now, tell me, just where is Miss Beacham? Or better still, where is Mama? Surely they could not have left you to chaperone." He opened the door once more. Oswald seemed to have moved closer to Phoebe. Reginald's hand tightened on the crystal door handle.

"Mama went into Upper Milburne to meet Lady Craddock. I do believe the lending library has got a parcel of new romance novels, you must know."

"Wonderful," he grumbled. "And Miss Beacham?"

"Beachie was here, of course, for Mama asked her to stay with Phoebe, but there was some trouble below stairs. Mrs. Rackett again. Something to do with primroses, and Mrs. L. is in a taking because Mrs. Rackett refuses to cook. It was Underwood who came up here for Beachie, saying there were pots and pans flying in the kitchens." There was a gleam in her eye that was much too worldly-wise for her years, and Reginald felt his head pound. It was the left side this time, and it was getting worse.

Suddenly Oswald possessed himself of Phoebe's hand, and Reginald burst into the room. "Why Oswald Hastings, good morning to you. And what brings you here?" he asked loudly. The sound of his own voice caused his head to ring.

"Oh, ah, Your Grace!" Oswald jumped up and bowed. "Servant, Your Grace." His shirt points were absurdly high, his clothing garish. But the yellow coat was the work of one of the finest London tailors, and Reginald supposed he had made his way into the dandy set. "I, er, came to ask Lady Phoebe to drive with me this afternoon."

"I see. Well, I am sorry, Hastings, but Phoebe is promised to Miss Beacham this afternoon for the linen inventory."

"Oh. Well, perhaps tomorrow." Oswald looked hopefully at Phoebe, whose face was becoming mutinous.

"Yes. I understand we are to dine at Beverwil tomorrow night," the duke replied as genially as he could. "Please convey my respects to your father and aunt, old chap. We all look forward to seeing you then. So kind of them, I'm sure."

Phoebe rose and pouted prettily. "But Reggie, tomorrow morning—"

"Yes, I know, dear. Miss Beacham has requested your company on an outing with the children tomorrow. But I do think you will be well rested by nightfall. Do you not agree, Hastings?"

Something unpleasant flashed in Hastings's cool hazel eyes for just a moment. But then he assumed his accustomed air of affability. "To be sure, Your Grace. Lady Phoebe, I look forward to tomorrow night." He bowed correctly all round and took his leave.

Phoebe stamped her foot. "How could you, Reggie?" she cried, big tears welling up in her eyes. "You have been odiously rude! Why, you—you practically turned him out! And now he'll go off to Elsie Craddock and you—"

"Elsie Craddock! She can't be above sixteen years old!"

Phoebe was turning into a watering pot by now. "She's my age, and ever so pretty. You have ruined everything, Reggie, and I will never—"

"Oh, do cease, Phoebe!" he scolded, handing her a handkerchief. "The man is no gentleman—taking your hand in such manner, nearly sitting in your lap! You are not yet out, Phoebe, and you may *not* have gentlemen callers!"

"You are merely set against him because he is a younger son! You do not understand him at all. I did not know you to be so odiously domineering and . . . and high in the instep, Reggie! I wish you'd stayed in London!"

Letty gasped, and Reginald ordered his sister to her room. She fled, leaving a trail of tears behind her. Reginald was beginning to feel as if someone were pounding a hammer behind his left eye. He heard an unmistakable "tsk tsk" and turned to see Letty regarding him disapprovingly as she leaned negligently against a doorpost.

"And just what does that mean, miss?"

"Well, if you truly want my opinion, I think Phoebe is making a perfect cake of herself. But, ah, you *had* ought to beware, Reggie."

"Of what?" he asked curtly.

"Well, I know you think he's a loose fish. Beachie says so too. But if you forbid her to see him, she's likely to think herself Juliet to his Romeo, if you take my meaning."

"No, I do not, miss! Of a certain Phoebe hasn't read that blasted play, which *you,* I might add, oughtn't to do either."

"Beachie says 'tis great literature. And what's more, she says Phoebe ought to be allowed to see a great deal of Oswald. You know, 'familiarity breeds contempt' and all that sort of thing."

"'Beachie' talks much too much. Does she never tell you to visit the schoolroom? Off with you now, young lady, and look up the author of that quotation you so glibly toss round."

"Very well, Reggie," she said, and tripped away, not the least cowed. "It's from Aesop," she called from down the corridor.

He was going to strangle that governess. But first he had to find her. In the kitchens, of all places. Well, he had better see what the brouhaha was about at all events. Things must have come to a rare pass indeed for Underwood to have come abovestairs with such goings on.

He hadn't been to the kitchens in years, he realized as he descended the narrow, winding stairs. And wouldn't be there now, undoubtedly, if not for the meddling, omnipresent governess who seemed to be everything *but* a governess! And it seemed to him, as he stood in the doorway of the first of the kitchens, that he had been doing too much skulking around his own house these three days past. Too much standing in doorways watching ludicrous scenes that could somehow always be laid at Miss Rose Beacham's doorstep!

This time he felt as if he were witnessing a bad play. It would have been funny had it not seemed that his very house was falling down on his ears. Mrs. Longbotham moved her ample form across the stone floor and banged a large cast-iron skillet on the butcher block table at which Cook sat, head in her hands. "You've got to *do* something, Mr. Underwood! How is a body to be runnin' a house without knowin' day to day whether there will be *food* at table?" Underwood and Miss Beacham hovered near Cook, their backs to the duke. Miss Beacham was wearing a peach dress of a fashionably lightweight muslin that looked far too thin to be decent.

Now Mrs. L. grabbed Underwood's immaculate black coat sleeve. "Please, Mr. Underwood," she pleaded, her booming voice suddenly sounding girlish. "Tell me what I had ought to do."

"Oh, Mr. Underwood, surely *you* can understand my sensibilities," Cook cried. "Why, when I saw Eliza carrying just three primroses in from the garden, and her sayin' as how Miss Beacham requested them . . . and everyone knows that if a body brings only a few primroses indoors 'tis bad luck for chicken hatchin'! And here I am with a new batch of eggs this very mornin'. Oh, Miss Beacham, are you certain they don't know 'bout the primroses up in Lancashire?"

"Why, of course they do, Mrs. Rackett," he heard himself say as he strolled nonchalantly into the room.

"Your Grace," Mrs. L. exclaimed, dropping the skillet to the floor with a clamor that made his head rattle.

Cook stumbled to her feet, turned about, and bobbed a curtsy.

"Your Grace," Underwood said, turning and bowing stiffly. He obviously did not care for such an invasion of his nether domain.

The duke heard whispers and the clatter of pots and pans in the shadows, and then absolute silence, as if unseen minions had suddenly realized an august presence had come among them. The governess, blast her, merely pivoted round and inclined her head, her eyes twinkling with amusement as she waited for him to continue.

"Miss, ah, Beacham did not realize you would be overset, because she knew I had commissioned Martinez to bring an entire bouquet of primroses from the garden into the herbarium," he lied blithely, appalled at himself. "And so naturally no one saw them, as *no one ever goes there.*" He said this last pointedly, his eyes staring fixedly at the governess. She raised a questioning brow. But now his wayward eyes fell lower. Why must she needs wear a dress that revealed every one of her womanly curves? Could she not wear something a little less distracting? He forced himself to go on. "And, of course, everyone knows that to bring a quantity of primroses into the house of a day signals good luck for a se'nnight." There, he thought. That should buy them all a week's peace.

Miss Beacham was biting her lip to keep from laughing, Mrs. Longbotham was regarding him suspiciously, and Cook thanked him profusely before collapsing, in sobbing relief, into Underwood's hapless arms. The duke beat a hasty retreat, dragging the governess with him.

A wave of nausea assailed him at the top of the dim first-floor landing, and he squelched it ruthlessly, pausing a moment to steady himself.

"Your Grace? Are you right?" she asked concernedly, putting a hand to his arm.

He took a deep breath, unwilling to let her see his

weakness. "Of course I'm right, dammit! Except for the fact that I have to interrupt my work to find Phoebe being mauled about by that scoundrel Hastings, with none but a child for chaperone!"

"Mauled about! Whatever—"

"And then I needs must descend to the bowels of my house to rescue you from a domestic brangle which is none of your concern!"

Her chin rose up haughtily, and she removed her hand. "I'll have you know that Underwood requested my help, Your Grace, and I assure you, I did not need rescuing!"

He quirked an eyebrow at her, his stomach momentarily settling down, though his head still pounded.

"It *would* have come about, Your Grace," she insisted, then a smile curled her lips and her chin came back down. It was a very nice chin, he thought, and quite adorable when she was in a huff. "Though I must own your intervention was most timely. You are quite an accomplished storyteller."

The landing was narrow and he stood very close to her. Close enough to inhale her scent—a heady combination of jasmine and sandalwood. Close enough to feel her breath graze his face, to see the rise and fall of her breasts beneath that shockingly thin muslin dress. Too close. He took refuge in anger. "I hardly think being able to tell a convenient clanker an accomplishment, Miss Beacham," he countered.

"I . . . I disagree, Your Grace," she said quietly, all traces of humor gone. "There are times when a judicious . . . clanker answers best, I think. Sometimes it is necessary, you, see, to . . . to protect the innocent." She stared at him out of eyes that looked suddenly haunted, and he had the distinct feeling that she was trying to convey some message to him. She looked of a sudden very vulnerable. For the first time it occurred to him that, rather than having schemed for some unknown nefarious end to gain a place in his household, she might be in some sort of trouble.

He felt a most improper urge to gather her into his arms. Instead his hand came up to brush a stray lock of hair from her face. "Miss Beacham, what are you trying to tell me?" he asked gently.

His nearness was doing things to her again, causing her to feel flushed all over. He stood so close, his shoulders so broad and well-formed beneath the charcoal gray suit. Somehow he had disarmed her. Why had she said what she had? She must not give him any cause to doubt the story of her background. But his hand on her face was so gentle; never had a man touched her so. His voice held such concern that she had the sudden urge to throw herself into his arms and tell him all. And if she did, would he . . . would he what? she asked herself. Help her? No, for he was a man for whom honor was paramount. And she had behaved dishonorably. She had defied her father and the law and run away. Run away after committing the most heinous of crimes.

The duke would dishonor himself by knowingly aiding her. But it would never come to that. For he would despise her for what she had done. And he would turn her out.

She could not tell him. She drew in her breath. "Merely that . . . that such stories are harmless, Your Grace. Poor Mrs. Rackett cannot help being so very superstitious, and we must do what we can."

He stared at her for a long moment, certain it was not

97

of Mrs. Rackett she was thinking just moments ago. He could not shake the feeling that she was in some difficulty, nor could he still a pang of disappointment that she had failed to confide in him. And why should she, he asked himself, when he lost no opportunity to ring a peal over her? "Come, my dear. I will escort you above stairs," he said finally, putting a hand to the small of her back.

His tone, the endearment, and the feel of his hand at her back caused a flurry in Susanna's stomach and so weakened her resolve that she was alarmed. She wished he would rail at her again; she felt much safer that way.

And so, as they came into the light of the upstairs corridor, she threw him a saucy look. "Tell me about your herbarium, Your Grace," she said.

"No, Miss Beacham, I will not! And do not go taking any notions about it into that head of yours," he growled, and realized that his headache was much worse, although he had forgotten it for several moments on the landing.

Now he knew there would be no working this day.

Chapter 6

The children having sat for as long as they could for their afternoon lessons, Susanna resolved to take them for a walk through the woods surrounding Milburne Hall. It was a warm day, and she promised to allow them to wade into the stream at the base of the North Wood. That promise placated Timothy, who much preferred to help Perkins in the stables. Thomas, who had at first pleaded some vague indisposition so as to be allowed, Susanna suspected, to continue dissecting roses, also seemed eager. And even Letty had been coaxed away from her books. As they marched down the stairs from the nursery, Robin Hood lumbered along with them, picking his head up only when Timothy bounced the red ball along the corridor.

Letty avidly recounted to Susanna, as they made their way out to the south lawn, that morning's debacle with Oswald Hastings. "So Reggie got his dander up, and now Phoebe is having a fit of the dismals, and hasn't come out of her room since," Letty said with superior disdain.

Susanna began to admonish her gently to show

respect for her elders, especially the duke. But her sentence was cut short as the red ball, and Robin Hood, came careening within inches of her. She yelped and jumped out of the way, and for the next few moments the North Wood was forgotten as she and the children giggled and chased the ball and the great big basset hound all over the lawn.

She was just righting her blue straw bonnet and calming the boys down when Martinez strode out from the house toward them. He seemed perturbed and drew her to the side. "Please, Señorita Beacham, if I may beg you. The duke's rooms are just above this lawn. He has a slight indisposition and I would not want him to be disturbed."

"No, of course not, Martinez. Do you mean to say he is ill, in bed?" she asked in concern.

Martinez looked decidedly uncomfortable. "Ah, yes, señorita. But it is nothing. Just something he ate, I think."

The duke did not seem to Susanna to be a man of weak constitution. And the food at Milburne Hall was always exceedingly fresh. Besides, they had all eaten the same things that day, more than likely. Suddenly she remembered that moment on the back stairs landing when he had looked very ill indeed. Then he had rallied, and she had taken the somewhat pained look that remained to be a reflection of his extreme vexation at the time. But perhaps it was something more. "Martinez, please. What is it? *Is* he ill?" she asked in agitation. "He . . . he did not look well this morning."

Don Reinaldo would have his head for this, Martinez knew. But if he did not tell her, she would learn of it soon enough. For when the duke did not appear for tea, or dinner, everyone else would realize that it had come upon him again. "It is a megrim, señorita. They do not come often, but they are very bad."

"Is there nothing to bring him relief? Some laudanum perhaps? Shall we have the doctor?"

She seemed quite overset, and Martinez regarded her thoughtfully. Don Reinaldo seemed always to be ringing a great peal over the governess, and yet she was so distressed. "No, señorita, he will not take the laudanum. It will pass."

"When? How long—"

Martinez shrugged, wishing he had not begun this conversation. "Two days, perhaps three."

"Oh, dear," she said, shaking her head and promising to keep the children quiet. Martinez thanked her and took his leave.

When he'd gone, Susanna gathered the children round and explained that their outing would have to wait as she had just recalled an important commission she must take care of. No one was overly disappointed, and as they scrambled back to the house she knew they would each be well occupied for several hours.

She paused in the front entry lobby, debating the wisdom of what she was about to do. Earlier the duke had not wanted to tell her what was wrong; Martinez had been most reticent. Clearly the duke would not take kindly to her assistance. And she supposed it was highly improper at first stop for her to go up to his rooms. But Martinez was there, she reminded herself, and it *was* broad daylight, after all. Besides, it would be the height of selfishness not to try to help him.

For her Aunt MacLaughlin, Jamie's mother, had oft suffered a similar affliction and Susanna had always

101

been summoned to her bedside. "Healing hands," the old woman had whispered. Susanna was not sure how or why 'twas so, only that some movement she did with her hands brought relief to her aunt's pain-wracked head. And once when Jamie had sprained his ankle she had been able to accomplish what all the hot compresses could not.

Squaring her shoulders, she lifted the skirts of her dark blue walking dress and headed for the stairs. She rapped gently at the outer door to the duke's apartment. It swung open to reveal a sitting room furnished in shades of gray and navy blue. It matches his eyes, she thought irrelevantly. "Señorita!" Martinez exclaimed in a whisper. "What are you doing here?"

"Forgive the intrusion, Martinez, but I—I think I can help His Grace."

"Thank you, señorita, but you do not understand. There is no—"

"Martinez. I had an aunt once who was felled by such megrims. Dreadful, violent ones that wracked her head, usually on one side. And I would massage her head, you see, and her neck, and finally she would sleep, and when she awoke, ofttimes it would be gone. Or at the least, be much lessened."

He peered at her out of dark, narrowed eyes. "He will not like this, Señorita Beacham."

"I know that, Martinez. It will not be the first time I have raised his hackles, you know," she said with a slight smile, and Martinez stepped aside to let her pass.

He led her into the bedroom, and at first she could see nothing. For the room was in near blackness, the windows obviously encased in heavy draperies. She stood a moment allowing her eyes to adjust to the darkness. It was a very large room, she realized, its

102

focal point a huge fourposter bed that stood in the center. She swallowed. Whatever was she doing in a man's bedchamber? Especially this particular man's!

"It's no use, Martinez. I cannot sleep." His voice sounded more like a moan, and she lifted her chin and moved silently forward. She knew exactly what she was doing here. She stopped, some five feet from the bed, as he said, "And the children have been making the most godawful racket. Wait until I get my hands on that sham of a governess! I'm going to wring her neck, Martinez, before the week is out!"

Martinez looked ruefully at Susanna, then approached the bed. "Do not excite yourself, Don Reinaldo. You know it makes the pain worse."

"I know, dammit! What is that I smell? These damned headaches play havoc with my nose as well as my eyes. I could swear I smell jasmine. That is *her* scent, Martinez. Did you ever hear of a governess who wears scent? And did you see what she wore this morning? A muslin so scant, hugging her in such a way—"

Martinez coughed and Susanna gesticulated rather expressively until she had his attention. She tiptoed back to the doorway, and he followed.

"I am sorry, señorita. You see it will not work."

"Blether! Yes, it will. But I need you to turn him round so he lies crossways on the bed. His head should be near the edge, and I should like a chair pulled up to the bedside."

Martinez looked most dubious. "And just how do I explain—"

"Why, tell him you have heard of a marvelous new remedy, unlike any he has ever before encountered. Now, do hurry. He is obviously suffering terribly. I shall wait in the sitting room whilst you rearrange him."

Moments later Martinez called her back, and she crept toward the bed. Martinez, she noted, stayed back in the shadows.

"This is ludicrous, Martinez. I always sleep with my head at the *head* of the bed. What sort of ramshackle remedy are you talking about? Surely not one of Cook's concoctions divined by the flight of magpies!"

Susanna reached the bed and held her skirts as still as possible as she sat down in the chair. She could not see Martinez but felt his presence.

"Answer me, Martinez! What is going on here? Why do I smell jasmine? I must be losing my mind!" She put her hands to his silver head. "That blasted governess— Ooh! Martinez, you . . . since when did you . . . ah. Yes, oh, yes, the pain is centered right there. The left temple. Ah. Lower. Mmmm." His voice became a moan of pleasure and Susanna kept at her work. "Ah, yes. My hair. So much tension. M-Martinez," he said in a soft, almost floating voice, "why do I smell jasmine . . . ?" Suddenly she felt him tense and the voice became harsh, but her fingers didn't stop. "Since when did you take to wearing jasmine? Answer me, Martinez!" he yelled and then one large hand reached back and grabbed hers. "So smooth and soft your hand is," he growled and twisted his head and pulled her so that she fell forward, nearly colliding with his head. His glittering gray eyes met hers, their heads only inches apart. "Where the devil is Martinez? And as for you, Miss Governess, I am going to murder you. Slowly." He shifted round and made as if to rise. She heard a stifled laugh in the background and knew there would be no help from that quarter. Which was just as well.

Gently she grasped his shoulders beneath the comforter and pushed him back down. "Hush, Your Grace. You really are a very bad patient, you know. I am aware that you wish me at Jericho just now, but the fact is that I am very good at this, and you are much in need of relief."

"What I need is sleep. And—"

"And I can help you sleep, Your Grace," she said soothingly.

Martinez coughed in the background. She began massaging the duke's head again, her gentle fingers pushing their way through his hair and making slow, sensual, circular movements on his scalp. It felt wonderful. She smelled wonderful. She leaned forward and he knew her breasts were only inches from his head. And he groaned with an agony that had nothing to do with his head.

"Martinez, don't do this to me," the duke called ominously into the darkness. Then he cursed audibly when he heard the click of the door. How *could* Martinez? Reginald was in too much pain to move and his valet knew it, damn him! And here *she* was, in his darkened bedchamber, this woman with her provocative perfume and clinging dresses and those soft, lovely hands. . . .

Good Lord, he might be ill, but he wasn't dead! And had she really said she would bring him relief and help him sleep? She obviously could not know what she'd said, what her proximity could do to him; but Martinez must know. Damn that Spaniard! Reginald would—

"Relax, Your Grace. You are much too tense. You will make yourself more ill," she said softly, as her hands continued their magical kneading of his scalp and temples.

Against his will and his better judgment, he felt himself relaxing as her fingers moved over his brow, his cheeks, and back to his scalp. Well, part of him was relaxing, at all events. For she leaned very close to him, her face but inches from his, her breasts, he imagined, nearly touching his head. He could feel her soft, sweet breath on his brow. He felt his loins tighten and was very glad of the darkness and the plump down comforter which covered him.

"It is mostly on the left side, is it not?" she asked, her fingers working at the left temple and above the left eye.

"Yes," he murmured, amazed as the pain seemed to lessen under her touch.

"I can feel it. Relax, Your Grace. That's right." Her voice was like fine chamber music, clear and dulcet and soft. And now her hands moved to the back of his head, which she lifted and rocked ever so gently before continuing the massage. Those slender, delicate fingers were amazingly strong and their slow circular motion was delicious. If he could just forget who was doing this to him, what she looked like and smelled like . . .

"Ahh," he murmured as she began to work on the back of his neck.

"So rigid," she whispered near his ear, and it took him a moment to realize she was talking about the left side of his neck.

"Ah, yes, lower," he breathed, then wondered why the devil he couldn't keep his mouth closed.

Nonetheless, those heavenly fingers moved lower and finally came to his shoulders. And then the delicious circular motion stopped. The fingers groped around his shoulders and down his back a bit, and he felt her tense.

And suddenly he chuckled, knowing exactly what was troubling her. "Did you expect formal attire, my dear?" he quizzed, then could not resist adding, "Surely you know that when you beard a gentleman in his bedchamber you must accept him at his most . . . comfortable."

Oh, Lord, why had he said that? He heard her gasp. "Yes, well, I am persuaded Martinez did right in making you . . . comfortable," she replied. Comfortable? he thought. If she only knew . . .

Her hands continued their rhythmic motion on his bare shoulders. By God, she had pluck, he thought. Either that or she was amazingly naive, or . . . or was it that she was simply familiar with a man's body? No. That he would not believe. He knew an innocent when he saw one. And she *was* one—dangerously, provocatively innocent.

Those hands were making him feel very heated as they kneaded his shoulder muscles, the soft skin of her fingers seeming to burn into his bare back. He imagined her hands coming round to his chest, going lower. . . . Oh, God, this was torture. Sweet, exquisite torture. How much more could he take before he forgot all about this blasted headache and simply grabbed her— headache, honor, and his gentleman's code be damned!

Oh, dear, Susanna thought, what had she done, coming here? She knew she was making him feel better, but she was beginning to feel very strange indeed. She was unaccustomedly warm and her stomach fluttered and her breathing was too shallow. And she had never expected him to be *naked!* Well, she supposed he must be wearing *something*—drawers at the least, mustn't he? Good Heavens, she'd never imagined he'd be so . . . so bare. Why, Aunt always wore her nightrail.

And besides, she was a female. Her back was not nearly so broad, so hardened with muscle, not punctuated with tiny, coarse, curling hairs. And the plains of Aunt's face did not have the strength of the duke's, nor was her hair so thick and silky. And her voice did not rumble deeply in her chest as she spoke.

She worked his shoulders for a bit, trying to distract herself with thoughts of Aunt MacLaughlin. She missed her and hoped her aunt was not too worried about her. And she wondered where Jamie was—off on the Continent with his regiment no doubt. Had Jamie been home, would things have been different? she mused. Probably not. Jamie had been her boon companion in their youth, but he was no match for her father and Mortimer.

Unlike Reginald Ayres, she thought irrelevantly, who held power in the very lift of one ducal eyebrow. And that power, she suspected, came not from his titles and dignities, but from the man himself. And she was no match for him. Lord, what *was* she doing here? In Devon, in his house, in *his bedchamber* for heaven's sake?

Her warm hands moved back to his nape, and she began again to massage his scalp. He could not hold back another moan of pleasure.

"Ye should be getting sleepy, Yer Grace," she whispered, leaning closer to him.

Not a chance, he thought. But his head was pounding less, of a certain. "Where did you learn to do this, Miss Beacham?"

"I dinna ken. I just—"

"An old Lancashire remedy, perhaps?" he asked. There was a mocking ring to his voice that she did not like. She did not answer.

"And do they speak like that in Lancashire, Miss Beacham?"

Her heart began to pound. "Like . . . like what?"

"'I dinna ken.' And 'Yer Grace.' And don't forget the 'burn' and the 'bairns.' Did you think I hadn't noticed?"

She willed her hands to keep working. "Yes, well in Lancashire we—"

"Miss Beacham?"

"Yes?"

"Winestead is in Yorkshire," he said slowly.

Her hands stopped and her stomach plummeted. "It . . . it cannot be, Your Grace. Why—"

"Miss Beacham?"

"Y-Yes?"

"Do you know what lies east of Winestead?" he asked in the tone of someone about to spring a trap. She was looking at his face upside down and could not discern his expression, which was just as well.

"Why, of course, Your Grace, I—"

"East of Winestead, my dear, is the North Sea!"

"Ohh!" she moaned.

"Methinks 'tis not a Lancashire lady at all that we have here, but a Scottish lass, whose name is undoubtedly *not* Rose Beacham!" His voice grew harsher and she jumped up, pushing the chair back. She turned to run and felt a strong, firm hand close about her left wrist and pull her back. She squirmed, but he was too strong for her. He yanked her down until she fell forward and somehow found herself seated on the bed next to him. He did not let go her wrist; she stared at his naked arm and that portion of his chest that was visible where the comforter had slipped down. She swallowed hard.

"Well now, my wee Scottish lassie, I believe 'tis time

we had a little talk," he said in a voice of deceptive softness.

"Surely not now, Your Grace. You . . . you are ill!" she protested, not daring to add that he was also at least half-naked. Massaging his head till he slept was one thing, but talking to him, sitting on his bed . . . Her wrist tingled where he held it, and her stomach did somersaults.

"Now!" he countered, his gray eyes blazing. "You may start by telling me who you are, where you come from, and what the *devil* you are doing at Milburne Hall!"

Susanna wondered if he could feel her shake. She *must* brazen it out, else be prepared to leave by nightfall. She took a deep breath and refused to meet his eyes. "My name *is* Rose Beacham, and I *am* from Lancashire. There may well be a village of Winestead on the coast of Yorkshire—and now you mention it I do recall such—but I come from the *parish* of Winestead, in *Lancashire.* As to what I am doing here, why I am teaching the children—"

"Enough!" he exclaimed. He shook his head, then grimaced with the pain of it. "You do amaze me with your ability to tell one clanker after another, ma'am. But I have traveled much of this country, not to mention the world, and I know well 'tis a bonny Scot I harbor under my roof. He tugged at her wrist and pulled her closer. Her breasts grazed his chest, and he knew he must be mad, for his body leaped to attention, but he had to know. "What are you running away from, Scotty?" he whispered.

He could not mistake the sudden tensing of her arm, of her entire body. "I . . . I am not running away, Your Grace," she replied, her voice trembling. "I merely

110

needed a position, as you know."

What he knew was that he ought to turn her off straightaway. He had known her a scant three days and already his life was one imbroglio after another. She was a liar and a meddler and certainly no governess. He ought to and yet . . .

"Look at me," he commanded softly. Slowly, she met his eyes. Even in the darkness he could see the fear and vulnerability in those deep blue eyes. Eyes that so often brimmed with amusement. He could feel her full breasts press against him with the rhythm of her breathing. This was madness. What the hell was she doing here, in his house, in his *bed* for pity's sake? The hand that held her wrist slid to her upper arm; his free hand came up to grasp the other arm. Her perfume assailed him and he felt himself pull her closer. "Scotty, what *am* I to do with you?" he breathed.

"P-please, Your Grace, I . . . I . . . your headache . . ."

"Is the least of my problems just now, Scotty," he muttered, and moved one hand to the nape of her neck. She was poised just inches above him, her rosebud lips slightly parted. She looked beautiful and confused and infinitely desireable, and dear Lord, how he wanted her!

"Your Grace?" she whispered tentatively, and suddenly he was recalled to himself.

He *was* His Grace, the duke, and she was an unprotected woman in his house, let alone his bedchamber. And whoever she was, wherever she came from, he knew her to be an innocent. Yet he had been about to . . . to kiss her! And the devil only knew what else. Good God, he hadn't got a stitch of clothing on!

He cleared his throat and dropped his hands. "Scotty, you . . . you'd better go."

"Yes, I . . . I shall. But I— Does yer head still pain ye?" she asked softly, and he was amazed. He had intimidated her, come close to dishonoring her, and yet she did not run from him, or dissolve into tears. Her first thought was for him.

"'Tis of no moment," he replied, dismissively. "I am right."

She rose from the bed and sat back down in the chair. "Hush now. Let me help you. Please," she murmured, her fingers beginning to work again. Such a musical voice. Such magical fingers. He could not find his own voice to object.

The duke was silent and finally Susanna heard the steady, even breathing that told her he slept. She stood quietly, looking down at him. His bare shoulders were visible above the coverlet. She did not dare cover him, lest the movement waken him. Such broad shoulders, such firm muscles. A man, she thought, was so different from a woman.

She felt warm all over again. And then she took a deep breath and walked away. The sitting room was empty and for the first time she wondered where Martinez had gone and why he had left at first stop. She shrugged her shoulders, let herself into the corridor, and went in search of the children.

And Martinez, having stationed himself just beyond the dressing-room door, where he just happened to have heard the entire exchange between "Scotty" and the duke, smiled in sweet satisfaction. He had been right. He knew he had been right.

Chapter 7

Susanna contrived to keep the children fairly quiet for the remainder of the day and hoped that the duke continued to sleep peacefuly. She did not dare go to his rooms again. He did not appear for dinner.

"Martinez informs me that he is asleep," the duchess told her as they took their places in the family dining room. "One of those dreadful megrims, you must know. Just came on him today. I own 'tis a miracle he can sleep at all. Martinez said something about a new remedy, but I could not get him to reveal any details. Have you any idea, Beachie, what sort of remedy?"

"Why, ah, no, Your Grace," Susanna managed, her eyes on her wineglass, which Underwood was just now filling.

"Undoubtedly one of Martinez's strange recipes from Spain. I declare he contrives things of which no one else would ever dream," the duchess said, then added in a near whisper, "I would not want Cook to know, but I daresay some of his remedies come from the Gypsies. There are so many there, you must know. In Spain, that is. He made a poultice for one of Reggie's mares last year—Hippolyta it was—well, we all thought she would have to be put down, poor thing, until Martinez got to her. But she's very superstitious about Gypsies, and—"

"Mama, how can the mare be superstitious about Gypsies?" Phoebe interrupted. A footman had begun serving the oxtail soup. Susanna noted that the soup sloshed ever so slightly in the tureen at her words.

"Is she? Hippolyta, dear? But what would the mare know of Gypsies, especially Spanish ones?"

"I think, Phoebe," Susanna began, seeing the shoulders of the poor footman shake suspiciously, "that what your mama means is the *Cook* is superstitious about the Gypsies."

"Yes, of course. Did I not say so?" the duchess went on. "Well, at all events, I do not care a rush where Martinez found this particular remedy. If it helps I hope he will employ it again and again. Though I cannot conceive why he is being so secretive."

Susanna nearly choked on her soup and silently blessed Martinez for his reticence.

As soon as the footman departed Phoebe said, "Perhaps it was the megrim that caused Reggie to be so unpleasant this morning."

"Whatever do you mean, Phoebe dear?" asked the duchess.

"Oh, Mama, he was perfectly horrid. Nearly ordered poor Mr. Hastings from the premises. And when he, Mr. Hastings I mean, invited me to drive this afternoon, and then tomorrow, Reggie said I was otherwise occupied. I own I was never so humiliated!"

Phoebe looked close to tears and Susanna set about soothing her. But Phoebe only sniffled and said accusatorily, "Reggie said you had requested my

114

company on an outing tomorrow morning, Beachie. But I don't recall any such thing. Did you—?"

"Well, I . . . ah . . ."

"What a splended idea, Beachie! And what's more, if Reggie is feeling more the thing, I think he had ought to accompany you. I do think he spends too much time with his books and his specimens. I am quite certain that contributes to his megrims," the duchess put in.

"Well, if Reggie goes, I shan't!" Phoebe declared petulantly, and Susanna was heartily glad that the servants came in to serve the next course, thereby terminating a most unpromising line of discourse.

As it was, conversation remained general and innocuous for the remainder of dinner. And while she had once enjoyed the light prattle of Phoebe and the duchess, had joined in and found their company soothing, now she found herself restless and bored. And she knew very well why, though she was reluctant to admit it to herself. She missed him. She missed his conversation, and the shared amusement conveyed as their eyes met across a room. Strangely, she even missed his ringing a peal over her, preferred it to his absence.

And she scolded herself severely, for such feelings were highly inappropriate. But her mind did not obey her conscience, and as she nibbled at the braised goose and potato pastry, she found herself thinking of his strong face, and of the way his smile could transform it. She thought of the way he looked, so tall and broad in his finely tailored coats. And she thought of this afternoon. She could almost feel again her fingers running through his thick silver blond hair, then massaging his neck and his shoulders. Those hard, muscular, naked shoulders. She felt herself flush and reached for her wineglass. And she scolded herself again. She was Rose

115

Beacham, governess. And a governess had no right to hold such thoughts about a duke of the realm.

It was a cool night. Martinez let himself out a side door, lit a cheroot, and strolled through the gardens. Don Reinaldo still slept, and so there was nothing for Martinez to do. Nothing to do but think. And he had come out here to do just that.

Underwood had come to him after luncheon to report that the little French maid had not, indeed, taken her luncheon with the upper servants in the butler's pantry. She had, in fact, taken it alone in the kitchen. Martinez had not understood, but nevertheless had continued in his self-imposed exile and had dined in the servants' hall with the underservants. He could not help overhearing the buzz of talk about how Angelique again did not appear in the butler's pantry for dinner. Cook had permitted her, once again, to eat at the butcher-block table in the largest kitchen.

He sought a private interview with Underwood after dinner. His dealings with the butler had always been amiable but tonight Underwood put on the stiff mask he used with the rest of the staff.

"I do not like such goings on below stairs, Martinez," he said with his nose high in the air.

Martinez responded in kind. "Of what goings on do you speak?"

Underwood sighed. "You are avoiding her. Now she is avoiding you. I do wish you'd have your brangles in a less . . . public manner, old fellow."

"Brangles? We have not had any such thing!" Surely the exchange in the duke's dressing room could not be called a brangle.

Underwood had looked at him most doubtfully, and Martinez had stomped off to the kitchens in search of Cook. Cook had been much more coming.

"A dear sweet little thing she is, so sorry to be causin' such a mort o' trouble. And *you* should be ashamed of yourzel', scarin' her in such a way—"

"Scaring her?" Martinez asked in astonishment.

"Well, she didn't *say* as how she was scared, no more did that dear Miss Beacham—"

"Señorita Beacham! What has she to do with this?"

"Oh! Nort, I'm sure, Mr. Martinez. Only that the little maid come to her a-crying'. Wouldn't say much, the governess, just asked if I'd have the little maid to be eatin' in the kitchen, But I got it out of Angelique, I did."

"I do not understand."

"Well, there be no way to wrap it up in clean linen, and that's a fact. Angelique said as how you have quite a temper, you do. But *that's* not why she won't break her bread in the butler's pantry, poor wee mite." She put her hand on Martinez's arm and leaned forward to whisper conspiratorially, "She says as how you're right handsome and kind, and she wouldn't distress you for the world. She's heard the talk, you see, and knows full well why you're eatin' in the servants' hall. Well, and 'taint no secret how you feel 'bout the Frenchies, now is it? And she says as how you be havin' more right to your place at Mr. Underwood's table than she, you bein' here such a long time. So she's gone instead."

Martinez had stared at Mrs. Rackett in chagrin and astonishment, and now as he paced the garden and puffed on the cheroot, he was no closer to solving this very prickly problem. The little French maid had left her rightful place at the table so as not to discompose him. And she had gone to eat in the kitchens, where even the lowliest scullery maids did not break their bread. And she thought he was kind, even handsome, Mrs. Rackett had said. All this knowing full well how he felt. His own feelings did not make sense, he knew. The little maid had had nothing to do with the war in Spain. Could he hate a whole people because of the brutality of their soldiers? And yet, how could he forget what they had done?

How strange that Angelique reminded him of his sister, Margarita. Even now, all these years later, he still felt a great lump in his throat as he remembered the day the French soldiers had come and dragged her off. He remembered her cries and the way they had beaten him senseless when he ran to her aid. When he had come to, he had found his old father with a bullet through his heart. And his beloved sister lay broken and bleeding in the barn. She died in his arms and he'd gone off to join his brother in the fighting. Gone to kill as many of *them* as he could. But they got his brother too, eventually, and would have had him as well had it not been for Don Reinaldo.

Angelique was one of *them*. And yet, she too had suffered at the hands of her countrymen. She was very sweet, the little maid, and pretty, with her dark hair and brown eyes and petite figure. So like Margarita. And he was making her suffer.

He tossed the cheroot down and stomped on it. What is wrong with you, Martinez? he asked himself. You have forgotten what it means to be a gentleman.

Martinez ran his hand over his eyes and the back of his neck. He had been raised in a family that demanded that a man shield and protect his women at all costs. He had failed miserably with Margarita, and since that time had not had a woman in his life for more than a half-hour at a time.

But though he had no woman of his own, nor wanted one, still he was always careful to be gentle with those who crossed his path. Even the village serving wenches who warmed his bed when he felt the need, even those he treated with a careful courtesy.

Only with Angelique had he forgotten himself. He had frightened her in the dressing room so badly that she ran away. And he had caused her to run from the dining table as well.

He must make amends. He did not know how, but it must be done tomorrow. Else he would have failed again.

It seemed so real. That was what Susanna would remember most about the nightmare. She was in the duke's bedchamber, massaging his head. He reached for one of her hands and began to stroke it; she felt warm and wonderful. And then suddenly he clamped his fingers down hard on her wrist, and he was not the duke any longer, but Duncan Mortimer. Susanna tried to run, but he sprang from the bed and grabbed her shoulders. His mouth bit down on hers and she could feel bile rise in her throat. He was backing her into a wall, ignoring her protests, his hands all over her body. And then she saw the glint of metal. He was stabbing her, over and over! "No!" she cried out. "Oh, God, no! All the blood! So much blood!"

She was crying now, curled up into a ball on her side. She became aware of someone shaking her, calling to her. But the hands were gentler than Mortimer's, the voice young and high-pitched.

"Beachie, wake up! Wake up, Beachie, you are having

a nightmare," the voice said. Slowly Susanna shook herself out of sleep. She peeled her hands away from her face and opened her eyes. Letty was crouched by the bedside, frowning in concern. Susanna sat up and managed a wan smile.

"I am right now, Letty, and so sorry to have disturbed your sleep. I cannot think what can have possessed me to cry out so."

"It must have been a terrible dream, Beachie. You were screaming about blood, that there was blood everywhere," Letty said softly.

Dear God, Susanna thought. Had she really said such a thing aloud? She reassured Letty that it meant nothing, for after all dreams needn't be rooted in reality, need they? And then, thanking Letty for waking her, she sent the child back to the nursery to sleep.

Sleep was long in coming to Susanna, however. For she had lied to Letty; the dream *was* rooted in reality. She *had* been in the duke's chamber. Mortimer *had* backed her against a wall. She shivered as she tried to force the memories away. She could still feel Mortimer's cold hands on her. And then there *had* been blood. All that horrifying blood. But the dream had been strangely inaccurate, too. For it had not been Mortimer whose hand had stabbed and—No! She would not think of it! Not again. She couldn't.

Raggedly she sat up and lit a taper. She gathered up the book that sat at the bedside table and lay back against the pillows, determined to read until sleep claimed her.

Susanna awoke feeling surprisingly refreshed, having finally fallen into a deep, dreamless sleep. Letty came to her room before breakfast to inquire if she was suffering any ill effects after her nightmare. Susanna assured her, quite truthfully, that she was fine and bade Letty put the incident from her mind. And Susanna sincerely hoped she would; it would not do at all for Letty to ruminate overmuch on the words Susanna had so indiscreetly cried out last night.

The children were particularly exuberant that morning. Word had filtered through the house and reached them that Beachie planned to take them on an outing. And Susanna was rather afraid from what they said that they did not consider a walk to the North Wood much in the way of an "outing." No, they rather meant a carriage ride to one of the seacoast towns, or perhaps along the Torridge to Milburne Damerel. But as Susanna herself had never been farther afield than the North Wood, she hadn't the least notion where to go.

She took the children up to the schoolroom straightaway after breakfast, intent on diverting their attention with some fascinating tale from Greek mythology, but for once she failed to hold their interest.

"Perhaps Reggie will be more the thing today," Timothy said eagerly, "and he can accompany us. Maybe he'll even take us to Maidenstone!"

"Don't be a nodcock, Timothy," Thomas retorted, "you know he never takes *anyone* there. It's his *private* island, you must know, Beachie. Smaller even than Lundy. Why, it's not even on the maps! He goes there to 'escape,' he says, and to look at the wildflowers."

"It sounds lovely," Susanna replied a bit wistfully.

Letty looked at her strangely, and Thomas said, "Well, he never takes us, but perhaps one day he'll take

121

you, Beachie, you being closer to his age and all."

"That's a capital notion, Thomas!" exclaimed Timothy. "And then you can tell us *all* about it!"

Susanna felt herself color and glanced over at Letty. Letty gazed at her with that strange, speculative look in her eyes. "Yes," she murmured after a moment. "Do ask him, Beachie, and perhaps he'll even tell you whence the island got its name. Such an unusual name, Maidenstone, but he always fobs us off, saying he doesn't know."

For some reason Susanna felt she didn't want to know either. And suddenly she thought of the duke, yesterday morning on the backstairs landing. And then in the afternoon when she'd massaged his head. She thought of his broad shoulders and silky hair, and the way his voice occasionally gentled with concern for her. And last night at dinner, she'd actually missed him! Unwittingly her thoughts flew to the dream, to the first part, when he'd stroked her hand. . . .

No! She did *not* wish to go off with him to his private island! No more did she wish him to accompany her and the children on an outing. In fact, she told herself emphatically, the less she thought of her employer, the better!

Reginald awoke early, amazed that it was dawn, that he'd slept the night through. What exactly had that governess done to him? Whatever it was, it had felt heavenly, he had to admit. But of course, he would never allow her to do such a foolhardy thing again—coming into his bedchamber, and he in his natural state! As to Martinez, he'd have the fellow's head on a silver salver!

122

He rose slowly from the bed and was amazed that while he still had some pain in his head, the devastating nausea had receded. And even the pain was a mere dull ache. The violent throbbing had gone.

He rang for Martinez, deciding that he would ride this morning as usual. Perhaps the megrim would not worsen with the day, and by some miracle the worst was over. No, not some miracle, he reminded himself. It was because of *her*, Miss Beacham. Scotty, he amended, bemused. Scotty and her beautiful, graceful, amazing hands.

Martinez was in quite a brown study when he arrived, and his obvious distraction and the somber cast of his dark eyes prevented Reginald from administering the scathing setdown he had prepared. It could wait, he thought, and took himself off to the stables.

The ride cleared some of the fuzziness from his head, although the dull ache remained. Still, it was with a more springy step than he'd expected that he strolled down the first-floor corridor to the breakfast room.

He heard his mother's voice from several feet away. "I think Beachie's idea of an outing just splendid, Phoebe. And, of course, you must go."

"Mama, Beachie never said—"

"Oh! But I have only just remembered, dear, that Lady Craddock might come by for a visit, and Elsie, too. Elsie did want to see you, you must know. She wanted to peruse the latest issue of *Ackerman's* with you. Perhaps Beachie will not mind your staying home if Reggie accompanies her. I do think the fresh air—"

That was all the duke had to hear. "Good morning, Mother, Phoebe," he said, striding into the room. He poured himself a cup of coffee from the sideboard.

Phoebe gaped at him, but his mother smiled broadly.

"So glad you're feeling more the thing, Reggie dear. That new remedy Martinez spoke of must indeed be a wonder."

"New . . . remedy, Mother?" he asked, nearly spilling his coffee as he quickly took his seat. There was no mockery in her expression or her tone; at all events he thought she was incapable of it. Still, whatever had Martinez—

"Yes, dear. Very secretive he was about it, too. But as it seems to work, I do hope you'll use it again and again."

This time he did spill his coffee. His cup clattered onto the saucer and he reached for the serviette.

"You *are* right, are you not, Reggie?" the duchess asked solicitously. "Perhaps some more of that remedy—"

"I am fine, Mother. Now tell me about this . . . er . . . outing."

"Why, the one Beachie has planned with the children. You must know of it, for you told Phoebe that Beachie had requested her company."

Phoebe was eyeing him with a rather smug look that he could not like. She daintily nibbled a piece of buttered bread. "But now it seems I cannot go, for Elsie Craddock—"

"Yes, I know, I heard that part," Reginald grumbled.

"So, you see, dear, the only help for it is for you to accompany Beachie and the children. I own I will feel more comfortable knowing they have a man with them, at all events."

Reginald chomped on a piece of sausage and began to wish himself back in bed, megrim and all. He was beaten and he knew it. Hoist on his own petard, as it

124

were. He wondered what "Beachie" would make of this, if she knew of it.

She did know, he discovered when he made his way upstairs after breakfast. Three very eager children seemed able to speak of little else.

"They seemed quite certain that it was my idea at first stop, but truly I—"

"Never mind, Scotty," he said wryly. She blinked at his use of such a nickname and looked delightfully confused. He wondered what was wrong with him, to address her so inappropriately, but somehow the name fit her. He wouldn't use it in company, of course. . . . "Now, where would you like to go?" he asked amiably. They stood close to each other, just outside the schoolroom, the door ajar.

"I know so little of the region, Your Grace," she replied, a graceful hand reaching up to tidy a wayward curl, "that I really cannot say. And I fear I might lose the way or—"

"Don't tease yourself. I shall accompany you."

"But, are you certain you are feeling up to it? Why, just yesterday you—"

"I am much better, and you know very well why. 'Tis just a dull ache today." She appeared so concerned that he forgot himself so much as to smile and say, "And if it worsens again, why I shall have my special remedy along with me."

When she colored to the roots of her auburn hair, he flicked his finger gently across her cheek. "Never mind," he said softly. "You ready the children, and I'll send word to Cook to prepare a hamper for luncheon."

With that he was gone, and Susanna stared after him. He had smiled at her, a rare occurrence indeed.

She did not think this outing a very good idea at all.

Martinez ran Angelique to ground in the dry laundry, one of the cavernous service rooms on the ground floor of the Hall. She was startled at his entrance and even more startled when he asked her to walk in the garden with him. She followed him out into the laundry garden, past a maid hanging up a basketful of clothes and through a narrow gate marking the path leading to the kitchen garden. He settled her on a small stone bench and stood looking down at her.

"Señorita," he began, and then when the dark brown eyes regarded him like those of a frightened doe, he said more softly, "Angelique."

"Yes?" The voice was a mere whisper. He hated it that she was so frightened.

"I think that we make trouble in the kitchens, you and I. First I go to the servants' hall, then you go to the kitchens to eat."

"Oh, but I only . . . I did not wish you to —"

"I know, Angel—señorita. What I try to tell you now is that I . . . I have behaved badly. We will both eat at Underwood's table from now on, I think."

"You . . . you do not mind? You do not hate me so much then?"

Martinez winced. There was not an ounce of guile in this child. "I have never hated you, Angel—Angelita."

She looked at him expectantly, and he sighed and sat down beside her. "It is your countrymen. They took . . . everything I had. And when I hear you speak, hear

126

the sound of the language—but that is no excuse, is it?"

"They . . . they took everything I had as well, monsieur."

He sighed and nodded slowly. It was true. He brought his finger to her chin and turned her to face him. She did not really look like Margarita, but something about her reminded him of his sister. "I am sorry I frightened you," he said softly.

She smiled tremulously and looked much too vulnerable. He did not like it. "I will see you at luncheon," he said at last, dropping his hand. She bobbed a curtsy and scampered away, leaving him with a jumble of very conflicting thoughts.

The weather had finally turned as warm as one expected for the end of June. The sun shone, and there was not a trace of the recent dampness in the air. It being a perfect day for an outing, the three children could hardly contain themselves as they clamored into the carriage yard. Reginald thought Scotty seemed rather subdued, but she looked utterly charming in a peach sarcenet walking dress. Her auburn hair glinted in the sunlight, under a saucy, chip straw hat that he was certain no governess ought to own.

He had ordered the landau readied. One of the grooms would accompany them to see to the horses, but would ride the rear. Reginald intended to drive himself. For one, he enjoyed driving and for another, the concentration required would distract him from the dull ache in his head. As everyone made ready to board the landau, there ensued an argument as to who would ride the box with him. Scotty, unable to resolve the brangle, looked at him helplessly out of those big midnight blue eyes. For one moment he had the impulse to take *her* up with him, the children be damned.

But he checked himself and chose Timothy to ride the box, the boy's enthusiasm for the pair of grays pulling the landau being quite unparalleled.

His land covered a good part of North Devon. They would see some of it on the way to Clovelly, the picturesque little seacoast town that he had elected as their destination.

He drove the landau slowly onto the gravel drive that wound like a ribbon round the Hall and all its outbuildings. Milburne Hall, graceful Palladian structure that it was, sat at the base of gently rolling hills that came from the south and the west. To the north was the home farm, and to the east the fertile land spread forth in large patches of deep green grass and rich red loam, much of it under cultivation by tenant farmers. Beyond, the land sloped in gradual terraces down to the valley of the Torridge.

Susanna sat across from Letty and Thomas, relishing the beautiful day and marveling at the lushness of the passing scenery, the farms, the little streams, the riverbanks. But what most caught her eye were the profusions of wildflowers. She saw primroses and lenten lilies and foxgloves in the hedges. They passed through wooded glades and coombs where bluebells carpeted the ground in layers thick enough to scythe, and where the scent of honeysuckle wafted toward them.

She was enchanted, as she had been from the very beginning, by the Devon landscape. She hadn't had the opportunity to see very much of it, other than what she'd explored with the children on foot, and so today was a special treat for her as well as for them. Milburne was so different from Ballincraig, beautiful in a completely different way, and she was glad of it, for it eased the ache for the homeland she would never see again. She did not want to think of the heather and the mists and the majestic black moors of Scotland. Instead she fixed her eyes on the bluebells and cornflowers, and enjoyed herself thoroughly.

Everywhere the land was dotted with thatched-roof, whitewashed cottages, about which cows grazed lazily in the sun. "Look!" she exclaimed at one point. "Aren't those orchids? Do not tell me the cows graze on orchids!"

"Oh, yes," Thomas replied offhandedly. "Wild orchids grow quite plentifully here, you must know. Reggie says they are actually much prettier than the cultivated ones. Don't you agree, Beachie?" She did, but still marveled at it. At home the only orchids were hothouse flowers.

The carriage now dipped into a valley along a river. They lumbered through lanes that were deeply rutted in the red earth. The lanes, banked steeply to the sky, twisted and turned amid clusters of wildflowers. Myriads of little humming things swarmed about the flowers and flitted through the air. Susanna suddenly longed to be able to talk to the duke, to ask him about this. But he was busy in front with Timothy, and Thomas and Letty were chattering away across from her. And that, she reminded herself, was just as it should be!

Then, suddenly, they entered a deep coombe, where the side of the lane seemed to drop sheer into the tangled green. She gulped in fright, but Letty only laughed. "Do not tease yourself, Beachie. Reggie's a capital driver. Look just there, to your right." Susanna turned her gaze to where Letty's finger was pointing and beheld, far below them, rocky granite cliffs falling into the sea. She sucked in her breath at the harsh splendor of it.

"Look, there's Milburne Quay!" Thomas exclaimed a few minutes later. "That's where Reggie keeps his ketch. And the yacht. Maidenstone is just across from there. I wonder where he's taking us? You don't suppose—"

"Don't be a ninny, Thomas!" Letty interrupted. "We're going west. I'll wager we're bound for Clovelly."

And so it proved to be. The path became somewhat pebbly as they climbed higher and higher, and then finally the duke pulled the carriage to a halt in front of a small timber-framed, gabled inn.

Reginald helped them all to alight, gave the groom instructions for the horses, then led the governess and the children round the corner to where the road ended and a cobbled, narrow, steep causeway took its place. They stood on a precarious perch just above the causeway, and Reginald watched Scotty's eyes widen with surprise as did the childrens'. Below them, the color-washed cottages of Clovelly tumbled like a waterfall into the sea. They were irregular, gabled houses perched along the winding cliffside lanes.

"I've never seen anything like it," Scotty breathed. "Why it's almost as if you could step out the doorstep of one house onto the roof of another!"

"And look at the donkeys!" Letty exclaimed, pointing to the causeway just below, where two donkeys labored up the hill. One carried a rider and odd bits of cargo, and the other pulled a wooden sled of sorts.

130

"Fish!" Timothy declared. "They're hauling fish. It rather smells, I should say. Can we have a donkey ride, Reggie?"

Letty looked at him with disdain. "Of course not, nodcock. They don't ride them for amusement, you know."

"I daresay that is the main method of transport here," Reginald said. "This causeway is called the High Street. Believe it or not, it's the main street of the town. You can see how it seems to crawl up from the jetty down there."

He stood next to the governess as his eyes scanned the panorama below. The day was growing warmer, and the sun was beating down on them. Scotty lifted one peach-clad arm to shield her eyes from the sun. He watched the sarcenet of her dress stretch across her breasts as she did so. There were tiny beads of perspiration along her upper lip. He felt a rush of warmth that had nothing to do with the sun.

Reginald took several steps away from her. It was only then that he noticed Letty watching him with a speculative look that he could not like.

"Can we go down, Reggie?" Thomas asked, drawing Reginald's attention. "I see market stalls just several feet below."

"The path is steep," he replied, "but perhaps we can descend a little way." He led them over to the cobble lane and placed them single file for the descent down to what seemed the center of town.

The boys went first, then Scotty, with Letty and Reginald in the rear. He expected Letty to scurry down, but she surprised him by holding back, staying him with a hand on his arm. She waited until the others were out of earshot before she spoke.

131

"Reggie, Beachie had a nightmare last night," Letty said, and he had the feeling she'd thought carefully about this before deciding to tell him. "Her screams woke me. She kept crying about . . . about blood. 'All the blood,' she was saying. I went to her and woke her and she claimed it meant nothing, but I . . . I do not think so, Reggie." Letty sounded genuinely worried. "It was something about the way she spoke the words in her dream. It seemed so real. You don't suppose she's been hurt, do you?"

Reginald was shocked at his reaction to Letty's words. He felt a tightening deep in his gut, fury that someone might have harmed Scotty, and an inexplicable regret that it had not been he who had comforted her last night. He thought it entirely likely that she'd been hurt. He had sensed before that she might be in some kind of trouble. But how the devil to ferret out the truth?

First he must insure that Letty was well out of it. To accomplish this end, he explained that nightmares often have naught to do with reality and that his sister was to say no more about the situation, lest she embarrass Beachie.

Letty gazed at him with narrowed eyes. "I am not addlepated, Reggie. I shall say nothing. But if *you* say nothing, well, I shall think you addlepated, indeed." With that rather cryptic remark, she left him and skipped down after the others.

Damnation! How could he question Scotty? She'd looked pale this morning, very likely because of that nightmare. But the drive had brought the color back to her cheeks, and he was loath to chase it away with painful reminders. Besides, each time he'd tried to broach a personal topic with her, she'd either spouted a

132

bag of moonshine or folded like a clam. She was hardly likely to tell him of her nightmares, let alone the cause of them. And at all events, they were her own business, were they not? They were no concern of his.

The boys scampered ahead and Scotty took Letty's hand. Without thinking, Reginald held Scotty's elbow, steadying her twice when she stumbled over an irregular cobble. Each time she looked up at him with a lovely flush on her cheeks, and an even lovelier, tentative smile on her red lips. He did not want to cause that smile to disappear, and yet perhaps Letty was right; he had got to say something. He looked up and caught Letty's all too shrewd eye on him again. Damn the chit, he thought irritably and in the next minute she charged ahead to join her brothers.

He drew Scotty a bit closer to him as they walked. "Scotty, you . . . ah . . . looked a bit pale this morning. Are you feeling quite the thing?" he ventured.

He felt her stiffen and inwardly cursed himself, and Letty. "Of course, Your Grace. The day is very beautiful. I am enjoying myself exceedingly," she replied in the formal, forced tone one expected in a London drawing room. He hated hearing it from her.

"Did you sleep well?" he persisted softly, and for a moment he thought she shivered. But that seemed impossible; the day was overwarm.

"Yes, thank you," she answered politely, "And you?"

He was saved the necessity of a reply to the meaningless query, for the children had fallen back to engulf them in their chatter.

Susanna was enormously relieved when the children came back to join them. Surely the duke was merely being solicitous; she *had* looked a bit peaked that morning. He did not mean anything specific by his questions, she assured herself.

They ambled for some time among the colorful stalls and she was glad of the distraction of the children. The duke made no further attempt to pursue their tête-à-tête, and she found herself relaxing once more. She listened to the strong cadences of his voice as he answered the children's questions. His presence lent a special excitement to the day for the children, she mused, and tried to squelch the thought that his presence did the same for her.

The scents of freshly baked bread and smoked meats assailed them as they walked. And everywhere there was the odor of fish. Thomas pointed out a quay down below, where they could see nets drying in the sun. And then the fishermen began to haul up a huge net full of hermit crabs, starfish, and giant rayfish. Suddenly, almost the minute the net hit the quay, some half-dozen young children tumbled onto the wharf, gesturing and chattering excitedly with the laughing fisherman.

Thomas and Timothy both turned eager, beseeching faces toward the duke, who shook his head. "No, my scamps. The last time I allowed you to join the fishermen it took me nigh onto an hour to drag you away. We have other plans for today."

Timothy opened his mouth to protest, but Susanna intervened. "Perhaps we can begin a study of the fish to be found on the north coast of Devon. And then we can come back and study them."

"Oh, capital, Beachie!" Thomas exclaimed. "Perhaps we could take some home. Especially the starfish. Why, we could dissect one! I've seen pictures of their inside parts and . . ."

Scotty began to look a bit green, and Reginald

smoothly changed the topic. After a few minutes they passed a small pub, and Reginald realized he was parched. But he couldn't very well take the children in there; he didn't even know if he could take Scotty along. It was time they headed back, he said, but a small grassy patch of shade had caught Scotty's eye. She put a hand to his sleeve and asked if they might not rest there for a moment. He assented and put his own hand to the small of her back as he ushered the group to the shade.

"Do let us go down to the beach," Timothy pleaded.

"There *is* no beach here, Timothy," the duke responded equably. "No sandy beach, at all events. Just those pebbly ridges you see. We'll go over to Milburne Quay now to have our luncheon. From there you can climb down to the beach."

The children looked pleased and jumped up, ready to leave. But Scotty looked a bit peaked, so Reginald stayed them with his hand and a glance at their governess. Reluctantly, they sank back down and lapsed into a debate about how many steps comprised the stone staircase from Milburne Quay to the sea. Scotty smiled ruefully at the duke. "Thank you, Your Grace. Sometimes the summer sun is a bit much for me. And here in the south it is much stronger than in— than at home." He looked at her speculatively for a moment. He knew questions were futile. Unwittingly, his hand went up to touch her chip straw hat.

"This is very fetching, Scotty, but perhaps you should wear a wider brimmed hat," he murmured, so that only she could hear. She colored and looked down at the cottages below.

"Why do I have the strange feeling that Clovelly is more Spanish—or Mediterranean, at least—than it is

135

English?" she asked after a moment. "It reminds me of pictures I've seen of Spanish seacoast villages."

He accepted the shift in subject; she would not discuss anything personal. "You are quite correct, Scotty. It *is* rather Spanish in character. And I do not think it accidental, you must know."

"Could Clovelly have been built by survivors from the wrecks of the Armada, Reggie?" Thomas asked, and the duke blinked. He had not thought any of the children were listening. "It most certainly could, Thomas, and probably was," he responded.

"Beachie told us all about the Armada, about how we licked Philip and became rulers of the sea!" Timothy said with relish. Reginald marveled at how much ground this nongoverness had covered in one short month.

Letty asked how it was that countries changed allegiances the way they did. "For in the last war we fought alongside Spain, did we not? To free the Peninsula from the French?" Her mind amazed him even more than Thomas's. Scotty deferred to him, and he launched into as simplified an explanation of international politics as he could manage. Then he wondered how the deuce he had come to this pass, discussing politics with three children and a beautiful woman on some overheated cliffside.

But Scotty beamed at him approvingly and he felt inordinately pleased. And then he brought himself up short, wondering how she dared be so condescending as to show approval of *him*! Never mind, he decided, and concluded by saying that countries often changed allegiances according to expedience and that enemies in one war might become allies in the next.

"But don't people hold grudges? I mean, look at the

Hundred Years' War," Thomas put in.

How did he know about the Hundred Years' War? Reginald wondered, his eyes flying to Scotty.

"Look at Martinez and the French!" Timothy blurted out.

"Just what do you mean by that, young man?" Reginald demanded.

Timothy looked stricken and Thomas intervened. "I'm sure he only means to say that Martinez dislikes the French, as everyone knows, Reggie."

"Yes, of course. That's why he's eating in the servants' hall, you must know," Timothy said with new confidence. "On account of Mama's new maid."

"What?" Reginald nearly shouted, but his mind was racing. Could this have anything to do with Martinez's obvious distraction this morning?

"Oh, yes," Letty chimed in. "Did you not know? And poor Angelique was so distressed she asked Cook's permission to eat in the kitchen!"

"What?" He was truly shouting now. "How the deuce do you *know* all this? Surely Mrs. Rackett did not give any such permission!"

"Oh, but she did," Letty insisted. "For Angelique could not think of any other way to bring Martinez back to his rightful place and—"

"But it doesn't signify, Reggie," Timothy put in helpfully. "For I heard Mrs. L. tell Cook that Martinez told Underwood he and Angelique would return to the butler's pantry after all. Mrs. L. said she saw Martinez and Angelique talking in the laundry garden, you must know."

"Scotty?" Reginald queried suspiciously, suddenly realizing that she had been all too silent during this entire exchange. His earlier concern for her was slipping away as his pique mounted.

"Yes?" she said uneasily.

"What do you know of this?"

"Why, nothing, Your Grace. How could I possibly have anything to do with your man and Her Grace's maid?"

He didn't know, but he'd wager . . .

"But Beachie," Timothy blurted, "Jeb told me Eliza—she's the dairymaid, you must know—well, Eliza overheard Mrs. Rackett say that you—"

Thomas suddenly jabbed him in the stomach and Letty jumped up, claiming she was absolutely famished and wasn't it time they set about having a go at the nice hamper Cook had packed. And Scotty said she was quite well rested by now and that she'd heard the view from Milburne Quay was quite beautiful.

He was going to throttle this governess. Sooner or later.

In the interest of fairness he took Thomas up with him on the ride to Milburne Quay, although he was more likely to get the full truth of the Martinez story from Timothy. But it didn't signify and he knew it. It was obvious she was involved, as she seemed to be involved in all sorts of goings on in his household. Either Angelique had gone to Cook and Cook to the governess, or Angelique had gone to Scotty at first stop. He thought it more likely that the timid little maid had gone to Scotty. She seemed to attract confidences, not to mention trouble.

He held the reins too tightly and turned the landau too abruptly, and then wondered whatever had come over him to treat his horses so barbarously.

Chapter 8

On the way to Milburne Quay they dipped south and skirted the outer reaches of Upper Milburne. It seemed to be a small but fairly bustling village with at least one winding tree-lined street of shops. Susanna saw that all whom they passed recognized the landau, and bowed or curtsied or doffed their hats as they shouted greetings to His Grace. There was affection in those greetings, and respect bordering on reverence. And she knew that Reginald Ayres was a very good landlord.

Milburne Quay seemed to be a tiered series of jagged, swirling rock formations jutting out from the cliffside into the sea. The quay was not very large, the natural formation having been augmented—ages ago, she surmised—by a man-made stone wharf. As they ascended the cliffside in the landau, she caught glimpses of the carved-stone staircase that wound from the top of the quay down the tiered, swirling rocks to the beach.

They disembarked atop the quay, where trees and several ancient-looking thatched cottages relieved the harshness of the rock. The duke directed the groom to set the hamper on a grassy patch shaded by a silver birch, and then groom and carriage disappeared.

In the next moment the children darted away toward the edge of the precipice, and as Susanna made to follow, the duke took her arm and led her there at a more sedate pace. She was very aware of his large hand at her elbow and reminded herself to concentrate on the children. But they were already scampering down the stone stairs.

"Oh, dear," she sighed. "I suppose I had ought—"

"No, let them go. They'll never sit still for luncheon 'til they've counted those steps," he said amiably and guided her to a low ledge that ran along part of the quay. He sat her down in a shaded area, and as she turned to look down at the sea she could feel his eyes on her.

He was silent, but she feared he might attempt to pick up the thread of one of their previous conversations. Instead he gazed down at the quay, and she sensed he was awaiting her reaction. Her eyes widened at the sight of a large and beautiful vessel berthed just below. Numerous workmen swarmed over it, and she knew it must be the yacht. The name *Midnight Lady* was painted on its bow. A sleek ketch was moored a few yards away, and there were several small crafts as well; two looked to be fishing boats.

Her eyes moved on to the sandy beach, visible to the side of the wharf. The pink and white sand glistened in the sunlight, and the water itself sparkled like a treasure trove of emeralds and sapphires. The sea was calm today, but the jagged rock formations told her 'twas not always so.

She turned and tilted her head up at the duke. "I do not know which is more beautiful, your seafaring vessels or your coastline."

He smiled then, a broad, almost boyish smile that transformed his face and caused her stomach to flip over. "The coastline, to be sure. I am very biased, you see, for I think my little corner of the world has some of the most beautiful scenery in all England." He said it without conceit; he sounded rather humble about it, actually. And his "little corner of the world" seemed to cover half of Devon.

"I can see why," she said. "And I am struck by how varied it is. These awesome cliffs, not far from wooded coombes and lush green farmland. I have never seen the like."

The smile, if possible, deepened, the gray eyes clear and warm. He put one foot upon the ledge and leaned close to her. "I'm glad you like it," he said simply, and something in his tone made her feel quite warm inside.

She turned again to the wharf. "The *Midnight Lady* is quite a vessel. The children told me she would be here."

"Yes, well, if they ask to board her, the answer is no. There is too much work going forth now."

"Ah. Well, perhaps *you* had ought to tell them that."

"I shall, but I do assure you, she's not nearly so glamorous as she looks."

She raised a skeptical brow, and he nodded. "She's a relic I inherited along with everything else. Probably not worth the trouble it seems to be taking to make her seaworthy again. For the first time in some fifty years I might add. The *Midnight Lady* was just another casualty of my noble ancestors' dissipation of the Milburne estate." He said this last with a bitterness she'd never heard from him before.

Instinctively she put a hand to his arm. "There is

141

nothing neglected about Milburne Hall now," she said softly.

He smiled faintly and sat down beside her. "That is because my father spent his entire life repairing the ravages of *his* father and grandfather. The house was a virtual ruin and half the land had been sold off. He spent his youth in India, amassing a fortune. Then he returned and bought it all back, even tracked down the paintings and antiques that had been sold to pay gaming debts over the years. And had workmen and architects swarming over the Hall for twenty years. He died before he could ever sit back and enjoy it all." The duke sighed. "He never did get to the yacht, which I suppose is why I'm seeing to it. For his sake. But for myself, I prefer my little ketch."

The ketch looked sleek and beautiful, and hardly little, but it was not that which was on her mind. Without thinking she said, "I have seen the rack and ruin that gaming and . . . other things can wreak on even the best of families."

The intensity in her voice surprised him. He turned her to face him. "And where have you seen that, Scotty?"

Abruptly she jumped up and moved several paces away, out of the shade. He rose and followed her. "Oh, a neighbor of ours, you must know. And of course, one hears tales . . . " she said vaguely.

Another Banbury tale, he thought in exasperation. Well, and what else did he expect? He wondered what the "other things" were, but knew there was not the least chance she would tell him.

She was staring out at the sea and her hand came up to shield her eyes. He stood at her shoulder, his head just inches from hers, inhaling that heady scent of

142

jasmine, and suddenly wanted to put his hands to her shoulders, to let her lean back against him. . . .

"That island out there"—she pointed out to sea—"is that Maidenstone?"

"I see the children have been talking. Yes, it is. I suppose you'd call it my hideaway. Sometimes I just need to . . . get away by myself." Why had he said that? Why was he even talking to her about such things?

She turned to face him, her eyes searching his face. Strangely, she seemed to understand. "It looks very beautiful, lush with greenery."

"It is. All trees and ferns and wildflowers. Rather looks like a large version of those bouquets you're so fond of making."

A twinkle appeared in her deep blue eyes. "And do you enjoy the flowers, my lord duke, or do you merely study them?"

"Well, of course I—" She raised a brow, and he softened his voice. "How did you know, Scotty?"

She smiled. "That you work too hard? Why I—"

A shout from below interrupted her, and they both turned to see the twins at the bottom of the stone staircase, gesticulating for permission to run off to the beach. Reginald shook his head and waved them back up.

They came reluctantly, but fell readily enough to the luncheon Cook had packed. Reginald thought the cold glazed ham, fresh bread, and Devon Brie delicious; and Scotty smiled as he poured her a glass of the madeira Mrs. Rackett had thoughtfully provided. He began to wish the children at Jericho.

"You see, Thomas, I was right," declared Timothy. "One hundred and eight steps."

"No, there are not!" retorted Thomas through a

mouthful of the ham. "One hundred and twelve! I counted 'em!"

The argument went on, until finally Scotty distracted them with speculation about how high the waves might come onto the quay in a storm. This set off a new debate. The noise was beginning to grate on Reginald. His headache buzzed a little louder.

"Letty, why don't you and the boys go down to the beach for a bit?" Scotty suggested, but her eyes, narrowed in concern, were on Reginald.

Letty, a wedge of juicy orange halfway to her mouth, looked pensively from Reginald to Scotty. She put down the orange. "Race you both to the sand!" she exclaimed and was off like a shot. The twins followed rapidly on her heels.

Reginald took a sip of his wine and gazed at the governess. She was sitting some three feet from him on the picnic blanket, her knees bent under her, the hamper to her side. She seemed to read him all too well, but that look on Letty's face and her willingness to curtail her luncheon troubled him almost as much.

"Is it getting worse?" Scotty's musical voice pierced his reverie. He did not pretend ignorance.

"A bit. How . . . how did you know?"

"Aunt's eyes used to cloud over, as yours have. Would you like—"

"I . . . I do not think so, Scotty. It would not be at all the thing, you know." Even as he said the words he realized how ludicrous they sounded. As if his bedchamber were more the thing!

Her eyes crinkled with what surely was unseemly merriment. Blast! She seemed to read his mind. He felt he had got to say something but first took two sips of wine. "Scotty, I . . . I have not properly thanked you for what you did for me yesterday. It was very good of you, and I will own it worked like a wonder. But you must not do such a thing again, my dear. Coming into my . . . my bedchamber like that. It is not at all—"

"The thing. Yes, I know, Your Grace," she said irrepressibly. "But you know, I do think propriety is all well and good—well, I mean to say, where should we be without it?—but sometimes one can take it a bit too far, don't you think? And choosing to suffer when there is a perfectly good remedy to hand is quite—"

"Scotty," he interrupted, unwittingly inching closer to her, his eyes locking with hers, "it is not only a matter of propriety."

Good Lord, had he really said that? He hoped she wouldn't understand what he meant, but she colored and looked down and he knew she'd understood only too well.

"Scotty, I—"

"Why do you not take laudanum, Your Grace?" she asked abruptly, raising her eyes once more. He was grateful for the change in subject.

He refilled both their glasses before answering. "My grandfather seems to have had these megrims as well. Toward the end of his life he was completely addicted to laudanum. He was a gamester before that, and was often in his cups, but with the laudanum he became totally reckless. My father inherited only what was entailed—the Hall, mortgaged to the hilt and a veritable ruin by then, plus its gardens and the home farm. It was fortunate he was able to buy the rest back. As for me, Martinez is always forcing some vile concoction down my throat, but none of it avails me aught. So, other than some brandy and cool compresses—"

145

"Aunt always says whisky makes the megrims worse. I would imagine spirits of any kind—"

"Whisky?" he queried. "As in Scottish whisky?"

"Well, I . . . I suppose 'tis made there, but Aunt drank it all the same, in Lancashire, that is."

"Another clanker," he murmured, but nonetheless put down his glass.

She bristled. "I'm sure I do not know *what* you mean, Your Grace."

"Don't you?" he asked, taking her glass and setting it down next to his. He inched closer and possessed himself of her slender, beautiful hands. "Scotty, I am not a fool. I know perfectly well that everything you've told me about yourself has been naught but one faradiddle after another."

"Fustian! It has—"

"Fustian exactly. You've told me fustian! Who are you, Scotty? Where in Scotland do you come from?"

She pulled her hands away and jumped up. She simply must make him believe her! He followed her to an ancient tree at the rim of the precipice. "I cannot think what you mean, Your Grace. Surely Lady Darnley's letter explains—"

"Exactly nothing." He stood behind her and put his hands gently to her shoulders. "Why won't you trust me, my dear? If you are in some difficulty, if . . . if anyone has tried to harm you, surely I can be of help."

Oh Lord, she thought, he is so good. But he would despise her if he tumbled to the truth. He won't, she assured herself. He could not possibly; Scotland was very large, after all. . . . She ought to be afraid. He might turn her off, he might . . . But his warm breath in her ear sent a tingling sensation throughout her body. And his hands on her shoulders—oh, God, how she wanted to lean back against his broad chest and tell him the whole, have him make it right. But such was the stuff of fairy tales. There was no one who could make it right, least of all the honorable duke.

And so she clamped her jaw rigidly shut, but she could not help the way her body relaxed against him. His hands moved to her upper arms and pulled her closer. And for one moment she forgot where she was, who she was—forgot everything but how warm she felt, how her stomach fluttered, how her entire body, stretched the length of his, seemed to vibrate with some new, delicious sensation.

He closed his eyes and inhaled her scent. There was no one in sight; the tree shielded them even from the children. And for just a moment he allowed himself to push the world away, allowed his body to revel in the feel of her softness. His lips brushed her hair. She fit so well against him. . . .

"Reggie! Beachie! Where are you? Look at all these seashells I've gathered!" Timothy's exuberant voice pierced the sweet, silent air.

Scotty started, and he let her go. She put a hand up to tidy her hair and stepped out into the sunlight. The mood, their reverie, was effectively broken. And just as well, he knew, for it was madness, all of it.

The children came scampering up the steps, beautiful pastel-colored seashells in hand. They prattled happily for a few minutes and then Letty said, "Did you see Maidenstone out there, Beachie?"

"Why, yes, I did. Your brother pointed it out to me."

"Can we not go there just *once*, Reggie?" pleaded Timothy.

"Don't be a ninnynammer, Timothy," Thomas said in a most superior tone. "Reggie goes there to be alone,

147

not to drag us with him. Or he studies the flora. Now if anyone ought to go, I think it ought to be someone with a keen interest in the study of plants," he concluded smugly.

"Never mind, Thomas. I have no intention—"

"I am persuaded it is not a place for children, Reggie," Letty put in, "but I'm certain Beachie would enjoy it. She *loves* flowers, you must know."

"Does she?" the duke heard himself say quietly, as Scotty flushed and looked everywhere but at him. And he knew suddenly that he very much wanted to take her there, unprecedented and improper though it was. But the voice of reason, and conscience, prevailed, and he supposed he never would.

For dinner at Beverwil Manor Susanna chose a gown of ivory lace over a peach satin slip. It was two years out of date, but she loved the dress with its very high waist, tiny puffed sleeves, and unusually full skirt. The skirt was trimmed with a deep flounce of ivory lace adorned with cockleshells of peach satin. It was a gown the duke had not yet seen. But of course, she told herself resolutely, that had nothing to do with her choosing it. Nor had the fact that the color, so she had been told, set off her creamy skin and auburn hair beautifully.

She settled the children early so that she might take time about her toilette. She was looking forward to dinner at the Hastings', although being included in the family party made her a trifle nervous. It would certainly not help convince the duke that she *was* what she claimed, to wit, Miss Rose Beacham, governess.

Standing in her petticoat before the glass, she

debated for several minutes about her hair. Surely it was more prudent to retain the severe chignon she had worn thus far. But that style, once she had pinned her hair back, seemed terribly at odds with the soft lines of the dress. Besides, she told herself as she ran the brush through her thick locks once again, if the Ayreses were kind enough to make her one of their party, then surely it was incumbent upon her to look her very best. And so she caught her hair up in a full knot at the crown and arranged the curls to fall artfully from it. Then she pulled several tendrils out to graze her nape. She loved working with her hair and achieved the look she wanted in a few minutes. The only thing missing, she thought, was one of the coral roses she had just this morning placed on the trestle table in the entry lobby. But she dare not . . .

It took a bit more time to struggle into the formfitting gown, but try as she might, she could not do up more than four of the myriad buttons at the back. She was loath to seek out a maid, for she knew word would get about straightaway below stairs that the governess's dress required a ladies' maid. That would not, she knew, help her credibility with the duke. And so she quietly tiptoed across the hall to the nursery. The corridor door led to a large sitting room, which was dark save for two tapers burning in the wall sconces. Several bedrooms led off the nursery. She peeked into the first and as she expected, Timothy was sound asleep while Thomas was reading by the inadequate light of a single taper. She closed the door softly and moved on to Letty's room. Letty jumped as the door clicked open and stuffed some magazine of sorts under the bedclothes.

"Letty, why ever are you hiding your magazine?"

"Oh, 'tis naught, merely an old— Oh, Beachie!" she exclaimed in wonder as Susanna strolled into the room, one hand holding the dress together at the back. "You look bea-*u*-tiful! Wait until Re—ah, Mama sees you! She will be delighted! And what have you done to your hair? I like it ever so much better than the way you usually wear it, as if . . . as if you were quite on the shelf!"

"Why, thank you, Letty. But I do assure you I am quite past my first blushes," Susanna replied, and wondered why she felt the need to emphasize that to Letty. She pivoted round and added "I am having some difficulty, dear. Might I prevail upon you to do up my buttons?"

Letty giggled and scrambled to the side of the bed. "'Course I will, but anyone as beautiful as you are had ought to have a proper ladies' maid." She fumbled a bit with the buttons and brought the bedside taper closer.

"Fustian! I do *not* need a maid! I can do up most of my dresses perfectly well," Susanna retorted, perhaps too vehemently. When Letty had done, Susanna swiveled back round, and the child reached out with tentative fingers to touch the fine satin.

Letty looked uncharacteristically wistful, so Susanna sat down on the canopied bed. "You know, Letty dear, someday you'll have dresses every bit as lovely as this, and some ever so much more magnificent, I am persuaded."

"Perhaps," Letty said doubtfully, then, brightening, added, "but you must know it will not signify, for I shall never look beautiful. Oh, but do not tease yourself about it, Beachie, for I warrant *I* do not. You see, I mean to become a bluestocking!"

"A bluest— You most certainly will not! Why, you'll

be a great beauty one day."

"Oh, Beachie! You must not offer me Spanish coin the way Reggie did. Anyone can see that my hair is quite insipid, and I am far too plump, and my nose is too—"

"Letty! Letty! You are but twelve years old. Did I never tell you that when I was your age I had the most dreadful freckles and was quite excessively plump?"

"Did you have pigtails, too?"

"Why, of course. All the—"

"You've been talking to Reggie, haven't you?" she said accusatorially.

"About this? I should say not!"

Suddenly there was a glint of wonder in Letty's eyes. "Oh," was all she said.

"At all events," Susanna went on, patting her hand, "a woman's charm is at least as important as her face and form. You already have intelligence and a deal of wit, and you shall acquire the rest as you grow older."

"Will you"—Letty fidgeted with the coverlet and her voice dropped lower—"Will you be . . . here to teach me?"

Susanna bit her lip, then whispered, "I shall stay as long as I can, Letty."

Letty nodded solemnly, and then Susanna asked once more about the magazine beneath the rumpled bedclothes. Reluctantly Letty withdrew a rather old issue of *La Belle Assemblée*.

"Why the secrecy, Letty? This is hardly a Minerva Press novel or—"

"I know. 'Tis just . . . I feel such a ninnynammer looking at the fashion plates. 'Tis just . . . 'tis just the sort of thing Phoebe would do," she said with barely concealed disdain. And then her brown eyes looked stricken. "I mean to say, she is the best of sisters, always kind and willing to spend a moment, and so beautiful, just like Mama, but . . . but you cannot deny that she is rather a peagoose."

Susanna sternly repressed a smile. "Letty, I do assure you that occasionally perusing a fashion magazine will not render one a peagoose, or a ninnynammer either. It is quite all right to intersperse it with your Shakespeare, you must know."

At that Letty began tentatively flipping the pages, so Susanna took her leave, for time was rather escaping her.

She completed her toilette rapidly, draped her lace shawl about her shoulders, and headed for the stairs. Once on the first floor, she peered over the banister at the lobby below. And then, unable to resist, she ran down the stairs and over to the trestle table. Glancing about to make sure no one was about, she quickly snatched a small coral rose from the bouquet. She peered into the glass above the table and secured it in her hair. Rather pleased with the result, she darted back upstairs and on toward the Blue Saloon.

She regretted her impulse as soon as she reached the threshold. The duke was alone in the room. He stood next to the mantel, a glass of sherry in his hand and what could only be described as a brooding, rather forbidding look on his face. But if his expression sent a wave of apprehension through her, the look of the rest of him was disconcerting in quite another way. He looked, well, beautiful in a superbly tailored, wine-colored coat, navy blue waistcoat, and cream-colored breeches. Her eyes lingered on those close-fitting breeches a moment too long, and to her mortification, she heard him call, "Scotty?" ever so softly.

Her gaze had quite unnerved the duke, but not nearly so much as her appearance. The peach satin dress outlined her figure and displayed her enchanting décolletage in such a way that he felt his breathing alter at the mere sight of her. His eyes traveled her length as she came slowly into the room, her skirts undulating around her, outlining her waist, her hips, her long, slender legs. He swallowed hard and raised his eyes to her face. Her head was slightly tilted, her big midnight blue eyes regarding him a bit questioningly. Two small sapphire drops, twinkling at her ears, caught the color of her eyes. Her red lips were slightly parted, her high cheekbones delicately flushed. And her hair. God, but it was beautiful, the curls falling in enticing disorder from the crown. Such rich, thick hair; it would be magnificent falling down her back. His eyes fell to her throat, long, slender, bare of jewels, and her shoulders, hardly covered by the tiny puffed sleeves. He took a step toward her. Her skin looked smooth and creamy, and he longed to run his hands, and his tongue . . .

He stopped short, a wave of heat coursing over him. Take hold of yourself, old chap! This is the *governess*, dammit!

"Would you"—he stopped and cleared his throat—"Would you like a glass of sherry?"

"Yes, please," she said quietly, and he was glad of the excuse to turn from her and walk to the decanter. He needed to compose himself.

When he turned back round he saw that she had gone to the window. She stood gazing out at the dimming light, one hand on the partially closed blue velvet draperies.

He went to her and handed her a glass. She stared down into it, and then her eyes met his. His mother and Phoebe were late, as usual. He was not sure whether to be pleased or sorry. "Scotty," he said softly, "you look very . . . beautiful tonight." Oh, Lord, that wasn't the sort of thing to say to the governess!

She did not blush or stammer, as any self-respecting governess would have done, but instead peered at him from under her lashes and smiled "Why, thank you, Your Grace. I must say you—well, you do look rather dashing, you know."

When, he wondered, had a woman ever complimented him on anything other than how vast his acreage or how lovely the bauble was that he'd just placed in her grasping little hand? He felt a slow smile spread across his face and inclined his head in acknowledgement.

"Do you know, Your Grace, 'tis rare that I've ever seen you smile so . . . so broadly," she said almost in a whisper. "I am persuaded you had ought to smile more."

He was unused to compliments, and felt his color rise. Perhaps to cover his embarrassment, he felt himself become piqued. He did not want instructions from the governess about when to smile! And furthermore, now he thought of it, how could he permit the *governess* to go anywhere looking like that? Dressed in a gown that . . . that left so little to the imagination!

"Scotty, much as I admire your dress, do you not think you might be rather chilly? The Devon evenings . . ."

That irrepressible twinkle appeared in her eyes again. "Well, I daresay, the evenings are not all *that* cold

154

here," she said quizzingly, but before he could contrive a suitable setdown she added quickly, "By the by, I had a most interesting conversation with Letty a few moments ago. Did you know that she seems to divide women into two categories? Where on earth can she have gotten such an addlepated notion?"

Reginald coughed and quickly set his drink down on a nearby table. "What, ah, sort of categories?" he asked. Surely Letty couldn't have gotten any such notion from him. . . .

"Women, according to Letty, are either beautiful ninnynammers or plain-looking bluestockings, and since she sees herself as plain—"

"Oh Lord, I know. She told me yesterday she means to be a bluestocking! I do hope you can disabuse her of that notion! And now I think on it, I've meant to tell you . . . well . . . when she was saying that she'll never be a beauty like . . . like you, Scotty"— Again she did not blush, merely smiled and if anything looked a bit amused— "well, I'm afraid I imbued you with a fat, freckled childhood."

Scotty let forth a light ripple of giggles. "And pigtails, I suppose?" He nodded. "No wonder she was so suspicious when I told her the very same. She thinks we're in collusion."

She raised her glass to her lips. "Did you really, Scotty?" he asked quietly.

"Did I tell her—?"

"No. Did you really have freckles and pigtails and the lot?" There was a certain gleam in his eye and a curl to his lips that made her pulse accelerate.

She smiled crookedly. "Aye."

"You were probably adorable. And full of mischief."

Her eyes danced. "I was always leading my cousin

Jamie into all sorts of scrapes. His mother, Aunt MacLaughlin, was quite in despair of me."

"And where is your cousin Jamie now?" Why was he asking? Why did he care?

"Jamie's been on the Continent with his regiment for three years."

She sounded a bit wistful. "Do you miss him?" he asked, feeling unaccountably annoyed.

"I miss . . . I miss the days gone by, when . . . well, it doesn't signify." How could she tell him that she missed her mother, and Ballincraig in better days? Susanna took a sip of sherry and despite his prompting would say no more.

She started to move away, murmuring something about an interesting painting on the far wall. Reginald clasped her wrist and drew her back. "Scotty," he said, gazing down at her intently and not letting go her hand, "MacLaughlin is a Scottish name."

Her eyes widened and she nearly spilled her drink. He took it from her and set it down, possessing himself of both her hands now. "Oh? Is it?" she said ingenuously. "I . . . I hadn't noticed."

He drew her closer. They were only inches apart. "Hadn't you, Scotty?" he whispered.

Oh Lord! Why did she allow him to call her that? Why did she not pull away from him? Why was she breathing so rapidly? And why ever had she mentioned Aunt's name? "No, I hadn't," she said unsteadily. "There are, ah, several MacLaughlins in Lancashire, you must know."

"Ah, Scotty"—he breathed out the words, his half-smile making her heart pound strangely—"when will you learn that you cannot gammon me?" He moved yet closer to her and his hand came up to cup her chin gently. She felt a wave of heat ripple through her. Why was she not more frightened? She had got to say something, had got to shift the subject. "I cannot think what ye . . . what you mean, Your Grace," she said haltingly and then, mustering her sense of humor, added, "Someday you must tell me how *you* classify women. Or do you agree with Letty?"

Reginald dropped his hand. No, he did not agree with Letty, but he had his own categories for women. "I do not think I shall tell you, Scotty," he finally managed to reply, and doubted that he ever would. For he was very certain of those categories, and she fit into neither one.

Chapter 9

Susanna knew within minutes of their arrival at Beverwil Manor, that she was not going to enjoy the evening. She was not certain why; it was not an accustomed reaction for her. And besides, she had ought to enjoy such an unusual evening out.

Perhaps it was the manner of their hosts as they greeted them in the large, cold drawing room. Oswald Hastings was ingratiating toward her, nearly obsequious toward the duke and his mother. And at Phoebe he cast contrived looks of incipient passion that would have been amusing had Phoebe not looked like she was about to melt. The Baron Hastings seemed to be making too much of an effort to be jovial, as if a great deal were at stake tonight.

And she realized soon enough that a great deal *was.* Tonight was a concerted effort by the entire Hastings family to further Oswald's suit with Phoebe. And Susanna realized that she herself must have been invited because they had divined that she had some influence with the duchess.

It was Ernestine Hastings, the baron's pinched-looking maiden sister, who made this most obvious. She had greeted the duchess as if they were long-lost friends, when in fact Susanna knew Her Grace only tolerated Miss Hastings because of the proximity of the two estates. And now Miss Hastings gushed effusively about how wonderful it was to see the duke back in residence after so *prolonged* an absence. Her hand came up to graze the duke's arm in a rather cloying attempt at flirtatiousness. Susanna saw the duke's jaw tighten in annoyance and wondered if anyone else had noticed. And then suddenly she met his gaze and could not keep a spark of merriment from her eyes. The duke's gray eyes crinkled in shared amusement, and she was pleased to see his jaw muscles relax. The baron's sister greeted Phoebe as if she were some precious china doll, and Phoebe cooed that it was such a delight to be with them all, before she glided off in the direction of Oswald.

Finally, Ernestine Hastings turned to Susanna. The baron's sister was a very tall, angular woman; she wore a lemon yellow dress with too many flounces, which unfortunately did not become her at all. She raised her chin and looked down at Susanna, only belatedly remembering to smile. "Ah, Miss Beacham," she said in clipped tones, "we are so pleased to have you. I don't suppose that in *your* position you have the opportunity to go about much, but dear Oswald assured us you would welcome such a chance." Susanna just barely kept her mouth from gaping open. A sideways glance at the duke told her he hadn't decided whether to be furious or burst out laughing at such condescension. "Besides, he tells me you are so much more than a governess." Miss Hastings went on in a low voice. "Almost like one of the family. Oswald said you would make a fortuitous addition to our little group tonight, and of course, as always, I see that my dear nephew is right."

She beamed fondly at her "dear nephew," who was standing more close to Phoebe than any notion of propriety allowed. To Phoebe's credit, Susanna saw her inch away. Unfortunately, the duke saw them too, and Susanna knew fury had won out.

Ernestine Hastings turned her very artificial smile back to Reginald. She actually took his arm to usher them forward to greet the others. He forced himself to relax, but his eyes kept wandering back to Phoebe.

Lady Craddock, who was dark haired where his mother was light, but just as dotty and dithering, sat on a green loveseat next to her daughter, Elsie. The duke had always had a soft spot for Lady Craddock, whose husband had left her only a modest jointure. For she seemed to manage admirably and was always exceedingly cheerful. Her husband, never having expected to come into the baronetcy, had become an army man, and Lady Craddock had spent most of her married life following the drum. She had settled in Devon after his death to be with her girlhood friend, Reginald's mother. And she had brought with her an avid but good-natured penchant for gossip as well as some rather odd souveniers from her world travels. These included several primitive statuettes glorifying various parts of the anatomy best left undisplayed on the drawing-room table. They also included exotic bits of foreign costume, especially headdresses, which she enlivened Devon society by wearing from time to time.

Tonight she wore some sort of gray toque, out of which danced numerous ostrich feathers. It was a rather large headdress but would have been fairly unexceptionable if not for the three tiny stuffed birds perched precariously therein. Her silver gray dress, thank Heaven, was pure English.

Lady Craddock seemed to relieve some of the boredom of country life for Reginald's mother, and for that he was grateful. But every so often Lady Craddock did get up to some queer start or other which worried him not a little.

What always amazed Reginald was that the gregarious Lady Craddock had managed to produce two children so totally unlike her. Elsie, at seventeen a younger, prettier version of her mother, was painfully shy, without a spark of her mother's originality, but she was a pretty, behaved girl whom Reginald thought a fitting companion for Phoebe. Elsie's brother, William, hovered at his mother's side. He was just a year older than Elsie and had aspirations of entering the clergy. As William was a rather overly sober young man, even by Reginald's standards, that was probably a good idea.

The baron, who'd had one too many glasses of sherry, had cornered Reginald's mother and was attempting to do the pretty. His mother was either being polite or believed every one of his overblown compliments, for she was batting her eyelashes and patting her hair.

Dancing attendance on Elsie, bringing her lemonade and inquiring as to her comfort, Reginald saw a tall, good-looking, dark-haired man. Miss Hastings called him over and made him known to Reginald. The man was Major Hayes, an old friend of the late Sir William Craddock. He looked close to forty, a bit old for Elsie, Reginald thought. But then, Lady Craddock had not the funds for a London Season, and Elsie might not have the opportunity to meet many men. As she was so very shy, an older, more settled man might do well. And certainly the child could do worse than the good-looking major. But Hayes eyed Scotty much too lingeringly when they were introduced, so Reginald decided he was *much* too old, and come to think on't, not all that handsome.

When Hayes finally went back to Elsie, Reginald ushered Scotty to a chair by the window and procured them each some sherry. Scotty did not touch hers, he noted, and her eyes were glued to Oswald and Phoebe, who were just now joined by Miss Hastings.

"My mother should never have accepted this invitation," he murmured into her ear as he stood beside her. "No good will come of the connection."

She concurred, but insisted that Phoebe must learn for herself what an odious young man Oswald truly was. Phoebe was dressed tonight in a pink lace gown that showed off far too much of her very young bosom. And Oswald, having seated her, was hovering next to her and availing himself of the view. That Reginald stood in exactly the same proximity to Scotty, he did not care to think on.

He saw Oswald bend his head to whisper something in Phoebe's ear and in so doing place his hand on her bare shoulder for a moment. Reginald felt himself go rigid, and he took a step forward. Scotty was up in a flash, one hand holding his arm surreptitiously.

"Don't, Your Grace, I beg you. Be careful," she whispered. He looked down at her slender hand on his coat, then back up at her beautiful face as she stood close to him. And suddenly he forgot about Phoebe and, in fact, wished the whole company, save Scotty, at Jericho.

"The Reverend Mr. Honeyworth," intoned the butler, effectively and fortuitously putting an end to Reginald's inappropriate thoughts. Mr. Honeyworth was a short, dapper man with wavy white hair. He might have been anywhere from sixty to eighty years old. No one could tell, and he certainly wouldn't, and as he'd had the living at Milburne parish for longer than anyone could remember, there was no way of finding out. He claimed partial deafness, a very convenient deafness, the duke had always surmised. For the rector used it too well to his advantage, ignoring conversations that bored him and listening avidly to those not meant for his ears. And though he was given to a bit too much to levity for a man of the cloth, Reginald thought he was basically a good sort.

He made straight for them after being welcomed by Ernestine Hastings. He greeted Reginald pleasantly and then broke into a broad smile and greeted Susanna as if they were old friends. She responded in kind; Reginald hadn't even known they'd met. "How perfectly delightful to find you here, Miss Beacham," he said. "I usually look forward to these evenings at Beverwil with the same enthusiasm as to a visit to the dentist. The baron has often shot the cat by the time I arrive, and Ernestine will forever badger me about singing for us in church." He leaned forward and his eyes crinkled up. "She has the most dreadful voice, you must know. Shrill and rather dried up, just like she—" At a look from the duke he stopped, cleared his throat, and said, "Well, at all events, 'tis a treat to have you among the company, m'dear. Of course, if *you'd* ever like to sing in church . . ."

163

"I do not think so, Mr. Honeyworth," Reginald said with barely concealed pique.

"No, no. I don't suppose so. Still, 'tis a pity."

Reginald was very glad when dinner was called.

Ten minutes later, he was downing madeira much too quickly, in the vain hope that it might help him relax. He did not care for the seating arrangement at all. Nor did he understand it. The fact that Phoebe was placed next to Oswald Hastings, he understood all too well, but Scotty between Major Hayes and the rector? She was across and some distance down the table from Reginald. He himself had been placed between Lady Craddock and Elsie, with William and the duchess on Elsie's right. Now why on earth was he next to Elsie? Surely Miss Hastings could not imagine he had any interest in *that* quarter?

And poor Elsie cast mooncalf eyes toward the major, her expression growing more and more desolate as Hayes continued to ignore her. For Hayes, damn the man, could not keep his eyes off Scotty. He poured her wine and leaned over to whisper something which made her laugh, and ogled her bosom when he thought no one the wiser. Dammit! Didn't he know one did not flirt with governesses, or ogle then, or single them out for any special attention? Next thing one knew he'd be paying court to her! Well, Reginald would put paid to any such notion straightaway. After all, the children *needed* their governess!

A niggling voice at the back of his head reminded him that he didn't believe she was any sort of governess at first stop. And further that even if she were, it was hardly fair of him to prevent her from having an occasional caller.

Certainly she might have a caller, he decided. A

female one! And it occurred to him that Major Hayes was not a bit too old for Elsie Craddock.

His attention was diverted, while the oxtail soup was being served, by Ernestine Hastings. Seated at the foot of the table, she fairly leaned across Lady Craddock, who sat next to her, to address the duke. "Oswald was telling me just the other day, Your Grace, about your *exciting* work in London. A magazine of botany! I own I am most impressed. Why, I cannot wait to read it!"

Doing it much too brown, Reginald thought disdainfully. He doubted she ever read anything more exacting than *La Belle Assemblée*. She tried to smile, and he reflected that the result was not worth the great effort it seemed to cost her.

"Indeed, Miss Hastings. *The Journal of Botanical Research*," he replied, and then on impulse added, "And I am currently studying the sexual theory as applied to the wildflowers of Devon." Lady Craddock sputtered into her wineglass and Miss Hastings's face turned the color of that very wine. Good God, whatever had possessed him to say such a thing? That governess's inappropriate sense of levity must be getting to him.

His hostess reached for madeira with a shaky hand, but Lady Craddock appeared to be smothering a giggle in her serviette. Reginald, unable to suppress the glint in his eye, blithely asked Lady Craddock about her plans for William's future.

They conversed for several lively minutes as Lady Craddock spoke rather candidly about her children. But her eyes, curiously, strayed across the table several times. Her expression was distracted, speculative, and he wondered in amusement what she was thinking. And then his amusement faded as his eyes focused directly across the table where Oswald and Phoebe sat. He could not hear what they were saying, for the table was quite wide. But it was obvious that Oswald, his lips at her ear, was importuning Phoebe about something. Phoebe blushed and shook her head, and thus they went on, back and forth, while the stuffed Dover sole and sautéed sweetbreads were being served, until finally Reginald watched Phoebe slowly nod.

He felt a vein begin to throb at his temple and wondered what the hell his sister had just consented to.

Susanna might have contrived to enjoy herself, for her dinner partners, Major Hayes and the rector, each exerted himself to be charming. But the undercurrents at table were all too obvious and disturbing. The baron, at the head of the table and already in his cups, quite ignored the major at his right as he leaned over to engage Susanna in some inane discourse about how clever Oswald was with estate management. Yes, Susanna thought, he is managing quite well to dissipate the estate. The duke was rigid with tension, which she could somehow sense all the way across the table. He kept glowering at her and at Phoebe in turn. Lady Craddock was casting odd looks across the table, toward either the rector or herself; she could not be sure. And Ernestine Hastings was trying much too hard to be pleasant.

Thankfully, after the Dover sole arrived, the baron decided it was time to exert his inebriated charm on the duchess, who sat to his left. The major took the opportunity to ask Susanna how she liked the Devon weather. She answered enthusiastically, but a surreptitious glance at Elsie's downcast face caused her to dampen her enthusiasm. Susanna certainly had no interest in the major, nor did she wish to cause Elsie distress. Really, Miss Hastings's seating arrangement left much to be desired. The major's bluff, amiable manner was beginning to wear on Susanna, especially as he punctuated his statements with pointed glances at her bosom. She was relieved when the Reverend Mr. Honeyworth addressed her in his soft, gravelly voice.

"You are looking especially lovely tonight, my dear Miss Beacham, though I'm certain there are those who would say a man in my position oughtn't to say so."

"Why, thank you, Mr. Honeyworth," she replied, smiling. She had met the rector several times briefly at Milburne Hall and had liked him immediately.

"Ah, perhaps you can tell me, my dear, why your employer, the good duke, is shooting dagger points across the table with his eyes."

She looked at Mr. Honeyworth sideways and saw the telltale twitching of his lips. "Well," she began, "he may be shooting dagger points for any number of reasons. He has so many, you see." She speared a bit of the sweetbreads with her fork. "I believe it depends on the time of day."

"So, my noble neighbor does not quite approve of you?" he asked, eyes dancing. "Could it be that you do not fit his notion of a governess?"

Susanna heard warning bells in her head and her eyes narrowed.

"Oh no, Miss Beacham. Do not look so. You have naught to fear from me," Mr. Honeyworth said quickly, then added, "I think you make a perfectly lovely governess. Not that you would not make a perfectly lovely something else as well."

She relaxed and raised her eyebrows, but her eyes were merry.

"Er . . . yes—well, never mind that. Now, tell me, my

dear, surely Milburne does not glower only at *you*. . . ."

He let the words dangle and Susanna ventured a glance at the duke's forbidding face. "Well, no, actually. I think it is Phoebe and Oswald Hastings that have . . . ah . . ."

"Raised his hackles? I daresay. I did not suppose he would welcome that suit. Then perhaps I had ought to tell you . . ."

"Tell me what, Mr. Honeyworth?" she prompted after a moment.

"Well now, I am quite deaf, you must know, my dear, and—" she raised a skeptical brow and he chuckled— "but I am, you know, when I . . . er . . . have to be, and so, of course, I hear all sorts of things." He broke off as the footmen served the next course, which looked like stuffed pidgeons and rather overcooked asparagus, as well as a huge nondescript piece of beef.

By the time the footmen had departed, the major had claimed her attention once more, and so it was some time before she was able to ask Mr. Honeyworth what "sorts of things."

"Ah, yes. Well, young Hastings does not know enough to lower his voice, you see. He said, I believe it was during the soup—too watery, don't you agree? And this meat, rather dried out. So was the sole, come to think on't. It's a wonder, isn't it, that Ernestine's bill of fare is as dried out as she—yes, well, never mind that." He gave up trying to cut the shredding beef with his knife and speared an asparagus tip instead. "Oswald was telling Phoebe to meet him secretly at the lending library in Upper Milburne. He will contrive to be rid of her maid, and then he means to take her driving. I believe he spoke of a picnic."

Susanna's eyes widened in dismay. "Oh, dear," she

said. "It is worse than I thought." A swift glance across the table told her the duke had witnessed her tête-à-tête with the rector and seen her distress. She knew she would have to tell him. And then what . . .

Dinner seemed to go on interminably, each course more overcooked than the last. And when the ladies retired, the duke found himself unaccustomedly impatient to join them. Well, to join her, he had to admit. He very much wanted to talk to Scotty, for many reasons. But Ernestine Hastings made that nearly impossible, once the gentlemen joined the ladies for coffee in the drawing room. Her tall, gaunt form darted about, seating people where they had no intention of sitting, so that Scotty was forced to make conversation with the evermore bosky baron. He was loudly proclaiming the fertility of his acreage and the soundness of the house, which Oswald would inherit, in case anyone was ignorant on that head. And Miss Hastings informed Reginald in her slightly nasal voice that Oswald was saying only the other day that it was time he settled down and began filling the Beverwil nursery. She looked pointedly at Phoebe as she spoke, a sharp gleam in her eye, and Reginald knew it was the Beverwil coffers that she wished to fill.

Lady Craddock was talking in some earnest to the rector, who was smiling and nodding with great interest. Reginald enjoyed a moment's conjecture as to what a man of the cloth could find to speak about at such length with a woman reputed to wear harem pants about the house.

But then this tête-à-tête ended, and Reginald let his gaze drift away. He sipped his coffee in unalleviated boredom, until his eyes met Scotty's across the room. They communicated to him the very same feeling, and he could not hold back a slight smile. Her eyes grew merry in response.

As he had feared, for surely it was *de rigueur* for such interminable evenings, Miss Hastings asked Phoebe to sing and play the the pianoforte and then, of course, she had to ask Elsie to do the same. Both girls played adequately, no more, and had sweet, quite unmemorable voices. Oswald feigned rapture during Phoebe's performance, but the major seemed genuinely entranced with Elsie's. All to the good, Reginald thought. It would take his mind off governesses.

Miss Hastings next began strutting to the piano herself. Reginald knew he could not possibly sit through a single rendition in her nasal, scratchy voice, and before he could stop himself he was on his feet, proclaiming that Miss Beacham had a lovely voice and that he would turn her pages.

Miss Hastings looked surprised, but consented with a forced graciousness and a hard smile. His mother seconded the notion, saying it was a wonderful idea, and didn't dear Beachie sing about the house quite often. The rector beamed at Scotty with what the duke hoped was fatherly approval. But Lady Craddock's eyes flitted from him to Scotty with a speculative gleam that made Reginald wish he'd opted for Ernestine Hastings shattering glass while trying to sing an operatic aria.

But there was no help for it, and he seated Scotty at the pianoforte. Then he realized that there was no music to turn; he remained standing beside her at all events. He'd never heard her play, but her graceful, slender fingers glided over the keys just as he'd imagined they would. She began with a light Shakespearean ditty, and then sang a sea ballad, her beautiful, deep, musical voice filling the large room. Next she played a slower song, a love song. It had a haunting melody, and must of a certain be Scottish, but then he'd known all along where she came from, hadn't he? He stopped thinking, and let the words and the music flow over him. Her voice somehow beckoned him; he moved closer and closer. And every so often her eyes, almost against her will, met his. His breath caught in his throat as she sang:

"Oh, I was a lassie that day we met,
And he was a soldier, I'll ne'er forget.
He kissed me but once, pledged his troth to me,
Way doon at the burn by the weepin' tree.

"But I was too young for to wed, they'd say,
And he must away to the wars that day.
I'll come for ye, lass, he cried oot to me,
Way doon at the burn by the weepin' tree.

"And so I did wait through the lonely years,
My hair turned to frost, the burn filled with tears,
And still my true heart was a keepin' me
Way doon at the burn by the weepin' tree.

"Till winter descended o'er all the land;
Then he came a-ridin', held oot his hand—
Come bide with me, luv, at last noo I'm free,
And I'll lay ye doon by the weepin' tree."

The words were bittersweet and Reginald felt a lump in his throat for the long-ago pair who had loved and parted and waited a lifetime for each other. Such a wretched waste, he thought, and again his eyes met Scotty's.

She repeated the song and he found himself mouthing the words, singing them softly, so only she could hear. . . .

And then it was over, and the room was silent. Still Reginald could not tear his eyes from hers, nor could he stop thinking of those words, of all those loveless years. His mouth felt dry. Why was Scotty looking at him so oddly? Why could he not move? It was almost as if he were . . . transfixed. He did not understand himself; his eyes searched hers in the stillness of the room. He was not aware of anyone but the two of them. She hadn't moved.

Susanna's eyes met his. She could not move. Something had happened to her during that last song. When he had sung the words with her, blended his voice, however softly, with hers, it was as if . . . as if . . . She swallowed hard. It was as if their bodies, not their voices, had been somehow intertwined.

Those last lines would not leave her mind. "Come bide with me, luv, at last noo I'm free, And I'll lay ye doon by the weepin' tree." Oh, God, she thought, if I am not careful, I will find myself falling in love with this man. Her employer. The man who could expose her and send her packing at the first excuse. The man who would be horrified and disgusted at what she had done, at what she was. She must be on her guard, must keep her distance. It was *she* who was not free.

Reginald saw the sudden distress in her eyes before she lowered them. And then, finally, the company broke into applause. The spell, or whatever it was between them, was broken. Scotty took her bow, and then, suddenly, she was surrounded by the men, all praising her performance with varying gleams of appreciation that seemed, in the case of Major Hayes and the baron, to encompass her face and form as well as her musical abilities. Reginald felt his jaw tighten.

Lady Craddock put a hand to his arm. "That was . . . quite a performance," she said with an enigmatic smile on her lips.

Reginald was very happy to see the evening end.

As they entered the house, Susanna contrived to brush past Reginald and whisper, "I must speak with you. 'Tis about Phoebe." She did not want to be alone with him, especially at night. But something had to be done about the planned meeting with Oswald, and Susanna could not do it alone.

The duke nodded briefly to her and bade his mother and sister good night. Phoebe moved toward the stairs, but the duchess turned to Susanna. "You play beautifully, my dear. And what a lovely voice you have. Don't you agree, Reggie?"

"Yes, Mother, I do," he said, a bit curtly, Susanna thought.

"Well, come up then, Beachie dear. You must be fagged to death. Such a long day you've had."

"Ah, Mother," the duke said quickly, "I should like a word with Miss Beacham. I shan't keep her long."

"Well, of course, dear. I'm sure you have a great deal to talk about. Perhaps you might plan another outing. The children couldn't stop talking about your picnic today." With that the duchess trailed off, leaving Reginald shaking his head. If he hadn't known she was incapable of it, he would have suspected his mother of cryptic machinations, for her suggestion was outrageous. Outings with the governess, indeed!

He led that same governess through the darkened corridor to his study, He held her by the elbow and was much too aware of her body as she walked beside him. Her hips brushed against him every now and again, and the faint scent of jasmine stirred his senses.

He groaned inwardly and vowed to make this interview as short as possible. He lit several tapers as soon as they entered the study. The more light the better, he thought, but knew that was a mistake when he turned to face her. How beautiful, how desirable she looked in her peach satin dress, her creamy skin glistening in the candlelight. Her shawl rested in the crook of her elbows; he resisted the urge to cover her bare shoulders.

He went to the sideboard and poured some brandy. He proffered a glass to her, but she shook her head. He poured himself a double, and then came to stand near her behind the sofa. Resolutely he kept a distance of several feet between them.

"Your Grace," she said softly, "I think you drink too much. Particularly with such headaches as you suffer from. How *is* your head, by the by?"

He tossed down a good amount of the brandy, then set the glass down. "Is there no end to your meddling, Scotty?" She opened her mouth to protest, and he shook his head, smiling slightly. "Never mind, my dear. My head, actually, is much improved. Just a twinge now."

She smiled in return. "I am glad. And truly, I do not mean to meddle. 'Tis only that sometimes, well, one cannot help but—"

"So I've noticed," he said dryly. "Now tell me about Phoebe."

"Well, I have it from the rector, you must know. I believe you noticed our little tête-à-tête."

174

He nodded, tight-lipped. "You seemed to be enjoying yourself rather well with *both* of your dinner partners," he said more sharply than he'd intended. But she had brought the matter up, and he might just as well make his point.

"I suppose you would have preferred it if I had not enjoyed myself?" she asked tartly.

He drew himself up and kept his face stern. "One can contrive to enjoy oneself, Miss Beacham, without being overly, er, friendly."

"At all events," she went on, "the major was merely being a bit foolish, I expect. But Mr. Honeyworth, I assure you, was all that was polite. Poor man, I suppose everyone expects him to be excessively sober and staid, just because he has the living here. But he really is a very charming, funny man."

Reginald wondered just how charmed she was, then chided himself severely. The man was old enough to be her grandfarther, for pity's sake! Surely he could not entertain any inappropriate designs on her, nor would she respond to such, even if they *did* share a similar irreverent sense of humor.

"Yes, well, what has all this to say to the matter of Phoebe?" he asked politely.

"Well, you know how deaf the rector pretends to be, when he really isn't anything of the sort."

He raised an eyebrow. How had she tumbled to that one so fast? Most of Milburne parish had yet to figure it out. "I'd rather suspected, you must know," she continued, "but then he told me so himself."

This shocked him even more, as did the fact that, not for the first time, she seemed to have read his mind. "And?" was all he said.

She took a deep breath. "Oswald asked Phoebe to

meet him at the lending library in Upper Milburne. He said he would contrive to rid her of her maid and they would take a drive and have a picnic."

Reginald felt his blood begin to boil. Desire fled as anger took its place. "And she agreed to this?" he asked through clenched teeth.

Scotty nodded. "You can see why I felt the need to tell you tonight. She may—"

"Blast!" He slammed a fist into the back of the sofa, then stormed to the window. He whirled round to face her. "Excuse me, Scotty. I quite forgot myself. But how dare she behave in such a reprehensible manner! And how could she be so criminally stupid! I am going to lock her in her room until—"

"Your Grace." She put a hand on his arm.

"I suppose you have a better idea," he retorted. "Well, do tell me. If you have some solution to this coil, out with it!"

"Well, first of all," she said hesitantly, "I . . . I do not think Phoebe is truly stupid." He arched a brow. "I mean to say, she is foolish, surely, but she is only acting this way because she fears opposition. And Oswald has turned her head with his compliments."

"The man is a scoundrel of the first order."

"Of course he is. And as I said once before, I think you had ought to let Phoebe discover that for herself."

"You give Phoebe too much credit."

"Perhaps. But still if you wish her not to meet him in such a havey-cavey fashion, you must make it clear that Oswald is welcome to call. And to take her driving with a chaperone, of course. If his intentions are honorable, which they must be if he has designs on her fortune, then he cannot cavil at that."

176

"No. I expect you are right," he replied. "And now I think on't, I might tell him that she will not come into the money until, say, her twenty-fifth birthday."

Susanna stiffened. Her eyes narrowed and took on a bitter, faraway look. "That may answer, but do realize that he will know that once married, or even betrothed to her, he can borrow a great deal on the expectation."

Reginald had the distinct notion that it was not of Oswald Hastings that she was thinking. "What is it, Scotty?" he asked softly, taking a step closer to her. His hand gently cupped her elbows. "Will you not tell me what . . ."

She blinked and tried to smile. "Well now, what is to be done about tomorrow?"

He sighed. Would she never trust him? "I suppose we must find some distraction for her," he said. He did not drop his hands.

"Distraction?" she echoed faintly, her eyes deep blue pools in the candlelight. Her red lips, so close to his, looked all too inviting. He was thinking of only one sort of distraction, but it did not involve Phoebe.

"I will have my mother take Phoebe to the village to commission a few dresses. There is a creditable seamstress there. I shall tell Phoebe I've noted how much she is in need of new gowns. I have never known a female to cavil at such."

"That will serve admirably, Yer Grace." Susanna was hardly aware of what she was saying. The candlelight illumined the strong planes of his face. His gray eyes held hers. She did not know what he wanted of her, nor why she was not frightened. But she could not move. "In time Phoebe—"

"I grow tired of talking of Phoebe," he rasped. His hands came up to her cheeks, and he traced her

177

cheekbones with his thumbs. She closed her eyes as a warm ripple of some strange sensation coursed over her. Her heartbeat was erratic. She felt an overwhelming urge to melt into his arms. "I want . . . I want to talk about *you*, Scotty," he whispered, and traced her lips with his forefinger. Warning bells sounded in her head, but still she could not move.

"Yer Grace, dinna . . . dinna ask me questions I canna answer." Dimly, Susanna heard herself slip into Scots. She could not seem to help it.

"Do you not think," he breathed, his mouth just inches from hers, "that you might call me by my name, at the least when we are alone?" He smiled down at her. That smile, and the deep, masculine softness of his tone, sent another wave of heat through her.

"Milburne," she said tentatively.

He shook his head, his left hand at her nape. "No, Scotty. Try again."

"'Tisna . . . 'tisna proper."

"Ahh," he murmured, a gleam in his eyes. "Well, you know Scotty, I do think propriety is all well and good, but sometimes one can take it a bit too far, don't you think?"

He lifted her chin with his right hand. "Scotty?"

"Reginald," she breathed. He had been holding himself in check, trying not to lean forward, to claim her lips as he'd ached to do for so long now. But the sound of his name on those very same lips sent a bolt of heat through him.

Slowly he lowered his head. He touched his lips to hers in a feather-light caress. Her lips were soft and full and warm . . . and ever so tentative, so innocent, yet full of yearning. They parted slightly; hesitantly, they pressed against his. It was that innocence that caused him to draw back, however reluctantly, to end the kiss before it had really started. He stroked her lips with his finger. Such a brief kiss, but it had been enough. Something had happened between them just now, some ineffable communication. He felt as if he had somehow defined their relationship. But of course, that was nonsense; he had rather made everything all the more confusing.

He gazed down at her in the candlelight and his hands gently grasped her shoulders. Her eyes were wide, unfathomable. He had started something that someday, somehow, he would finish. But now was not the time. Slowly he lowered his hands. "Go to bed, Scotty," he said softly.

She reached up and touched his cheek with the palm of her hand. And then, suddenly, she turned and ran from the room.

Reginald stared after her into the dark and silent night. Then he poured himself more brandy. He did not retire for a very long time.

Susanna was shaking and tingling all over when she reached her third-floor rooms. She did not understand what had happened, or how, only knew that it must not ever happen again. She must never be alone with him again. It was too dangerous. And it was not, she admitted as she undressed under the cover of night, of the duke that she was frightened. Strange that Duncan Mortimer's touch had repelled and terrified her, but her reaction to the duke was so different. She did not understand why. There was something about him that drew her, and she must fight that strange attraction, *would* fight it, for both their sakes.

There was no other way. Perhaps for some other duke of the realm and Rose Beacham, governess, there might have been a way, albeit an unprecedented one. But for Susanna Fergusson, fugitive, and *this* duke, such a noble, honorable man, there was not, and could never be, a way. They had met in the wrong place and the wrong time. Tears welled up in her eyes as she climbed into bed, and she wondered how long she could bear to stay at Milburne Hall.

Chapter 10

Susanna dreamed again that night of the duke of Milburne. They stood under a tree at the edge of a cliff, his gray eyes smiling down at her. He reached out to touch her and then suddenly the gray eyes turned dark. And it was not the duke reaching out to her, but some huge and hideous snake with the face of Duncan Mortimer, pushing her closer and closer toward the precipice.

She woke up screaming and jerked to a sitting position, her face bathed in sweat. It was another nightmare, she thought, trying to calm herself. Only a dream. And then she realized that it was not she who was screaming. The sound was coming from across the hall. Dear God! One of the children!

She flew off the bed, brushing her tangled hair from her face, and yanked on her ivory satin wrapper. She fumbled for her slippers, then darted across the wooden floor and ran to the nursery. It was a terrible, piercing cry, coming from the boys' room. Quickly she lit a taper and went inside. Timothy was lying on his side in his bed, clutching his ear and shrieking.

Thomas was at the bedside, gently shaking him. "Wake up, Timothy! What's wrong? Oh, my God, what's wrong?"

Susanna set the taper down and touched Thomas on the shoulder.

"Oh! Beachie! Thank goodness! I can't get him to—"

"What is it? What's wrong?" Letty exclaimed, bustling bleary-eyed into the room.

Susanne peeled the frantic Thomas from the bed, handed him to Letty, and sat down beside Timothy. His little body was rigid, and she had all she could do to roll him over onto her lap.

"Timothy," she yelled over his screaming voice, "What is it?" He did not answer, just clutched at his ear so tightly that she could not tear his hand away to have a look. Oh, Lord, she had no idea what to do for ear pain. Where the devil was Annie, the nursery maid? Perhaps she would know.

She sent Letty in search of Annie and rocked Timothy and tried to soothe him. Thomas stood next to her, staring with terrified eyes at his brother. After what seemed an age, Annie came scurrying in, Letty on her heels. Annie took one look at Timothy and clapped her hands to her cheeks.

"Oh, my poor lamb! Such an age it's been since he had such an ear pain!" She sat down on the bed and put out her hands for the child. But her arms were no more able to soothe him than Susanna's.

"Annie, is there not something we can give him? What can we do for him?" Susanna asked urgently.

"Oil of almonds, we were used to use, miss. Like as not we've got some in the stillroom. 'Tis fer throat ailments, too."

"All right then, Annie, you go down to the stillroom

straightaway. I'll stay with Timothy."

Timothy was moaning now, and together the two women settled him back into bed. When Annie hurried away, Susanna turned to Letty. "Letty, will you go to Underwood? Have him send for the doctor straightaway. And Thomas, why don't you go to sleep in the spare bed in Letty's room. It will be quieter there." Thomas's young face looked crestfallen, and Susanna realized she'd hurt his pride. Quickly she added, "On second thought, why do you not accompany Letty, Thomas? The corridors are very dark, and I think she'll be glad of your escort."

Letty seemed about to protest, but Susanna silenced her with a look. Thomas drew himself up, enormously pleased. "Of course, I shall accompany Letty," he said soberly. "I was about to suggest the very same thing myself." Just so must the duke have been as a child, Susanna mused as she watched the two depart. A little boy already cognizant of a man's responsibilities.

She turned back to Timothy, murmuring words of comfort and stroking his face. He felt a bit warm, and she knew a fever might well accompany the ear pain. So she bathed his brow with water from the ewer, and waited anxiously for Annie. She thought of awakening the duchess, but Timothy wasn't asking for her, and Susanna somehow doubted she would be much help in a sickroom.

When Annie finally returned, she was carrying a basketful of all manner of vials and jars. "I . . . I can't read all them labels, miss, nor see the colors of the potions in that dark stillroom," she explained, and it took several minutes before Susanna was able to locate the tiny vial of oil of sweet almonds. She held Timothy down while Annie put several drops into his ear from

183

the corner of a white lawn handkerchief.

Timothy continued moaning for what seemed an endless time. Susanna sat at the bedside while Annie wrung her hands and paced. Neither could do any more at the moment. Susanna began to wonder where Letty and Thomas were and whether the doctor had been summoned. The two appeared minutes later and reported that Underwood was dispatching a messenger straightaway for Dr. Fairleigh. Then the children insisted on standing vigil at the bedside near Susanna; nothing she could say would induce Letty or Thomas to go to sleep. Then, finally, Timothy quieted, his moans subsiding to soft whimpers, his rigid body relaxing beneath the covers. Susanna felt the tension ease from her body as well.

She sent Annie to put Letty and Thomas to bed in Letty's room and tried to settle Timothy comfortably. She thought he would sleep, but he felt warm again and seemed restless. She bathed his brow and face, and wondered anxiously when Dr. Fairleigh would arrive. It also crossed her mind that perhaps the duke ought to be informed, but as Underwood was nowhere to be seen . . . Presently she became aware that Timothy was tugging at her sleeve, trying to tell her something.

She leaned forward. "Reggie. I want Reggie," he whispered.

"All right, dear. As soon as Annie returns I'll send for him."

He asked for the duke three more times and became increasingly restless before Annie came back to say that the others had fallen asleep. But Annie was horrified when Susanna asked her to go to the duke.

"Oh, I couldn't, miss. Why, he will be asleep, he will, and no tellin' where his man will have got to. He's a strange one, that Martinez, he is. And I never *have* been in the family wing, miss, and that's a fact. Oh, please don't be makin' me go, when it be dark and His Grace'll be like to rail at me and mayhap turn me off." The little maid became rather incoherent, and Susanna knew it was hopeless. She could send Annie for Underwood, and have Underwood rouse the duke, but that would take twice as long. Besides, Underwood was awaiting the doctor.

"Where's Reggie, Beachie? Why doesn't he come?" Timothy whined. He was beginning to thrash about. Susanna signaled for more water. Annie brought the ewer and several strips of linen to the bedside table.

"I'll bathe him, miss, like I done when he was in leadin' strings."

Susanna supposed she had no choice. Ridiculous as it was in a house full of dozens of servants and several family members, it was she who would have to go. She brushed the hair from Timothy's face and told him she would bring the duke. Then she yielded her place to Annie and lit the candelabrum that sat on the mantel. Pulling her satin wrapper more tightly about her, she took the candelabrum and headed for the corridor.

As she approached the door to the duke's rooms, she knew a fleeting hope that Martinez would be rattling about. But no one answered her soft knock on the sitting-room door. She moved a few yards down the corridor to what she thought was the dressing-room door; both the dressing room and sitting room led, she knew, to the duke's bedchamber. Perhaps Martinez slept in the dressing room.

It was a vain hope, for silence greeted her knock. Susanna took a deep breath and opened the door. She moved quietly through the large, comfortably appointed

185

dressing room and tapped on the bedchamber door. Then she held her breath. There was no answer. Oh, Martinez, she thought, where are you when I need you?

Silently, she pushed the door ajar. She could not make out the figure in the large four-poster bed in the center of the chamber. She stayed where she was and called, "Your Grace?" He did not stir.

Taking another deep breath, she ventured forward. The candelabrum threw eerie shadows about the large room. As she drew closer to the bed she could hear his deep, even breathing. She stopped at the foot and called to him. He turned onto his side, his large figure entirely covered by the satin quilt, but he did not awaken.

Slowly, reluctantly, she went to the bedside, near his head. "Your Grace. Wake up. Please . . . Timothy is ill." This time he did not move, merely snuggled deeper beneath the covers. Sighing inwardly, Susanna set the candelabrum down on the bedside table. She bent over him as he lay on his side. His silver blond hair was tousled, and the stern lines of his face were relaxed in sleep. She had an urge to brush the locks of hair from his brow. Instead she touched what she thought was his shoulder beneath the blanket and gently shook him. "Your Grace, wake up," she repeated.

"Hmm? What is it, Martinez?" he mumbled, his eyes closed.

She held him with two hands now and shook a little less gently. "I'm not Martinez. Oh, do wake up, Your Grace! Your Grace? R-Reginald! Wake up!"

"What the devil!" The eyes snapped open, and he grabbed one of her wrists and suddenly scrambled up to a sitting position. He was bare, completely bare from the waist up. That is, she could only see from the waist up.

"Scotty! What in hell are you doing here?" he growled. "Have you taken leave of your senses?"

She forced herself not to look at the way the tiny golden curls on his chest glistened in the candlelight. Such a broad chest, so well-muscled . . . She swallowed hard. "'Tis Timothy. He woke up screaming with ear pain and we've sent for the doctor and—"

"Good God! How long ago was this? Why didn't you wake me before?" He began kicking the covers aside, and a small gasp escaped her. "Hand me my robe, Scotty," he said with a slight smile, "and then you can turn around."

She did as he bade and heard him rise from the bed. "Don't go missish on me now, Scotty," he whispered into her ear from behind. "You're doing fine." She felt those strange flutters in her stomach again and did not reply.

"It's all right now," he murmured, and she turned to see him sash the burgundy dressing gown. She tried not to think of what he was, or more likely, was *not* wearing beneath that gown. He donned his slippers and took her hand. "Come on. You can tell me about it as we go."

"The . . . the candelabrum, Your Grace." Her voice came out unsteadily. He was standing very close to her, peering into her eyes.

"A moment ago I was 'Reginald.'" He breathed the words out softly. She felt herself color.

"Ah, Reginald, the . . . the candelabrum."

He nodded, snatched up the light, and, still clutching her hand, led her from the room. She explained what had happened as they went along, but the feel of his large hand clasped around hers, and the sight of him

187

in his dressing gown, were causing her heart to pound most erratically. She silently chided herself for being so distracted at a time like this.

The corridors were chilly and dark, despite the candlelight, and Reginald kept his hold on Scotty's hand. The steps up to the third floor were rather narrow and Reginald thought it prudent to take them single file. He led the way, pulling her behind him. He nearly collided with Underwood on the landing. Amazingly, the butler was fully dressed, his white hair combed neatly, not even his twirled moustache out of place. On second thought, not amazing at all, not for Underwood.

"Your Grace," Underwood said, bowing slightly and using the same formal tone he used in the drawing room. "I've just been to see the lad. He's sleeping, but the maid says he's rather warm. The doctor's been sent for and I was just coming to your—Oh!" The uncharacteristic exclamation escaped Underwood as he peered behind Reginald at Scotty. Remembering his manners, Reginald moved farther onto the landing and drew Scotty up beside him.

Underwood tried to hide his shock at the sight of the two of them in deshabille. But when the shock receded from his eyes a spark of interest took its place. Reginald thought it prudent to say, "As you see, Underwood, Miss Beacham has done just that. Timothy was asking for me, you must know." Underwood's long, thin face relaxed a bit, and he murmured something about awaiting the doctor.

As soon as he departed, Reginald rounded on Scotty, right there on the landing. "Whatever possessed you to come yourself, Scotty? Did you not consider the impropriety of it? A governess ought to have a care for her reputation, you know," he chided, rather more harshly than he'd intended. But dammit, he hadn't liked that look of Underwood's at all. And here Scotty was in a thin lawn nightdress and a satin wrapper, with her hair tumbling in glorious disarray about her shoulders. The butler was usually discreet, but something told Reginald Mrs. Longbotham would have a recounting of this episode out of Underwood by morning.

Scotty's hands flew to her hips, the movement pulling her wrapper partly open and accentuating her lovely shape. "For heaven's sake!" she snapped, "Would ye have wished me to consider propriety over the child's health? There was no one else about, and I hadna the faintest idea where to find Martinez, nor Underwood for that—" Her words were cut off by the moan coming from the nursery. They both ran and found Timothy thrashing about, the maid trying to soothe him.

"I'm here now, Timothy," Reginald said calmly, sitting beside the boy and feeling the heat of his brow. Scotty handed him a wet cloth which he quickly applied; he heard her send the maid for fresh water. After a while he was able to quiet Timothy and rose to bring two straight-backed chairs to the bedside. He sat Scotty down and took for himself the chair closer to the bed. "How long has he been like this?" he asked.

"His screams woke me. I suppose it's an hour gone, by now."

His eyes met hers. "You should have come for me sooner." He hoped the gentleness in his tone would constitute an apology for his earlier harshness.

It seemed an eternity before the doctor arrived. Reginald and Peter Fairleigh had grown up together, had tumbled over the hills and fields of Milburne together, and under any other circumstance the duke would have been most pleased to see him. Reginald went to meet Peter in the sitting room when Underwood announced him. They greeted each other with warm bear hugs.

"Peter! It's been an age! Thank you for coming so promptly."

"'Tis good to see you, Reggie. I was not even aware you were home. But come, where is my patient?" Fairleigh returned warmly. He looked handsome as always, his tall figure lean and trim, his dark hair combed fashionably forward and his brown eyes as shrewd as ever.

Reginald took Peter into the bedroom. The maid was off in the corner lighting more tapers and Scotty rose at their entrance. Peter's eyes widened at the sight of her and then twinkled in appreciation. Reginald frowned. "Ah, this is Sco—er, Miss Beacham, the new governess. Miss Beacham, Peter Fairleigh, my oldest friend."

"The governess?" Peter, blast him, did not trouble to hide his astonishment. His eyes swept over Scotty, who was looking damnably delectable in her deshabille. Then his gaze flitted between Reginald and her with a speculative gleam.

Scotty extended her hand for all the world as if they were in some overcrowded ballroom festooned with hothouse flowers. Peter took it eagerly, a note of amusement in his voice as he greeted her. Decidedly piqued, the duke reminded them both of the reason for this nocturnal visit.

As Peter sat down at the bedside, Reginald took Scotty's elbow and none too gently pulled her from the room, shutting the door behind him. Two lights flickered in the sconces near the mantel of the sitting room. "Scotty," he said, taking a deep breath, "I think you had ought to go back to bed."

"Oh, but I—"

"Or, at the least get dressed, for pity's sake!" he blurted.

Her hands flew to her hips again, and the blue eyes flashed. "I can assure ye, Yer Grace, that had there been time, I would have. But what with Timothy screaming, I didna think to stop and peruse my wardrobe! Next time, of course, I shall!"

He took her hands and smiled. He couldn't help himself. "Scotty. Calm down," he said soothingly.

"I willna calm down, Yer Grace. 'Tis absurd to invoke the proprieties at—"

"What happened to 'Reginald'?" he queried, moving a step closer to her.

"Reginald, then. And *ye* talk of pr—"

"Your Scots is showing, Scotty," he interrupted, grinning. She went pale and very still. He flicked her cheek gently with his finger. "Never mind," he said softly. "I know 'tis absurd, my dear, and you did right in coming to me. But Timothy does not need you just now and I—I cannot like the thought of half the men in Milburne seeing you in . . . in such a delightful state of disarray." He put his hands to her shoulders and pulled her closer to him. Their bodies were only inches apart; he could feel the heat emanating from her. His breathing was too rapid. This was wrong. It was dangerous. It was certainly not the time. "And for myself, I find it far too . . . distracting."

"Ye are also in yer . . . deshabille, Reginald."

"And does that distract you, Scotty?" She was so

close to him that he could almost feel her heart beat. He knew it was not at all steady.

For a long moment she didn't answer. He fought the urge to crush her against him and kiss her. "Aye, that it does," she finally whispered and then broke from him and ran from the room.

He cursed softly into the night, then strode back into the sickroom.

Peter was just standing and closing his black bag. "Well?" Reginald asked. Peter motioned him outside.

When they were once more in the sitting room, Peter said, "I do not think this is all that serious, Reggie. The fever is not too high, nor the ear too red. He must be watched, of course, and bathed regularly. But he is young and resilient. He will come about."

Reginald nodded. "Is there anything we can give him?"

"The oil of sweet almonds, as you've done. Every two hours or so, unless he feels the pain rise before that. And if the fever should happen to rise very high, remember to bathe his legs."

"Thank you, Peter." Reginald clapped his friend on the back. "I would it were not the middle of the night. We have a good deal of catching up to do. I don't think I've seen you for nigh onto a year. Perhaps tomorrow—"

"I'll come back to see my patient in the afternoon, and you can offer me a brandy."

"Excellent."

"Oh, and I'll expect to hear all about the new governess," Peter said, an all-too-knowing glint in his eyes.

"Peter," Reginald began warningly, "There's nothing—" The door burst open, and Scotty stood on the

192

threshold, clad in a dark blue dress. Both hands were held behind her; he suspected she was holding her dress together. Surely she couldn't do it all up herself so fast. In truth, now Reginald thought on't, he didn't know how she could dress herself at all. She needed a maid, he thought, then realized how absurd it was to suggest the governess—

"Miss Beacham," Peter said, bowing slightly. His lips twitched as he took in her hastily clad form.

Reginald cursed inwardly. Not only was her back undone, but her hair still fell in the most improper, luxurious waves, and her small feet were bare.

"Ah, Scotty—"

"Dr. Fairleigh," she interrupted, her voice filled with concern, "how is Timothy?"

Peter took a step closer to her and smiled all too charmingly. "I don't think there's a need to worry overmuch, Miss Beacham. He'll be right as rain in a day or two. I told Reggie, er, His Grace," he amended, in a tone that said he assumed the formality unnecessary, "what needs must be done for the boy, but really you've done all you can for now."

"Thank you, Doctor," Scotty replied, all graciousness, and then to Reginald's horror she brought her right hand forward. Thank God the left hand seemed able to hold the damned dress together.

Peter took her hand and bid her good evening, or good morning, as the case might be, with wry amusement. "I hope to see you again soon, Miss Beacham," he concluded. "Under more auspicious circumstances, of course."

"I should like that, Dr. Fairleigh. It is a pleasure to meet a friend of His Grace."

Damnation! Reginald thought. Did she think this

was some sort of tea party? "Miss Beacham?" he said in his most formal tone, "I was about to see Dr. Fairleigh down. Good night." He bowed slightly to her in dismissal, but his eyes promised that he was not at all finished with her.

"Oh yes, do, Your Grace," she said too genially, "and I shall see to the sickroom." And with that she sidled past them, keeping her back to the darkness. But her eyes met his squarely and Reginald wanted to strangle her.

Peter made only one reference to her, and that as he stood on the threshold donning his hat. *"All* about her, old chap," he said, grinning, and then set off jauntily down the gravel path to his carriage.

Tomorrow, Reginald vowed, he would set Peter straight. As for Scotty, he would set *her* straight about her penchant for flirting with every man in her path! But when he arrived back in the nursery, he was greeted by the sight of her tempting derriere, displayed to delightful advantage as she leaned over Timothy and arranged the bedclothes. At least she's dressed, he thought, and noted that her buttons had been done up. He felt a pang of disappointment at that and sternly stifled it. He moved a few steps toward her, and on closer inspection noted that the buttons were misaligned; she'd missed the second and fourth. He found the disarray oddly sensual and steeled himself against the thought. He cleared his throat.

"Scotty!" She stood gracefully; only she could extricate herself from such a position with such fluidity of movement.

She turned and walked toward where he stood at the foot of the bed. She put her finger to her lips to caution him to silence, and he saw that Timothy was asleep. He

194

led her back to the sitting room. She looked beautiful, despite the shadows under her eyes. The candlelight cast a burnished glow that caught the red highlights in her long, flowing hair. He swallowed hard and felt his anger slipping away.

"Where is Annie?" he asked abruptly, determined to hold on to his very justified ire.

"I sent her to bed. She—"

"You sent her to—Scotty! *You* can't mean to stay up with—"

"Of course I do, Reginald. After all, he is my responsibility."

"Scotty." He shook his head and came forward, taking her hands. They felt soft and slender. Then he recalled his vexation and dropped them. "He is not so very ill; Annie is perfectly capable of staying with him," he said curtly. "You are the governess, after all, not the nursery maid. And tomorrow will be a rather busy day, I fear. We'll all take shifts in the sickroom. Even my mother and Phoebe can—" He paused as she quirked an eyebrow. "Well, Phoebe, at all events, can take her turn. But for now, you need your sleep."

"But the fever—"

"Is not all that high now. Do cease arguing with me, Scotty! Annie can wake you if the fever rises. I have a notion he will sleep the night through at all events."

"I do not see why—"

"It is not for you to see, merely to obey orders, Scotty! And I'm giving you an order. I want you in bed now!" Her eyes widened, and he realized that that last was a rather unfortunate turn of phrase. "What's more, Scotty, you have got to behave in a more seemly manner around, er, gentlemen."

Her eyes flashed. "More seemly? Would ye care to

195

explain that?" she asked haughtily, her chin high.

"Yes, dammit, though you know perfectly well what I mean! Flirting with Major Hayes and the rector and—"

"The rector?" she nearly shouted.

"Yes, dammit, the rector! And now Peter!"

"I was *not* flirting, Reginald! How dare ye accuse me of such!" She stamped her foot, her lips pursed. "Why, the mere suggestion is . . . is . . ."

"You are supposed to be a governess, which I take leave to remind you I seriously doubt, but as long as you are here in that capacity—for *however* long you are here—you will damn well conduct yourself appropriately!"

Susanna blanched and bit her lip. For a moment there was silence as she regarded him warily. Then she took a deep breath and said, "Very well, Your Grace. I . . . apologize for any untoward behavior. I shall endeavor to school myself appropriately in future." She spoke with a quiet dignity though tears glistened in her eyes, and he felt a cad. He had virtually threatened her, and he hadn't meant to. But he knew it was better this way. And he was back to being 'Your Grace'. He knew that was for the best as well. Whatever had possessed him to allow such familiarity between them?

"Good night, Miss Beacham," he said formally, and added, "I want your word that you will wake Annie now and go to sleep yourself. You have the other children to see to in the morning."

"Yes, Your Grace," she said almost meekly. He found he missed that twinkle in her eyes. He whirled round and stormed out of the room.

Susanna stared at the closed door, unable to move, a tumult of emotions assailing her. Earlier this evening, in his study, he had been so warm to her, had held her and . . . and even kissed her. She'd known it was improper, but she had not been able to resist the warmth of his touch or the light in his gray eyes. And just earlier, before he'd sent her to dress, he'd held her against him. But now, he had been so angry, had become so formal. And to have accused her of . . . of . . .

But the worst of it, she knew all too well, was the fact that she had so far forgotten herself and her precarious position as to allow their relationship to take a dangerously informal and improper turn. His rather rude reprimand had served her well. She was the governess, and she must act like one. Governesses did not allow their ducal employers to call them by nicknames, and certainly did not address employers by their given names—the fact that he had requested it being quite irrelevant. And they did not meet their employers' gazes so boldly, no matter how compelling their masculine eyes. Nor did they allow those strong arms to hold them, however briefly . . .

Susanna felt tears pricking at the back of her eyes and wrapped her arms around herself. She would contrive to remember her place. She must, for she had no place else to go.

Slowly, she turned and walked back into the sickroom. She would not wake Annie. She would stay with Timothy herself, knowing she could not sleep now at all events.

Chapter 11

Reginald slept fitfully at best and, plagued by unpleasant dreams, rose just after dawn. He remembered all too well the events of the night before. Without ringing for Martinez, he hurriedly donned breeches and a white lawn shirt. He didn't bother with a cravat, just slipped on a pair of gray half-boots and set out toward the nursery.

It was just before the east stairwell to the third floor that he heard the rustle of skirts and the sound of wood banging against metal. Probably the maid carrying a bucket and mop, just around the bed. But then she spoke, and he knew there were two of them. "I had it from the night footman, the one what went for the doctor. And he had it from Mrs. L., what had it from Mr. Underwood hisel'!" one of them said.

"You baint meanin' it, Lucy! In their night clothes? Both of 'em? The duke and—"

"Like I said, Sally. And His Grace holdin' her hand, and she with her hair down like some—"

They were coming closer. Cursing profusely under his breath, Reginald hurried up the stairs. He was feeling murderous as he strode down the corridor toward the nursery. He didn't know whom to murder first—his butler, his housekeeper, or the damned governess! Never, in all his years as head of this ramshackle household, had his peace been so cut up! Not until *she* came . . .

He heard her voice before he reached the nursery rooms. Silently, he approached the threshold of Timothy's room. Scotty—Miss Beacham, he reminded himself—sat at the bedside, singing to Timothy in her low, melodious voice. The rustle of bedclothes told him Timothy was still awake. He tiptoed into the room and stood, some five feet from the bed, looking down at the two of them. Scotty's back was to Reginald. She was stroking Timothy's brow and the child's lids were growing heavy. Her blue dress, the same one she'd donned last night, looked sadly rumpled; her hair was still disheveled. Her shoulders dropped tiredly, and he wondered whether she'd gone to bed at all. Probably not, damn her! Did she never obey instructions?

He realized Timothy had fallen asleep. Scotty bent her head and kissed the child's brow, and the simple gesture produced an uncomfortable tightening in the pit of Reginald's stomach. A wave of tenderness swept over him, and he told himself it was for Timothy. But he could not prevent the flash that came before his eyes—Scotty with another child. A small child. Her own. And with it the thought that someday some man would—

Abruptly he turned around, grinding his teeth and forcing his mind to dwell on the fact that she had disobeyed him and on his resolve to set their relationship back onto a proper footing.

"He's asleep now, Your Grace," she whispered from

behind him. He'd not even realized she was aware of his presence.

He followed her out to the sitting room. "You gave me your word that you would wake the maid," he said sternly. "That you would go to sleep."

. Her chin came up. "And so I did. But then I awoke just before dawn and—"

"Miss Beacham," he interrupted ominously, and without ceremony put his hands to her shoulders and whirled her round. The same second and fourth buttons were undone. Just as he'd suspected, the dress had never come off; she'd not been to bed at all. He turned her back round and dropped his hands. "You are an inveterate liar, ma'am."

A look of wide-eyed injured innocence crossed her face, and she splayed one hand across her chest. "Why, Your Grace, I—"

"And you do a dreadful job of dressing yourself," he couldn't help adding, but his tone was not nearly as severe as he could have wished.

Her right hand flew to her back. "Oh dear," she said ruefully, grasping for the buttons, "I *have* made a muck of it. In truth, I . . . I couldn't sleep." Damnation! It was impossible to remain angry with her.

He was about to ask why she could not sleep, but clamped his mouth shut. It was not a very prudent question; he hadn't slept well himself. The candles had long since guttered in their sockets, and the early morning sun cast an eerie gray light about the room. For the first time he could see the deep shadows under her eyes.

"How is he?" he asked.

She smiled slightly. "I think he's better. He began crying from the pain again some while ago, and I gave

200

him more of the oil, then he subsided. But I think the fever is down and that the doctor may be in the right of it. Another day or two and he'll be fine."

How, Reginald wondered, could he be angry at her for watching over his brother so carefully? He felt himself smile in return. "I'm glad. And now you take yourself off to bed. I'll ring for Annie, and I'll see that Letty and Thomas are occupied for at least several hours."

"There's no need—"

"There is every need. Now, come along." Against his better judgment he took her arm and began to propel her toward the door, but she resisted, trying to pull away from him.

"I will, Your Grace. Truly. But I . . . I want to tidy up a bit here," Susanna stammered. Did he not understand that she did not want his escort, did not want him coming near her rooms?

"Devil take it, Scotty, must you gainsay my every word?" Reginald demanded in exasperation and half dragged her out of the sitting room, into the corridor, and to her own set of rooms.

He kicked open the door of her small sitting room and ushered her inside. He kept one hand on her arm and, unthinkingly, closed the door with the other. This room was darker than the nursery, having only one small window. The bedchamber beyond was in shadows, but still he could make out a small fourposter and a narrow washstand. He'd never seen these rooms before and suddenly felt uneasy. This woman belonged in beautiful, spacious rooms surrounded by light and flowers. Not here, where the sparse oak furnishing, bare floor, and shabby sofa could depress even the most cheerful of spirits. Why the devil hadn't something been done about this years ago? But in a flash he knew why. There was nothing incongruous about a Miss Pritchard or a Miss Talwin living in these rooms. It was only Scotty, with her grace and beauty, and that merriment that always threatened to overtake her, only Scotty who was out of place here.

She turned, and he had to let her go. Still, they stood just several feet apart. And suddenly, in the dark silence of her rooms, the air vibrated with a tension that had not been there moments ago. He had vowed to keep his distance; instead he moved closer. His eyes swept the length of her. The crumpled silk dress fit her like a glove, outlining her figure all too well. Her hand came up to her nape, and she stretched her back.

"Can I trust you now to go to bed?" His voice sounded hoarse to his own ears.

She swallowed hard, and her eyes swept over him. Over his thighs, bulging in the tight-fitting breeches, and over the fine white shirt stretched across his muscular chest. It was open at the throat, the golden hairs just visible.

He repeated his question, more softly this time. He stood too close. Oh God, why did he not leave? His tall masculine presence filled the small room, overwhelming her in a way it never had before. She had vowed to keep her distance from him, to remember her place. Had he not admonished her last night to do just that? Why was he making it so difficult by lingering here?

She clasped her hands at her waist and raised her chin a trifle. "Yes, Your Grace. I shall try to get some sleep."

There was no merriment in her eyes now, he noted. Her shoulders slumped with fatigue and she rubbed her stiff neck with her hand.

"Poor Scotty, you've been bent over Timothy's bed all night; you need a good massage." He moved inexorably closer to her.

"No, thank you. I'm all right. I—"

"It's the least I can do, after you cured my headache so neatly," he murmured. He put his hands to her shoulders. "Here now, just relax." He drew her closer and began to massage her shoulders. Her muscles were stiff, as he'd expected, but so was her entire body. "Come, you need to lie down," he said softly, and put a hand to the small of her back.

He nudged her toward the sofa, but she refused to lie down. She sat, instead, at the far end, and he came to sit beside her. She pivoted so her back was toward him, her hands resting on the arm of the sofa. He touched her right shoulder. "Put your arms down and try to relax," he whispered.

Susanna knew she should never let him do this, but she was stiff all over, and the thought of his strong hands easing away the tension had been irresistible. She sat erect. She would not give in to the urge to lean against him, to let down her guard.

"Ahh, that feels good," she murmured. Blissful utterings of "Mmmm," and "Ahh," escaped her. Reginald tried not to think of other circumstances in which she might make the same sounds. He felt her body relax bit by bit while his grew warmer and warmer.

His hands slid to her upper arms. "Scotty," he whispered. "Perhaps this wasn't such a good idea after all."

She knew she should rise, agree with him, tell him to leave. But his breath was warm in her ear, and his hands made her skin tingle, even through the silk of her dress. She felt herself leaning against him, even as she willed herself not to.

He felt her warm body against his chest once more and his hands tightened on her arms. He could feel her rapid breathing and he bent his head to lightly kiss her soft nape. A slight moan escaped her and she turned her head toward him. He groaned and twisted her body round to face him.

"Scotty," he rasped, as he pressed her back against the corner of the sofa. Her lips looked soft, pliant, ready. Her warm, full breasts were crushed against him. His hand caressed her shoulder and then trailed down to stroke her breast. He felt her quiver with desire and he pressed his lips to the hollow of her throat.

"Reginald," she breathed raggedly, arching toward him. He felt his blood begin to pound, and suddenly he knew that if he kissed her now, truly kissed her, he would not be able to stop. Dear God, what was he doing here, in her chamber, with his brother ill just across the corridor?

Reginald heaved himself shakily from the sofa, his body still heated. She did not move, and her supine position brought forcibly home to him what he'd almost done. Cursing himself for a bounder, he extended his hand to her.

She took a deep breath and gave him her hand. He drew her to her feet.

"Forgive me, Scotty." He held onto her hand and looked down into her blue eyes, dark now with confusion. "I never meant for this to happen. I have quite forgotten myself." She looked mortified, and he wanted to gather her close, to comfort her; but he didn't dare. He could not trust himself. He let go her hand and pulled himself together. "You have my word that such will not happen again, Miss Beacham," he said soberly.

His sudden formality cut her to the quick, for all she knew it was best. And she was chagrined to realize that she did not want him to make that promise. For she had *wanted* his caresses, had wanted him to kiss her!

He watched the tormented expressions play across her face. "I think we'd best forget this happened, my dear," he said gently. "Do go to sleep, and I will see about keeping the children occupied and Timothy cared for." She nodded, and he bowed himself out.

Susanna went to bed and slept the sleep of pure exhaustion. But her last thought was that she would not forget. And she would always wonder what it would have been like if he had truly kissed her.

The duke strode down the corridor, down the narrow stairwell to his own rooms. He shrugged himself into his riding clothes and went out to the stables, knowing he had to ride and clear his head. But he knew even that would not help. For Reginald wanted, for the first time in his life, that which he could not have. His women had always been experienced and very available. And Miss Rose Beacham was neither of those things.

The blood pounded in his temples as he gave his stallion its head over the green meadows. His desire for her was completely irrational, completely unlike him. She was the bloody governess! Such things simply did not happen! Not to him in any event. He had always been master of his emotions, and certainly master of all his encounters with women. Lord above! What had she done to him? And whatever was he to do with her?

He strode back up to his room and rang for Martinez. He would have a bath, go down to breakfast, and then convince his mama to take Phoebe shopping. And he would see to the children. Anything to keep his mind off that governess!

He was already savagely tearing off his riding coat when Martinez appeared. "Ah, Martinez. See about a hot bath, will you? And hurry. I've a great deal to do today," Reginald snapped.

Martinez tried not to smile. "Certainly, Don Reinaldo, without delay. And good morning to you, too."

Reginald stopped in his tracks and grimaced. "Oh, Lord. As bad as that, old friend?" he said quietly, sliding into the upholstered wing chair by the fireplace.

Martinez nodded. "Do not trouble about me, *amigo*. But you . . . I do not know when I have seen you so . . . so up in the boughs." Deftly, Martinez relieved him of his riding boots. "It cannot be, I do not think, that you are worried about the boy. He will be fine, the doctor said."

Reginald nodded. "I know. Forgive me for snapping. I—I am tired. That is all." He stood and began pacing, yanking off his shirt as he spoke.

"Of course, Don Reinaldo." The abject tone was belied by the curling of his man's lips.

"Well, I am, dammit! 'Twas a difficult night."

"Was it?" There was a decided gleam in Martinez's eye as he picked up the garments the duke kept tossing to the ground.

"Hellfire, Martinez! Whatever you've heard, it's . . . that is . . . Timothy was screaming, calling for me. She came straightaway to get me. Naturally she didn't have time to change into—" Reginald paused midsentence as he realized Martinez's moustache was twitching suspiciously. "Oh, never mind," he said dampeningly.

"You do not have to defend yourself to me, Don Reinaldo," Martinez said quietly, helping the duke into a silk brocade dressing gown. "But I think that is not what sends you up into the boughs, is it? They will have a good gossip below the stairs, but in the end, everyone will understand, and the charming Señorita Beacham will not suffer for it."

"I am not quite so sanguine as you, my friend." Reginald paused to gaze out the window and his voice lowered. "Her . . . her hair was down . . . and she wore naught but a light satin wrapper and—" Recalling himself he turned to face Martinez and ran a hand through his hair. "Oh, blast it all, you meddlesome old woman, 'tis not the gossip, as you well know. It's . . . it's . . . ." Bleakly, he put his right fist to his clenched teeth, then pounded it into the palm of his left. "Goddammit! I do not know what is wrong with me! I . . . I can't seem to keep away from her! I've never acted so . . . so . . . ." He turned away again. "And she's the bloody *governess,* for Christ's sake!" He rubbed the back of his neck wearily. "What the devil am I to do, Martinez?"

Reginald felt a momentary surprise at his own words; it was not his way to confide so in any man. Except, he admitted ruefully, to Martinez. It had happened in several of his darkest hours on the Peninsula. And each time, with his comforting fatalism and clear good sense, Martinez had helped him see the way to go on. And so the duke of Milburne waited expectantly for his valet and closest friend to speak.

But when he did, there was a curious lightness in the Spaniard's voice, a glint in his dark eyes. Reginald did not like it one bit. "It is quite a coil, is it not? But I think, you know, that you will come about. *Sí*, in the end, you will come about," Martinez said smugly.

"Your faith is touching," Reginald drawled derisively as Martinez departed to fetch his bath. It was most disconcerting that for once his friend did not understand his predicament. And of course, short of telling him such things as a gentleman never spoke of, he could not *make* Martinez understand it. Nor did he want to, dammit! There were certain problems a man must solve for himself. And, ruminating on this particular one, he began to wonder why he had requested a hot bath. Surely a cold dousing in the nearest stream would be more to the point!

Having finished with the duke's toilette and watching him stride out irritably with the intention of repairing to his study, Martinez betook himself below stairs. His destination was the dry laundry, but a dreadful caterwauling coming from the region of the kitchens drew him instead.

"It is cruel what you do to *le petit chat!*" shouted the little French maid in a most indignant voice. Martinez was quite taken aback; he'd no idea she could shout like that. The reason for her indignation was curled up in her arms, mewing and licking what seemed to be an injured paw. "Such an innocent as Horatio—" Angelita stopped when Mrs. Rackett shook her frying pan at her.

"There be nowt innocent about *him*. 'Tis the Devil hizel' inside that cat! And he come into *my* kitchen, walked across my very hearth! And now I don't know how I be servin' that soup, not to mention the bread and—"

"Mrs. Rackett, what seems to be the problem?" The staid butler appeared. The large form of Mrs. Longbotham, hands on her very large hips and a scowl on her face, loomed up behind him.

At the appearance of Mr. Underwood, Cook dropped her frying pan and put her head in her hands and began to sob. Martinez was much amused to see the butler awkwardly put his long arms around Cook's shoulders and attempt to soothe her. Mrs. Longbotham was not amused; she glowered at Cook and at Angelita in turn.

Mr. Underwood demanded an explanation, into which Cook and the little maid launched at the same time. Martinez collected that Cook had found Horatio sniffing near the oxtail soup and come at him with the skillet. The black cat, wisely attempting escape, had stepped on a red hot trivet and let out the shattering cry that brought Angelita running. Now everyone began talking and shouting at once, and Martinez wondered if he ought to intervene. But truly he was much too amused to do anything but watch, and very quietly inch over to stand near Angelita. For little by little, he saw the other three draw together and begin shouting more at the little maid than at each other.

When Reginald heard the ear-piercing scream, his first thought was of Timothy. It came through the open window of his study, but when he heard it a second time, he knew it came from below stairs. More vexed than overset, he made his way to the stairwell.

The sight that met his eyes was no surprise, although seeing his mother's maid hovering near Martinez, as if for protection, certainly took him aback.

His appearance caused only a momentary hush, for when he demanded an explanation, everyone save Martinez began talking and gesticulating at once. As near as he could ascertain, the chief opponents were, once again, Mrs. Rackett and Horatio. He set about trying to soothe Mrs. Rackett, his already taut nerves becoming more jangled by the minute, and he wished Scotty were there.

He did not seem to be making much headway with Cook until Martinez had the presence of mind to lead the maid, and hence Horatio, away. The fact that Martinez actually had his arm draped protectively about Angelique's shoulders Reginald decided to speculate over later.

First he had to remind Cook about black cats and shadows and the noon hour. And then he informed her—for didn't she know?—that oxtail soup, and certain herbs, and oysters and the juice of eels . . . well, they warded off the devil's own evil and so naturally they were proof against a black cat, a mere substitute for Satan, after all.

And when the woman had finally calmed down and he'd once more reached the more civilized regions of his home, he wondered if he were losing his mind.

Martinez led a tearful little maid holding a moaning black cat up to his rooms in the west wing of the third floor. His quarters were directly above the duke's chambers, with a convenient bell pull connecting them. Years ago Don Reinaldo had insisted on connecting two bedchambers to create this suite and Martinez had not caviled. The outer room was his workshop-cum-library-cum-sitting room, the inner was his bechamber. The arrangement suited him admirably and he had twice thwarted the duke's attempts to enlarge his quarters still more. The war had changed Martinez; he knew it well. He asked very little of life now, and he was content. The only luxury he did permit himself was the lighting of both his fires all winter long. He did not know if he would ever get used to the English climate.

It was to his sitting room that he took the little maid and her injured burden. He sat her down in a chair by the window and searched the rows of vials and pots, until he located what he needed. He applied the salve to Horatio's paw, which was red and raw from the burn. And then he bandaged the paw, although he imagined the cat would not put up with that for long. Horatio was very subdued and allowed himself to be ministered to. But when Martinez was done, the cat leapt from the warmth of Angelita's lap and escaped out the open window and onto the nearest tree branch.

Angelita ran to the window. "Oh no!" she cried. "Horatio, you must come back!"

But the black cat merely looked at her before making his way with careful determination down to the ground. The little maid looked most overset. "He needs to rest," she said tearfully. "Who knows what may happen to him with—"

"Angelita," Martinez said softly, taking her by the shoulders, "he will not do anything foolish. The

211

animals—they know how to heal themselves. Much better than human beings, I think."

She looked up at him, her dark lashes wet. *"Oui,* monsieur. Sometimes, human beings . . . I . . . I think we do not heal at all. *N'est-ce pas?"* she said tremulously.

She was so sweet, so tiny and vulnerable. He knew what she meant, and he had no answer. "I do not know, Angelita. In truth, I do not know." And then without quite realizing it, Martinez drew the little French maid close to him and encircled her with his arms. She did not seem to mind, and she felt good to him, soft and sweet smelling, barely coming to his chin. He was not a big man, but she felt very fragile and he somehow sensed that she was all broken up inside.

A feeling of protectiveness rose in him, such as he had not felt in many years. He moved his hand slowly up and down her back. He was all broken up inside too, but his body was strong and hard. He'd made sure of that, so that nothing could touch him inside. But she would, he realized, if he let her.

Very gently, he put her away from him. "You had better go now, Angelita," he said quietly.

She nodded and did not meet his eyes, her delicate shoulders slumping. Then she turned and padded silently out of the room. A moment later he ran after her, but she was gone, probably down the back stairs. Cursing to himself, he began to walk down the corridor. He rounded a corner and let his eyes scan the entire hallway. At the far end, the nursery wing, he saw a flash of something dark. It looked like a man's coat. And if his eyes did not deceive him, it was going into the wrong room.

Frowning, Martinez quickened his pace. First he

checked the nursery. Letty's door was closed. Thomas was gone, and Timothy was sound asleep, Annie bustling about the room. Nodding briefly at her raised brows, Martinez silently made his way across the corridor to Miss Beacham's rooms.

Don Reinaldo was standing at her bedside, his fists clenched as he looked down at the sleeping woman. The curtains on the little window had been drawn against the morning light, but still from the threshold Martinez could see clearly the expression on the duke's face. For a moment he looked away; never had he seen such a look on a man's face. It was hunger and desolation all at once. Martinez looked back at Don Reinaldo. The duke was fighting a battle with himself, and Martinez wondered what the outcome would be.

He felt his friend's despair; it vibrated in the air as Don Reinaldo gazed down at the governess. Then the duke bent to brush a strand of hair from her face, and suddenly Martinez smiled. Don Reinaldo need not despair, after all. And perhaps, one day soon, he would realize it.

Discreetly, Martinez coughed. The duke did not move, but whispered over his shoulder, "There is no need to play nursemaid, Martinez. I shall leave presently."

Martinez went in quietly and tapped the duke on the shoulder. "Come now, Don Reinaldo. You cannot stay here."

The duke sighed deeply and nodded. And then without a word, he turned and left the room. Martinez waited a few moments before leaving himself. He was startled when he reached the corridor to see Letty standing in the doorway of the nursery, book in hand. She was staring down the corridor at the duke's retreating back. Then she turned to Martinez, and he was even more startled when she smiled conspiratorially and actually winked at him! A twelve-year-old winked at him! He looked down at the book in her hands. *Romeo and Juliet*. *¡Dios mío!* Don Reinaldo was in worse trouble than he knew!

Chapter 12

Reginald found his mother finishing the last of a late breakfast. Phoebe, thankfully, was nowhere about. He greeted the duchess with a cheerfulness he was far from feeling and poured himself a cup of coffee. Sitting down at his usual place across from her, he spoke to her about Timothy. She had already been to see him this morning, and Reginald assured her once again that the lad would be right. Then he gradually and deftly brought the conversation round to Phoebe and the suggestion that she had ought to purchase several new gowns.

The duchess put her Limoges coffee cup down delicately on the saucer. "Oh, but dear, I do think her wardrobe is quite adequate enough for now. Of course, we'll need to replenish when we take her to London. I do hope you'll consider taking her for the Little Season. It does seem the most sensible course. Oh, but do not think I mean to rig her out in anything too sophisticated, Reggie dear. Indeed not. For a girl just out, and one so young as Phoebe, only the most demure constumes will do, you may be sure. White and aqua and lemon yellow and—"

"Mama!" Reginald finally interrupted.

The duchess looked surprised. "Yes, dear?"

"I am not speaking of London. I am speaking of here and now. I should like Phoebe to have several dresses made up. Take her to the dressmaker in Upper Milburne. Today. I believe she has a creditable collection of fabrics."

The duchess nibbled a piece of toast. "Oh, but my dear, that will hardly be necessary. Mrs. Coombs will be happy to come to the Hall. Why—"

"No, Mother!" Reginald exclaimed, and seeing no help for it, began to explain. "I wish Phoebe to be distracted with a trip to the dressmaker today because I have reason to believe that she means to keep an assignation with Oswald Hastings today at the lending library."

"The lending library!" The duchess was dutifully shocked, and then she shocked Reginald by adding, "That is hardly the place for an assignation, I must own. Why, everyone is always shushing one and—"

"That hardly signifies, Mama." Reginald felt himself gripping the table very hard. "I do not wish her to meet him *any*place. And at all events, 'tis a picnic he has planned. Now will you please do as I say and take her to the dressmaker?"

"But dear, you cannot have thought. Timothy is ill and—"

"And he will be well cared for, Mother. And 'tis only for a few hours. Truly I would not ask, did I not deem it important. Now, will you go? And don't, for pity's sake, tell her why, or even that I suggested you go!"

"Of course, Reggie dear. I'll do just as you ask. Though I cannot understand why you think buying

Phoebe new dresses will discourage the Hastings boy. I should think quite the reverse. A girl always looks in her best bloom in new gown, you must know."

Reginald was beginning to feel exhausted and was grateful for the light footfall in the corridor which caused him to caution his mother to silence. Phoebe appeared a moment later, looking altogether too fetching in a yellow cambric muslin walking dress. She brought her coffee and two blueberry muffins to the table and declared her intention of going to the lending library this morning.

"Oh, but Phoebe, dear," began the duchess, "I own 'tis much too beautiful a day for the lending library. Perhaps a picnic or—oh!" Reginald nearly knocked the Limoges cup from her hand. He bit his tongue to keep from groaning. But then his mother smiled apologetically at him, that certain smile that he knew must have melted his late father's heart. "But at all events, it doesn't signify, Phoebe dear, for I mean to convey you to the dressmaker today. I have decided you need several new gowns, you must know."

"Oh, Mama, aren't you a dear! But truly I do not think—that is, of course I should always *love* a new gown, but it is not as though I truly *need* one just now. And I did so have my heart set on the lending library. And you need not trouble about a chaperone, for of course I shall take my maid. I am persuaded that must be quite unexceptionable here at Milburne," she said, calmly buttering her muffins.

The duchess looked at him helplessly and Reginald grit his teeth. Damn the chit! How dare she stand there and lie so blithely! He willed himself to calm down and opened his mouth to speak, but was forestalled by the sound of a musical voice coming from the doorway of the breakfast room.

"Good morning, everyone!" she chimed and glided into the room wearing her lime green morning dress and a lovely smile. Only the smudges under her eyes attested to her lack of sleep. Sleep! Reginald blinked. He'd just left her asleep less than an hour ago!

She poured herself coffee, her hands moving with their usual grace. "Phoebe, dear, I could not help overhearing, and, well, isn't it lovely that you are to have new gowns. Not but what you have a beautiful wardrobe, but it would not do to fall behind the fashion, now would it?"

"Do you really think so, Beachie?" Phoebe said doubtfully. "I did so want to go—"

"I know, Phoebe," Scotty said, sliding into a seat between Phoebe and the duchess. Then she leaned forward, so that the duchess could not hear, and murmured, "But, you see, it would be such a good distraction for your mama. We don't want her fretting about Timothy, now do we?"

Phoebe was immediately contrite, and said that of course she would go, whereupon Scotty turned to the duchess and engaged her in a lively discussion of which styles and shades would be most suitable for Phoebe's delicate beauty. Phoebe seemed to glow under all the attention, and Reginald had all he could do not to stare open-mouthed at Scotty. How *ever* did she do it?

When the company made to disperse, Reginald contrived to whisper to Scotty, "A word with you please. In my study." She nodded, and he allowed her to precede him while he lingered a moment with his mother.

"Keep an eye on Phoebe, Mother. Do not allow her to go off on some errand of her own."

218

"Are you sure, dear? She did say something about the lending library. Perhaps . . ."

Reginald rolled his eyes heavenward. "I am sure, Mother. *No* lending library. *No* other errands," he said sternly, "Do you understand what I'm saying?"

Whereupon his mother, not understanding at all, nodded and patted his cheek.

Seeing Scotty in his study was like taking a breath of fresh air. He smiled as he watched her peruse his bookshelves. What she was, or who, was a question Reginald had become increasingly reluctant to pursue. Why, he could not say, but he would have to face it soon enough. His reply from Penderleigh would come, and with it, no doubt, his confirmation that Scotty's reference was a sham. Not that he needed confirmation, of course. 'Twas just that once he had it, he would have to act upon it. Wouldn't he?

Clearing his throat, he advanced into the room, closing the door behind him.

Susanna heard him enter and forced herself to take a deep breath. After what had happened at daybreak in her sitting room, she'd hardly known how to face him that morning. There had been others in the breakfast room, which had made it easier. Now they were alone. She could not, as he had suggested, forget the way he'd held her. She could however, *pretend* it had never happened.

She braced herself, turned round, and smiled. "I could spend hours here if I but had the time. All these histories and journals. Plays too, I see. And poetry." She lifted one finely arched brow. "Do you read poetry, sir?"

"I do not ordinarily have time for poetry, Miss Beacham," he said dampeningly. "I assume that neither do you."

She came to stand in front of his desk, just several feet before him, and lifted her chin. "You are quite right, Your Grace," she said stiffly. "I do not have the time. Was there something in particular that you wished to speak to me about?"

He hated hearing that tone from her, hated hearing "Your Grace" on her lips instead of "Reginald."

"Yes, Miss Beacham. I, ah, wanted to thank you for your timely intervention with Phoebe."

She smiled slightly and relaxed, leaning back against the large mahogany desk that was rather littered with papers. Unthinkingly, he stepped closer to her.

"It was nothing, really," she said. "I just happened to overhear."

"Yes, well, what I do not understand is how you happened to be there. You were . . . that is, I told you to go to sleep—"

She shrugged. "I cannot sleep for very long in the daylight."

He forebore to comment that she had seemed to be sleeping very deeply but a short while ago. He could not very well admit he had been watching her. And he ought not to have been; it only made things worse. He recalled all too clearly what she'd looked like, her slender shoulders encased in some flimsy piece of white lawn, her face in sweet repose. Her red lips had been slightly parted, her beautiful auburn hair fanned out on the pillow and down her back. When he'd seen her last night in her night clothes, he'd been too distracted by the rest of her to notice how long, how truly beautiful, her hair was. Didn't governesses sleep with their hair all tidily braided? he'd wondered.

And now, as he gazed at her and unwittingly moved closer, he had to resist the urge to pull the pins from her hair, to see it fall loose once more.

"You look very tired, my dear. Why don't you rest for—"

"No, truly, Your Grace. I . . . I am right." She seemed a bit nervous, as if his proximity disconcerted her. A sensible man would put the space of half the room between them. Until last week, he had considered himself an eminently sensible man.

"I mean to set Letty and Thomas to their lessons now. But I was wondering if you might help me."

"In what way?" The change of subject both relieved and annoyed him.

"It's Thomas. He does so want to pursue his study of plants. But what few materials he has seem inordinately complex. I thought perhaps you might help me devise a plan of study."

"My dear, the materials are complex because the subject is so." Reginald sighed and stepped round behind the desk. She turned to face him. "Just look at my desk. I assure you it does not please me to work with papers strewn about in such manner. But there is so much controversy still upon the subject of the article I am writing that—"

"I do not think that a bit of chaos when in the throes of some creative work is all that harmful. I should think, in fact, that it might be helpful." She had moved round the side of the desk and come to stand next to him, her eyes on the array of papers and books before them.

"I am surprised you consider this creative work. Scientific study is usually not regarded so."

"No, I collect that most of the time 'tisn't. Classification is not, I don't suppose. But leaps of intuition are creative, are they not? As is taking known facts and seeing them in a new light." He stared at her. "I . . . I have read some of your work, you see," she added softly, a flush on her cheeks.

"Have you, indeed?" he murmured.

She met his eyes. "I . . . yes. I don't pretend to understand it all, of course, but enough to see why you've already achieved such distinction. What are you working on now?"

"Well, ah, several things simultaneously. My classifications of . . . of Devonian wildflowers, for one," he said with difficulty, but she seemed interested, so he forced himself to go on. "I've already collected a good many specimens that need cataloguing. And this article"—he pointed to the desk top—"is to be the leading work for our new journal. It will also be the beginning of a new treatise I am . . ."

She watched him color as his eyes focused on the material before him. He quickly flipped a page over so she could not see it. "Well, it doesn't signify, for none of this will help you with Thomas," he said briskly. "'Tis far too, ah, complex." He took her arm to steer her away; her curiosity mounted. "Let us peruse the bookshelves to see if—"

"Oh, but I assure you Thomas is most interested in *your* work." She twisted within his grasp and peered down at his desk. She could not resist. Her eyes narrowed as she read the scrawled heading at the top of one of the pages: "The Sexual Theory of Plants as Propounded in Ancient Times." She turned, wide-eyed, to Reginald.

"Scotty," he said warningly, but she ignored him and

some imp in her caused her to lift several papers and begin to read scattered notes.

"'Male and Female Plant Reproductive . . . Organs, According to Nehemiah Grew, 1676.'" Her voice became lower and her cheeks pinker. Abruptly, he dropped her arm. She kept reading. "'The Linnaean Sexual System . . . Debates over the . . . one fertile and four sterile stamens of the . . .'" She looked up at him, her eyes a deep blue. She was aware that her breathing was a bit shallow. "I had no idea that was what Linnaeus—that is, when I gave Thomas that book, I . . ."

"Obviously," he said dryly. "Now, I think that's enough, Scotty." He reached for the papers, and she scooted a foot away and shielded them with her body.

"I also had no idea botany was so fascinating. Although you did speak of controversy." She turned to face him; he saw that gleam in her eye and wanted to strangle her. Instead he merely stepped closer to her. Her eyes scanned another page of notes as she continued reading. "'According to the Reverend Goodenough . . . a literal translation of . . . Linnaean botany is enough to shock female modesty.' Oh dear." She looked up at him again, that imp of mischief in her eyes. "Am I supposed to be shocked?"

Oh, God, he *would* strangle her. He drew himself up. "It is certainly not drawing-room conversation, ma'am. Now if you don't mind . . ."

"But it all seems such a tempest in a pot of tea, Reginald. I mean to say, they *are* talking about plants, are they not? How can one really liken the orga—I mean to say . . ."

"Dammit, Scotty! Give me those papers!" he shouted, snatching them from her. She responded by turning to the desk.

"Well, and here's the one you flipped over so hurriedly," she said ingenuously, picking up the paper. "Why, it's a poem! And here you said you had no time for such things. And you're even analyzing it! 'The Botanic Garden,' by Erasmus Darwin, describes the . . . floral harems, the impatient male stamens pursuing the' . . . ah . . . 'recumbent pistils, pistils being the female repro—' Ah, this poem, Reginald, is—"

"Is not fit for the schoolroom, my dear," he finished softly and slid the paper out of her hands. She did not lower her eyes, as he expected, but met his gaze. "It is actually a defense of the Linnaean theory. But it is no more fit for the students than the governess, I think." She bristled, and he sighed, setting the paper down and putting a gentle finger just under her chin.

"When will you learn to obey me? I tell you to go to bed and you—"

"I am not a child, Reginald," she snapped, drawing away. "I can decide for myself when to sleep *and* what to read. Obviously I would not teach that sort of thing, but as for myself, I can assure you I am no green girl to—"

"Aren't you?" he interrupted, amused by the sparks in her deep blue eyes. He let his hands lightly cup her elbows. "You don't look many years out of the schoolroom to me. How old *are* you, Scotty?"

Her chin came up. "I am five and twenty, Reginald, as you know full well from my—"

"Another clanker, Scotty?" He drew her closer. "Can you not even tell me the truth about that? I promise I shan't cast you out at midnight." He saw the unmistakable flash of fear in her eyes and felt her stiffen. "Scotty, what is it?" he asked gently.

224

She shook her head and tried to pull away. "'Tis nothing, Your Grace. I . . . I must see to the children."

"Scotty, please." He held her firm, drawing her closer until only a hairsbreadth separated them. "I think you are in some kind of trouble. If you will only tell me what it is, I can help you. I am not without influence, you must know, or resources."

"You . . . you talk fustian, Your Grace," she declared, knowing she must divert him, wishing he would ring a peal over her instead of being kind. It was much more difficult this way. "There . . . there is no problem. Now, I really must be going. We . . . we can discuss Thomas's lessons at another time." With a sudden jerk she twisted away from him and darted to the front of the desk.

He caught her in a minute, unable to take any more. He grabbed her by the shoulders, and pulled her close. "Devil take it, Scotty! For how long do you think to fob me off with your Banbury tales?" he demanded harshly. "I'll have the truth from you sooner or later." He saw her eyes dilate with fear and willed himself to calm down. He hated seeing that look in those beautiful blue eyes. "I had rather it be sooner," he finished evenly, and touched the palm of his hand to her cheek. "Who *are* you, Scotty?" he asked intently. He *had* to know; perhaps then he would understand this maddening, inexplicable attraction he felt for her. She shook her head mutely, and he felt his temper rise again. His hands went back to her shoulders and tightened. "For the love of God, Scotty, tell me the truth!" he railed.

"No!" She tried to tug away from him, but he held her fast. "There is nothing more I can tell—"

"Goddammit, don't you know you're driving me

225

crazy?" he exploded, then crushed her against him. And with no thought at all, only his anger and hunger to guide him, he covered her mouth with his.

His lips were hard and brutal as they enveloped hers, his tongue strong and urgent as it thrust inside the sweet warmth of her mouth. One hand wound its way around her nape, his fingers stabbing into her chignon and dislodging several pins. The other massaged her back, searching for buttons, then slid down to caress her hips. The feel of those lovely rounded hips sent his blood racing. His body was taut with desire, his loins afire. He ground his hips against hers, knowing it was madness, knowing he could not stop.

He had taken her by surprise, she told herself; that was why she hadn't stopped him. And now, he was kissing her with such force, such urgency that she could not pull away. But to her shame she did not even try. His warm lips engulfed her; his tongue was touching every recess in her mouth, sending tingling waves of pleasure through her. And his hands. Dear God, his hands were setting her afire. She must stop him. She wedged her hands between them, against his chest. But instead of pushing him away she grasped his lapels and clung to him for dear life. Her knees began to feel weak. Without realizing it, she inched her hands up until they were wrapped around his neck. And she was kissing him back; God help her, she was letting her tongue meet his in a sensual, forbidden dance.

He began to caress her breasts, and the ripples of pleasure threatened to explode. Then he thrust his hips against hers, and she felt the heat of his desire even through the layers of their clothes. She could hear herself moan. Never had she felt this way. When Mortimer had touched her she had felt naught but cold revulsion, but Reginald's touch drew her like a magnet. She did not want him to stop, only wanted more. More of what, she did not know. But she wanted it desperately.

It was her soft, sensual moan of desire that stopped him, for he realized she would not; she was as caught up as he. Maybe more so, for she could not comprehend the consequences. And if she would not call a halt, then he must. Else he would dishonor her and, in so doing, himself as well.

His breathing was labored as he lifted his head and forced himself to step back from her. "Scotty, I . . ." he began raggedly.

"No, please. Do not say anything," she whispered brokenly, turning her head away.

He put a finger beneath her chin and forced her to meet his gaze. "You make me forget who I am," he uttered softly, and dropped his hand.

A wave of pain washed over her. How *could* she have forgotten, even for a moment, who he was? And that there could be no room in his life for her, not as Rose Beacham nor as Susanna Fergusson. "I . . . I'd best be going, Your Grace," she whispered.

He had seen the pain in her eyes. He had caused it, and he felt an answering jolt of pain himself. The beautiful blue eyes misted over, and he cursed inwardly. He touched her cheek, ever so briefly, with the back of his hand. "Do not be so formal with me, Scotty," he rasped. "It . . . it doesn't seem to help."

She closed her eyes for one brief moment, and then he stepped aside to let her pass. When she had gone and closed the door behind her, he wandered to the window and ran a distracted hand through his hair. Oh yes, they had gone beyond the point of formalities. But where the devil were they to go now?

Susanna ran down the corridor, not knowing where she was going, only that she had to get away, had to be alone. She did not stop until she was in a remote corner of the formal gardens, where a hedge hid a stone bench that overlooked a tiny fish pond. She sank down onto the bench and willed the shaking to stop.

The entire scene in his study replayed itself in her mind. She willed the images not to come, willed her lips not to feel the warm tingle his had left there, willed her body not to feel again the ripple of desire his hands had caused. But the images, the feelings, came anyway. She ruthlessly dashed away the moisture in her eyes. She would not allow herself to cry. For it would weaken her, and that must not happen.

She must be strong, just as Beachie had cautioned her. She remembered the older woman, sitting on the veranda of her little cottage, her deft hand moving in and out of the tapestry as she plied her needle and spoke softly to Susanna.

But even dear Beachie, when she'd warned Susanna of the pitfalls of this desperate masquerade, had not thought of this. That a man in the house where she worked might importune her, yes. But that she might respond? Never! Susanna flushed with shame at the realization that not once, when Reginald came too close, had she pushed him away.

She stared unseeingly at the tiny gold and amber fish that swam busily in the pond. The day was warm, she realized, very warm. June would end this week, July begin. Week blended into week, month into month. How long could she stay here? Her own weakness terrified her. She could not trust herself alone with the duke. Reginald, she thought. Handsome, honorable, strong Reginald. Oh, God, where would she go if she left here?

She did not notice the tears that began to fall, or the sound of footsteps coming down the path behind her. "Señorita?" The gentle voice of Martinez broke into her reverie. "Are you all right?"

Startled, she jumped up and swiped at her damp cheeks. "Yes, I . . . I am right. I just came out for a . . . a breath of air."

"Ah," Martinez said knowingly. "Of course." He turned to stare down at the fish. "It is a bit hot, the air, is it not? Well, never you mind. Ah, tell me, I saw Don Reinaldo just now, stalking about the Hall, looking most—ah—blue-deviled. Do you happen to know why?"

"No, I . . . I have no idea." She stood rigidly, hands at her waist, not looking at him. She thought she heard amusement in his voice; she did not like it, but she could not move.

"Señorita." Gently he took her arm and turned her to face him. She found the gesture oddly comforting. "I think that you must give him more time. He is very confused right now, I think."

Her mouth fell open, and he dropped his hand, smiling softly. "Do not look so . . . so shocked, señorita. I am not blind. But you know it would help if you would, ah, tell him the truth."

She knew she could not hide the leap of alarm in her eyes. "I don't know what—"

"Do not tease yourself, señorita. I do not know your secrets. But Don Reinaldo, well, someday you will tell him. You must learn to trust him and to trust that things do have a way of working themselves out."

"Do you trust, Martinez?" she rasped.

He sighed deeply. "I am trying, señorita. It is the only way."

Something in his tone caused her defenses to crumble. Her eyes welled up again. "I . . . I can't tell him," she whispered. "He would despise me. And I would have to leave."

Martinez cocked his head at her. "I do not think you understand. It is all a matter of trust, Señorita Scotty. Just as I said." And with that he patted her hand and sauntered off down the path, leaving her staring, open-mouthed, after him.

Chapter 13

Reginald spent the remainder of the day trying to avoid Scotty. But he was very aware of her, knew very well that she divided her time between Timothy and the other children. And he could tell, even from a distance, that the dark smudges under her eyes became more pronounced as the day wore on.

In the late morning he worked with Carleton, his steward, going over estate accounts. He did not like what he was seeing. Carleton was getting careless. Undoubtedly he was merely getting too old. Reginald knew he would have to think about replacing him in the near future. But not now. He had enough on his mind just now. After lunch he closeted himself in the herbarium. Phoebe and his mother were still at the dressmaker's and so, telling himself he could relax, he attempted to lose himself in the cataloging task before him. But when he began sifting through his notes on Devonian wildflowers, he realized that he would need another trip to Maidenstone, his island hideaway.

The doctor came in the afternoon to pronounce Timothy on the mend and to prescribe another two days' rest. Scotty exited the nursery just as Reginald arrived with Peter, who again eyed her departing form appreciatively.

When they had finished with Timothy, the duke led Peter down to his study for that glass of brandy he'd promised him.

Five minutes later, ensconced with Peter, drink in hand, he tried to steer the conversation away from the so-called governess. But Peter was having none of it. His shrewd brown eyes regarded the duke speculatively.

"She's very lovely," Peter said without preamble, his eyes on his brandy snifter, "I can see why you—"

"Peter," Reginald interrupted soberly. "What you saw last night, well, it was not what you think."

Peter lifted his eyes; Reginald did not like what he saw there. "How can you have any idea what I'm thinking, Reggie?"

"'Tis written all over your face." Reginald sipped his drink, then snapped it down. "I can assure you there is nothing untoward going on between Miss Beacham and me."

"Oh, I would not call it *untoward,* old chap. I would rather say 'tis all quite normal, given the—"

"Dammit, Peter!" Reginald said softly. "She's a dependent in my house. You don't actually believe I'd—"

"No, actually, I don't. You've always had too damn many scruples." Peter grinned. "Sometimes it's not all that healthy, you know."

Reginald sank back into his chair with a cool smile. "For all your talk, Peter, and your reputation, I do not think even you would seduce an innocent living under your own roof."

232

"Wouldn't I? Well, perhaps you are right." Peter drained his glass. "However, as she is not living under *my* roof, I don't have your obstacles," he said enigmatically.

"And just what do you mean by that?" Reginald asked tensely.

Peter flexed his knee and crossed it over his left leg. "Well, I'm considering calling upon her myself." His voice was serious but his eyes twinkled. "Honorably, of course," Peter added. "That is, if you are quite sure you are not looking to secure your own succession in that quarter."

Reginald refused to rise to the bait and adroitly shifted the subject.

Ludicrous, Reginald repeated to himself when Peter had gone. Utter fustian! One didn't marry governesses. Certainly not those of origins unknown or suspect. The dukes of Milburne had always been leaders of Britain, and their wives had a certain position to uphold. In Devon, in London, at Court. The future duchess of Milburne must be a woman of impeccable family, a woman bred from birth to just such a position.

Reginald had always known that choosing the correct sort of wife was one of the responsibilities of his position. He had always accepted it and still did. That he had not heretofore entered the married state was testimony to the fact that every eligible woman he encountered was either too grasping or too hen-witted for him to consider paying his addresses to. Or perhaps, he mused, it was that they became so when the possibility of a coronet dangled before them.

He did not know, but he had not lost hope of

contracting a suitable alliance. A woman whose lineage was impeccable, whose demeanor was amiable, biddable, suitably dignified. Nor did he despair of finding affection within his marriage. Such did not happen often, but it was possible. His parents had had it. Of course, he thought ruefully, half the time his mother hadn't known what his father was talking about, but that hadn't seemed to matter. That Reginald was cut from a different cloth from the former duke only meant that his quest would take longer. Not, of course, that he was particularly diligent in his search. He had, after all, two brothers to succeed him.

And none of that signified in the slightest, he thought as he sloshed more brandy into his glass. For he didn't intend to marry the damned governess! He sauntered to the empty chimney grate, and her image rose in his mind's eye. Scotty, that morning, in her clinging lime green dress. Scotty, last night, in her thin satin wrapper, her auburn hair falling about her face . . .

Suddenly he raised the full brandy snifter and dashed it into the grate. The crystal shattered into a myriad tiny shards that mingled with the liquid sliding inexorably down into the crevices of the cold, empty chimney grate.

"Damn her!" he said under his breath, and ran a jagged hand through his neatly combed hair.

Letty was curled up with her book in a corner of the morning room. Mama and Lady Craddock were there too. They'd met during Mama's outing with Phoebe, and Lady Craddock had been invited to tea. It was still an hour before that appointed time, so the ladies were enjoying a comfortable coze.

Letty loved the times when she was permitted to sit with Mama. Even though a great deal of what her mother said was nonsensical, Letty loved the soft cadences of her voice, loved watching her do her exquisite needlework. Letty knew her own samplers would never equal Mama's work. But best of all at these times was that Letty could read when the conversation was tedious, and only *pretend* to read when it became interesting.

The conversation had suddenly become *most* interesting, and Letty made sure to appear most absorbed in her book.

"But do you *never* think of marrying again, Arabella?" Lady Craddock was asking Mama.

"No, dear Louisa, I cannot say that I do," Mama answered. "I miss my dear Milburne so very much, you see. And then there are the children. They keep me quite busy."

"Yes, I suppose," said Louisa, Lady Craddock, doubtfully. "In truth, Elsie occupies me fairly well, but I hope to see her settled in the near future, for I do think Major Hayes will come to the sticking point. And then, with Elsie gone, there is only William. But the dear boy is such a prosy bore! He cannot possibly need much of my time," she finished good-naturedly.

From the corner of her eye Letty could see Mama lean over to pat Lady Craddock's hand. "Perhaps the rector might have some charitable works for you to do, Louisa. He is forever—"

"Yes, I know, Arabella, but that . . . well, truth to tell, I *have* been thinking of the rector, but, ah, not of charitable works."

"Oh. Has the rector suggested another project, then?" Mama asked.

"Er, no. Not precisely, Arabella. I miss dear Lord Craddock, you must know, but I miss, ah, being married, as well. Do you know what I mean to say?"

"Oh, yes, of course, Louisa. A husband is always there to advise one."

"No, Arabella. That . . . that is not what I mean." Lady Craddock lowered her voice but Letty, her curiosity mounting and her hearing acute, could hear her well enough. "I miss, well, someone to . . . to sleep with at night, to warm my toes and, well, other things."

Letty's ears were burning. She wished she could see Mama's face. Of a certain she would be blushing. But Letty dared not look up.

"Oh," Mama said faintly. "I . . . I see. And you wish the rector to perform the ceremony."

"Ah, not precisely, Arabella." Letty could sense Lady Craddock moving closer to Mama on the sofa. "The rector is a very charming man, I am persuaded, and I think perhaps he is lonely, too."

"Oh! Do you mean to set your cap for the Reverend Honeyworth, then? But, my dear Louisa, is he not a bit old?" Mama sounded most flustered. She had stopped plying her needle.

Lady Craddock's light laughter tinkled in the quiet room. "I do not think he is nearly as old as everyone thinks, nor as deaf. And I cannot see that it would signify. Why, I remember a sultan in Turkey once. Quite past his prime, one would think, but that did not stop him from . . . Well, never mind. I shall simply have to find an opportunity to walk about a bit with the rector. Perhaps a moonlit garden . . ."

Lady Craddock's voice trailed off before she changed the subject, and Letty decided she would very much like to be a rosebush in that very garden when

Lady Craddock led the Reverend Honeyworth down the path.

Angelique stared at Martinez across the table in the servant's hall. How kind he was, yet strong. But there was so much sorrow inside him, locked away, visible only if one looked deeply into his dark eyes. She knew; she too had sorrow locked away. He had been so kind to her, she wished she could do something for him. And he had held her. She had felt so safe, so warm. She could not remember the last time anyone had held her.

The conversation at dinner was all about the duke and the governess and what had transpired last night. Angelique listened with only half an ear. Her mind was elsewhere. Her eyes kept coming back to the dark, handsome man across from her. Smiling slightly, Angelique made her decision.

She assisted the duchess to undress, saw her into bed. Then she went up to her own room, slipped on her nightdress, and sat down to wait. The Hall quieted, finally. Angelique took a single taper and tiptoed out of the room. Silently, she made her way down the rambling corridors of the third floor. When she reached the west wing, her heart began to beat rapidly, but still she went on, outwardly calm.

She tapped lightly at his door, not knowing if he would answer. He might be asleep. . . . She heard the scrape of a chair against the wooden floor, and then the door opened. He wore a nightshirt; his dressing gown was open. She kept her eyes on his face.

"Angelita?" he whispered. "You should not be here." He could not take his eyes off her. She looked so tiny and frail in her big, billowing nightgown. So delicate.

"May I come in, monsieur?" she asked in a tiny voice.

He smiled and drew her inside, taking the candle from her and setting it down. He felt suddenly very warm; he left the door open.

Martinez took her hands. "What is it, Angelita?" he asked gently.

"You . . . you were very kind to me today. I . . . I wanted to thank you." Her eyes looked large, lost, beautiful.

"You are most welcome," he answered slowly. "But you could have told me that in the morning, no?" Why was it becoming difficult for him to speak?

Oui, but I . . . I . . ." Nervously she broke away from him and walked to the center of the little room. She kept her back to him. "I know I should not have come. But you have been so kind to me, and I . . . I wanted to do something for you."

He closed the door, then padded to her and stood just behind her. "What, Angelita?"

Slowly she turned around. She would not meet his eyes. "I think, monsieur, that you are lonely, as I am."

In the flickering candlelight he could see the hints of the soft curves beneath the flannel nightdress. He felt his body tense. She must not be here. He was not made of stone. He must send her away, before it was too late. "Angelita . . ." he said hoarsely.

"You held me," she whispered, and finally her head came up. Her eyes glistened with tears. "I do not know when was the last time someone held me."

His mouth was dry, very dry. Slowly his hands came up to her shoulders. He wanted to pull her close but dared not. "Angelita, you . . . you do not understand. If, if I hold you now, I . . . I will not be able to . . . to stop at that." Her eyes were deep, dark pools. He bent

238

down and brushed his lips lightly to hers. "You are a child, little one. You do not understand."

"I am not a child, Martinez. I am four and twenty years old. I . . . Let me stay with you."

Four and twenty! Was it possible? Her lips trembled. He realized he was making her beg; he could not bear it. She was so innocent.

Very gently he pulled her closer and took her face in his hands. "I want you, *querida*. But you, you are . . ."

"Martinez." Her breathy whisper stopped him and her small hand came up to cover one of his. "There is something I must tell you. When I was fourteen, my aunt's husband—he was not a very nice man—and he . . . he . . ." She took a deep breath. "I am not a . . . a maiden, Martinez."

He felt a hard knot of pain in his stomach, and his jaw clenched in impotent fury. Sensing his distress she dropped her hand.

"But . . . but never before have I—"

"Hush, Angelita," he said raggedly, crushing her to him. "It does not matter. Not anymore. Not anymore." He kissed her eyes, her nose, and gently brushed her lips. And then he effortlessly picked her up in his arms and carried her into his darkened bedchamber. She was so light, so fragile. He felt as if he were carrying a little wounded bird. And that was exactly what she was, he realized. And he vowed, as he lowered her to his bed, that he would make her whole again.

Reginald awoke Saturday morning feeling decidedly unrefreshed. He would ride out over the estate, he resolved. There were several tenants with whom he needed to speak; Carleton's books were unfortunately becoming a bit muddled. And in the afternoon, he thought as he stumbled from the bed and rang for Martinez, he would go to Maidenstone. There he could relax, lose himself in solitude, and, of course, collect more wildflower specimens.

Martinez's smile was much too cheerful, his step too jaunty for this hour of the morning as he came into the dressing room. Reginald's head was fuzzy; he supposed he'd downed too damned much brandy last night.

"You do not look good, Don Reinaldo. Are you not sleeping well?" inquired his valet in a solicitous voice belied by the twinkle in his eye.

"Cut line, Martinez," Reginald grumbled. "You know perfectly well why I'm not sleeping well."

Martinez calmly began to lay out his riding clothes. "Do I?"

"Yes, damn you." Reginald plunged his face into the bowl of freezing water on the nightstand. Fumbling for a towel, he muttered, "And I don't see any relief in sight." He threw the towel over his shoulder and sighed. "She's driving me crazy, old friend. And short of dismissing her, there's not a blasted thing I can do about it."

Martinez paused in the act of opening the drawer of a highboy and gazed at the duke with a rather odd, faraway look in his eyes. "You are a man of principle, Don Reinaldo. It is one of the things I have most admired about you. But sometimes, *amigo,* you have to put aside your scruples." With that enigmatic statement the valet closed his mouth and would say no more.

Reginald thought, as he made his way to the stables

in a state of ill humor, that too many people were commenting on his scruples of late.

He gave his sleek stallion its head; both he and the gray seemed to need the speed of the early morning gallop. Later, after breakfast, he would visit several of the tenant farms. For now, he would enjoy the exercise, the solitude, and the sense of freedom he always derived from these early morning rides.

He ate a solitary breakfast, no one else being about, and made his way upstairs. He hadn't yet had the chance to speak with his mother about yesterday's little outing with Phoebe.

The duchess's sitting-room door was ajar. He stepped in, but seeing no one about, advanced toward the bedchamber. He rapped lightly; when no one answered he went inside. That was when he heard the voices, coming from the dressing room. First a man's voice. Curious, he silently padded closer to the partially opened door, then stopped in his tracks. Martinez stood with his back to the door, his hand cupped lightly to the face of the pretty little French maid. The one Martinez had not wanted to sit at table with. The maid—Angelique he thought her name was—faced the doorway but did not see Reginald. She had eyes only for Martinez.

"Are you all right, Angelita?" Martinez asked in a voice Reginald had never heard him use before.

She smiled, her eyes limpid. "I am very much all right, Francisco," she whispered.

Francisco! Reginald stood riveted, shocked. He hadn't even known Martinez *had* a given name! And then Angelique turned her face to kiss Martinez's hand, and Reginald finally bestirred himself enough to leave them to privacy.

241

He shook his head, bemused, as he sauntered down the corridor. He had no doubt at all as to what that little scene signified, and he realized it explained Martinez's unusual mood this morning. Martinez and the French maid! Despite himself, the duke grinned. He could hardly credit it.

And then he remembered how Angelique had looked up at Martinez, and the grin faded. It must be damned nice to have a woman look up at one in such a way.

He recalled now Martinez's words. *Sometimes,* amigo, *you have to put aside your scruples.* Well, my friend, Reginald thought ruefully, I am happy for you. But for me, I am afraid it is not at all so simple.

He found his mother at the little gold escritoire in the morning room. His humor was not improved by his mother's intelligence that they'd encountered Oswald Hastings, coming out of the lending library yesterday. Of course, they'd stopped to chat—only a moment, she assured him when his expression became thunderous— and wasn't it nice that Oswald enjoyed reading and visiting the lending library now and again? "I know the reservations you have about him, Reggie dear, and truly I share them, but he *is* such a well-mannered young man, now, is he not?"

The duke groaned and asked about her and, more specifically, Phoebe's plans for the day. The duchess surprised him by saying that they were returning to the dressmaker's, as she had still been unpacking several new bolts of fabric when they'd arrived yesterday. Lady Craddock, apparently, was to meet them there. "For you may be sure she has such a marvelous eye, Reggie dear. And I do want Phoebe to appear in the first stare of fashion. Elsie will be there, and we'll all take tea at the Ginger Shop," his mother concluded. Reginald forebore to point out that Lady Craddock's idea of fashion had occasionally included wearing something suspiciously resembling harem pants to a country ball, not to mention a certain headdress that included live birds.

Instead he wished his mother a good day, relieved that Phoebe's time would be accounted for, and made his way to the nursery to see Timothy. Timothy, to his astonishment, was sitting up in bed laughing. Someone—his back was to Reginald—was regaling him with an apparently very funny story about an old gray carthorse. Closer inspection revealed Jeb, one of the grooms, still smelling of the stables, sitting at Timothy's bedside!

Jeb bolted from his seat at the sight of the duke. His face was red, and he twisted his cap mercilessly in his rather grimy hands. "Beggin' yer pardon, Yer Grace, but . . . you see I . . . I'm here on account of—"

"Beachie sent him up, Reggie," Timothy chimed in, and Reginald groaned; he might have known. "I'm feeling right as rain, don't you know, or almost so, but Dr. Fairleigh says I still have to stay in bed." Timothy's face eloquently expressed his displeasure. "I'd much rather be in the stables, of course, so Beachie told Annie who told—"

"I take your meaning, scamp," the duke interrupted, ruffling Timothy's curly light brown hair. And then added, "Carry on, Jeb," before sauntering from the room.

He meant to check the schoolroom next, but a rumble of laughter from Letty's room sent him there instead. Letty was in bed in her nightdress, her pigtails rather a hopeless tangle. Thomas, though fully dressed, sat crosswise at the foot of the bed.

Reginald frowned, looking from one to the other. "What's wrong, poppet?" he asked Letty. "What are you doing in bed at this hour?"

Letty's eyes suddenly took on a forlorn look. "I'm not feeling quite the thing, Reggie," she said in a scratchy voice. "My throat hurts dreadfully, and I ache all over. Beachie said I should stay in bed today."

Reginald put a hand to her brow. "Well, thank God you are cool to the touch. No pain in your ear?"

She shook her head. "Do not trouble about me, Reggie. I shall just read to pass the day."

There was an odd note in her voice. It made him uncomfortable. "And you, Thomas?" he asked pointedly. "Why aren't you in the schoolroom?"

Thomas looked down at the coverlet. "I, ah, was sick this morning, Reggie. Lost my, er, breakfast."

Reginald stood over his brother. "How do you feel now?" he asked concernedly, wondering why the lad wouldn't look at him.

"A bit, ah, dizzy. Beachie said Letty and I might just as well keep each other company. And Timothy, too."

"I see," the duke said quietly. All three of them sick? he thought. That hadn't happened since they'd been in leading strings. He bade Thomas raise his head. The boy's face was flushed, but otherwise his color was good. Reginald frowned. Some illness or other was spreading through the nursery or . . . But no. That was too farfetched. Certainly Timothy wasn't feigning illness and the others would have no reason to. They enjoyed their lessons with Scotty and of a certain could always coax her into an outing if they were bored.

Well, he sighed, perhaps a day of bedrest *would* do them good. They didn't look all that sick, so he wasn't unduly worried, but he would have Peter look at them

244

later when he stopped to see Timothy. When he said as much they both answered almost simultaneously.

"Oh!" Thomas exclaimed. "That won't be—"

"Of course, Reggie. I do not want my sore throat to worsen. Perhaps he'll have a potion for me," Letty said, a bit too eagerly.

"Perhaps," Reginald said noncommittally, and left them soon after to go in search of Scotty.

He heard a scuffling behind the closed door of the schoolroom. As he knocked and opened it, that black and white kitten, Desdemona, sprinted out, with Robin Hood, his great drooping ears brushing the ground, loping after her. Reginald had half a mind to go after them but heard Scotty giggle and stepped into the schoolroom. She was in the process of arranging papers on her desk.

"'Tis hardly a matter for merriment, I should think," he snapped, advancing forward. "How can—?" The sound of furniture toppling to the floor stopped him. The noise was coming from the nursery. He dashed out of the room, Scotty on his heels. As they rushed into the nursery he thought he heard stifled laughter, but there was no further sound of furniture moving. He threw open the door of Letty's room; Scotty stood at his shoulder.

The scene that greeted them was not what he expected. Letty was still in bed, although the cover had slipped lower and now *her* face looked flushed. Thomas was still at the foot of the bed, but he shared that space with the troublesome loping basset hound. Desdemona sat on the window sill, calmly licking her paw. The entire scene was too calm, too still. Almost like a tableau. A very posed tableau.

"Are you two right?" Scotty broke the silence and

245

brushed past him into the room.

The children nodded, but Letty said her throat hurt and Thomas reiterated the fact of his dizziness. Scotty shot a concerned look at Reginald and moved toward the bed, but he caught her arm. "Never mind," he whispered. "Let them rest."

He tugged her gently toward the door, but Letty's voice stopped him. "Ah, Beachie, are you sure *you* are right?" He and Scotty pivoted toward the bed; Reginald felt himself frowning. "You do look rather peaked, you must know," Letty went on. "Do you not agree, Reggie? I daresay dear Beachie is in need of a bit of fresh air. I know! An outing would be just the thing! Oh, but that won't do at all, would it? What with all of us confined to bed, and Mama occupied with Phoebe. . . ."

She let her voice hang in the air and Reginald cast a sharp glance at Scotty. She did look a bit tired, but otherwise fine. Too good, as always.

"I daresay Beachie can sit in the garden," Thomas put in. "After all, she doesn't need to look after us today."

"Nonsense," Scotty said quickly. "Of course I shall. We may not have lessons but—"

"I'm very sleepy," Letty interjected, yawning delicately.

The entire exchange was decidedly odd and Reginald escorted Scotty out of the room moments later. He took her to the schoolroom and, leaving the door ajar, turned to face her. She was wearing a peach muslin dress that made her skin look fine and delicate.

"Scotty, do you know just what is going on here?" he asked in a carefully neutral tone.

246

Her face was all concern. "No, but I fear that they may all have the same illness. I hope—"

"Somehow I do not think so," he murmured. "Do you have any reason to believe that they—Letty and Thomas, that is—might be trying to gammon us?"

She looked genuinely shocked. Still, given her penchant for meddling and telling clankers, he wasn't totally convinced. On impulse he shifted the subject. "What do you know about Martinez and Angelique?"

She flushed just slightly. "Well, of course, Martinez did not wish to eat across table from her, and so she went to eat in—"

"I don't mean that. I mean last night."

"Last night?" Again the puzzlement was genuine. Well, if she didn't know, he was certainly not about to tell her.

"Never mind," he muttered and took a step closer to her. "You do look a bit peaked," he said softly. "You still haven't recovered from that night with Timothy. Perhaps you should sleep."

"Ahem, Don Reinaldo."

They jumped apart at the sound from the doorway. Reginald frowned as Martinez cheerfully came forward. There were times when Reginald wished the man were merely a servant he could dismiss at will.

"Don Reinaldo. Señorita, good morning. I came up to visit with Timothy and I heard your voices. A beautiful day, no? Oh, but, señorita, you do not look at all the thing. You are in need of fresh air, no? A ride, perhaps. You do ride, señorita, do you not?"

"Well, yes, actually, but I—"

"That is excellent. I am certain Don Reinaldo will take you riding today."

Reginald felt his brows come together in a frown;

247

Scotty looked decidedly uncomfortable. What the devil was Martinez about? He said blandly, "A fine idea, Martinez. As you must know, however, there is the little matter of the children."

"Yes, the children," Scotty chimed in quickly.

"Do not tease yourself, señorita. Annie is already with them, and I will check on them. After all, I will not have all that much to do while Don Reinaldo is away." There was a gleam in Martinez's eye, a certain smugness that Reginald did not like above half. When he got his sometime valet alone . . . But for now, Reginald was cornered and he knew it. Although why everyone seemed to want to be rid of him—of *them,* he amended—he could not fathom.

"Well, then, Martinez, now that 'tis all settled, why do you not go straightaway to the children," Reginald suggested. "Oh, and perhaps today would be a good day to show Thomas your herbs and potions. He's quite interested in plants, you know." A flash of annoyance went through Martinez's eyes. It was fleeting, and soon replaced by a glint of grudging amusement, but it was enough to give Reginald a small sense of satisfaction.

A moment later Martinez departed and Reginald turned to Scotty. "Do you have a riding habit?"

"Yes, but—"

"Go and put it on. I needs must visit several tenant farms, and I should like to leave straightaway."

"Truly, there isn't any need to take me. I shall just sit in the garden and—"

"Now, Scotty, we have our instructions," he admonished gently. She did look a bit pale, he thought, but no less beautiful. He suddenly wanted to see those eyes and her hair in the sunlight. He took several steps toward her and cocked his head. "Besides, I should like to take you. I'll have Mrs. Rackett pack a light luncheon. We can explore for part of the afternoon and still return home before the doctor arrives. I should like Peter to look in on all three of them."

Susanna knew it was not a good idea to go with him. But the joy of riding again was too much to resist. She pushed aside the thought that a day alone in the duke's company was also too much to resist.

Chapter 14

Twenty minutes later, when she met him in the stableyard, he knew he had ought to have his head examined for going along with Martinez's machinations.

She looked, very simply, good enough to eat in a snug russet brown riding habit with a row of tiny buttons down the front. She wore no hat over her smooth, neatly pulled back auburn hair. He wondered what it would look like when the wind tousled it.

One of the grooms led Hercules, his gray stallion, into the yard. Scotty's face lit into a smile, and he wondered just how well she knew horseflesh. "How well do you ride, Scotty?" he asked abruptly. "And no clankers, please. I will not have you endangering your safety or my horseflesh with one of your remarkable Banbury tales."

"Quite well," she replied in clipped, lofty tones, and he grinned.

"Saddle up Stardust," he called to the groom.

The mare was a sleek chestnut, not as powerful as Hercules, but equally beautiful. He watched in silence as Scotty ran her soft graceful hands over the mare's flanks, murmuring in a curious lilt all the while. He was not surprised that she mounted with ease, nor that she sat in graceful comfort in the saddle. She seemed quite familiar with horses, and she certainly knew quality. One more nail in the coffin of her clanker about the impoverished vicar's daughter.

As they rode out at a mild canter, it was neither her glowing face nor her all too lovely figure that caught his attention. It was her hands. Slender, ever graceful, even encased in the supple leather gloves, they held the reins so lightly, yet with a quiet strength.

Susanna tried to concentrate on the mare, on the sunny day, on the lush greenery of the meadows. On anything but the man riding beside her. He looked as powerful as his gray as he sat in the saddle, his body almost one with the animal he controlled so easily. He was tall and broad, the strength of his muscles visible even through the black riding coat that fit him to perfection. Her eyes swept over him, from his torso to the thighs pressing against the stallion's flanks, and she flushed at the memory of what it felt like to be crushed against him. She forced her eyes to his face. The granitelike set of his features was tantamount to a splash of cold water. He was, she knew, regretting having brought her with him. And well he might, she admitted ruefully. She was mad to have consented.

They rode eastward, and Susanna was struck anew by the sheer lush beauty of his land. The meadows were green and rolling, the soil rich and red, the cottages pristine and whitewashed. And everywhere brightly colored wildflowers danced in the light morning breeze. There was a certain dampness in the air that was not unpleasant, and a halo of mist seemed to rise above the flowers. It reminded her, quite suddenly, of Scotland, and for a moment she felt a pang of homesickness. She let it wash over her, and then it faded, and she gave herself over to the vista before her. She longed to stop and run through the fields, but instead followed the duke as they skirted a carpet of bluebells and then plunged into a thickly wooded coombe and down one of the deeply rutted lanes that she knew were Devon's own.

When Reginald finally slowed their pace, she smiled at him, remembering what he'd said on their last outing about the scenery in his "little corner of the world." "'Tis so beautiful here, Reginald. But do you never stop just to roam among the wildflowers?"

"Not here," he answered. "I need to visit several farms, so I'm afraid I'm not paying all that much attention. When I want to amble through the wild-flowers, I go to Maidenstone."

He ventured a glance at her. She looked like a flower herself, beautiful and ripe and ready to be plucked. Hellfire! He kicked Hercules to a gallop as they ascended the lane. He had work to do.

The morning was a revelation to Susanna. They visited three farms, and at each one the same thing happened. It was as if unseen eyes had watched their approach, for no sooner had they reined in than the stableyard was filled with people. The farmer and his wife, children, dairymaids, farmhands . . . They all greeted "His Grace" with the reverence she had come to expect, but there was an underlying affection as well. And most unexpected was the way the duke seemed to return that affection.

At the last farm Reginald introduced her to his tenant, Ned Browning, and his buxom, pink-cheeked wife. They were a middle-aged couple surrounded by a bevy of children and several grandchildren. The Brownings seemed to know very well who she was and accepted her being with the duke without a murmur of surprise. A little toddler of perhaps two years tugged on Reginald's breeches and pointed to the gray already being led away. Reginald laughed openly and scooped the child up, calling for the stableboy to lead Hercules back. Reginald sat the child in the saddle and carried on an inane conversation with the toddler for several minutes before returning him to the ground. Susanna could only stare, marveling. Never had she seen the duke so light-hearted and carefree. Certainly he was never so with his own siblings. Why, she did not know that she had ever seen him laugh! Perhaps it was that his responsibilities to his family weighed heavily on him. Still, she thought he had ought to laugh more. His face looked almost boyish when he did.

Mrs. Browning plied her with questions about the Ayres children as she shepherded them toward the timber-framed farmhouse, insisting that Miss Beacham and His Grace simply must taste her lemon curd and clotted cream. Susanna listened with only half an ear, for she was attuned to Reginald's conversation with Ned Browning. The men spoke of seed drills and the new steam pumps and the projected vegetable yield. Once again, Susanna was amazed. Reginald seemed so knowledgeable, so interested, so concerned with any problems.

She watched the sunlight brush his thick silver blond hair and knew the startling urge to run her own fingers through it. His fine gray eyes looked clear, intent, so very intelligent. And his lips, sensuous, warm . . . Susanna felt a ripple of heat course over her and could

253

do nothing to stop it. In truth, Reginald was unlike any other man she had ever met. It was not only the way he made her feel when he . . . Well, never mind that, she told herself sternly. It was much more than that. It was that she admired him in a way that was wholly new to her.

As she sipped Mrs. Browning's good strong tea, she thought about the men in her life before she'd come to Milburne Hall. Jamie, her cousin and childhood playmate. Goodhearted, kind, but rather malleable, she thought, with never the strength of character she sensed in the duke. And Duncan Mortimer, with his cold, thin lips and open leer. Mortimer, who made it clear that he wanted her at any price and whose cruelty was evident in all his dealings with those weaker than he. And her father, who never concerned himself with his tenants unless they neglected to pay the rent. Her father had never considered that his responsibility to his land or his only child ought to dampen his enthusiasm for gaming and drink. He was a rather coarse man, insensitive; and in the end, he had proven himself cruel as well. She had seen the look that passed between him and Mortimer that last night and had known that her father had betrayed her. That had hurt most of all and had given her strength to leave. There had been nothing to stay for.

How different Reginald was from all of them. His strength allowed room for kindness. His formidable intelligence gave him interests far beyond the normal pursuits of men of his exalted station in life. His anger and his concern for propriety masked a passion with which she was all too familiar. She felt herself color. . . .

Suddenly Mrs. Browning touched her arm and

repeated her question. Susanna apologized for wool-gathering and focused her attention on her hostess. But all the while her mind was whirling. No, she thought. I do not want to admire him. I do not want to think of how I feel in his arms! I must not!

Yet as she and Reginald came once more into the sunlight and mounted their horses, she could think of nothing else.

They rode south, along the banks of the Torridge. She ignored the occasional clouds that obscured the sun and hinted of rain. Of a certain she did not wish to see their outing cut short and assured herself it was the pleasure of the countryside, not the company, that she did not want to relinquish.

The countryside was indeed beautiful, the flowers adorning the riverbanks a rainbow of color. There were yellow iris, tower thistles, and meadowsweets, partially hidden in the midst of ripe green grass. And above it all, dragonflies and devil's darning needles hovered and hummed. Reginald had slowed their pace, and impulsively she called ahead of him to ask if they might stop a moment.

He fell back and came abreast of her. "You and your flowers," he said, and smiled in a way that made her stomach flutter. "But we shan't stop just yet, Scotty. There's something ahead I want you to see. I promise you a multitude of flowers before day's end."

Susanna nodded and returned his smile, realizing with a jolt that she did not at all wish for the day to end. They skirted a village nestling in a valley of the Torridge. It was Milburne Damerel, Reginald told her, an ancient market town, still the sight of the annual fair at Michaelmas time.

Soon after, they ascended a rise of lush green grass

dotted with birch and sprinkled with bluebells and orchids. Here they reined in and tethered their horses to the trees. Reginald took her elbow, then led her to the edge of the rise, where an ancient spreading oak had provided a sturdy V of low branches. He seated her on one side and propped his foot upon the other.

She tried to concentrate on the scenery, not on the feel of his hand at her elbow as he seated her or his warm breath in her ear as he bent over her. "The river is below us," he pointed out, "and that arched bridge is more than two hundred years old." The bridge was beautiful, a stone carving of graceful arches spanning the river.

"Why, it looks as much a part of the landscape as the hills and trees," she murmured.

"I know," he replied softly, and then put his hands to her shoulders and turned her southward. "What do you see there, in the distance?" he asked.

What she saw were the rolling hills and fertile valleys of Devon. And then beyond, suddenly the scenery changed. Even at this distance she could see the change from green grass to scattered heather, from rich, red-brown loam to black granite rock. The vast and stark rocky ground, only occasionally softened by clusters of leafy trees, rose in a compact mass of tumbled hills and dales, well above the surrounding country.

It was a moor, she realized, and judging from the location, knew it for Dartmoor. She said as much to Reginald, and he smiled, pleased. "I have always loved the moors," she said wistfully, rising and staring out across the miles. Once again she felt that pang for a home she would never see again. "Despite their loneliness, even savagery, there is a beauty to them, a splendor." She turned to face him. "Reginald, can we go there?"

"Not today, I fear. 'Tis a trip in itself. Perhaps another day." She nodded, and turned back to Dartmoor. He could sense the sadness in her, could see it in the droop of her shoulders. He moved to stand behind her and grasped her upper arms lightly. "You miss them, don't you?" he asked softly, and when she turned, puzzled, he added, "The moors of Scotland?"

He felt her stiffen, saw fear flash through her eyes before her expression became carefully guarded. Damnation! What was she afraid of? "No, I . . . I have never been to Scotland," she stammered. She's a poor liar, he thought, albeit a tenacious one. "I was referring to the moors of . . . of—"

"Of Lancashire?" he asked with a glint in his eye.

"Yes, of course," she replied with a stiff, endearing dignity.

Hellfire! he thought. He had baited her and to no purpose. He was not proud of himself and thought he would give anything to have her relax again. "Of course," he echoed, smiling reassuringly.

He brushed a hand over her cheek; if anything, her expression grew more wary. He told himself it was to remove that look, to wring a smile from her again, that he made his suggestion, but later he would wonder if he had not meant to take her there all along. "I promised you more flowers," he said lightly. "Let us make quick work of our luncheon and then ride north to Milburne Quay." At her raised brow he added soflty, "I thought we might go to Maidenstone."

Her mouth opened and she tilted her head in complete bewilderment. "Oh," she uttered, drawing the one syllable out in dawning surprise. "I didn't think—that is to say . . ." She stammered, and he watched caution war with her irrepressible spirit, her emotions plainly written across her face. "Oh, Reginald, the flowers!" she finally exclaimed, her eyes sparkling, her hand unwittingly reaching out to touch his forearm. "I should love to go!"

Reginald felt absurdly pleased. They did not linger over the cold repast Cook had packed into his oversized saddlebag, and very shortly were headed north again. The air was still damp, pleasantly warm but not too hot. He would have preferred fewer clouds but otherwise it seemed quite perfect. She asked him dozens of questions about his lands and his tenants as they rode, and he was careful to ask none about *her* home.

Their arrival at Milburne Quay caused the usual excitement, and by the time they'd come within twenty feet of his ketch, *Silver Fox,* there were several men and a swarm of children on the quay ready to see them off.

The sleek vessel was even more beautiful than Susanna had thought at a distance. She sailed effortlessly through the clear, blue water, Reginald guiding her with the ease of long experience. It seemed a short time before he was mooring the ketch and handing Susanna up onto the sand. She walked uphill without speaking, Reginald at her side, carrying his saddlebag.

And then she stopped and simply stared, awestruck. It was a harmony of blues. The cornflower blue sky above, the blue green sea below, and all round a carpet of bluebells and blue iris, with merely a hint of buttercup to break the harmony. The only sound was the murmur of honeybees at work in the flowers, and the gentle lapping of the waves on the beach.

She hardly noticed when Reginald took her hand to

lead her farther inland, so enchanted was she by the riot of color now at her feet. Wildflowers—pink, blue, violet, gold—of myriad shapes and sizes, many of which she had never seen before, tumbled over each other and swayed in the gentle breeze. The air was fragrant with their scent.

Reginald guided her over a twisting path and up onto a grassy knoll from which they could see much of the island. "Oh, Reginald," she breathed, "It's more beautiful than I'd imagined."

"Yes, it always is," he said with quiet pride, and smiled in a way she'd never seen before.

It was then that she realized he'd been holding her hand for some time and that they were quite alone, as alone and isolated as a man and woman could possibly be.

Suddenly very nervous, she disengaged her hand and took several steps away. "How, ah, how big is the island?"

His eyes swept over her and he knew very well why he'd brought her. She belonged here. She, with her vibrant coloring, her perfect curves and graceful movement, was like a flower herself.

He realized that he had ought to answer her question. "Some two miles long, less than a mile wide. Not all that big, but 'tis enough."

"It's wonderful, Reginald. Are there any buildings?"

"Yes, actually. A small, rather primitive cabin. I keep some supplies there. It has little more than a cupboard, a rudimentary table and a . . . a bed."

Their eyes locked and she flushed.

"Shall we explore?" he said quickly, and led the way down the knoll. The cabin, he knew, was one place they would avoid.

He took her through patches of goldenrod and blankets of heather. The constraint lessened between them as she ran through the wild, haphazard clusters of flowers. She exclaimed over the plentiful orchids and trailing roses and the innumerable wildflowers whose names she did not know and could not pronounce once he'd identified them. He took pleasure in her unabashed joy and in her astute observations.

"There are so many ferns, Reginald. But hardly any two seem alike."

"Quite right, Scotty. Devon is as known for its varied ferns as it is for its wildflowers."

She cocked her head. "And you're studying them, aren't you?"

He nodded. "Among other things."

She asked him how he preserved ferns for his herbarium, and he explained the painstaking process. "The leaves, the fronds, that is, must be dried under pressure among sheets of absorbent paper. The paper must be changed daily whilst the plants give out moisture. These large fronds are preserved singly, and since they are larger than my folios, I must fold them, whilst they are yet fresh, to prevent them from cracking. Once the specimens are thoroughly dried, they are arranged on stout white paper and fastened with gummed straps, or egg white."

"Would it not be more conducive to examination to have them loose in a folded piece of paper?" she inquired, fascinated.

"Indeed it would, but the probability of injury to the specimens becomes much greater. Of course, they are labeled and enclosed in paper covers, and then put in narrow drawers to protect them from insects and various other casualties."

"Such as younger brothers?" she quizzed, under-standing his protectiveness of his work a little better.

He chuckled. "Yes, and basset hounds and—"

"And governesses?"

He gave a shout of laughter. "And governesses, too. Especially the mischievous ones."

She flushed and quickly bent to pluck an intricately patterned fern leaf. She stared down at it and then back at him. "I think you are something like this leaf, Reginald. From a distance it looks quite simple in design. 'Tis only when one looks closely that one sees how very complex it is. And from a distance, one might assume this leaf to be quite like all the others. But it isn't. It is quite unique. Amazing, I should say." After which pronouncement she turned and strolled off, leaving Reginald to stare after her bemused.

He found her next beside a small pond, sitting with her legs dangling over the grassy bank. She was staring out at the lily pads.

"Shhh," she whispered, "I'm watching that frog. He's made his way nearly all the way across, hopping on the lily pads. And that dragonfly—I've never seen one quite so big. It seems to prefer the white lilies to the yellow. I wonder why."

"I haven't any idea," Reginald murmured, amuse-ment rising to the fore.

"Even the reeds here sprout flowers. I own 'tis quite extraordinary! Why, the whole island is a most exquisite garden, all the more so for being untouched by hoe and pruning shears." She turned and peered up at him, smiling.

Suddenly he thought of the song she'd sung at Beverwil. This was a pond, not a burn, and there was no "weepin' tree," but he longed to hold out his hand and lay her down. . . . He swallowed and sat down, just inches behind and to the side of her, his legs outstretched, his hands on the ground. If he leaned forward he could brush her hair with his lips; resolutely, he did not. He saw that she had unbuttoned the top two buttons of her habit. Her skin looked creamy white beneath it. She smelled of jasmine. He thought the day had grown overwarm and shrugged out of his coat.

"Thank you for bringing me here, Reginald. I know you did not truly wish to, and I—"

"On the contrary," he interrupted. "I very much wanted to bring you, you must know. I wanted you to see . . ." He paused, seeing what looked like a shredded flower in her hand. A water forget-me-not. Curious, he lifted hand and flower. Not shredded, he decided, for stem and floral blossom had been carefully split open.

He arched a brow, turning her body partially round to him, forgetting his resolve not to touch her. She tilted her head back to look at him; her lips were much too close to his. "I, ah, I was looking at . . . that is, what with Thomas studying the differences between . . . I mean to say . . ." She coughed and lowered her eyes. "Well, we *were* discussing it in your study, you must know and I . . ."

Reginald sternly repressed a chuckle and lifted her chin with his forefinger. "I begin to understand, Scotty. Pistols and stamens." She tried to turn her head away, but he cupped her chin and held her fast. "You know," he murmured, not quite thinking clearly as they sat so close together, "the male and female differences in plants are rather subtle, for all they do exist." She gazed at him mutely, her red lips slightly parted. His hands went to her shoulders, and he felt her quiver. The sun beat down on them; in the background the bees hummed about their work. "But it might be more illuminating if you made a study of, er, animals." Her eyes widened, and he drew her closer. "Or perhaps . . ." His voice grew lower as her breathing grew more rapid. He hardly knew what he was saying. "Perhaps we might make a . . . a study of our own."

"R-Reginald . . ." she whispered. Her eyes were wary, but her body swayed to his.

"Scotty . . ." He groaned, and crushed his mouth to hers.

Susanna melted as soon as his warm lips met hers. Her lips parted of their own accord, and she allowed his tongue to taste and savor, and finally to dart into her mouth. His hands moved over her shoulders and down her arms, warming her skin, making her tingle all over. And then the kiss deepened; sweetness yielded to urgency as his lips bruised hers and his hands swept over her in a frenzy. Hardly aware of their surroundings, she felt her legs being swung up and over the grassy bank. Her hands wound their way round his neck as her tongue met his, thrust for thrust.

He pressed her down onto the soft grass. She went willingly, her every nerve alive as he stretched out beside her, partially covering her with his body. His gray eyes were dark; he seemed beyond thought, and so was she.

She was pliant and responsive, like molten liquid in his arms. He wanted to touch her everywhere; he could not get enough. She ran her fingers through his hair and moaned into his mouth as his hands stroked her sides, her hips, her breasts. His entire body was taut, throbbing with desire. A niggling voice at the back of his head reminded him he had no right to take her. But she wanted it too, he insisted silently, and then shut his mind. Only sensation remained. She was beautiful and perfectly rounded and soft and sweet smelling. He had never wanted a woman so much. Never.

He kissed her eyes, her smooth cheeks, her throat where the habit had been opened. And then, impatient with the barrier of her clothes, he began unbuttoning the next few buttons. The blood pounded in his head as he bared her skin and saw the soft rise of her breasts at the top of her chemise. "God, but you're beautiful," he breathed, and caressed her with a gentle finger. She quivered beneath him and he took her mouth again, fiercely this time, and shifted himself further on top of her.

He never knew when he became aware that something was wrong. That she was fighting him, not urging him on. Her hands pushed at his chest and she wrenched her mouth from his.

"Nae, Duncan!" she tried to scream. But her voice came out in a horrifying, hoarse whisper. "I willna let ye do this!" She pounded his chest, and he finally lifted his head. The look in her eyes turned him cold. It was the glazed look of fear. Terror, even. He'd seen that look on her before, he realized, but he'd forgotten. She had, after all, been as eager as he moments ago. She was staring at him but not seeing. She was shaking. He put his hands to the sides of her face. "Scotty, look at me. 'Tis all right," he rasped. "I won't hurt you."

She shook her head and closed her eyes. He eased himself off her slender body, but kept his hands at her face. When she opened her eyes again, he knew she was back with him. Slowly, he rose and extended a hand to her. She took it, and he helped her up. They stood facing each other, the very air around them vibrating with tension and desire and remorse. His eyes searched her face; her gaze met his, bravely, he thought, and he admired her for it.

"Reginald," she said at length, quickly fastening several of her buttons, "I'm sorry, I—"

"No! It is I who must apologize." He ran his hand along the back of his neck and walked several paces away. "Oh, God, Scotty, we've played this scene before. I should never have . . . I've no right to . . ." He stalked back to her. "Hellfire! I—I cannot seem to keep away from you. 'Tis the damnedest coil. 'Tis just as well you . . ." He paused and put a hand to her cheek. "What I am most sorry about," he said very softly, "is that I frightened you. I would not for all the world—"

"I . . . I ken that, Reginald. I . . . I dinna ken what came over me. Silly, really. I—"

"Scotty," he interrupted very softly, "Who is Duncan?"

He saw the momentary flash of alarm. "Why, I have no—"

"Scotty," he said ominously, his hands lightly grasping her upper arms.

Susanna fought down panic. Had she really said that name aloud? Now she must dissemble, give him a partial truth to throw him off the scent. She turned from him and walked several paces away. "He . . . he was a very bad man," she said wearily. "It was all a very long time ago." He must believe me, she thought desperately. He must not connect Duncan with anything in the present.

She felt his hands on her shoulders, his warm breath behind her ear. She longed to lean back against him but instead stood up straight. She must always stand

265

straight, and alone. That was the only way for her, had been so ever since that fateful night in Ballincraig. "Did he hurt you?" he asked. She could hear the tension in his voice and knew she had got to allay it, to preclude further questioning.

"He tried to, but he—I got away," she whispered.

Relief swept over him. Slowly he turned her round and gazed into her eyes. "Did you love him?" he could not help asking.

"Did I . . . oh, God," she moaned and, breaking away from him, began to laugh hysterically. It was a strange, unpleasant sound, and it was answer enough. She had said Duncan *was* a bad man, and so perhaps he was dead. All to the good, Reginald thought, but knew he could not ask that, or anything else. Not now.

Silently he went to her and shook her gently until she calmed. And then he gathered her into his arms. She tried to pull away.

"'Tis all right, Scotty. Relax. I merely want to hold you," he said soothingly.

He held her in silence for unknown minutes, his hands softly stroking her hair and her back while his mind worked furiously. If this Duncan were not already dead, Reginald knew he would gladly have killed him. And the intensity of his feeling jolted him. He wanted to make love to Scotty, but he realized that he also wanted to protect her. And the thought of her with another man made his blood boil.

Good God! he thought, releasing her. Whatever was happening to him? She was the governess. He could not make her his mistress, could not consider her for his wife. Instead he was slowly going mad.

"I think it time we returned," he said quietly.

She nodded. "Oh, but did ye not wish to gather

several of the fern leaves? And the flowers, too? And in any event, I should like a few minutes to . . . to wander on my own. Would that be all right?"

He assented but bade her not to wander too far. She slowly ambled off to the left, where the land dipped and then rose again. She pinned her scattered hair back into place, all the while trying to bring her scattered wits to order. It was madness to have come here. She was playing with fire, and one way or the other, she was going to be badly burned.

She did not understand herself, did not understand what happened to her body every time Reginald came near. She only knew it mustn't be. She mustn't allow it. She climbed a rather steep hill, laden with wild orchids and honeysuckle. At the top was a very large, unusual stone. Almost white in color, its edges were rounded. It was molded in such a way that several people could sit on it, or, she realized, one could lie upon it, quite comfortably, in fact.

It was even big enough for two, she thought, and felt herself flush. Oh, Lord! She sat down on the stone. To distract herself she let her eyes wander far afield. The vantage point was high enough for her to see a good part of the island. And, she noted, she was nearly in the center.

Maidenstone was every bit as breathtaking as she had expected. Abruptly, her eyes looked down at the great white rock on which she sat. She wondered whether the island took its name from this very stone. She must remember to ask Reginald. Perhaps he would tell her the story behind it.

Suddenly the vista before her darkened, and she looked up to see a huge fluffy white cloud drifting in front of the sun. A moment later the sun shone through again and Susanna was relieved, for she remembered the earlier feeling of dampness in the air. This was not, she thought, the time or place to be caught in a downpour.

She let her eyes scan the landscape once again. Off to one side she thought she saw the thatched roof of a cottage hidden in the trees. Everywhere the flowers danced in the gentle breeze. And then she espied Reginald. He was crouching in a cluster of deep green ferns, and even at this distance she could see the intensity on his face as he worked. The sun beamed down on him, illuminating his thick, silver blond hair. She rose and gazed down at him. Quite suddenly, he turned and looked up at her. He uncoiled his tall body and stood, breaking into a smile. It was the kind of smile that softened his face and warmed his eyes. And Scotty felt her breath catch in her throat. No! she told herself as he waved briefly with a handful of leaves and bent once more to his work. It cannot be, she assured herself. I will not let it be so!

Feeling weak she sank back onto the stone and put her hands to her overly warm face. She could not be in love with him! It made absolutely no sense. He was the duke of Milburne and she was . . . she was . . . Oh, God, what she was was far too complicated for words. It was utterly foolish and futile for her to love him. She closed her eyes and pictured him in her mind's eye. Reginald holding her, kissing her. Reginald storming at her. Reginald with his family, his tenants, his plants. Reginald singing softly with her at Beverwil Manor. *Come bide with me, luv, at last noo I'm free, And I'll lay ye doon by the weepin' tree.* Love. She had been afraid then of this very thing, but she had not heeded her own warning. It made absolutely no sense, she told herself again. But she opened her eyes and looked down at him once more. And she knew, with a physical pang, that it made all the sense in the world.

When she met Reginald down below some minutes later, it seemed that every part of her body vibrated with awareness of him. She could hardly find her voice but answered in monosyllables when he asked if she was ready to go. He placed his carefully packed specimens into his saddlebag and threw it over his shoulder. He put a hand to her lower back as he guided her toward the ketch, and she found that his touch disturbed her more now than before. Before she'd realized . . .

Only when he commented on her unusual reticence did she venture to ask whether the large white stone was indeed "Maidenstone."

He stopped and turned to face her, arching a brow. He was too close to her and she tried to step back, but he caught her arm. "Yes," he said softly. "It is."

She could not keep her eyes from his, could not still her rapidly beating pulse. "Why is it called 'Maiden-stone'?"

He stared, mesmerized, at the pulse beating at her throat. Two buttons of her habit were still undone. He remembered too well what loveliness was hidden beneath the others. He forced his eyes back to her face. "Well, it was a very, very long time ago. There was the duke and the maiden, and the stone, big enough for, ah . . ."

"Two?" she supplied in a threadbare voice.

"Yes," he said. "And the duke was not a gentleman, you must know, and he, ah . . ." He stopped. "But I—I *am* a gentleman, Scotty, and I do not think I ought to tell you the rest." He took a deep breath.

"We'd better go now," he said quietly, and she did

not demur.

The sky darkened as the ketch sailed to the mainland, the water a bit choppy. This time the sun did not reappear. Having landed, they mounted their horses with due speed and set off at a gallop. Milburne Hall had just come into view when Reginald felt the first droplets. He cursed and urged his horse faster. Scotty followed suit, but only moments later the skies opened up and the downpour started.

Drenched to the skin, they reached the Hall. Reginald led them round back to the stableyard. He jumped from the gray and helped Scotty dismount, threw the reins to a stableboy and ran, one arm around Scotty, into the nearest of the rear doors.

They stood together in a dim passageway, lit by a single small window way above their heads. Scotty was shivering, and he ran his hands over her arms to warm her. Her hair had long since tumbled down her back in long, wet clumps. Even her dark eyelashes were dripping with water. He let his eyes sweep over the rest of her.

His breath stopped coming for a moment; he was certain of it. Nothing had prepared him for this. Not Scotty in her nightclothes, not Scotty warm and willing beneath him. Her rain-drenched clothes were plastered to her body, revealing every curve and valley almost as plainly as if she'd been wearing nothing at all. He didn't dare move, didn't dare touch her. He felt his loins tighten and was suddenly quite warm, despite all the water. He swallowed hard, and then he saw that she was subjecting him to a very thorough perusal of her own. He hoped to God his desire was not evident to her eyes, but found himself growing more heated by the second.

When finally she raised her head, her face was flushed. She was no longer shivering. Unable to help himself, he moved close to her. Slowly he traced her soft lips with his fingertip. And then he put his hands to the sides of her face. His mouth was only inches from hers.

"Scotty, oh, my dear Scotty," he heard himself rasp before he resolutely released her.

Chapter 15

Reginald had hoped to spirit Scotty to her rooms with no one the wiser, and it was just outside her door that he admonished her to change her clothes as quickly as possible lest she catch a chill.

"You needs must take care of yourself, Scotty. I'll see that a hot bath is sent up and a fire laid for you straightaway," he said softly.

To which she protested that a fire was not at all necessary, nor a bath. She did not wish to upset the servants' routine, and she would be right straightaway. He sensed her discomfort, knew the source, and felt a surge of anger.

His fingers gripped her shoulders more firmly than they should have. "Dammit, Scotty! I'm concerned for your health! Now, for pity's sake, do not argue with me! You are to have a hot bath, today and *every* day, and a fire whenever you wish it. I shall give orders to that effect. You will agree that it is *I* who give the orders around here?" he demanded.

"Y-yes, Reginald, of course."

"Scotty," he said, his voice softer now, "have I or has

anyone in this house given you to understand that you are to be treated as a servant?"

"Of course not."

"Very well, then, my dear. Do cease acting like one. You are beginning to shiver again. Now, off with you and do as I say." He kissed her on the brow, and nudged her through the doorway.

It was only then, when he turned back to the corridor, that he espied Peter Fairleigh across the way, leaning against the closed door of the nursery. On his handsome face was a silly grin which he immediately wiped away. But a twinkle remained in his eye as Reginald, cursing inaudibly and wondering how long his friend had stood there, came toward him.

"How are the children, Peter? Care for any brandy?" Reginald managed.

"No, thank you. Don't have the time. And you look like you could use a hot bath yourself, first stop. Timothy will be right after another day abed," Peter went on. "Thomas can get up tomorrow, and Letty . . . Letty can do as she sees fit."

That last pronouncement seemed rather strange to the duke. As did the smug look in the doctor's eyes, but Fairleigh refused to be more forthcoming and took his leave straightaway.

It was a very perturbed and preoccupied duke who sank into a steaming hot bath a short time later. Never in his life had he known such a coil. Scotty. He was torturing them both and he had no idea what to do about it. Even now, he could not help picturing her in her own bath on the floor above, and his body reacted accordingly.

He forced his wayward mind to consider, once again, his options. He could seduce her, of course. He could overcome her strange fear with gentleness, and he could win her. She wanted him. Even in her obvious innocence, she wanted him. But such a course was against all his principles. And when it was over, then what? Of a certain she would not be able to stay on here. Would he then give her enough money to live on her own, to insure that she needn't work again, or . . . or take another lover? Another protector. The whole notion was so distasteful to him as to make him feel sick. He would be pensioning her off like a loyal servant or a discarded mistress. Which was, of course, he admitted wearily, exactly what she would be. Why it would be so much more distasteful than giving some other mistress her congé he was not sure. Because she was a dependent in his house? Because she was innocent? Yes, all that, but something more; he knew not what.

Martinez had said that one must sometimes put aside one's scruples, and it seemed he had followed his own advice. But the same rules simply did not apply between a duke and a governess as between a valet and a lady's maid.

Marriage, of course, was not possible. Not that he wished to marry her! It was a preposterous notion! They'd known each other less than a se'nnight. He knew nothing about her background, nothing of the truth at all events. And they had little in common; a powerful physical attraction was simply not enough grounds for marriage.

No, he did not wish to marry her, but even if he did, it would have been impossible. Dukes of the realm, and in particular dukes of Milburne, did not wed Scottish lasses of dubious origin who'd found it necessary to run away from home and masquerade as governesses!

Hellfire! Who the devil *was* she? Where did she come from and from whom was she running? Or hiding? Certainly she was well hidden here in the depths of Devon. Was it a father, a guardian from whom she ran? A husband? He forced himself to calm down. No, not a husband. She was innocent; he would stake his life on it. He knew innocence because he knew the lack of it all too well. Scotty had never lain with a man.

And just who, he wondered with a sense of unease, was Duncan? He had frightened her, to be sure, but she had said it was a long time ago. Was it? Suddenly he recalled the dream Letty had told him about, a dream of blood. Could that have to do with Duncan? The thought chilled him, as did the possibility that the episode might have been more recent than she'd let on. Might she not have just now run away from Duncan?

And then suddenly, a sickening fear descended upon him. Scotty had run away once. Might she not do so again if . . . if he pushed her too hard? Either physically or by demanding the truth from her? If she fled, he would have no idea where to look for her! What did he know of her other than that she sprinkled her speech with Scottish words and probably had had a governess named "Beachie"?

Unsteadily, he rose from the tub, grateful for Martinez's uncharacteristic absence. He reached for the thick bath towel, his mind working furiously. There was one more option, and he knew in a flash that he had got to take it.

If he did not want her to leave, then *he* must. He would go to London. There was more work to be done on the journal; he had wanted more time to peruse Sir Joseph Banks's herbarium. Later perhaps he would tour his other estates. There was always work to be done. He must make Scotty believe that it was all very necessary work; never must she suspect his real reason for leaving. For he had no doubt that did she know, she would leave first.

He would wait only for a reply from his friend Penderleigh in Lancashire regarding Scotty's dubious reference. Perhaps such confirmation might include some clue as to her true identity.

Until the arrival of that correspondence, he would take pains not to be alone with Scotty. His decision thus made, he should have felt relieved. Instead he felt a curious emptiness.

Susanna's body luxuriated in the feel of the steaming hot water, but her mind could not be easy. She should never have gone with the duke. And yet, she would not have missed a moment of their time together, even though in the end, it would only bring her pain.

Oh, Beachie, you did not warn me of this, did you? she cried inwardly. 'Twas bad enough that she responded to him so shamelessly, but now to discover that she was in love with him . . . How had it happened? And what did it matter? She had been unable to prevent it, much as she'd tried.

And how futile was such a love, for it could lead nowhere. She could not give herself to him; a man of his principles would lose all respect for her if she did. And there were her own principles as well. She was a lady, had never acted as anything less. But besides—and this was the most wrenching of all—she did not know, after that last night in Scotland, if she was free to give herself at all.

She had squelched the memory of that last night for two months, but suddenly it clamored for release. Perhaps it was because of what had happened in the afternoon. Reginald had kissed her and eased her down onto the grass. And, God help her, she had wanted him never to stop. Until somehow, as if she'd completely lost her mind, she could no longer see Reginald, feel his body close to hers. It was Duncan Mortimer kissing her, his cold, hateful hands roving her body. And in those few moments before Reginald released her, she had relived all the terror of that dreadful night.

Her father had invited Duncan Mortimer to dine. Duncan Mortimer, to whom her father had forcibly bethrothed her one month before and whom she'd steadfastly refused to wed. Neither confinement nor beating had induced her to go willingly to Mortimer as his wife. She had wondered what her father's next ploy would be, but none of her imagining had come close to the terrible reality.

After dinner her father had disappeared, leaving her with Mortimer. And Mortimer, an ugly leer on his sharp, angular face, had dragged Susanna to her bedchamber. But first he had announced to two gaping maidservants that she was his wife. She did not understand what he had done until they'd reached her chamber. He had just declared, before two witnesses, he smugly told her, that they were wed. And so, according to Scots marriage law, they were.

Susanna remembered shaking with revulsion as Mortimer began to stalk her and disrobe her. He'd meant to claim his husbandly rights, to rape her, with, she knew, the full consent of her father. She was shaking even now in the warmth of her bath as the memories flooded her. Mortimer's wet, slimy kisses, his rough hands bruising her body, clawing at her clothing . . .

She had felt as if she were suffocating. Panic had welled up in her throat as she'd kicked and thrashed about in a vain attempt to evade him. She had hardly known what she was about, only that she had to stop him. She had groped blindly for something to hit him with and had seized the nearest thing to hand. It was her letter opener.

Susanna's heart was beating rapidly now as she remembered the next horrifying moment. She had stabbed wildly, only knowing that she had to escape him, hoping that she could hurt him just enough to make him release her. And then she would run.

Susanna's hands trembled as she tried to soap herself. For it had not happened that way. The letter opener had been a far more lethal weapon than she'd supposed, and her fear had given her a strength she had not known she possessed. Somehow the blade had found its way to Mortimer's throat. And suddenly there was blood all over as he stiffened and slithered against her to the floor.

She was crying now, her tears falling into the rapidly cooling bathwater. She remembered her dream of a few nights ago. Even in her sleep she had been unable to face the hideous truth. The truth that she could no longer suppress. No one had stabbed *her*. *She* had done the stabbing! She had murdered a man, or so she supposed. For surely one could not survive such a loss of blood. Only later had it occurred to her that there was a slight chance Mortimer had survived. And if he had, then she was a married woman, a runaway wife. That or a murderess. And neither one was worthy of

Reginald Ayres.

She choked back her tears and rinsed her face. How could she go on, seeing him day after day? She remembered Martinez's words. He told her to trust, to give the duke time, that Reginald was confused. But Martinez did not understand that Reginald's feelings were only part of what separated them, for he knew nothing of Susanna's background.

Besides, Reginald was not confused. Only his scruples, and perhaps the irrational fear that had come over her, prevented him from taking her. She felt herself flush, for she knew that, save for that fear, Reginald might well have taken her right there and then, on the grassy bank of the pond. And she, her body refusing to obey her mind, might well have let him, have welcomed it, in fact!

For a moment she allowed herself to wonder whether he felt anything for her beyond the strangely irresistible desire which haunted them both. He was always ringing a peal over her, yet she thought of his concern and his gentleness and suspected he *might* have some feeling for her. But still it did not signify. The duke of Milburne could not marry a governess! It was too ludicrous to consider. Of course, she had not been born to be a governess. But, she reminded herself bitterly, even though her birth was acceptable, even should he wish to wed her, she could not marry him. Not him, not anybody.

Slowly, mechanically, she rose from the tub and reached for the towel. She knew now, with an awareness that she supposed had been growing for some time, that she would have to leave Milburne Hall. Not tomorrow, perhaps, but soon. Staying would simply be too painful. She did not know whether she was drying bathwater or tears from her face.

The duke resolved to spend most of Sunday closeted in the herbarium and to avoid Scotty as much as possible. This he accomplished neatly until he arose to take a break in the midafternoon.

It was her voice that drew him; it was sweet and sultry all at once. He recognized the song that she'd played at Beverwil. "'He kissed me but once, pledged his troth to me, way doon at the burn by the weepin' tree'," she sang. He wished she would sing something else, but he could not resist going to her.

He found her in the Blue Saloon, her back to him as she arranged another of her endless bouquets. She was clad in her midnight blue morning dress. He stood in the doorway and told himself to go no farther. But his feet did not listen. Of their own accord, they silently crossed the Aubusson carpet to stand behind her, inches away. He did not say a word, did not touch her.

Abruptly she stopped singing and her hands became still. He clasped her shoulders and drew her back. She relaxed against him, and he felt the desire surge through him.

"Scotty," he whispered into her ear. Nothing more.

"Reginald," she answered, her voice faint.

She did not turn to look at him. Neither said another word. There was nothing to say. He simply held her, his hands unmoving, his lips brushing her finely coiled hair. And then, slowly, he released her.

"I shall go back to work now," he said.

"Yes." She lowered her head. He turned and walked from the room and back to his study.

The encounter had shaken him badly. She had

understood him, without words. The devastating need, the frustration, the futility of it all. And she felt it as well. He knew she did. He poured himself a glass of brandy and drank deeply. It did not help.

The reply from Damon, marquis of Penderleigh, arrived on Monday afternoon. Reginald should have been relieved. Now his curiosity would be satisfied. Now he could depart for London.

He wasn't at all relieved.

It had been, at all events, a rather uncomfortable day. The children, who seemed to have made a miraculous recovery since Saturday, all eyed him strangely. Martinez regarded him with open speculation, and Scotty was nowhere to be found. This morning there had been another ridiculous contretemps belowstairs. Something about Mrs. Rackett refusing Cleopatra's milk because Horatio had crossed her path. And when a much beleaguered Underwood had come to him, Reginald had wondered where the devil Scotty was when he needed her.

And now here was the missive from Lancashire. Slowly, Reginald broke the seal. First there were the usual greetings and then an invitation for the duke to visit Damon and his bride up in Lancashire. They had no plans, he wrote, to travel south for quite some time, and Reginald could only conclude that his old friend was quite as besotted as the on dits had it.

And then, stealing himself, Reginald read on. There was, indeed, a Lady Darnley of Hapworth Manor. She was, however, generally considered to have weathered more than eighty summers. She had at the least five known great-grandchildren who did not reside in the vicinity. Damon doubted whether Lady Darnley had employed a governess in the recent past.

As to one Sarah Beacham, Damon had not yet located her, but would pass on any information as he received it.

Damon went on to say: "My enchanting Penelope is quite intrigued by your mysterious governess"—not *my* governess, Reginald thought irritably and read on—"especially as she looks nothing like a governess." Good God, had Reginald really written that? "We wish you luck with her and hope to see you if you should decide to come north to investigate for yourself. Pen sends regards and bids you bring your incorrigible Miss Beacham with you." Not *my* Miss Beacham, dammit! And incorrigible . . . she was that, and more, but had he really written as much to Damon? He frowned, scanning the missive again. He recalled hearing that the new marchioness was quite a handful, and he could well believe it. Actually suggesting he travel north with the governess!

No, he would travel himself, to London, not to the north country. She was not Lancashire born and bred, of that he was certain. And he simply could not hightail it off for Scotland without knowing even her name! No, he would simply have to wait until some time in the future when she could bring herself to trust him. For now, he must insure that she stay here. Safe. Within reach.

He had thought, when he originally penned his letter to Damon, to confront her with the evidence of her duplicity and demand the truth. He had even thought to turn her off. Lord, was it but a se'nnight ago? Had so much happened in so short a time? He knew he would not turn her off, would not even confront her with his evidence and demand the truth. For she would not tell him, and might well flee in the night.

Strangely enough, he was no longer concerned with her qualifications as governess. The children obviously adored her and appeared to be making remarkable progress with their lessons. Of course, some of the subject matter was objectionable, and some of her methods exceptionable but still . . .

No, it was not Miss Beacham, governess, that he wished to unmask, but Scotty herself. He could not say exactly why, but he needed to know everything about her. Partly so that he could alleviate her fear of Duncan, partly so that he would know where to find her should she decide to run away again. But it was more than that and he knew it. He wanted to feel closer to her, and that sentiment was too dangerous to contemplate.

He stared down at the missive for a moment and then went to the empty grate. He struck a match, set flame to the paper, tossed it into the grate, and watched it burn. And then he sighed heavily. It was time to tell Martinez to pack his bags. He would leave at first light.

He would not appear for tea today; dinner with Scotty would be difficult enough. He would tell his mother at the table. It would not alarm her unduly. True, he had only just returned, but she was accustomed to his traveling.

He also needs must speak to Phoebe. A word in the Blue Saloon before dinner would do it. He would simply inform her that he expected her to behave with circumspection and that—he grimaced at this but knew Scotty's advice to be sound—Oswald Hastings was welcome to call in a gentlemanly manner. Then he would add that he was indeed considering allowing her

283

to make her come-out in London next Season. Even Phoebe had ought to perceive the connection between her behavior and her come-out.

But as for Scotty, he needs must tell her privately of his journey. He owed her that much and besides, he wanted to be certain that she did not think his sudden journey had aught to do with her. And so, he would see her alone, one more time. He would meet her in his study and be certain to leave the width of the desk between them. He sent her a message to come straightaway after tea, and then made his way upstairs to his chamber.

"I have some unfinished business with Sir Joseph. He is the president of the Royal Society, you must know," he explained to Martinez in response to his valet's unspoken question about the journey.

"I am aware of who Sir Joseph is, Don Reinaldo. You attend his breakfasts every Thursday whenever you are in London."

"That is correct. And his herbarium—"

"You are running away, *amigo,*" Martinez gravely put in.

"I am doing no such— Running away from what, pray tell?"

Martinez quirked a brow at him, even as he pulled a leather portmanteau from the cupboard in the dressing room. "Did you enjoy your little trip to Maidenstone?"

It was a seeming non sequitur, but the twitching of the valet's moustache told Reginald it was nothing of the kind. Reginald sighed. "Yes, I enjoyed it. Rather too much if you would know. Does that answer your question?"

"Yes. It is as I said. You are running away."

"Dammit, Martinez!" Reginald ran his fingers

through his hair. "I have to leave! Do you not see that?"

"As I said, you have an overabundance of scruples."

"Perhaps. But it is not simple for me as for you, my friend."

Martinez straightened up, bristling. "Would you care to explain yourself, Don Reinaldo?"

Reginald found himself smiling. "Come down off your high ropes, old chap. I am happy for you. Truly I am." He noted that Martinez began to relax. "She is very lovely."

"Yes," Martinez responded, a fond look in his eye, "and you—"

"For me it is different, *amigo mío,*" Reginald said with a finality that effectively terminated that particular line of discourse.

For several minutes there was silence as Martinez folded the duke's linen and Reginald stared unseeing out the window. At length Martinez asked, "How long will we be gone?"

It was an unusual question for Martinez to ask. He was a man who lived in the present and concerned himself little with the future. Reginald turned to face him. "I do not know, Martinez. I need time. I will go and wait upon events. I—" Reginald paused and gazed intently at his friend. There was an uncharacteristic bleakness in the Spaniard's eyes which he tried to hide by busying himself with the duke's cravats. Reginald realized with chagrin that he'd been behaving like an unfeeling idiot. "Martinez, I . . . You do not have to go with me. If you would rather—"

"No!" Martinez raised his head, his expression now unruffled. "I go with you. Don Reinaldo does not travel without his valet," he declared with the same finality of tone Reginald had used moments before.

285

And the duke knew there was nothing more to be said.

Scotty tapped at the door and glided into his study at the appointed time. He stood behind the desk; she stopped near the sofa, hesitant to come any closer. She wore a pale peach sarcenet dress that made her auburn hair glow and her skin look like fine, fragile porcelain. He told himself that she was not fragile and that what he was doing was best for both of them. They would both be strong.

He resisted the urge to join her at the sofa and instead gestured for her to take a seat in front of the desk. She came forward but remained standing, her beautiful hands resting lightly on the polished mahogany surface. He stared for a moment at those hands, remembered what they looked like weaving flowers into a bouquet, what they felt like on his head, massaging away the pain, and around his neck, when he'd kissed her. . . .

He raised his eyes to her face. "Scotty, I wanted to tell you that I am leaving for London on the morrow."

She went pale and quickly looked down. "I . . . I see," she murmured.

"Yes, I . . . have business there," he said slowly, his voice low, "and then there is some research that—" When she raised her eyes, his voice caught in his throat. She looked the way he felt—bleak, empty, as if she were fighting despair.

"I . . . I understand," she whispered. "Ye needn't explain." What did she understand, he wondered, and then she lowered her eyes again and added in a soft undertone, "It is best."

Good God! Did she know, then? Did she understand

the true reason? Yes, she must. Scotty was no fool. And now it behooved him to assure himself that *she* would stay. Without thinking of the wisdom of it, he came round to stand before her at the front of the desk.

Gently he lifted her chin with his fingertips. "I do not know how long I will be gone. But I . . . I should like you to be comfortable here. To treat this as your home. Do you understand me?"

Some of the tension seemed to leave her. "Aye, Reginald."

Unwittingly, his finger traced the line of her jaw. Her soft smooth skin felt very warm. Quite deliberately, he dropped his hand. "Take care of the children for me. And my mother. They all need you." He did not add that he needed her, did not even like to admit it to himself. That was why he was leaving.

"I will, Reginald. Ye are not to trouble yerself about them."

He nodded, half-smiling. "Keep an eye out for Phoebe."

She returned the faint smile. "I willna let her do anything foolish."

He nodded again. "Will you," he began, keeping his hands rigidly at his sides and trying to ignore the pulse jumping at her throat, "will you write to me? About . . . about the children?" He added this last hastily.

"Aye, Reginald, I'll write to ye. Ye have . . . have a care for yerself."

"Scotty," he rasped, finally yielding to impulse and putting gentle hands to her shoulders. He felt her shudder at his touch. It was not, he knew, from fear.

Her eyes searched his face. "Godspeed, Reginald," she whispered, her eyes moist.

He leaned forward and lightly brushed his lips to hers. It was all he would permit himself but he needed that moment of warmth, just as he needed the feel of her shoulders beneath his hands, just one last time. It was all he had to take with him.

Susanna could not sleep. Dinner had been torture. Knowing it was the last she would see of Reginald for some time, having to pretend that his departure meant no more to her than to the duchess, or Underwood for that matter. It was all too much, and she hadn't wanted Reginald to see the strain it was causing her. And so she'd put a brave and lively face on it, and now here she was, huddled in the merino cloak worn over her nightclothes, wandering the gardens in the wee hours.

It was not just the fact of his departure that was keeping her awake. It was the reason. For despite what he'd said, she knew well that he was leaving because of her. He wanted her; she had, much as it shamed her to admit it, responded to him. Responded in a way she had never thought possible. But he was a gentleman, and the situation had become untenable. Milburne Hall, with all its myriad rooms and acres of land, was not large enough for the two of them.

She sank down onto a cold stone bench. The night air was brisk and she pulled the cloak more tightly about her. She ought to be the one to leave. It was not right that he had to leave his home. But she knew that he did not wish her to go. He wanted her here, for the children, for Phoebe and his mother. And perhaps for . . . But she would not pursue that line of thought. He did not love her, she reminded herself. He desired her, and that was quite a different matter.

How, she demanded inwardly, how could she have been so foolish as to fall in love with him? Such could do naught but add to the torment she had already felt since she'd fled her home.

She saw the light of the cheroot before she heard his approach. Martinez started when he saw her, then smiled and sauntered toward her.

"Can you not sleep, señorita?"

"No." She didn't think explanations were necessary.

"Ahh," he replied. He stood before her, looking down. "It is as I told you. He is confused. He will come about."

She shook her head. "It is very good of you to say so, Martinez. But I'm afraid you do not understand."

He did not say anything, merely took a long drag on the cheroot. At length she asked, "And you, Martinez? Why can you not sleep?"

He sighed. "Sometimes, señorita, we do not know if we . . . if we have done right."

She peered at him. "I think perhaps you do not follow your own advice."

He propped his foot onto the bench. "Which advice is that, Señorita Scotty?"

"You told me to trust." He frowned, puzzled, and she added softly, "I saw Angelique just before dinner." She did not know exactly what had passed between Angelique and Martinez, only that it was enough that the maid was quite overset at his leaving.

"Ahhh, I see." He took a drag on the cheroot and then tossed it away. Straightening up, he asked, "Will you . . . have a care for her, señorita?"

"Yes," she whispered, then rising, added, "Take . . . take care of Reginald."

For the first time Martinez smiled. "I will. Perhaps our return will be sooner than either of us thinks."

Chapter 16

London was rather unbearably hot. Unfortunately it was not hot enough for the ton to have begun their annual exodus to Brighton. The Season still had several weeks to run itself out. And so, invitations poured in every day to Milburne House. Invitations to balls, soirees, musicales, breakfasts that started at three o'clock in the afternoon. Reginald grumbled to Martinez that it was uncanny that word of his return had reached so many hostesses so soon. But Martinez pointed out with his inevitable logic that many people probably never knew he'd left.

"After all, Don Reinaldo," Martinez had said rather dryly, as he brushed the duke's hair forward in the Brutus haircomb he favored, "you were not away in Devon a very long time."

No, he thought now as he sat in his study. Not a very long time. Merely a se'nnight. A se'nnight that had changed everything, and changed nothing.

Outwardly nothing *had* changed. He could not allow it to do so. He met with his secretary and discussed his various holdings, did his research, refused as many invitations as civility allowed. Last night he'd put in a brief appearance at some ghastly, overcrowded ball, a sad crush to make any hostess proud. All the things he'd done the last time he was here. But this time his mind had been on none of it. For though outwardly nothing had altered, inwardly he did not know if he would ever be the same.

He could not stop thinking of her. She filled his thoughts during the day and kept him from sleeping at night. He burned for her. He had given his last mistress her congé weeks ago, but there were others he could visit. Women who would be warm and all too willing. But Reginald was not a fool, and he knew very well that the physical release would, for the first time in his life, not assuage him. He did not want a paid and painted companion. Nor did he want one of the several "ladies" of the ton with whom he occasionally spent a mutually satisfying evening.

He wanted Scotty, and all the miles he'd put between them had not made a whit of difference. In truth, it was worse. His body still ached, but it was more than that. He wanted to talk with her, hear her voice, watch her arranging flowers—his flowers. Yesterday, he'd attended Sir Joseph's weekly breakfast for members of the Royal Society. In the past Reginald had been content to share what scientific tidbits he'd gleaned with his secretary, what humorous anecdotes with Martinez. This time he'd wanted to tell Scotty.

Last night at the odious ball, he had barely noticed his partners, only wondered all the while what it would feel like to partner Scotty in the waltz. Would she dance as gracefully as she did everything else? He'd gone into supper with a particularly insipid blonde, and each time he'd seen the back of an auburn head, he'd held his breath until the woman had turned and he'd felt the foolish, puerile disappointment that it was not Scotty.

He'd only been gone four days, one of those spent in travel. Twice already, his secretary, Benton, had asked if he were ill. And thrice he'd been on the verge of telling Martinez to pack his bags.

And the post. In the past he'd always looked upon it as a bothersome nuisance. The post always meant more obligations—scientific, financial, social. True, occasionally there was an item of interest, but more often than not he was content to wait for Benton to sift through it and present to him those items which needed his attention.

But these last few days he'd pounced on the post the minute it arrived. Rather, he thought in self-disgust, like a lovesick schoolgirl. Yesterday, Thursday, there'd still been no letter from her. And he'd told himself that, of course, there hadn't; he'd only left on Tuesday, for heaven's sake, and the Quicksilver Mail, London-Devon run, took two days. But this morning there hadn't been a letter either. Not from Scotty. There *had*, however, been correspondence from Milburne Hall. It was addressed in a feminine, foreign hand to Martinez. Amusement warred with envy as Reginald stared down at the missive; then he'd thrown it back onto Benton's desk amid the pile of invitations and bills. Let Benton give it to Martinez. Reginald would be damned if he'd suffer another of Martinez's lectures on relaxing his scruples. Some time later the duke had heard his valet's unmistakable whistle coming from the corridor. It had not improved his humor one iota.

And now, in the afternoon, Reginald toyed idly with the quill in his hand and tried to concentrate on his article for the *Journal*. Instead he counted days. He'd suspected that she would not write until he did, and apparently he'd been right. To that end he'd written a short missive to her on Wednesday. He'd simply asked after the children, Phoebe, his mother. Not knowing what else to say, but wanting to put words to paper, he'd even asked after Desdemona and Robin Hood! And only at the end had he asked Scotty how *she* was. Was she getting her proper rest? he'd written, when what he'd really wanted was to ask if she was any better able to sleep than he was. Was she excessively busy? he'd asked, when he'd really wanted to know if she missed him as he missed her.

"Hellfire!" he exploded audibly. He had got to snap out of this! He would go to that blasted card party tonight, and tomorrow he would spend the day at White's. He would keep himself occupied and he would forget!

The words blurred on the page before him. She would receive his letter today, he thought. Next week, he would receive an answering missive. If she wrote at all. Perhaps she was a poor correspondent. Perhaps she would not wish to write. . . .

Good God! He thrust his chair back and paced the room. Never before had he been prey to self-doubt. Never had he been so obsessed with anyone or anything. He was poor company for himself and everyone around him. What had she done to him?

Susanna felt a headache come upon her. Oh, dear, she thought, most disconcerted. She *never* suffered from headaches! But then, never before had she known sleeplessness as she had these few nights since

293

Reginald's departure. And for the first time since she'd come here, she'd found herself being irritable with the children. Thomas had been quite put out when she'd scolded them this morning for allowing Desdemona to play hide-and-seek with Robin Hood in the schoolroom. Timothy had asked if she were feeling quite the thing, but Letty had simply gazed at her with a very slight, but unmistakably smug smile. Susanna was not at all comfortable with that smile.

She had brought the children out here to the gardens for luncheon. But instead of joining in their games, as she usually did, she'd wandered a little way off and sat down on a gracefully carved stone bench.

It was Friday. He'd only been gone four days. She had known she would miss him; she hadn't known thoughts of him would invade her every waking hour. When she'd been arranging the bluebells and goldenrod in the morning room yesterday, she kept expecting to hear him pad quietly up behind her. She'd closed her eyes and imagined the feel of his warm breath in her ear. Then she'd opened them and whirled about, and the emptiness of the room had made her shiver. And this morning, Robin Hood had tracked muddy paws all over the freshly washed marble entry lobby and had knocked down the hapless maid, spilling her bucket. Susanna had heard the maid's shriek from upstairs, and she imagined Mrs. Longbotham's bellow could be heard all over the Hall. It hadn't been terribly difficult to calm the maid, or to assure Mrs. Longbotham, who threatened to banish Robin Hood to the stables or leave him to the tender mercies of Mrs. Rackett. But Susanna kept looking about the lobby, expecting to see the duke, hoping to exchange a glimmer of amusement with him.

And he wasn't there. She'd received a letter from him that morning, had read it and reread it while the children were working on various projects in the schoolroom. There had been little personal in it, other than an admonition that she get her proper rest. But at the least it was some form of contact. He had signed it "Reginald." The letter rested now in the pocket of her gown; she would pen a reply at the earliest opportunity.

She chanced to look up at that moment, and a flash of yellow color caught her eye. It was across the expanse of the rolling green lawn, beyond the rose garden where the gazebo sat on a mossy rise. She blinked, thinking that it had been her imagination, but instinct took over. She glanced over at the children and ascertained that they were well occupied, the boys with Robin Hood and the red ball, Letty with her sketch pad. Satisfied, she rose and made her way across the lawn.

Her first letter arrived on Tuesday morning. He snatched it from the tray before Benton even saw it. She wrote in a beautiful hand, with smooth, curving sweeps to her letters.

It was a colorful communication, full of all the news of home. He chuckled as he read her account of Robin Hood's contretemps with Mrs. Longbotham and the slop bucket in the entry lobby. And he rolled his eyes at her recounting of tea with Lady Craddock and her children on Friday. Major Hayes had come as well, as had the Reverend Mr. Honeyworth.

"Lady Craddock and the duchess enjoyed a comfortable gossip," she wrote, "while William Craddock bored poor dear Mr. Honeyworth to tears with his very knowledgeable theological comments on the rector's last sermon. When William was finished I do believe Mr. Honeyworth regretted having given any sermon at all. William will make a very earnest cleric, I daresay, and I deem it only fair to warn you that he has his eye on the living here, should Mr. Honeyworth decide to retire.

"You will be happy to note that Major Hayes and Elsie seem to have come to an understanding; he had eyes only for her the whole while. I do believe that despite their age diffference, Elsie has a tendre for him, which of a certain simplifies matters for Lady Craddock." Reginald did not at all care for this reminder of how he'd made a fool of himself the night of the Hastingses' dinner, accusing Scotty of flirting with the major. He read on: "Letty comported herself with dignity and seemed to go on quite well with the rector once William released him." She would, Reginald thought fondly. Of all his siblings, Letty had the best sense of humor.

"There was one rather unusual note to the proceedings," the letter went on. "Lady Craddock, garbed in an unexceptionable lavender gown and some Indian turbanlike headdress, did the most extraordinary thing. At the first lull in the conversation, she strolled over to Mr. Honeyworth and asked him whether he thought there was any similarity between Hindu philosophy and one of the finer points of his last sermon. The rector looked momentarily startled, for indeed dear Lady Craddock has never been known for her interest in such matters. But he did not look at all displeased, nor did he object when Lady Craddock took his arm for a turn about the room. The subject seemed to engross them both for some minutes,

Reginald, and I own I did not know what to make of it!

"As to Phoebe, she was somewhat reserved, and though I hesitate to overset you by relating to you the reason, I know you will ring a peal over me should the situation worsen without your having been apprised."

Frowning, Reginald read her description of the flash of yellow just beyond the gazebo. He knew what was coming before he read the words. She had known too.

"Phoebe and Oswald were seated on your mama's lovely wicker loveseat, engaged in whispered conversation. They jumped when they saw me, but I followed my own advice and invited him to tea. He declined and I reminded him that he was welcome to call on Phoebe in the prescribed manner. No, do not clench your jaw, Reginald." He paused and smiled. Scotty knew him well. "I truly believe it is the only way. At the least in the house I can keep an eye on them. At all events, as we walked back to the house, I contrived to mention to him alone, lest you hadn't had the chance, that Phoebe's fortune would not be released to her until at the least her twenty-fifth birthday. Whereupon Oswald turned to me and in all innocence declared that he hadn't given her fortune a thought. Somehow, my dear Reginald, I do not think I have discouraged him."

Reginald was not at all happy with this state of affairs, but he liked the "my dear Reginald" part rather well, indeed. Only in the last paragraph did she ask after him. She hoped that his work was going well but that he was not overtiring himself. Was he sleeping well? Ah, Reginald thought, she was more daring than he. He had merely asked if she were resting. And now he knew that sleep, or lack of it, was as much on her mind as his.

"Angelique sends her warmest regards to Martinez.

She is lonely, I think, but happy." So, Reginald mused, Scotty had figured that out, had she?

"Everyone here misses you, Reginald," she concluded, but he only cared about one person missing him.

She signed the missive simply "Scotty." Not "Beachie" or "Miss Beacham" or "Rose" but Scotty.

He read the letter again and ached for her.

Somehow, Reginald contrived to pass the week. He worked, he spent time at his club, he graced several balls. He wrote to Scotty and awaited her reply. On Friday night, no longer able to endure another crowded ballroom where he would search in vain for auburn hair and midnight blue eyes, he opted for a quiet dinner at White's. It was there that he met his old friend Charles, the earl of Ainsley. He had seen Charles and his beautiful countess earlier in the Season but was most surprised to encounter the earl now. For Lady Ainsley was breeding and, if Reginald recalled correctly, had ought to be nearing her confinement.

"I arrived just this morning," Charles told him as they took their seats at a quiet table for dinner. "Some unavoidable business matter, you must know, but I leave for Somerset at first light. I do not like to be away, especially now." There was a fond, far-off look in the earl's eye, and Reginald felt an unaccustomed stab of envy. He found himself wondering what it would be like to have a wife waiting at home for him. He tried to picture Amanda Ainsley, and instead he saw Scotty, reclining on a sofa, his sofa, her body stretched with child, *his* child. The image was fleeting, but his hand shook as he reached for his wineglass.

Somehow, he kept his voice steady and asked after the countess's health. Then, as dinner was served, they spoke of politics and their mutual preference for their country houses over London. As the stuffed turbot was followed by a glazed duckling, Reginald noted a contentment about Ainsley that hadn't been evident years ago. It had, Reginald suspected, come only recently, with his marriage. And again the duke could not keep Scotty's image from his mind's eye. He sighed inwardly for what could not be.

It was then that Ainsley asked him why he was preoccupied. The question jarred Reginald. Had he been that obvious? He seized on the nearest problem he had to hand, other than that of a certain governess, and told Ainsley his concerns about Phoebe and her fortune-hunting suitor.

To his amazement, Ainsley threw his head back and laughed. "Heaven spare us all from chits just out of the schoolroom," he said. "I had a similar brouhaha with my ward, Kitty. Round about the time I met Amanda. And, of course, I did exactly what Amanda cautioned me not to do."

"What was that?" the duke asked cautiously, his fork poised midair.

"She advised me to allow them to meet, under my watchful eye, of course. Instead," the earl sighed, "Instead I ranted and raved and forbade Kitty to see him. And so, of course, she ran off with him. Which was precisely what Amanda had said she'd do," he concluded ruefully.

"Amazing," Reginald murmured. "Scotty said much the same to me about Phoebe."

"Scotty?" Ainsley queried.

Reginald recalled himself. "The, ah, children's governess, you must know."

The earl raised a brow. "I see. And the, ah, children's governess was advising you about your sister. Unusual name, Scotty, is it not?"

Reginald felt himself squirm and signaled for more wine. "Yes, well, 'tisn't her name, actually, just a nickname."

"Yes, I see. Children do find the most amazing apellations for governesses," Ainsley mused nonchalantly, but his eyes were sharp.

Reginald reached for his newly filled wine goblet and drank deeply of the fine claret. "As it happens, I . . . well, the, ah, children call her 'Beachie.' For 'Miss Beacham,' you must know." The earl's eyes began to twinkle. "'Tis a rather long story," Reginald muttered.

"What happened to your ward?"

Ainsley grinned. "Kitty's mysterious fortune hunter turned out to be . . . well, not a fortune hunter at all. They make their home in Essex now. Raising racehorses, and, I suspect, from the last I saw Kitty, children as well."

Reginald smiled in return. "All's well that ends well, eh? Well, Phoebe's suitor is no mystery. He's our nearest neighbor—an inveterate gambler who comes from a long line of wastrels. Younger son of the Baron Hastings. Young Oswald is quite desperately hanging out for a rich wife. And Scotty writes that the situation is getting worse."

"You must introduce him to Lady Gresham and her daughter Eloise," Ainsley said with just the faintest tightening of his jaw.

"The Dragon Lady? But—"

"She's been trying to marry that daughter of hers off for several seasons now. Never did succeed with her elder daughter." Charles's slate blue eyes took on a rather grim, faraway look, as if he were seeing into the past. Intrigued, Reginald knew there was a good deal more to the story. But somehow he suspected he daren't ask. And then Charles leaned back in his seat and abruptly changed the subject. "Tell me about Scotty."

Reginald nearly choked on his asparagus. "I cannot think what you mean, Charles. She is the governess. There is little more—"

"My dear Reggie," chided Charles, a smile tugging at the corners of his mouth, "I have known numerous governesses in my day. And never have I had the urge to correspond with them, nor allow them to advise me on any matter whatever, nor to call them endearing little nicknames."

"'Tis not endearing!" Reginald protested, then stopped as the earl raised a skeptical brow. "Oh, hellfire!"

The earl chuckled. "I've known you since the Peninsula, Reggie. A man gets to know another fairly well in war time. But you are under no obligation to tell me aught, you know."

Reginald took another sip of his claret and regarded the older man. No, he did not have to answer Charles. But he suddenly found the urge to speak about it overwhelming. He smiled fondly. "She does not look at all like a governess, you may be sure. She is beautiful, with auburn hair and deep blue eyes and—" Something in the earl's eyes brought Reginald up short. He cleared his throat. "Yes, well, she is the most meddlesome female, does not know the meaning of obedience, and has the most inappropriate, irrepressible sense of humor." Charles was grinning now, and Reginald

301

frowned. "'Tis not a laughing matter, Charles. The house is at sixes and sevens, what with the children—"

"And they rather adore her," Charles put in.

"Well, yes."

"And you . . . miss her," the earl said carefully.

Reginald sighed deeply and nodded. "But I . . . I had to leave Milburne. I . . . I could not keep away from her."

"Is that such a problem?" There was a damn sight too much amusement in the earl's voice.

"She's the bloody *governess,* Charles!"

"Ah, I see. Not quite good enough to be—"

"No, dammit! You do mistake the matter! 'Tis . . . Oh, blast it all, Charles! 'Tis much more complicated than that." Reginald ran his hand through his hair and wished he were home in his study so that he could pace. The earl regarded him blandly and continued eating his minted peas. "I do not know who or *what* she is! She has told me naught but one great clanker. I suspect that she is in some sort of difficulty and has run away, but she will not let me help her. And, God help me, I do not even know where she comes from. If she were to run away again, I . . . I do not know if I should . . . even find her." Reginald's voice trailed off as he voiced his deepest fear.

"So instead *you* have, er, run away," the earl observed.

"It seemed the better part of valor," Reginald said dryly, and was relieved when the waiter came to collect their plates. They remained silent as a trifle was served.

"It is only a temporary solution, my friend," the earl said at length.

"There *is* no solution, Charles. Surely you can see

302

that. Men in our position have certain responsibilities—"

"It is as I said, then. She will not suit as the duchess of—"

"No, dammit! You do not see at all. I am not thinking of marriage. 'Tis out of the question."

The earl smiled. "Forgive the presumption, old chap, but it seems to me that the other alternative would not require nearly so much cogitation. No, I daresay you would still be in Devon, happily enjoying—"

"It would be simpler by far, Charles, but . . . she is a lady," Reginald interrupted.

"A lady but not lady enough to—"

"Will you cease saying that, Charles!" This time Reginald did rise and began pacing between the near window and his chair. "Merely because I . . . I miss her, think about her, even write to her, is hardly cause to leg-shackle myself. And even did I wish to wed her, which I take leave to remind you I do *not,* but even did I wish to, why, I know naught about her people. Good God, I do not even know her name!"

"Reggie, do sit down," the earl suggested mildly. When the duke complied he went on, "No man can see into another's heart, nor direct his conscience. I can only tell you what I learned when I met Amanda. One is that things are often not what they seem. Nothing made sense when I met her, and I desperately needed to know the truth. Oh, I knew her name, to be sure, but of her past I knew naught but the stories I'd heard." The earl sighed. "They were rather . . . unpleasant. And well, suffice it to say that I felt the need to ferret out the truth. Until I realized—thank God before it was too late—that it didn't signify. In point of fact, Reggie, I would have wed Amanda no matter what. Of course, those tales were proven false, but it would not have signified in the least if they hadn't been. That she was worthy to be my countess I think I knew from the first. That I loved her . . . well, that is a very difficult thing for a man to admit."

Reginald stared at the earl. It was rare that he was so forthcoming. But then, Ainsley had changed since his marriage. He smiled more, seemed more at his ease. Reginald, at the moment, was anything *but* at his ease. Love? Of a certain, he did not *love* Scotty. He wanted to bed her, to talk with her, laugh with her. That did not—could not—mean he loved her. As to marriage, why it was the furthest thing from his head!

His mind awhirl, Reginald was most grateful when the earl, with supreme tact, deftly shifted the subject.

The duke's second letter began with "My dear Scotty" and asked after her in the second, rather than the last paragraph. Susanna could hardly wait to put pen to paper to reply. She raced through several paragraphs describing the latest crisis in the kitchens, as well as giving him a schoolroom progress report and a description of Phoebe and Oswald casting mooncalf eyes at each other at Lady Craddock's dinner party. She took time to mention, however, that Lady Craddock had worn a most unusual garment consisting of layers of some diaphanous material arranged in what surely must be an Eastern style, for it bore no resemblance to anything British. And that the Reverend Honeyworth, seated to her right, had been hard put to keep his eyes from her.

And then she lingered over the last three paragraphs,

where she asked how he was, what London was like now that the Season was drawing to a close, whether his work was going well. She closed the letter "With warmest regards, Scotty" and had barely time to seal it before Timothy and Thomas came barreling into her sitting room in pursuit of the wayward red ball.

It was in his third letter that Reginald told her he missed her and thought of her often. A surge of joy went through her at his words, and with it came a great sense of freedom, for she could finally tell him in her answering letter that she missed him, too.

But the schoolroom rebelled against Mrs. Marcet's *Conversations on Natural Philisophy* that morning. And Susanna had to talk Letty out of reading Fielding's *Tom Jones* and Thomas out of dissecting a bird that Horatio had obligingly killed. There was another contretemps with Cook, and then Lady Craddock came to tea. It was then that she and the duchess hatched their little scheme, and continued discussing it the very next day so that Scotty had to stay close to hand, lest their plans became far too fanciful.

And so in the event, it was not until that next evening that Susanna was finally able to pen her reply.

Reginald had downed too damned much brandy the past night. It had been the only way to bring on sleep, a heavy oblivion in which Scotty visited him and the longing was assuaged, however briefly. But now he had the devil's own headache and Martinez's latest concoction helped not a whit. Reginald damned Scotty for putting him in this predicament and simultaneously longed for the feel of her soft hands on his temples, her fingers massaging his scalp. He remembered her telling him how whiskey brought on her Aunt MacLaughlin's megrims and wondered grimly why he hadn't heeded the warning.

Gritting his teeth against every sharp sound and flash of sunlight, he made his way to his study, determined to lose himself in work. Instead he lost himself in her letter, just now arrived and placed on his desk by a suspiciously grinning Benton.

"My dearest Reginald," she began, and he smiled as he read.

She opened, as usual, with a cheerful account of the schoolroom and of Mrs. Rackett's latest exploit. Reginald laughed aloud at Mrs. Rackett's reaction to Horatio nestled asleep next to Cleopatra. He wanted to hug Scotty, to be there with her, to share her amusement.

And then the missive became less amusing. "I am persuaded that the duchess will write to you presently, but I thought perhaps I had ought to warn you that she and Lady Craddock have hit upon the notion of giving a ball here in the beginning of August. I believe your mama said it would 'be just the thing to liven up the summer,' and Lady Craddock's rather fertile mind immediately began working on decorating schemes. Lady Craddock, bless her, wants to help as much as possible, especially since the duchess has assured her she may announce Elsie's engagement to Major Hayes at the ball.

"I have tried to curb Lady Craddock's more exotic fancies; indeed, I am certain that I have scotched the notion of bolts of silk draped tentlike from the ceiling, with snake charmers and camels for authenticity.

"I have not, however, attempted to dissuade them from the notion of giving a ball at first stop (though I

306

shall if you wish it). For I am persuaded that your mama was in the right of it when she said, quite as an aside, you must know, that perhaps at the ball 'dear Phoebe will meet someone more suitable than that dreadful Hastings boy.'

"And there, my dear Reginald, is the crux of it. Phoebe might be unofficially brought out at the ball (for of a certain you will wish to give her a London come-out), and at the least she will meet other young men. The situation here with Oswald does not improve, and I own a ball might be the very thing! Of course, if you are most assuredly opposed to it, then perhaps taking Phoebe to London for the Little Season might answer, though that is months away. Do let me know your wishes in this matter, Reginald."

Reginald chuckled at this last. His wishes, indeed! She had given him a choice which she knew was no choice at all. A ball at Milburne or the Little Season! She knew well what he would choose. And that, he supposed, was what his life would always be with Scotty—she would seem to accede to his wishes, having first assured that she would get her way! He wondered why the notion troubled him not a whit, and then he brought himself up short. What the devil was he thinking? But he knew. Scotty. In his life, in his bed, at his table. Permanently. No! The notion was preposterous! He couldn't. Besides, he did not love her. Did he?

And then he read the final paragraph of her letter and felt his breathing stop. "I do not know if I miss you more at times such as this, when I need so much to talk with you, or at night, when I walk in the gardens because I cannot sleep. Godspeed. I remain, with warmest regards, Scotty."

Scotty, he thought, I miss you so.

His head began to pound, the dull ache from overimbibing settling on the left side. He would have a full-blown megrim within the hour.

He rose and went to stand at the window overlooking Grosvenor Square and rubbed his throbbing temple with his hand. He needed her. Not merely to still the burning desire in his loins, not merely to massage away the pain in his head. He needed, simply, to be with her, to speak with her, to see her smile, to hear her laugh. Was that—he felt himself swallow hard—was that what love was? To feel a constant longing for another, to feel oneself incomplete without her? And—he sighed deeply—if it were true, if he did love her, what then? Could he, as the earl had implied, simply cast aside all considerations of lineage and the training from childhood necessary for a future duchess of Milburne? And even if he could push such aside, would society accept her? That Scotty was a lady of breeding, that she was capable of presiding at his table, running his house—hellfire, a dozen houses—he did not for a moment doubt. But he had not a clue as to her antecedents, her life before coming to Devon. And she had run away. Why?

Charles said that he, too, had searched for answers, and in the end, the answers had not signified.

But they *did* signify, Reginald's conscience screamed. He was the duke of Milburne! He had a responsibility to his family, his numerous tenants, his country. He could *not* do as he pleased.

No, his heart countered. He was the duke of Milburne. He could do *precisely* as he pleased.

He strode to his desk, sat down, and pulled out a sheet of writing paper to pen a reply to Scotty. He perused her letter again and thought of the ball. It was, he realized, probably a good idea for Phoebe's sake. He did not at all mind that he would not be there for the endless preparations, and was thankful that Scotty was there to manage things. Lord knew what queer starts his mother and the dithering Lady Craddock would get up to if left to their own devices.

He would return for the ball itself. By then he would have been away some six weeks. Long enough for the need to fade or . . .

He would know as soon as he saw her. Suddenly, he was certain of it. He would look at her and he would know if he could live without her, or if he must, at whatever cost, find a way to live with her.

Susanna sat in the garden and pulled from her pocket the letter that had arrived that morning. Letty, as had become her habit, had brought the missive to her governess, a secret smile on her child's face. Susanna suspected that Letty sensed there was something personal in her relationship with the duke. But Letty never spoke of it, and Susanna appreciated her silence as well as what seemed her tacit approval.

Susanna smiled as she unfolded the missive. She had read it earlier, but she'd been in a hurry and now she wanted to savor it.

"I miss you," he wrote at the end. "The days are interminably long without you. Yet I must stay for a while longer. I shall come home for the ball."

He was coming home. The ball was in a little over a fortnight, and he would be here. She smiled and felt tears prick the backs of her eyelids. Her joy was bittersweet, mixed with a feeling of impending desolation. She longed to see him, to have him hold her, talk to her, even scold her in that way he had of feigning anger even when he did not quite feel it. He would do all of those things. And he would kiss her and tell her he'd missed her, perhaps even dance with her at the ball.

But when the music stopped, nothing would have changed. He was the duke of Milburne and she . . . She was not free to become his mistress, would she consider it, nor his wife, would *he* consider it. She was not free, nor was she fit for Reginald Ayres. And this time, *she* would have to leave. She'd known for a long time that it would come to this. The fact that she loved him, that he perhaps cared for her, made it so devastatingly painful. But it did not change what had to be.

Slowly Susanna rose. It was time to begin, quietly, to make preparations for her departure.

Chapter 17

July was drawing to a close. London was emptying itself of people, but still Reginald stayed. His work was going well. The article for the first issue of the new journal was almost finished. He was catching up on his correspondence with some of the continental botonists he'd met on his expeditions. And he'd begun his work on the ferns of Devonshire.

There were fewer distractions in the tomblike quiet of Milburne House in Grosvenor Square than there ever were at the Hall, especially now that the Season had come to an end. At Milburne Hall one could open one's study door and be pelted by a red ball, accosted by a loping basset hound, or assailed by the scent of jasmine and the sound of a woman singing. Of a certain one would not get as much work accomplished.

Still, it was not work which held him in the stifling metropolis when he longed to be home. And he was honest enough to admit, finally, that it was not, as he'd tried to make himself believe, that he wanted to give Scotty and himself a long enough separation, time to know their own minds and hearts. It was rather, very simply, fear. Fear not of facing Scotty, but of himself, of how he felt and what it would mean.

Martinez had said Reginald was running away by coming to London, and he had been right. But Reginald had not realized the extent of what he was running away *from*. Now he did, and still he stayed away. The ball was in less than a fortnight. He would arrive a day or two before and not sooner.

Scotty's latest missive apprised him of plans for the ball and recounted a fishing expedition with the children that ended in an unplanned swimming excursion as Timothy caught a fish too large for all four of them together to reel in. They never did see what it was he caught, but they did drench their clothes and cool off rather nicely.

Reginald stopped reading as his wayward mind conjured the image of Scotty emerging from the stream with her wet clothing clinging. . . .

He forced himself to read on, but it didn't help, as she wrote of how he disturbed her dreams at night and how she counted the days.

Reginald, too, counted the days, his longing mounting even as did his fear.

Susanna had an hour to herself. Lessons were of shorter duration in the summer, outings more frequent, and she had sufficiently tired the children out today so that they were now resting. Or at the least, they said they wished to rest. She suspected the boys were in the stables and Letty was huddled in some corner with her latest book.

Susanna turned her face toward the afternoon sun as she sat on the stone bench in the rose garden. The trickle of the fountain was soothing and the sound of birdsong delighted her.

Today was Thursday. He'd be home in a se'nnight— he'd said as much in yesterday's letter. And the ball was Saturday week. She would stay until the ball, and then . . .

Susanna had not yet answered his latest letter. It was becoming more and more difficult not to tell him that she loved him, especially when his letters grew warmer and warmer. He had signed this last, "Your own fond, Reginald."

She so much wanted to write "With all my love," but she did not know if he wanted to hear that. And at all events it would inordinately complicate matters. Would he understand that she had got to leave *because* she loved him?

There was another letter which she awaited, and which had not yet arrived. Her answer from her own Beachie. She needed it, watched for it, and dreaded it. For it would finalize her plans to leave.

The sound of Letty's light footfall on the gravel path stirred her from her reverie.

"Beachie! I am so very sorry to disturb you, but Mama obliged me to find you."

Susanna jumped up. "What is it, Letty? Is your mama ill?"

"No, 'tisn't Mama at all. 'Tis Angelique. She appears ill, but . . . but more than that, she cannot cease crying and . . . and Mama says she has been most distracted of late."

"Well, then, we must see to her straightaway, musn't we," Susanna said briskly, taking Letty by the hand and leading her back down the path.

But Letty stopped her for a moment. "Beachie, I

think you should speak with Angelique alone."

"Why is that, Letty?" Susanna asked curiously.

"Well, you may be sure I do not know what it is ails her but I, ah, I am persauded it has something to do with Martinez."

"Martinez! Why ever should you say that?" Susanna tried to keep her voice calm. The child was rather too perceptive for her own good.

Letty cocked her head. "I really cannot say, Beachie, except that she gets a certain look in her eye when his name is mentioned. Rather like the way you look when someone mentions . . . Reggie."

Oh, Lord, thought Susanna. She'd known for days that she'd have to speak to Letty sometime soon, but she'd been putting it off. Now, however, she felt obliged to speak. And she must remember that Letty, while a child, was more adult than Phoebe some of the time. She took both of Letty's hands and gazed earnestly into her brown eyes.

"Letty dear, attend me, please. Martinez and Angelique aside—well, I will see about her in a moment's time—but that aside, you must understand about the duke and me. We . . . we are . . . friends, my dear, and that is all. That is all we shall ever be, even if . . . if you might fancy you have cause to think otherwise. You must contrive to remember that he is the duke of Milburne and I am the governess."

Letty's lips curled in a subtle gesture that Susanna knew would someday have men falling at her feet. "You must think Reggie a great fool, Beachie," she said, and then skipped off, leaving Susanna staring openmouthed after her.

She found Angelique in the duchess's dressing room with Her Grace, Phoebe, and an upstairs maid hovering over her. Very gently, Susanna disengaged a tearful Angelique from the baffled, overset group and led her upstairs to Susanna's own rooms. She sat Angelique down on the sofa and put her arm about her.

"Tell me, Angelique, what is wrong. Perhaps I can help," Susanna said softly.

Angelique sniffled into an already wet cotton handkerchief. "No one can help me, mademoiselle. I shall be turned off and—"

"Of course, you shan't. The duchess would not—"

"She will have to, mademoiselle. You see I—" her voice dropped to a whisper and her eyes welled up anew—"I am with child."

Susanna supposed she ought to be shocked. Any maiden would be. Except that she had dealt with similar situations any number of times, with the maids and village girls at home. And the shock then had not been that the girls were increasing, but that several claimed her own father was responsible, and she'd known it for the truth!

And so she very calmly asked Angelique if she'd written to inform Martinez.

"No! Oh, I could not! He—"

"He might be rather pleased, Angelique, you know."

"No! He must not know! He will . . . will . . ."

"What? Surely you do not think he will cast you off?"

Angelique shook her head and straightened her shoulders. "No. He is a very good man. He will feel obliged to marry me, and I could not do that to him. He is not a man disposed to marry. I know—"

"Angelique. My own dear governess, Bea—,ah, Bertie, always used to say that no man is disposed to marry until he meets the right woman. I do not know Martinez's mind, but I do know you must give him the

315

choice. It is his child, as well, after all."

The little dark-haired maid smiled tremulously. "Very well, Mademoiselle Beacham. You . . . you will not tell the duchess?"

Susanna shook her head and inquired if Angelique was ill. Only in the early mornings, the maid informed her, and Susanna promised to ensure that Angelique was able to rest in the mornings. "An upstairs maid can bring Her Grace's chocolate, after all, and she does not require her toilette all that early."

That settled, and a calmer Angelique dispatched with a hug, Susanna sat down at her desk to write to Reginald.

"Martinez, what is it? You haven't said a word this half-hour past and you're nervous as a ninnynammer. 'Tis a wonder you haven't sliced my face with that razor!" Reginald declared as his valet slipped him into his coat of navy blue superfine.

Martinez sighed heavily and apologized. "'Tis only that I have not had a letter. It is at least a se'nnight now. Something is wrong, I can feel it."

Reginald clapped his hand on his friend's shoulder. "I am sorry, Martinez. But we will be home in a few days' time."

Martinez nodded and said hesitantly, "The, ah, Señorita Sco—ah, Beacham—she does not write that anything is amiss?"

Reginald smiled and shook his head. "Only that Oswald Hastings is still dangling after Phoebe and that Lady Craddock had to be talked out of having live swans in large copper tubs at the ball."

Martinez chuckled and turned his attention to His

316

Grace's hairbrushes.

It was later that morning that Scotty's letter came. Its tone was warm and filled him with longing, and funny, as always, as she recounted the latest antics of his ramshackle household. But on the last page she grew serious.

I do not know if it is my place to tell you this, my dear Reginald, but I would feel remiss did I not. I know how close you are to Martinez. You must decide whether to relate this to him or have him wait until Angelique tells him herself, as I have persuaded her she needs must do. She is increasing, Reginald, and quite distraught at the thought that Martinez might feel obliged to marry her. I have calmed her and seen to it that she rests in the mornings, when she is a bit unwell. But Martinez mustn't worry, as I believe she is in excellent health.

I am counting the days, Reginald, until you return.

Your own,
Scotty

A whistle escaped Reginald's lips as he held the missive in his left hand and tapped it with his right. He thought he knew what Martinez would do, but of course, it was the man's choice. So, Martinez's presentiment had been correct. Reginald wondered, not for the first time, if there were some gypsy blood in the fellow. He gazed pensively at that last page, and then rose quickly and made his way upstairs.

"Scotty has written something that may be of interest to you, old chap," Reginald said to Martinez.

"You will oblige me by not reading the closing," he added as he handed the last page to his valet.

They were in the duke's dressing room, and Reginald sat down on the velvet wing chair to await Martinez's reaction. He watched the Spaniard's face go rigid, then narrow in concern, and finally break out into a grin of pure joy. And suddenly Reginald felt, once again, that heretofore unaccustomed pang of envy.

"I . . . Don Reinaldo . . . she . . . she's . . ." he sputtered.

"Yes, I know, old chap," the duke murmured, his lips curling.

And then Martinez, the grin on his face becoming rather more pronounced, sank down onto the sofa and stared off into space. At which point Reginald slipped Scotty's letter from his hand and left his valet alone.

It was after luncheon that Martinez sought the duke out in his study. "I would like your permission to wed with Angelita," Martinez said without preamble.

Reginald smiled and came round the desk to shake Martinez's hand. "You do not need *my* permission, Martinez. You are free to do as you please. You always have been."

"I know that, *amigo mío,* but you see, I would like to continue in your service. Although I am afraid that Angelita will not be able to continue as—"

"I daresay not," Reginald countered. "A pregnant lady's maid would have a rather hard time with the duchess's more voluminous gowns, wouldn't she?" He watched Martinez color and, thoroughly enjoying himself, went to the cabinet to pour two glasses of brandy. He sat down in the plush leather armchair and gestured Martinez to the sofa. "But do not tease yourself, for of a certain Her Grace will find a

318

replacement. As for you, Martinez, I should think your duties as valet would conflict with your duties as a husband and father. As, for instance, when I am required to leave the Hall to go about my business. I'm afraid I should take rather a dim view of traveling with all the accoutrements of babies, old fellow."

Martinez grew pale and the duke went on imperturbably. "All this racketing about the country simply won't do, now that you are bent on leg-shackling yourself, *amigo*. Besides, I have long thought that concerning yourself with the cut of my coats and the folds in my cravats does not begin to tap your abilities." Martinez made a grumble of protest but the duke silenced him with a raised hand. "I do remember our days on the Peninsula, old chap. You could have run Wellington's headquarters with your eyes closed. I think it high time I availed myself of your many hidden talents."

Reginald rose and went to the window, then turned to face Martinez. "You may be aware," he said, "of my growing problem with Carleton. It is long past time I pensioned him off. But 'tis so hard to find a competent, trustworthy steward, one capable of administering the extensive Milburne lands."

"Oh, but I could not, Don Reinaldo. I—"

"You can and you will," the duke said sternly, then added, "Of course, my steward will need his own cottage, close to the Hall and large enough for the growing family I do not doubt he will have in short order."

At that point Martinez finally smiled and came forward to engulf the duke quite unceremoniously in a great bear hug.

"We can leave on the morrow instead of Wednesday,

if you like," Reginald offered when they had each remembered their dignity once again.

"No, Don Reinaldo. I can wait. It is only one day more."

"Ah, but I think, my friend, that *I* have waited long enough."

And so it was that at teatime on Wednesday, one day earlier than expected, the duke's two gold-crested traveling coaches pulled up before his stately Palladian home in Devon. Reginald jumped from the coach and strode toward the stairs of the great portico. He expected Martinez to follow, as eager as his valet was to enter the house. But when he turned back, he saw Martinez was already instructing the footmen about the luggage, which had traveled in the second coach.

"Martinez," the duke called from the foot of the horseshoe staircase, "I do believe you are needed inside."

Underwood, who'd just come down the stairs, was in the midst of a very proper though effusive greeting, and Reginald, smiling, cut him off and asked him to see to the unloading of the luggage.

The butler's mouth quite gaped open in most unbutlerlike fashion at this request, and it remained open as duke and valet bounded up the staircase and into the Hall.

Martinez disappeared into the nether regions immediately, and Reginald made straight for the Blue Saloon. He did not even take time to remove his travel-stained clothes. He had to see her first, and besides, Martinez was otherwise occupied.

He stood on the threshold and let his eyes sweep the

room before anyone saw him. They alighted straightaway on Scotty. She looked beautiful, dressed in the same midnight blue dress she'd worn the first time he'd seen her. He felt his body warm immediately. She did not see him, but held out her cup, and he realized that his mother was just now pouring out. Which meant the hour for tea was just beginning. Blast! And what was worse, he realized as soon as he dragged his eyes from Scotty, was that they had company. Lady Craddock, Elsie, the major, and Oswald Hastings. Good God! He'd never extricate Scotty from this.

Suddenly she looked up and her eyes met his. He felt a jolt all the way across the room. It was as if a huge magnet were pulling them together. His mouth went dry and his hands became clammy. Her cup rattled in her saucer. Good, he thought. She felt it too.

He schooled his expression to one of mild interest and strolled into the room. He endured the greetings, the exclamations of surprise at his unexpectedly early arrival, and allowed himself to be seated and served. Conversation buzzed around him; he had no idea how he responded to the questions asked of him. Scotty said not a word. She tried, once, to lift her teacup to her lips, but it shook too much and she placed cup and saucer down on the sofa table. She sat across from him; he dared not meet her eyes. He forced himself to survey the room. Elsie and Major Hayes sat on the blue damask loveseat, quite oblivious to anyone else. No doubt about the way the wind sat in that corner.

Lady Craddock and the duchess prattled endlessly about the ball, and Phoebe and Oswald Hastings sat on the other loveseat. Oswald had moved several inches away from her, but still sat too close. Reginald would have to speak to Scotty about that. Letty sat in the powder blue Hepplewhite chair, ostensibly concentrating on her cherry tart. But her eyes kept flitting between Reginald and . . . and Scotty! He watched the expression, the secret smile, on his little sister's face. Good God! he thought. She knows! Of all this company, of all this ramshackle household, Letty was the only one who knew, excepting Martinez, of course. Reginald was not sure whether to be pleased or horrified.

His eyes sought Scotty again. He ached for her; he had got to get her alone. Very deliberately, he set his cup down and put his hand to his temple. He waited a few moments until Letty piped up, "Reggie! Are you feeling quite the thing?"

Good girl, he thought, and then looked at her sharply. Just how much *did* she know?

"Reggie?" his mother inquired solicitously. "Have you the headache again?"

Slowly he rose. "I fear so, Mother. If you would excuse me, ladies and gentlemen . . ."

"Of course, dear," the duchess clucked. He took two steps toward the door. "Be sure and have Martinez prepare his secret remedy for you."

Really, it was simpler than he'd thought. "Of course, Mother. Oh, but I do not believe Martinez is available just now. Ah, Miss Beacham, did he not explain to you about his special remedy?" he asked nonchalantly.

Scotty rose to the occasion. "Why, yes, he did." She turned to the duchess and Lady Craddock, who were regarding her with some curiosity. "My poor dear aunt suffers wretchedly from megrims, you must know, and I finally prevailed upon Martinez to reveal his little secret." She smiled mischievously. "But you mustn't ask me, for I'm sworn to silence," she added and exited in Reginald's wake.

322

They did not speak as they walked down the corridor. He did not touch her, kept a good six inches between them. He couldn't very well take her to his bedchamber, supposed headache or no, and so led her instead round the corner to his study. He ushered her inside and firmly closed the door behind them.

She glided to the center of the room and whirled round to face him. He let his eyes sweep her length, drinking in the sight of her. The thick, smooth auburn hair, the finely arched brows, the creamy skin and deep blue eyes. The lush figure clearly, beautifully outlined in the midnight blue dress. He did not trouble to keep the hunger from his eyes, and he saw an answering longing in hers.

"Scotty," he rasped. She took a step forward, tentatively. Then another.

"Reginald, I . . ." she began, and then slowly, calmly, she walked into his arms. He crushed her to him, afraid to let her go. A rush of feelings assailed him, desire only one of them. He felt tenderness as well, and protectiveness, joy, and peacefulness all at once. Most of all, he felt as if he'd come home. It was no longer Milburne Hall which gave him that feeling, nor his family. It was Scotty.

He held her tightly, her face pressed to his shoulder, his hand splayed across her back. He felt her warmth, her softness, and inhaled the scent of jasmine, the scent that haunted his waking hours, even as her image haunted his dreams. And then, very gently, he took her face in his hands. He gazed at her in wonder and he knew. He loved her. Against all odds, he loved her.

He brought his lips close to hers but then hesitated. It was different somehow, knowing he loved her. He had never before felt unsure of himself with a woman. Now, suddenly, he did. He searched her eyes, wondering if she felt what he did. She was gazing at him intently, her eyes unfathomable pools of deep blue. Her lips parted slightly and he saw that they trembled.

And then, finally, he kissed her. What was meant as a gentle kiss exploded the moment their lips touched. Suddenly, there was no gentleness, only fire and longing as he pulled her close and crushed his mouth to hers.

Susanna melted the moment his lips came down onto hers. She felt his longing and answered it with her own, letting her hands come up to clasp his neck even as her mouth opened to his seeking tongue. His hands caressed her sides, her back, her hips, and she moaned deep in her throat.

And then, suddenly, he broke the contact of their lips and pressed her face into his strong shoulder. Her hands slipped around his waist and she held him as he stroked her hair with one hand, her back with the other. She could feel his heartbeat racing as rapidly as hers and knew he was trying to calm them both.

Slowly the heat of passion was replaced by a gentle warmth, and Susanna breathed deeply, evenly. It felt so wonderful, so . . . so right to be in his arms like this. He'd held her before, kissed her before, but there was something different about today. There was a new underlying tenderness in his touch. She recalled the way he'd gazed at her a few moments ago, and suddenly she knew that he'd truly come to care for her. And that only made it more difficult.

She fought back the tears that threatened to spill out. There was such a bittersweet joy in being here with him. She must concentrate on the joy; they would only have a few more days. Now, more than ever, she was determined to leave. There was no future for them, and the present was fraught with peril.

Martinez ran Angelita to ground amid a pile of lingerie in the duchess's dressing room. She was sitting on a stool, deftly plying a needle. At the sight of him she gasped, went pale and jumped up.

"Martinez!" she exclaimed in a startled whisper, the lacy confection she was mending falling unheeded to the floor.

"Francisco," he corrected firmly, and strode forward. He stood before her, not touching her. "You stopped writing," he said.

"I—I was much . . . occupied." She twisted her hands nervously at her waist.

"I see. You are too thin."

"I . . . I have not been hungry."

He stared at her, his mouth set grimly. Why would she not tell him? It was his child, too! Why was she silent? He wanted to shake her. He wanted to grab her and hold her close. He stood with his fists clenched at his sides, waiting. Waiting for her to speak. To trust him enough to tell him.

But the silence stretched out between them. And then he looked into her eyes. He saw the fear, the despair, and was suddenly furious with himself. She had suffered enough, and he was making it worse.

"Angelita," he said very gently, and moved to take her in his arms. But she jumped back and turned away.

"You . . . you had better go now, Francisco. I have much work to do," she said quietly. So stubborn, he thought, and proud. He came up behind her and lightly clasped her shoulders.

"And what will you do when you can no longer work, Angelita?" he whispered into her ear, and felt her entire body stiffen. Very slowly he turned her round.

She stared at him, wide-eyed, terrified. He kept his hands on her shoulders. "You little fool," he said with a half-smile. "You did not write. You will not tell me. Did you think I would not find out?"

She was shaking her head, fighting back tears. "How . . . I . . . I did not want you to feel obligated. I will be leaving here soon and—"

"Obligated? Leaving?" he nearly shouted. "What nonsense do you speak, Angelita? You are not going anywhere! Obligated? Of course I am obligated! A man is always obligated to the ones he loves."

"L-Loves? But you . . . you cannot love me, Francisco. You hardly know me. And . . . and I am French! I will not let you sacrifice—"

"You will have little choice in the matter," he said firmly. "We will be married within the fortnight." He stopped, seeing her stormy expression, and smiled down at her. "Angelita, once before I lost everything, everyone that I loved. Must I lose it all again? Will you deny me your love and the pleasure of watching my child grow? Can it be that you care so little that—"

"Oh, Francisco!" she cried, and threw herself into his arms. He held her tightly as she wept. At length she sniffed back the tears and mumbled, "I have been so frightened, and Mademoiselle Beacham said I must tell you, but I . . . I . . ."

He took her face in his hands. "If you ever again keep secrets from me, I shall beat you," he warned, his voice soft.

Her hand came up to clasp his wrist. "Forgive me, *mon amour*. But you see, I was frightened for you as well. I do not want you to lose your place."

"That has all been taken care of, little one. I will explain it all later," he answered, and drew her closer, his hands now closing about her shoulders.

"But—"

"Later," he repeated, and bent to kiss her.

After several minutes he raised his head. "Come with me now, Angelita, upstairs," he said quietly.

"Now? B-but I must work, and . . . and you must unpack for the duke! Besides, it is the middle of the day! We could not possibly—"

"Don Reinaldo does not expect to see me for quite some time. And we most certainly can." He grinned at her. "It is time, I think, for you to learn how to be an obedient wife. Do you walk or do I carry you?"

"I . . . I walk," she replied, and blushingly took his hand.

It was in the Blue Saloon before dinner that Reginald was able to take a really good look at Phoebe. He did not like what he saw. She was glowing a bit too much. There was a look about her eyes, a softness to her lips. Why, she looked as if she'd just recently been thoroughly kissed!

He contrived a moment alone with Scotty. "What the devil's been going on between Oswald and Phoebe? They looked too damned much in each other's pocket this afternoon! And now . . . well . . . I cannot like what I see."

If he was hoping Scotty would dispel his uneasiness, he was disappointed, for she merely nodded in concern and said that she would speak to him about it after dinner. And then she smiled at his mother as the duchess glided over to ask Reginald whether the Regent had yet gone to Brighton.

Dinner would have been interminable had Scotty not caught his eyes numerous times and shared his amusement over his mother's and sister's account of the ball preparations. He nearly choked on his wine as Phoebe recounted Lady Craddock's disappointment when it was decided that the live camels and snakes simply would not work. And he almost spilled his claret as the duchess casually mentioned the dozen swans that Lady Craddock had sent over, so everyone could see how they would grace the ballroom.

"I own I was quite taken with them, Reginald dear," his mama said between delicate forkfuls of salmon mousse, "but dear Beachie pointed out that they do tend to squawk noisily in crowds, and have been known to bite."

"Yes, but they would have been so lovely, swimming in their copper tubs, and that nice man would have stayed with them, Mama, keeping them in place," Phoebe put in.

"Yes, well, 'tis a pity, Phoebe, but it simply would not answer," the duchess countered. "Actually, Reggie, 'twas Timothy who finally convinced me. For he reminded me, dear boy that he is, that swans do fly and they *could* escape their tubs. And then they might walk about and, well, he said, they do tend to leave rather nasty little packages behind them. Rather like horses, you must know, but much smaller, of course. Still, it would be rather unpleasant, I daresay, for ladies do wear such delicate sandals to balls, do they not?"

At that point Reginald did spill his claret, all over the white damask cloth. Dinner could not end soon enough.

He declined to drink his port and went straightaway into the family drawing room with the ladies. And finally, after coffee and polite leave-takings, he was able to usher Phoebe and his mama out. He closed the door and turned back to Scotty.

He knew immediately that it was a mistake to be here with her, alone. The candlelight danced across her face, making her skin seem fragile, so delicate, irresistible. Her deep green evening dress shimmered over her body and there was just enough décolletage to make him swallow hard.

Still, it could not be helped. He left half the width of the room between them and asked her, once more, about Phoebe.

Susanna sighed, knowing she would have to tell him, hoping he would remain calm when she did. Her eyes swept over him, and she was glad he was keeping his distance. She found his nearness all too disconcerting. Tonight he wore a beautifully cut charcoal gray coat, and white knee breeches stretched very tightly across his powerful thighs. Susanna felt her face flush and forced her eyes back up to his face.

His brow lifted at her scrutiny and she was chagrinned to realize that he was regarding her with some amusement. Nervously she rose and moved to stand at the back of the sofa.

"Phoebe?" he prompted. She turned round to face him.

"Yes, of course. Phoebe. I, ah, I fear you will not like it above half, Reginald. You see, yesterday, some instinct sent me in search of her. I have been attempting to, ah, keep apprised of her whereabouts, you must know, as your mama has been . . . well . . ."

"I understand, Scotty. Go on." He was standing

straight, his hands behind his back. She tried to ignore how handsome he looked, the strong planes of his face illuminated by the candlelight.

"Yes, well, I found her in the gardens. Or rather, I overheard her conversing with Oswald and I, er, eavesdropped." She paused, her chin raised a trifle.

But Reginald did not take her to task. Rather he strolled to within three feet of her and said quietly, "I did not assign you an easy task, did I? Pray continue, my dear."

She tried to ignore the warmth of his gray eyes and took a step back. "Phoebe was saying something on the order of, 'You know how much I dearly wish it, Oswald. But the duke is away, and you needs must apply to him for permission.'"

"Good God!" Reginald exclaimed. "The blackguard offered for her, didn't he?"

"I fear so, Reginald. He replied that of course he meant to speak to you, but that he loved her and wanted to be certain she returned his regard. He said he hoped they might be married by September."

"September! I'll see him in Hell first! Trifling with the emotions of a young innocent! Why, she's barely out of the schoolroom! I hope you sent him to the rightabout!"

"Well," she began slowly, "I could not see them, you must know, and then they were silent for a time and . . ."

His eyes flashed, and she reached out to put a calming hand on his sleeve. "You may be sure I intervened at that moment. He *was* kissing her, but not the way . . . that is it . . . it seemed to me a rather, ah, chaste kiss, you must know."

"I see," Reginald murmured, much amused. So,

Scotty knew the difference in kisses now, did she?

She removed her hand from his arm; he immediately drew it back and covered it with his own. "Pray go on, Scotty. *Did* you put a flea in his ear?"

Scotty took a deep breath and said in a rush, "I told Oswald that you would return shortly and would be most happy to receive him and listen to his suit."

"You did *what?*" he exploded, dropping her hand and clenching his fists at his sides.

She raised her chin again. "We did agree, did we not, not to precipitate any rash and ruinous action on their part? And you may be sure I admonished him that any improprieties would of a certain *not* advance his suit."

Reginald stormed several feet away, then whirled to face her. He ran a hand through his hair. "I do not believe I'm hearing this! Have you gone mad? To encourage—"

"I did *not* encourage him, Reginald!" she exclaimed, her blue eyes glittering. "I merely fobbed him off!"

"Hah! You all but gave him permission to pay his addresses to her! You have overstepped yourself, ma'am!" he shouted.

"Blether!" she retorted, sashaying toward him with a hand on one hip. Amazing that she refused to be cowed. "I wouldna dream of so usurping yer position, Yer Grace! In truth, 'tis a great favor I've done ye. I make no doubt Oswald will apply to ye straightaway, and ye have only to hold him off until after the ball. By then I warrant Phoebe will have changed her mind."

"I would not wager a groat on that, Scotty. Phoebe can be very stubborn. 'Twould have been far better had you sent Oswald away with his tail between his legs and confined Phoebe to her room."

Her hand went to her bosom in dramatic astonish-

331

ment. "I? Surely I havena the authority to do such, Reginald." She was toying with him. He wanted to strangle her, and kiss her, all at once. He loved the way her eyes flashed, and the way she slipped into Scots, especially when she was the least bit excited. "But do *ye* send them to the rightabout, then. Of course, I daresay they'll hightail it off to Gretna Green at first light. Do ye fancy a trip to Gretna just now, Reginald?" she asked ingenuously, fluttering her luxurious lashes.

Yes, he thought suddenly, wish you, my little Scottish lassie. "Obviously, I do not with to precipitate an elopement, Scotty." He sighed, suddenly remembering the earl of Ainsley's story of his ward and what happened when he did not follow Amanda's advice. Perhaps Scotty *was* right. At all events the ball was only three days hence. They would simply have to wait upon events.

And so he told Scotty, who smiled sweetly and said she knew he'd made the right decision.

He grinned down at her and shook his head. She was doing it again. Maneuvering him, contriving matters so that he had virtually no choice, and then making it seem as if 'twere all his idea at first stop. And strangely enough, he didn't mind at all. Especially since he knew he could put his foot down did he believe himself right. As it was, he was willing to allow that she might, after all, have acted correctly.

"Of course, my dear," he finally said.

She cocked her head, her lips pursed in suppressed merriment. Life with Scotty, he thought suddenly, would never be dull.

His eyes swept over her. She looked, in a word, delicious. The creamy skin of her bare shoulders and throat gleamed in the candlelight. Her bosom and rounded hips pressed against the fabric of her dress, and he itched to trace her contours with his hands. He raised his eyes once more to her face. Her beautiful, beloved face. He felt a surge of longing which he tried to control. No, life with Scotty would never be dull. And life without her was unthinkable.

He knew it, had known it from the moment he'd seen her that very afternoon. He swallowed hard, the ramifications of what he was thinking just beginning to hit him. He would not say anything to her yet; he must come to terms himself with all that it meant.

"Reginald?" she inquired softly, reaching her hand out and then abruptly withdrawing it.

The urge to touch her was too great. Unceremoniously, he pulled her into his arms. "Ah, Scotty," he said laughing, "even arguing with you is a joy. However could I have stayed away so long?" He kissed the top of her head and wrapped his arms round her back. She tried to lift her head, but he pushed her face down onto his shoulder. "No, stay, love. I only mean to hold you. I shan't even kiss you—I do not trust myself." When she would have spoken he did not let her, merely held her until her hands crept round to clasp his waist. And then he tightened his hold, pulled her yet closer, and felt the warmth of a deep, harmonious unspoken communication.

Chapter 18

All the next day Reginald resisted the urge to seek a private interview with Scotty. For much as he wished to see her alone, to touch her, he had as yet no idea what to say to her. And so he spent Thursday, the day after his arrival, alternately pacing the corridors of his ancestral home, making feeble attempts to deal with the correspondence that had accumulated in his absence, and thinking. But most of all, he watched her.

It was two days before the ball. The household was all at sixes and sevens. He could not imagine it getting any worse, although he knew that in the next two days it would.

And in the center of it all was Scotty. He watched her flit back and forth from schoolroom to ballroom to kitchens. In the kitchens she made order out of chaos. Mrs. Rackett, skillet in hand, had the poor French caterer in a quake with her dire warnings about Horatio and evil spells. And the kitchen maids and caterer's men were ranged on opposite sides of the huge butcher-block table, arguing about who would make the eel soup and whether there was to be orange trifle or clotted cream and lemon curd for dessert.

Mrs. Longbotham bellowed for silence from her stance before the hearth, and Underwood, standing next to her, clapped his hands and cleared his throat imperiously. Both were ignored. In a far corner one of the men had waylaid one of the maids, who did not seem to mind at all.

Reginald lounged, unnoticed, in the doorway and watched Scotty survey the chaos and sashay around the room, talking quietly to this one and that. The noise level did not abate, however, and he wondered what she would do next. His eyes widened as she grabbed a kettle and wooden spoon, pushed through the crowd and actually climbed atop the butcher-block table! His mouth fell open as she banged the kettle with the spoon and shouted for silence.

In a moment she had it and handed down the kettle and spoon. She remained where she was, however, and though he thought it a most undignified position, her voice when she spoke held all the dignity and imperiousness of . . . of a duchess. She began by reassuring the French caterer that Horatio had been locked in the stables and explained to Cook that of course she would prepare all the Devonshire specialties. Cook beamed. Monsieur Alphonse would have charge of the "foreign foods," Scotty said, such as *les poulardes à la Périgueux,* and *le potage d'orge perlée à la Crécy.* As there were a great many more "foreign foods" on the menu than aught else, Monsieur Alphonse was quite mollified. Then Scotty neatly recalled the couple from the corner and gently admonished the young man to do his courting on his own time. Everyone began to go about the business of the day, and as Underwood patted Mrs. Longbotham's arm consolingly, she too was content.

Monsieur Alphonse gallantly assisted Scotty down from her perch, then turned back to the hearth. It was as she was shaking out her skirts that she looked up and met Reginald's eyes. He grinned at her and silently clapped his hands, before he disappeared into the shadows. This time, he saw, it was Scotty whose mouth was open.

If she brought order out of chaos belowstairs, she brought chaos into order in the ballroom. His mama was calmly directing two florid, rather rotund delivery men in the placement of what looked to Reginald's disbelieving eyes like Greek statues. They had already placed several—Zeus, Artemis, and Aphrodite, he guessed—in rather odd stances in the center of the ballroom. Several maids were following with bolts of sheer flowing fabric which they laced round the top of each statue to connect them. Dancers would either have to dip or be decapitated. Reginald was fairly certain he could lay this bit of flummery at Lady Craddock's door and was most relieved when Scotty swept into the room. She did not notice him standing at one of the windows.

In her wake tumbled Thomas, Timothy, Desdemona, and the red ball. They immediately began a game of tag, darting between the various statues and the huge potted palms being set up by the footmen. The red ball suddenly flew across the room and landed in a potted palm. Desdemona flew after it and landed on the bow of Artemis.

Scotty nonchalantly plucked the ball down and sent the children to a far corner of the huge room with the admonition to roll the ball, not throw it. Reginald, who on behalf of the priceless chandeliers was much relieved, did not even consider the absurdity of the children being here at first stop. He turned his attention to Scotty, who was complimenting his mama on the wonderful job she was doing and suggesting that she take a much-needed rest to preserve the beautiful color in her cheeks. And once the duchess was gone, Scotty rolled up her sleeves and began. Within minutes, she had workmen moving every statue, had the bolts of fabric floating to the sidelines. The potted palms were up and moving as well. They collided several times with the statues and became entwined with yards of silk chiffon.

Scotty remained unruffled and Reginald was reminded of her comment about creativity thriving in chaos. When finally she espied him she smiled and glided to the window, all the while gesturing to the maids and workmen.

"Mount Olympus?" he inquired wryly.

She smiled ruefully. "Well, at the least the statues do not fly about and squawk, or leave nasty . . . ah, well, at all events, this was the least of the evils, believe me. I do wish I'd been able to talk the duchess and Lady Craddock out of the Parthenon, however."

"The Parthenon?" He was almost afraid to ask.

She sighed and then her eyes twinkled. "Aye. 'Twill be arriving on the morrow. 'Tis for the orchestra, ye ken."

"Ah. I see. Come here, Scotty." Gently he drew her closer.

"Reginald, please," she whispered, alarmed, "there are people—"

"You've a smudge on you cheek," he said softly, and proceeded to brush it away. He felt the heat between them, even with just the slight contact.

"Th-Thank ye," she said breathlessly, her deep blue eyes locking with his, and he knew she'd felt it, too.

Not thirty minutes after she'd arrived, Scotty left the ballroom, Timothy, Thomas, Desdemona and the red ball in tow. He stayed a moment to survey the room and smiled with pleasure. It looked lovely, if a bit unusual. The statues now stood at the sidelines, forming, with the draped chiffon and the help of the potted palms, graceful arches that looked like they hid gardens beyond. Knowing that the flowers were yet to arrive, he thought they might well do so. He found he couldn't wait to see what Scotty did with the flowers.

Scotty. Pensively, Reginald left the ballroom and made his way to his study. He poured some brandy and sank into his deep leather sofa. She would never be conventional. She would never mind sacrificing a bit of her dignity for a kitten under a sofa or peace in the kitchens. She would disobey him when it suited her and flare with anger when his will prevailed. But she would run his household like a charm—devil take it, she was already doing so! She would be a wonderful mother, a gracious hostess, a true lady bountiful to the tenants. She would be everything a duchess of Milburne needs must be, and so much more.

For she would be his wife, his laughing companion, his warm and loving bedmate. He'd never quite known what he wanted in a wife, but now he did. One word— Scotty. He wanted Scotty.

And Ainsley was right. He didn't give a damn where she'd come from. He simply could not live without her. Society, however, might well give a damn. Scotty was every inch a lady, and his own title would confer upon her its own mantle of status. But still there were those high sticklers who might find it difficult to accept the daughter of some obscure Scottish laird or parson or whatever into their circle. However, his mama still held a great deal of power in society. So did he, for that matter. And Scotty herself could charm most anyone round her finger. Except, perhaps some vengeful mama who'd had her eye on the ducal coronet for her own daughter. He did not suppose that would trouble Scotty overmuch; of a certain it would not signify to him.

No, he thought. Society was not the problem. It was Scotty. He thought he knew her heart. She revealed it with her eyes and her body. But he did not know her mind. She might well love him, but he did not know if she would marry him. There was fear in her; there were secrets that he would have to fathom. Not, he realized, to ease his own mind, but to ease hers. He would choose his moment well, and then he would speak.

It was at tea that Reginald learned that Oswald Hastings had been invited to dine that evening. He was not best pleased and glowered at Scotty from across the room. She smiled placatingly back at him, and he thought he'd like to throttle her. But considering the plans he had for her, he knew that was not at all politic. Sometime later he heard Phoebe, with a nervous glance at him, beg of Scotty a private interview. Reginald thought he would like to be a fly on the wall during that particular discussion. But as Scotty and Phoebe left the saloon while his mother was describing her ball gown to him in excessively tedious detail, Reginald was left to grind his teeth in frustration.

"Oh, Beachie, I just know he'll never allow it," Phoebe was saying in some agitation as she paced the floor of the morning room. "He dislikes Oswald excessively."

"Now, Phoebe, you must have patience," replied Susanna, choosing her words carefully. "Oswald has not yet applied to the duke. And truly, your brother only wishes for you to meet more young men before making your choice. You are very beautiful, you know. I daresay you will become an Incomparable when you make your come-out."

Phoebe paused and cocked her head, her pretty blond ringlets dancing charmingly. "It is so good of you to say so, Beachie, and of course, I wish to have a Season. But I can be betrothed at the same time, can I not?"

"Well, I—"

"Beachie," Phoebe interrupted, coming to sit beside Susanna on the sofa and gazing at her out of limpid blue eyes, "have you never been in love?"

The question caught Susanna off guard. "Yes," she replied before she had time to dissemble. "Once," she added in a soft voice.

"I . . . I'm sorry," stammered Phoebe. "It must have been very painful for you. Oh, Beachie, don't you see, Oswald and I love each other, and Reggie dislikes him because of his family. Truly, Oswald is nothing like his father or elder brother."

Susanna knew she had got to take care about what she said. It would not do to let Phoebe know her true feelings, lest the girl cease confiding in her. "That may be, Phoebe dear, but you must own that the family coffers are low and that Oswald has been known to be in Dun territory. Not"—she held up a hand as Phoebe began to protest—"not to say that that is his reason for wishing to marry you, but you *shall* have a rather large portion, and so naturally your brother wishes to look into the matter."

"Oswald has made some very sound investments of late," Phoebe declared, her rosebud mouth pouting prettily. "We could live without my money, if need be."

Susanna's heart sank. Phoebe was eventually going to be very hurt. By Oswald Hasgings, not by the duke. But she ignored that and focused for the moment on the words "if need be." Was there a veiled threat there? "Perhaps, Phoebe," Susanna said cautiously, "but I daresay it would be excessively uncomfortable for you to be obliged to do so. And if Oswald indeed has a deep regard for you, he will certainly want to await your guardian's permission. There is no hurry, is there?"

"Why no, although Oswald—"

"And the duke has not forbidden you to see him, has he?"

"No. And I must own I am surprised, for 'twould be just like him to—"

"The duke is not an ogre, Phoebe," Susanna admonished gently.

Phoebe looked at her oddly. "Do you know, Beachie, I do believe you and Letty are the only two people in this household who are not afraid of Reggie. Excepting Martinez, of course." The girl paused and cocked her narrowed, lovely blue eyes. "You're very pretty, you know. It's a great pity that . . . well, what I mean to say is Reggie will have to marry someday, and I do so wish he could marry someone like you."

It was meant kindly, but the words cut Susanna to the quick, nonetheless. "Someone like you," Phoebe had said, for of course the duke could never marry *her*, a governess. Even Phoebe knew that. Whatever Reginald's feelings, his responsibilities would have to come first. But even if he *could* wed her, she reminded herself briskly, she was not free to marry *him*.

He'd been watching her all day. Smiling, instead of scowling. Yet he hadn't sought her out alone; he knew how dangerous it was. They could not go on in this way.

Susanna glanced at Phoebe and felt a surge of regret that she would not be here when the girl needed a shoulder to cry upon. And good Lord, what would happen if, as Reginald warned, Phoebe did not have a change of heart after the ball? Perhaps, Susanna thought, she had ought to stay a few days after the ball. Just a few.

Reginald suffered through dinner with Oswald Hastings, trying not to glower, trying to take comfort from Scotty's beatific, everything-is-going-according-to-plan smiles. He desperately wanted to see her alone, but Oswald stayed rather late and Scotty seemed tired. Which was no wonder, considering all she'd done today. It was hardly, he was well aware, the time for a declaration he was not at all certain she would want to hear.

The next day was more chaotic than Thursday had been, however, and hardly more conducive to the private discourse Reginald had in mind. Scotty was even more harried, as streams of delivery men poured in with baskets of food, the pillars of the Parthenon, and more potted palms. And in their wake came Lady Craddock quite ready to hatch a new decorating scheme at the eleventh hour. Scotty seemed unfazed by it all, but by day's end he saw her several times rubbing her neck and shoulders. He longed to do it for her, but prudence as well as the presence of his mama, Lady Craddock, Underwood, Mrs. L., Monsieur Alphonse, and numerous underservants held him back.

And then it was Saturday, the day of the infernal ball. Tonight, Reginald thought, he would dance with her. And tomorrow, he would speak.

By midmorning the harum-scarum state of the household grew too much for the duke, what with the florists running hither and yon and the caterer's men staggering under the weight of twelve-foot tables draped in lacy cloths. In the interest of self-preservation he buried himself in his study and did not emerge until it was time to dress for dinner.

Reginald took care about his toilette for the evening, choosing his favorite wine-colored coat and black knee britches. For once he did not groan with impatience when Martinez discarded the third cravat and started on the fourth.

Martinez, as was usual these last few days, went about his work with an all too smug smile that said, I've solved my problems; now, you solve yours. Well, Reginald thought, he meant to do just that, beginning with tonight.

He was relieved, as he strolled into the Blue Saloon for sherry, that the Hastingses had not been invited to dine before the ball. That far, at the least, Scotty was not willing to go. They were to be a rather intimate group, including the Craddocks, Major Hayes, Peter Fairleigh, the Reverend Honeyworth, and their south Devon neighbors, the earl and countess of Garnsworth. Lady Garnsworth was not among his mama's favorite people. But she did wield a great deal of power in the ton, having the ear of several of the patronesses of Almack's. Of a certain the Milburne name was sufficient to open all doors for Phoebe, but Reginald supposed it never hurt for a young girl making her come-out to have such an influential person in her corner. His mama, Reginald reflected, occasionally surprised him with flashes of good sense.

Reginald himself was rather ambivalent in his feelings toward the countess of Garnsworth. She was a tall, thin woman with a sharp tongue whose husband had long ago retreated into his club and his stables. The countess's judgments about people were quick and merciless, and Reginald had seen her dash a young lady's hopes with a look. On the other hand, those judgments were based not on lineage or pounds sterling, but rather on what she saw of the person standing before her. As Reginald often enough agreed with those judgments, and as he occasionally enjoyed her biting sense of humor, he was hard put to dislike her too much.

It occurred to him now that he would do well to cultivate Lady Garnsworth a bit himself and to see that she and Scotty became acquainted. Scotty had not put in an appearance yet, and so he exerted himself to charm the countess and to engage the earl in a brief but interesting discussion of horseflesh.

And then Scotty was there, poised for a moment on the threshold. With effort, Reginald finished what he was saying to Lord Garnsworth before excusing himself and taking several steps toward the door. His mouth was suddenly dry as his eyes swept over her. She wore a gown of peach satin edged at the bottom with a light wreath of flowers. It was open on the left side, draping sensuously to reveal a slip of ivory lace lined with satin. The satin rustled softly against her hips as she moved slowly toward him. The corsage of the gown was cut rather snugly, and low across the bosom. His rational sense told him there was no more of Scotty visible than there was of any other lady of ton at a London ball. But another part of him, a very fierce part, wanted to cover her up and whisk her away where he could admire her in private. Trying to ignore the warmth that swept over him, he took her hand and raised it to his lips.

"Scotty," he said in a voice too husky. "You look ravishing." Her blue eyes shone as she smiled at him, and her skin looked luminous. Her auburn hair was coiled high on her head, its only ornament two peach roses.

"Reginald," she whispered, "I have never seen you looking quite so . . . so dashing."

He grinned then, and remembering his manners, turned with Scotty to introduce her to the Garnsworths. Lord Garnsworth professed himself delighted to meet her. His wife, whose curiosity was obviously piqued by Scotty's entrance, and, Reginald supposed, his own reaction to it, was rather taken aback at being introduced to the *governess*. She masked it well, good manners coming to the fore, but she received another jolt when the duchess blithely credited Scotty with organizing much of the ball. And yet another jolt when Peter greeted Scotty much as an old friend of the family and she responded in kind. After that Lady Garnsworth seemed to watch carefully as Scotty moved about the room, and Reginald knew that for once the countess was reserving judgment.

Dinner was an unqualified success. The food, which he knew well Scotty had chosen, was delicious and the conversation flowed smoothly. His mama, as always, was a lovely if somewhat scatterbrained hostess. But dinner ran rather more according to the prescribed schedule than usual. He wondered if anyone but himself caught the eye signals flitting between the duchess and Scotty. For though his mama appeared to set the pace at dinner, in fact, it was Scotty doing so.

Phoebe, thankfully, comported herself well, and Lady Garnsworth went so far as to say she was a diamond of the first water and a pretty-behaved girl. This Reginald took to mean that the countess approved of her but was bored. The countess's sharp eye scanned the table for more interesting quarry, lighted on Elsie Craddock for a moment, dismissed her, and focused instead on Scotty. It was quite obvious to the entire company that Lord Garnsworth was taken with her. As were Reginald's friend Peter, the rector, and even the about-to-be-betrothed major. Reginald schooled himself to take it in stride. He supposed it would always happen this way and he had got to remember that it was all rather innocuous, especially since Scotty seemed not to take any of it seriously.

And the truth of it was that the major was only too happy to turn his attention to Elsie whenever politeness allowed. Even the rector kept glancing across the table at . . . well, it seemed he was watching Lady Craddock with a decided glint in his eye. And well he might, Reginald mused, and found himself wondering whether the birds in her outlandish headdress were live, and whether her gown, which looked to be composed of strips of floating chiffon, would completely unravel if one were to step on a part of the irregular train.

If Reginald viewed the dinner proceedings with equanimity, however, Lady Garnsworth was not best pleased. Scotty sat between Major Hayes and the rector, but Lord Garnsworth was near enough to converse with her, and laugh with her, as well. As Lady Garnsworth's frown deepened, Reginald's heart sank. But then Scotty, once again, amazed him. For she leaned forward to speak with the countess, who sat to the rector's right, and said, "Lady Garnsworth, I have been admiring your gown all evening." Reginald thought it a hideous shade of green. "And your coiffeur is most becoming." Reginald thought it something akin to a bird's nest. "I do wish you would share the secret of how you wrap and coil it so gracefully," Scotty bubbled. And Lady Garnsworth, whose looks clearly had always taken a backseat to her clever tongue, visibly preened and began to relax.

So much so that when the gentlemen rejoined the ladies after partaking of port and cigars, Scotty and Lady Garnsworth were deep in amiable conversation. Good Lord, Reginald thought, did Scotty wind *him* around her finger in just that way as well?

Scotty raised her eyes for a moment and he caught the gleam of mischief in them, and answered it with one of his own. So, he thought, she knew exactly what she was doing. And she *would* do it to him as well, but only, of course, when he allowed it.

Reginald opened the ball by dancing with Phoebe and then relinquished her to a growing cadre of admirers. His sister looked charming in a pale pink and lace confection of a gown, her blond hair caught in ringlets and her pale blue eyes sparkling. He sincerely hoped the young swains signing her dance card would keep her too busy to spend overmuch time with Oswald Hastings. Hastings stood to the side, drink in hand, glowering at the group surrounding Phoebe.

Susanna was enjoying herself hugely. She'd been

hostess in her father's house often enough, albeit not at so grand an affair as this, not to be fazed by the dozens of little tasks that required her attention. Nor was she fazed by the occasional snide snippets of conversation that floated to her ears.

"I do not know who she is, my dear Alicia, but 'tis a deep game she is playing. You may depend upon it, no governess of *my* acquaintance ever looked like that, nor comported herself half so prettily," she heard one woman say.

"Much too coming for a governess," sniffed another lady disdainfully.

The gentlemen, however, put themselves forth to be charming, dancing and flirting with her. A few importuned her insolently, but most treated her with a respect they might not ordinarily afford a mere governess. That, she knew, was because Reginald and the duchess had made clear it was what they expected. She smiled a bit sadly. The Ayres treated her as one of the family. They had from the very beginning, and that would make it all the more difficult for her to leave.

But she refused to dwell on that now. Now she let her eyes drift about the room. It looked quite beautiful, the gracefully draped statues and the plethora of flowers serving as a backdrop to the elegantly clad guests. Dozens of lights twinkled in the magnificent crystal chandeliers and even the orchestra looked resplendent, perched upon Lady Craddock's "Parthenon."

Sir Randolph Somebody-Or-Other was at this very moment trying to persuade Susanna to take a turn about the garden with him. But before she could formulate a reply, the first strains of a waltz issued forth from the "Parthenon."

Reginald strode across the ballroom toward Scotty.

The crowd seemed to part for him, and whispered voices drifted in the air.

"Why, I do believe he means to dance with her!" came one disbelieving voice.

"With the *governess?* I own I can hardly credit it!" came another.

"My dears," purred a rather haughty voice, "You may be sure she is *no* governess, and obviously the duke knows it."

"But who is she, then? Not a French émigré, I daresay. She doesn't sound French at all, does she?" was the ingenuous reply.

The duke registered the words at the back of his mind; he would deal with them later. For they reminded him that somehow Scotty's background would have to be established suitably to satisfy the ton. If, that is, he cared to retain his place in society. He gazed now at Scotty as she stood several yards in front of him, her beautiful eyes gazing expectantly at him. And he knew without doubt that all of society could go to the devil if he could but have her for his own. Slowly, he moved forward.

She watched him come to her, watched the crowd part, heard the excited murmur of voices. But she could not distinguish any words; her attention was focused entirely on Reginald.

He looked every inch the duke, his tall, broad frame encased in a magnificent claret-colored coat, his muscular thighs clearly outlined in his tight black satin knee britches. She felt herself quiver and raised her eyes to his face. How handsome he was, how strong the planes of his face, she thought. His gray eyes were intent on her, his square jaw set with determination. She felt her pulse race and he extended his hand to her.

And when she placed her hand in his, there was a sudden, charged silence all around them. In the next moment he pulled her into his arms and spun her into the dance.

Was it her imagination, or did the crowd fall back to give them more room? She felt as if she were floating in his arms, and all others had ceased to exist. She was aware only of Reginald and herself and the music. Neither of them spoke. He pulled her closer, his large hand firm at her back as he pressed her body to his. He smiled down at her, a secret smile of future promise. There *was* no future, she knew it all too well, but she refused to think about that. She would not think at all. Instead she smiled back, reveling in the heady pleasure of being held in Reginald's strong arms.

He pushed her head gently onto his shoulder and increased their pace in time with the music. His thighs brushed against her each time they turned with the dance; his chest was firm and hard. Her mouth went dry; her body felt overwarm. And when he slowed, she lifted her head. Her lips parted slightly; she wanted, suddenly, for him to kiss her.

As if he could read her mind, his eyes grew smoky, his lids half-closed. "I know, love," he murmured huskily. It was the second time he'd called her that. "But not here, not yet." The seductive promise in his voice nearly made her knees buckle. He caught her tighter against him and smiled knowingly. Her heartbeat raced. She felt no embarrassment, only pleasure and impatience.

Before she even realized it, he had danced her to the side of the ballroom and through the terrace doors. The air was warm and fragrant. The music floated through to the garden; he did not stop until they'd reached the darkest corner of the terrace.

"Reginald," she whispered, and he took her face in his hands and bent to kiss her. His mouth was gentle, teasing, his tongue playing tantalizingly over her lips and teeth. She did not want gentleness. She opened her mouth and wrapped her arms about his neck.

He groaned into her mouth, enfolding her in his arms as he deepened the kiss. She could feel his desire, a living pulsing thing. Her own body turned into hot, flowing liquid. She wanted more, though she was not sure of what. His lips trailed down to her throat and she moaned softly.

"Beachie? Oh, there you are, my dear," trilled the duchess. Reginald and Scotty immediately jumped apart. He kept his hand firmly about her waist to steady her as they turned to face his mother. "Oh, 'tis *you,* Reggie. I own I am much relieved."

"You are—Devil take it, Mother, whom else did you expect?" Reginald blurted out, quite forgetting his embarrassment.

"Why, no one else, Reggie. That is why I am so relieved," his mother replied with irrefutable logic. "Beachie, dear, I do hate to interrupt you, but Monsieur Alphonse is quite up in the boughs over the placement of the ices. I fear he'll listen to no one but you, my dear."

Scotty's eyes flew up to meet his, and he saw the barely suppressed twinkle. "Of course, Your Grace, I shall see to it," she said calmly. "Reginald, if you'll excuse me . . ." He nodded, his own eyes glinting. She gathered up her skirts and without troubling to put her hair back into place, glided back to the ballroom.

"She looks beautiful in that gown, does she not, Reggie?" his mother asked.

351

"Exquisite. You had it commissioned, did you not?"

"Yes. She did not wish it, but I insisted."

He smiled at her. Sometimes his mother surprised him. "I am glad, Mother. I should have thought of it myself, but—"

"Fustian! Men never do think of such things," she said blithely, waving her hand lightly in the air. And then his mama surprised him even more. "You really had ought to marry her, you know."

"What?" he nearly shouted.

"Well, you have to marry sometime, do you not? She's quite fetching, and truth to tell, I've never seen you look at any other gel quite the way you look at her. And she does seem to have a fondness for the children, which is rather important, since they do have a way of making their presence known. And I do not think she would insist I move to the Dower House, which is all to the good because it might be rather crowded with all the children. Of course, we *would* move if you wished it. I *could* turn the upstairs sitting room into a nursery, I daresay it would only mean moving the furniture and changing the curtains. Oh dear, there *is* the matter of the tapestries . . . but it doesn't signify. Beachie would know what to do. If—"

"Mama, Mama, a moment, please!" Reginald finally put up a hand to stem the flow of words. "Do you . . . do you realize what you are saying? Sco—Miss Beacham is the *governess*," he said soberly.

"Yes, dear, I know that. She *has* been for months now. And I collect 'twill be difficult to find a new governess, but still, 'tis even more difficult to find a wife, I should think."

Reginald coughed, striving for suitable gravity as he probed delicately. "Yes, I . . . I do agree, Mother. But

352

what I meant is . . . well . . . it would be a bit odd, would it not, for a governess to become duchess of Milburne."

His mother's eyes blinked in incomprehension. "Well, I own I cannot think why, Reggie dear. She would no longer be the governess if she became the duchess, now, would she?"

And with that inane bit of logic, his mama patted him on the cheek and drifted back to the ballroom.

Only when she had gone did Reginald permit himself a whoop of laughter. Scotty did not know it yet, but they had just passed the first hurdle.

Chapter 19

Reginald forced himself to dance with several of the young females put in his way by hopeful mamas, for he knew this was incumbent upon him as host. And in between he continued to hear whispered speculation as to the origins of the mysterious governess. He decided he had ought to use the rumor mill to his own advantage. He circled the ballroom, grateful for once to Lady Craddock, for the draped statues afforded him the opportunity to listen without being seen.

The tattlemongers seemed to be divided as to whether Scotty was a French émigré, a parson's daughter from Ireland, or a royal duke's by-blow. This will never do, Reginald thought, and sauntered about the ballroom and into the cardrooms. At length he encountered a loquacious young gentleman well enough into his cups as to have no idea to whom he was speaking. As he was still capable of semicoherent speech, Reginald thought him the perfect quarry. So he let slip into the conversation the fact that in the very next room there were wagers being placed about the Milburne governess. Was she the granddaughter of a

Russian princess or the daughter of a Highland chief?

"A wager?" The gentleman's bloodshot eyes lit up, and he soon after excused himself and made his way to the second card room.

Satisfied, Reginald whirled round to return to the ballroom and nearly collided with Peter Fairleigh. "A Highland chief, old chap?" Peter asked, his eyes dancing.

Reginald felt himself flush and then shrugged, grinning. "Yes, or perhaps the daughter of a nabob from the subcontinent."

"I see. I collect that you are trying to cloud the waters, is that not so?"

"Would you care to help me?"

Peter leaned back against the wall and folded his arms. "Does this mean the great duke is finally relaxing his scruples?" he queried.

Reginald's lips twitched. "Something of the sort. It may not be easy."

"No. I see that. There is more here than meets the eye." Reginald nodded. "I don't suppose you can simply let fall the truth?" Reginald shook his head and his friend's grin deepened. "Very well. I shall mingle among the tattlemongers, on condition that you let me wring the truth from you in the very near future."

Reginald agreed and the two parted amicably. On his return to the ballroom, he was accosted by his mama and Lady Craddock, who asked that he announce the betrothal of Elsie to Major Hayes. This he did with pleasure, and watched the happy couple lead the country dance. Reginald partnered Scotty; she danced with that special grace with which she did everything else. But he was not best pleased to see Phoebe and Oswald also making up part of the set. It

355

was their second dance together. Blast it all, he thought, and took only small comfort from the fact that at the least Phoebe had enough sense not to waltz. *That* would have to wait until her London come-out.

Reginald was even more wrought up when he led Scotty out for the supper dance and noted Phoebe and Oswald again dancing together.

"Dammit, Scotty! That is their third dance together! You know very well what interpretation the ton will put to that. Why, 'tis as good as a betrothal announcement!"

"But Reginald, is this not *our* third dance as well?" she asked ingenuously.

He pulled her closer. "That is another matter entirely," he said firmly. She lifted a questioning brow. "I shall explain later," he whispered, before the movement of the dance separated them.

Letty had thought it entirely unfair that after being privy to all the ball preparations, even helping with some, she was unable to attend. Everyone else was going, except, of course, the twins. But they didn't signify, because they didn't *want* to go. Letty did.

She wanted to watch the dancers, and to see Phoebe be the belle of the ball. For all she was rather a nodcock, Phoebe was kindhearted and Letty loved her. And she was beautiful in a way that Letty knew she herself would never be. Phoebe would be surrounded by beaux, and perhaps one would take her mind off Oswald Hastings. Letty wanted to be there to see. And besides, all manner of interesting things might happen at a ball, especially behind the potted palms or in the garden. Hadn't Romeo wooed Juliet in a garden?

Perhaps Reggie might finally kiss Beachie, or Lady Craddock might contrive to dance with the rector. Did rectors dance, she wondered, and then thought anything might happen at a ball. It would be a magical evening. . . .

But Letty knew that no one, not Mama or Reggie or even Beachie, would ever permit her presence at the ball. And so Letty had taken matters into her own hands. She wanted to see and not be seen. A twelve-year-old girl would be impossibly visible. She needed to be *in*visible. Servants, she thought, were invisible. No one noticed them, and some were very young indeed. And especially tonight, when the household staff was supplemented by the caterer's serving maids and a few extra village girls, who would notice an extra young servant girl? She would stay in the shadows, careful not to show her face. . . .

And so here she was now, in a pilfered uniform a trifle big for her, carrying a tray for camouflage and standing behind one of Lady Craddock's silken-draped pillars. Reggie was dancing with Beachie. They looked so beautiful together. . . . And then Letty's attention was diverted as she caught a glimpse of Lady Craddock, leading . . . leading the rector out one of the French doors to the terrace! She recalled what Lady Craddock had said that day at tea. She wanted to walk in the garden with the rector. She also wanted the rector to warm her toes, and Letty wondered if he would. Letty knew an almost overwhelming urge to follow them, to listen to their conversation. But she resisted, for eavesdropping was surely highly improper!

A few minutes later she espied Phoebe stepping out onto the terrace alone. Letty had read enough Minerva Press novels to know that a young lady could be importuned most improperly on a darkened terrace, even in her own home. Phoebe was undoubtedly too addlepated to realize that, and when she did not step back into the ballroom straightaway, Letty resolved to go after her.

Phoebe was not on the terrace, however, nor on any of the well-lit garden paths. And so Letty began a search of the more secluded corners of the garden. The bright moonlight illumined her way, but she did not find Phoebe. She *did,* however, hear familiar voices coming from the little arbor behind the yew hedge. Lady Craddock and Mr. Honeyworth. I must move on, Letty told herself, but her feet would not carry her. Instead she found herself peering through the hedge.

Lady Craddock was seated on the stone bench, the rector standing close to her. "You are quite right, dear Lady Craddock," he was saying. "My wife has been gone for ten years. It is a long time."

"Mr. Honeyworth," Lady Craddock began, turning her face up to his.

The rector cleared his throat. "Ah, yes, my dear?"

Now Lady Craddock stood up, and they were very close indeed. "My . . . my name is Louisa," she said in a small voice.

"Louisa," he repeated. "A very pretty name. My name is Aldous."

"Aldous? I might have guessed. I own 'tis a most distinguished name."

They kept looking into each other's eyes, and Letty was amazed. They seemed rather . . . old for this sort of thing. She wondered if they were going to kiss. Did rectors kiss ladies in gardens? She did not think so. . . .

"Do you know what I dislike most about widowhood, Aldous?" Lady Craddock was saying. Her hand fluttered to the rector's arm and he covered it with his own.

"No, Louisa. Do tell me," the rector responded, leaning very close to her. Letty could see a silly smile on his face.

"My feet are always cold. At night," she whispered.

The rector chuckled. "Do you know, my dear, I was, er, rather effective at, er, warming toes. I am sadly out of practice, but I do believe I could be so again."

"Oh, Aldous, I think you could too," Lady Craddock replied in a tone Letty had never heard before. And then somehow, Lady Craddock was in the rector's arms, and Letty knew they were going to kiss.

She was suddenly recalled to herself. It was bad enough that she had listened to what she had, but to stay there any longer would be reprehensible. She beat a hasty retreat, smiling to herself. She was glad the rector was kissing Lady Craddock. It seemed so . . . right somehow. She wondered about the toe-warming though. Did one do that in the garden too?

It was only when she was back on the lighted pathway that Letty remembered about Phoebe. She found her soon enough, however. Or rather, she heard the sounds of copious weeping, and something about the little sniffles that accompanied each sob told her it was Phoebe. She was in the rose garden, just off to the side of the main path, not far from the house at all. Phoebe seemed to have collapsed upon the ground, one hand thrown over the seat of a wooden bench, her golden hair spilling down in the moonlight.

Several times Letty tried calling her name, but Phoebe didn't hear her. Finally, Letty shook her gently. "Phoebe! What is it? What's wrong?"

Phoebe made a pitiful attempt to lift her tear-stained face. She did not open her eyes. "I cannot bear it," she cried. "My life is over." Letty was beginning to have some idea what was wrong with her. She took her sister by the shoulders and forced her to lift her head.

"Now, Phoebe—"

"Letty! What on earth are you doing here?"

"Never mind about that. Come and sit on this bench and tell me what's wrong. Maybe I can help."

Phoebe complied, amid much sniffling and groping for a handkerchief. Letty handed her one she found in the pocket of the uniform. Phoebe did not seem to notice the coarse linen, nor did she again question Letty's appearance. She merely looked down at her hands and spoke brokenly. "'Tis Oswald. I . . . I saw him leave the ballroom with—oh, I do not recall her name. She is the wife of some baronet whose land is somewhere to the east. She was wearing a shockingly low-cut gown, you must know, in a color that did not suit her at all. But that . . . that did not seem to signify to Oswald." That statement prompted another fit of weeping, and Letty patted her back and waited patiently. She was glad she had happened along. Phoebe needed to talk; she did not seem to see anything incongruous in pouring out her story to her younger sister.

"He . . . he took her down a darkened path," Phoebe went on. "I could not see them very well, but I could hear them. She was miffed at him and Oswald told her not to be overset. He called her—Mary, it was. He'd almost got the chit into the parson's mousetrap, he said, and once the deed was done, he'd come back to her and they'd go on as they had before. Surely she understood how he needed . . . needed to do it that

360

way. And then . . . then he kissed her. I could see him bend his head to her, and I knew," she said pitifully. "And I ran and ran. I know you cannot understand but I—Oh!" Suddenly Phoebe pushed her hair back and looked at Letty. "You must not tell Reggie, Letty. He is always so odiously right. I do not think I can bear— Why, I don't even know if I want to tell Beachie. Not yet. Even she did not like Oswald."

This pronouncement was greeted with another paroxysm of tears, and Letty despaired of even getting Phoebe to rise. She had got to get her into the house and up the back stairs before somebody saw her. She felt a moment's fury at Oswald Hastings and thought that he deserved a watering pot for a wife. But Phoebe did not deserve Oswald.

Letty set about to comfort Phoebe as best she could and wondered whether she had ought to look for Mama. But Mama would undoubtedly have the vapors did she see her daughter got up as a serving maid, and then Letty would have the two to deal with. Only minutes later she heard footsteps, and then suddenly Lady Craddock and the rector were there in the rose garden.

Lady Craddock's mouth fell open when she saw Letty, but she closed it and clucked over Phoebe. The rector merely winked at Letty and then bent to pat Phoebe on the shoulder as Letty explained everything to Lady Craddock.

"Oh, no, indeed, we must not tell the duke or Miss Beacham, nor your Mama. Not just now, for I own they are much too occupied with the ball," Lady Craddock said briskly to Phoebe moments later. "No, you must come home with me. We shall leave straightaway and you'll spend the night with Elsie.

Everything will look brighter on the morrow. And I do believe several of your dance partners this night might come to call in the afternoon. Come now, Phoebe, you'll mar your complexion with so very much weeping. And we shall have to bathe your eyes in camomile if you are to look beautiful again by the morrow. Come along now, child."

The birds in Lady Craddock's headdress bobbed up and down as she bent to Phoebe, but she paid them no mind. Letty was astonished with the way she contrived to stop Phoebe's tears and lead her out of the rose garden. Lady Craddock turned back to smile at the rector, and he grinned at her in return and said he would be happy to accompany them.

And then he turned to Letty. "You've done your sister a good turn, my dear. But, ahem, that uniform is a trifle large on you, would you not agree?"

Letty giggled, and the rector took her arm as they brought up the rear.

If the duke hoped for a tête-à-tête with Scotty over supper, he was disappointed. The earl and countess of Garnsworth joined them, and the earl proceeded to lavish rather a bit too much attention on Scotty. Reginald and Lady Garnsworth held their own conversation, although he suspected the countess's ears were tuned to the other two at the table. After a moment he gave up trying to engage her in discourse and concentrated on his lobster patties. Lady Garnsworth, her jaw set tightly, tried to feign interest in her truffled chicken.

Scotty appeared unmoved by Lord Garnsworth's compliments. She laughed gaily and tapped his wrist with her fan. "Oh, la, sir, how you *do* offer Spanish coin. And I know 'tis so, for your wife is one of the loveliest women here. Such elegance and grace that I cannot hope to emulate."

Reginald fought to keep his mouth from gaping open, and watched as, once again, Lady Garnsworth relaxed, unfurled her petals, and joined in the conversation.

It was sometime later, as Reginald stood watching Scotty flirt with her coterie of admirers, that Lady Garnsworth approached him. She stood to his side, her eyes following his. "I do think you had ought to look for a new governess," she said, staring straight ahead.

Reginald felt himself stiffen and turned to her. "I beg your pardon?"

The countess met his gaze and smiled. "She's quite wasted in the schoolroom, Milburne, and well you know it."

The duke relaxed and felt his lips twitching. "And what would you suggest I do with her, Lady Garnsworth?"

"Oh, I am persuaded you know that as well. But, ah, if I may suggest, you hadn't ought to wait too long." She turned to look pointedly back to the dance floor. Scotty was being partnered for the waltz by a very tall, handsome captain of the Horse Guards. Lord, where *had* his mother found all these people in the middle of summer? The captain was smiling down at Scotty, but there was a calculating look in his eyes that Reginald could not like. . . .

"I take your point, Lady Garnsworth," he said after a moment. "I have, you may be sure, thought much the same myself. But there may be problems. For instance, are you not curious as to who she is?"

"Of course I am. Who isn't? I rather favor the Russian nobility theory myself. Somehow I do not see her as obscure Irish gentry, you must know."

"Neither do I, dear lady," Reginald replied, striving for gravity.

"You are not going to tell me, Milburne, are you?" Her dark eyes twinkled. He did not think it happened very often.

"With all due respect, Lady Garnsworth, I believe 'tis Miss Beacham's story to tell," he said in all truthfulness.

"Well then, I shan't pry. Yet," she countered.

Reginald took a deep breath. "Countess, we may have need of friends," he said quietly.

She looked up at him piercingly. "Yes, that is so. But I apprehend that you have many friends, Your Grace."

"And Miss Beacham?"

The imperious lady smiled. "She, too, has friends." Reginald smiled in return. The second hurdle had been passed.

There remained only one more. And she was just now disappearing out through the doors with the captain from the Horse Guards! Quickly he excused himself and, ignoring Lady Garnsworth's grin, strode after Scotty.

"No, Captain Davis. I only came out for a breath of air. Thank you for that, but now I must return to the ballroom," Scotty was saying.

"Surely you'll not be missed for a few more moments, Miss Beacham," the captain replied smoothly. "The garden below looks most . . . inviting." He took her arm and began to lead her toward the garden stairs. Reginald stood frozen in his spot, watching.

Scotty tried to pull out of the captain's grasp, but he

would not let her go. "Please, Captain, I—"

"Oh, come now, Miss Beacham," the man said, a rough edge to his voice. Reginald clenched his fists at his sides, forcing himself to remain where he was. "I do not know what sort of game you play, but I own 'tis a deep one. You are no more governess than I, and I daresay this is not the first time you've gone down to the gardens with a man. But, perhaps, on second thought, there is enough privacy right here."

With that, the captain pulled Scotty into his arms, and Reginald, filled with an icy rage, strode forward. "Captain Davis." He tried to keep his voice calm. "I believe the lady has made her wishes known," he said coldly.

The captain jumped, releasing Scotty immediately. "Y-Your Grace, I—"

"The lady is living in my house, under my protection. Do I make myself clear, Captain?"

The veiled threat was not lost on the captain. The calculating look, and the lust, had gone from his eyes. Now he looked afraid. All to the good. He nodded cautiously, and the duke added, "A lady needs must be treated as a lady, and *spoken of* as a lady. Do you not agree, Captain?"

The captain's eyes narrowed a moment, and then he sighed almost imperceptibly. "As you say, Your Grace," he said between clenched teeth, and, without a glance to Scotty, took his leave.

Scotty stood trembling by the terrace railing. Reginald went to her and gathered her in his arms. He was amazed at how relieved he felt to hold her. If he hadn't been here . . . "I-I suppose you mean to scold me for coming out here with him," she mumbled, refusing to meet his eyes.

"Do I? I shouldn't think so. I am persuaded you know very well that it was a mistake." She raised tear-filled eyes to his. God, how he loved her, wanted her. Not a moment too soon, he thought, echoing Lady Garnsworth, and decided to put his fortune to the touch.

"Scotty," he said softly, and took her face in his hands. "I want you to give me the right to protect you."

The words struck her, like a blow, in the stomach. The pain was so acute it was all she could do to keep standing. She'd been half expecting it, yet even that did not soften the blow. He was offering her his protection. A beautiful cottage somewhere perhaps, where they could love and laugh and watch the seasons change. His protection. Not his name. She'd known he could not offer that; indeed, she could not accept it. And yet . . . she supposed that somewhere, deep down, she'd harbored the hope that he loved her, loved her enough to thumb his nose at society and offer for her. And she supposed in her schoolgirl fancy he'd found a way to set her free, so she could accept him.

Very deliberately she backed away from him. Fool! she scolded herself. The world is not made of schoolgirl fancies. It is made of men who sell their daughters in marriage. Of men who take women by force. It is not a world where dukes offer marriage to governesses. Reginald was offering, she knew, all he could. A carte blanche. A life of shame. She could not bear it.

"Scotty?" He came toward her. "I—"

"No, Reginald." She held a hand up and forced back the tears. "P-please, I . . . I cannot accept your . . . your offer."

He took her hand and pulled her close. "Scotty, please hear me out. It will be right, you'll see. There *is* a

366

way for us. You must learn to trust me. I—"

"Nae! Please let me go, Reginald," she pleaded, looking up at him. "I ken there is no alternative, that ye meant no disrespect, but still I . . . I cannot live that way."

"Live that— What the devil are you talking about, Scotty?" he demanded, abruptly letting her go.

"I must return to the ballroom, Reginald. Excuse me," she said quietly, and turned and fled the terrace.

Reginald stared after her, baffled, hurt, even angry. What sort of game was she playing? Why would she not at the least let him speak? Was it that she did not return his regard? Could he have so misread her?

Shaken, Reginald returned to the ballroom. But for the rest of the evening he was hardly aware of what went forth around him. He thought of their conversation on the terrace. There was so much he hadn't said. He hadn't told her he loved her. But she hadn't given him the chance, dammit! And why did he have the feeling that she would not have welcomed hearing it? He thought of their letters, of previous conversations, of the way she responded to his touch. It made no sense, blast it all!

Reginald downed a glass of brandy and watched Scotty make her way about the ballroom, charming everyone in her path. But she looked pale, and her movements were jerky, almost frenetic. She was as overset as he was. Oh, God, he had got to get her alone again. To hold her in his arms. To tell her of his love and kiss her until she admitted her own. It was there; he knew it was. Perhaps her refusal came from some misguided notion about differences in their stations. Or perhaps, he mused, recalling several encounters with her, it had to so with some fear of intimacy and a man named Duncan Mortimer. A man he could easily strangle right here and now!

It was a rather lowering thought that he had bungled the one and only marriage proposal he'd ever hoped to make. But it did not signify; he would do it right the second time. He accepted another brandy from a footman and reviewed in his mind every word they'd exchanged on the terrace. That leering captain had left. Reginald had asked Scotty for permission to protect her, and before he could say another word she'd backed away from him, refused an offer he'd not even finished making. He'd tried to reassure her, told her to trust him, and then she'd spouted some fustian about there being no alternative, and knowing he meant no disrespect. Well, of course, he hadn't! How could offering his name be construed as disrespect? What the devil was wrong with her? He'd offered protection and she—Good Lord! he thought, aghast. She'd totally mistaken his meaning. There were, after all, different kinds of protection. She thought he was offering her a slip on the shoulder! Little idiot! How could she think such a thing of him?

Well, he would correct her misapprehension straight away. And he would shake her till her teeth rattled! And then he would kiss her breathless.

But within half an hour, he knew he would do none of those things. For Scotty was very deftly, very successfully avoiding him. So successful was she, in fact, that before he knew it, he was bidding the last of the guests goodbye. Oswald Hastings was one of the last and he realized guiltily that he'd given Phoebe nary a thought for the past two hours. And then Scotty was declaring her fatigue and making for the stairs, carefully avoiding his eyes. But Reginald's attempts to

368

detain her were thwarted, however unwittingly, by his mama.

For despite urgent looks from him, the duchess insisted blithely that Scotty retire straightaway and not rise until noon at the least. So each of the ladies disappeared upstairs, and Reginald was left to pace the huge entry lobby, and then his bedchamber, in great consternation.

He could not let Scotty go to sleep thinking what she was thinking. Indeed, she mightn't sleep at all. Of a certain he would not be able to. Reginald tore off his cravat without stopping his pacing. But if he burst into her chamber at this hour, he would only give credence to what she already believed he wanted of her.

It didn't signify, he decided. He would go up there, and he would not leave until she understood. And accepted!

He took the stairs two at a time and tiptoed down the corridor. It would not do to wake the children. He rapped gently at the door; there was no answer. Either she hadn't heard, or she knew it was he and chose not to answer. If he called out or rapped louder, the children might wake. Slowly he turned the knob and peered into the murky shadows of the sitting room. He let himself in and called her name. Silence.

Sighing, he walked to the closed bedroom door. He rapped again. "Scotty, please, open the door. I must speak with you." He could hear movement inside, but she said nothing for several moments.

Then very softly came her voice. "Please, go away, Reginald. 'Tis late and I . . . I . . . there is naught to say."

There is everything, Reginald thought, but he'd be damned if he'd do it from behind a closed door.

"Either you come out or I go in, Scotty," he growled.

A moment later the door opened. She stood on the threshold holding a brace of candles. Her hair, its red highlights glistening like firelight, flowed over her shoulders. She wore a thin silk wrapper over an equally thin nightdress, neither of which did much to hide her lovely curves. Forcing himself to swallow, he took the candles and set them down, then led her into the sitting room. She stood before him, refusing to meet his eyes.

"Scotty," he said gently, "look at me." She raised her beautiful face to his. "I think we have been talking at cross purposes, my dear." She opened her mouth to speak, and he put a finger to her lips to silence her. "Hush, love. For once." He smiled down at her and drew her into his arms. He tried to ignore how warm and delicious her body felt next to his; that would have to wait. "When I offered you my protection, my little nodcock, I meant the protection of my *name.*"

Her eyes widened. "Your na—"

He chuckled. "Of course. And I begin to think you are as addlepated as my mama, thinking aught else." He felt her relax, almost collapse, against him.

"Oh, Reginald, when you said— And I truly could not blame you, for I know well that we can never—"

"Never what, Scotty?" he asked, frowning. "Never marry?" She nodded, and he tightened his hands on her shoulders. "Scotty, attend me. I *love* you. Those last weeks, when I was in London, were sheer torture. I cannot bear to be apart from you. You know well how much I want you, but it is much more than that. You've become a part of me. I need you with me. Always. Can I have been so mistaken in *your* feelings?"

She felt her eyes well with tears. She'd been right all

370

along! He loved her! A surge of joy filled her and quickly died, for in truth naught had changed. But he had asked her a question, and she needs must answer. She could not lie to him—not about this. And yet, would he understand that she could not wed him?

She reached a hand up to touch his cheek. "Oh, Reginald, I . . . I love you so. I shall never love another," she said, her voice hoarse.

"Wherefore the tears, then, love?" He brushed the moisture from under her eyes with one hand as the other began to stroke her back. No, she thought. He mustn't do that. His hand was sending little ripples of pleasure down her back, making her limbs weak.

"Y-You are the duke of—"

"I know who I am, Scotty; I know well my responsibilities. And you shall help me fulfill them. I shall be so proud to have you as my duchess. Everyone at Milburne already loves you. The ton will love you as well. There is no problem that we cannot surmount." He pulled her closer, one hand at her nape.

"I am not—"

"Hush," he whispered, and brought his lips to hers. She mustn't let him kiss her, she thought. But she wanted him, needed him so terribly, and knew they had little time left.

He meant to be gentle; he thought it was what she needed. But she deepened the kiss, parting her lips, offering herself. He groaned and crushed her against him; she was warm and pliant in his arms. But he sensed something else, an urgency, almost a desperation in the way she kissed him, clung to him. It was this last that gave him the fortitude to push her gently back. He kept his hands on her shoulders and peered down at her intently, struggling to catch his breath. His senses were swimming; he wanted her desperately, but not here, like this. They had waited this long. . . . But more important still, something was wrong. And it did not seem to be the fear of intimacy she'd shown before.

"Scotty, what is it?" he managed, his voice somewhat hoarse.

She stepped out of his grasp. "Reginald, I . . . I canna marry ye."

He reached for her again. "What fustian is—"

"Nae, Reginald," she interrupted, evading his hands, inching back toward the bedchamber. "Ye dinna understand. There are things, things ye dinna ken—know—about me."

"I am well aware of that, my love." He forced himself not to touch her again, lest she retreat further. "And it *would* help if you told me who you are. So much simpler when we post the banns, you must know."

"'Tis not a laughing matter, Reginald. I canna—"

"Scotty, attend me. I want to know the truth about you, partly because I love you and want to know everything about you. But mostly because I have reason to believe you are in some kind of trouble and I want to help you."

She was shaking her head, tears once more brimming in her magnificent blue eyes. "But understand, Scotty," he went on, "that nothing, I mean to say *nothing* you can tell me, will alter my wish to wed you." He went to her and gathered her close. "Please, love, tell me what it is that troubles you."

She rested her head on his shoulder. "Ye are so noble, so good, to have offered for me without knowing aught of my . . . my background."

"It does not signify, Scotty."

"But it does, Reginald. There are situations, things— unforgivable things—that cannot be undone. I would not bring dishonor upon—"

"No, Scotty. Nothing is—"

"Reginald." She pulled away from him and turned her back, then took a deep breath. "I am not . . . free to marry you," she rasped, the words sounding as if they'd been torn out of her.

Reginald felt an icy chill invade his body. It couldn't be, he thought. She was innocent, had never known a man. He'd stake his life on it. "What are you saying, Scotty?" he demanded, his body rigid with tension. "That you are already . . . married?"

She heard the tremor in his voice as he asked the question she'd been dreading. Slowly she turned to him. His face looked ashen. For once she could not lie to him. She swallowed the lump in her throat. "I . . . I do not know," she whispered. She could not bear the shock, the horror that came over his eyes. She whirled around and put her face in her hands. "Please believe that I love you. But even you cannot help me. No one can," she whispered, and then fled into her bedchamber and locked the door.

Then she fell upon the bed and gave way to wracking sobs. Dimly she heard the banging, heard him call her name, but then it stopped and there was only the sound of her own weeping. And finally that, too, stopped. She had wept enough, and there was precious little time.

The moment she'd dreaded had come, sooner than she'd expected, but there was no help for it. She could not stay another day. If she did she would bring more pain to both of them.

The letter had come from Beachie just days ago. Susanna hadn't wanted to think about it, but now she was glad that Beachie was seeking another position for her. It was the only way. Slowly, her heart numb and her eyes swollen beyond recognition, she began to pack her things.

Chapter 20

Reginald had tossed and turned for hours and finally fallen into a troubled sleep near dawn. When he awoke it was well past the noon hour. He was not at all well rested, nor had he come any closer to understanding what Scotty had said to him. How could she not know if she was wed? But one thing *had* become clear to him in the eerie predawn quiet when his mind had hovered between sleep and wakefulness. She might be married in the legal sense, but he'd wager his life she'd never been touched. And therefore, any such marriage, which obviously must be distasteful to her, could be annulled. It should not be all that difficult; a duke of the realm had certain influence, after all. In the shock caused by her statement last night he hadn't thought of that.

But he was thinking now! He jumped out of bed and rang for Martinez. He would speak to Scotty straight-away. It was obvious she hadn't thought of an annulment either. And, once and for all, he would ascertain just how this whole rather odd set of circumstances had come to pass.

Martinez had not seen Scotty and assumed she was still abed. So did Underwood. The children, happily ensconced in various parts of the house in which they had no business to be, had not seen her and assumed the same. Phoebe, he'd been told, had spent the night at the Craddock's, and the duchess had not as yet put in an appearance. But Scotty was not the duchess, and as the hour was advancing on one o'clock, Reginald found it deuced odd that no one had seen her. In point of fact, he did not like it one bit.

He strode through the corridors and made his way to the third floor. The nursery was empty. So was the schoolroom. His unease mounting, he knocked peremptorily on the door of Scotty's sitting room and, receiving no answer, went inside. It was still and quiet. Too quiet. He felt a sense of rising dread somewhere in the region of his stomach as he walked across the room to the bedchamber door. He knocked once, twice, then opened the door. He knew without looking at the bed that it was empty, that the entire room was empty. With heavy tread he went to the wardrobe and threw it open. Only one gown hung there, the beautiful peach satin ball gown.

He stumbled to the bed. He felt as if someone had just punched him in the gullet. He sat down and put his face in his hands, elbows resting on his knees. He'd been afraid of this. But somehow after last night, he hadn't thought—

God help him; he hadn't a clue as to where to look for her. And she was out there alone, unprotected, traveling heaven knew where. Tears pricked his eyes. He hadn't cried since his father died. Swallowing, he raised his head and let his eyes slowly wander the room.

It was then that he saw the letter, propped on the

mantel. He darted to it and grasped it with shaking fingers. His name was printed on the envelope. Quickly he tore it open. And then, holding his breath, he began to read:

My dearest Reginald,

I must ask you to forgive this precipitous flight, but you must believe me that it is the only way. There could never be a marriage between us, for reasons you cannot begin to fathom.

I should have known that you are so noble as to offer for me without knowing the truth of who I am. It is because you are so good, so honorable, that I could not tell you the truth. You would despise me, and I could not bear your contempt. Or you would try to become involved in some way, and I could not bear to be the cause of your disgrace.

I have come to care deeply for the children and your mother. Please make some excuse for me— that my aunt has suddenly taken ill or somesuch. They will all believe it, I am persuaded, save perhaps Letty. When she is bit older, take her aside and tell her—tell her that I loved you too much to bring dishonor down upon you.

I have loved you for a very long time. I will love you till I die. But I cannot be your duchess. I beg you not to attempt to find me; I shall come about.

Forever,
Scotty

P.S. I have absconded with ten pounds from your desk drawer. Please forgive me; I was too cowardly to venture forth penniless. I shall repay it as soon as I am able.

He read the letter a second time. His face was wet with tears when he finished. No, he thought. Not a coward. Never that. A coward would have accepted his offer and married him before he ever found the supposedly terrible truth she was hiding.

He heard footsteps in the outer room. He dashed the moisture from his face and went to stare out the window. "She's gone, Martinez," he said without turning round.

"So I see, Don Reinaldo. And you will go after her," the valet stated calmly.

Reginald whirled around. "I—yes, of course I shall." A smile tugged at the corners of his mouth. "Is everything so simple to you, old friend?"

"I have learned that many things are, Don Reinaldo. I am glad that you have relaxed your scruples."

"It is long past time for scruples, *amigo.*" The duke waved his hand in frustration. "But I haven't a notion where to look for her! I know she is from Scotland, but I doubt she'd go back there."

"Did you not make certain inquiries in, ah, Lancashire was it?"

The duke's reluctant smile turned into a grin. "Yes, you meddlesome old woman. And never quite received an answer about the possible existence of one Sarah Beacham, governess."

"Ah. Well, it seems to me, *amigo,* that Señorita Scotty"—at the duke's raised brow Martinez merely grinned—"that Señorita Scotty has several hours on you. But if we hurry, we can still pick up the trail."

"Pack my things, then. But Martinez, I go alone, with just a groom. No, do not grumble. I shan't be needing any intricate cravats nor formal attire, and I believe you are more needed here."

378

Martinez stiffened. "Don Reinaldo, my place is with you."

"Come down from the boughs, *amigo mío*. Angelique may need you, and I haven't a clue as to how long I'll be gone. Besides, I wish you to use the time to find yourself a replacement. It is time, I apprehend, that I pensioned off my all too old steward."

This time it was Martinez's turn to grin, and the two men repaired to the duke's chambers.

He was ready to leave in three-quarters of an hour. He went in search of his mama, but before he could say a word she launched into a tearful recital of Letty's encounter with Phoebe the night before. The gist of it seemed to be that Phoebe had finally learned the truth about Oswald Hastings. Reginald could only feel profound relief on that head, but in view of his mama's concern for Phoebe's broken heart, he tried to sound sympathetic.

And as the duchess dabbed at her eyes, Reginald informed her that Scotty had gone off to care for her sick aunt and that he was following to make certain she arrived safely. His mama clucked her concern and had no difficulty believing that ridiculous clanker. Nor did the boys, who expressed the hope that this did not mean they would have to have another governess. As Scotty predicted, only Letty tumbled to the truth.

She ran out to the carriage just as he was preparing to mount. "Reginald," she murmured, smiling mischievously, "do bring me home a new sister."

At first his mouth fell open, and then he smiled. "You read too many gothic novels, poppet," he admonished gently. "But I'll try."

* * *

379

Reginald kept to the main roads through Devon and Somerset, and the information he garnered at various inns which enjoyed his patronage told him that a Miss Phoebe' Beacham had indeed proceeded him. But somewhere north of Bath, Miss Beacham seemed to disappear, and it was only on the back roads that he picked up her trail again. This was no mean feat; indeed, it was only after numerous wrong turns and blind alleys, not to mention a hearty number of gold coins dispensed into the eager hands of innkeepers, that he learned that a woman answering Scotty's description had, indeed, stopped the night. But Rose Beacham was no more; 'twas Sarah Bertram now traveling north.

Did she really think he'd forgotten the name she'd invented for her former governess? Well, it didn't signify; the chase was on. And even though her circuitous machinations and penchant for back-road inns had cost him near to half a day, thus giving her almost a full day on him, he was confident he would find her.

As he'd surmised, the trail of "Sarah Bertram" led him north, and once he'd crossed into Lancashire, he also began asking after the direction of one Sarah Beacham, former governess. She, however, remained elusive. It was early on Wednesday morning that he found himself approaching a most ramshackle inn somewhere in the vicinity of the sleepy village of Little Cottsgreave. Its timber frame was well weathered and its green paint was peeling, but it had a rather friendly aspect for all that.

A cheerful ostler met him in the stableyard. "Cor, guv'nor, I never *did* see sich a bang-up carriage! Right up to the rig! You be a fine nib cove, I be bound." The young man's eyes rolled as they took in the gleaming carriage with its ducal crest and the sleek grays at its head. And his eyes sparkled even more at the sight of the gold coin Reginald pressed into his fingers.

Thinking that this encounter augured well, Reginald stepped through the door of the Hawk's Nest Inn. The vestibule was dark, even dank, and the corridor beyond no less so. He had only gone several feet when a balding little man emerged from a room several feet away. He had small beady eyes that darted about as if he worried that trouble might come upon him from any corner. He bustled forward in the manner of one who always has more to do than hours in which to do it and introduced himself as Mr. Chugley, innkeeper. Then he bowed low and said that his lordship was most welcome.

"I am the duke of Milburne," Reginald returned with suitable gravity, "and I should like breakfast in your best private parlor."

"Yes, yes of course, Your Grace." The innkeeper bowed again. "But, ah, beggin' Your Grace's pardon, there is one small problem."

"And that is?" Reginald arched a brow.

"Oh dear, oh dear," Mr. Chugley squeaked, shaking his little head and looking most perturbed. "Well, you see, we have only one private parlor, and it is, ah, occupied e'en now! Course, I could ask the gentleman to leave."

"That will not be necessary, Mr. Chugley. The taproom will do."

"Yes, of course, Your Grace, but . . . oh dear, oh dear. I do not think you would care for the company e'en now. Oh, but we have a sitting room. Perhaps you'd care—"

"Yes, the sitting room will be fine, Mr. Chugley,"

Reginald interrupted, torn between exasperation and amusement. The innkeeper looked vastly relieved and led him to a cozy room with well-worn, plump yellow furnishings.

A serving maid carrying a feather duster dropped a curtsy and shot him a saucy look before departing with Mr. Chugley's instructions for Reginald's breakfast.

Mr. Chugley made to follow her, but Reginald, tossing his hat and driving gloves onto the sofa table, detained him. "Tell me, Mr. Chugley, has a Miss Sarah Bertram been here of late? Yesterday, for instance?"

Mr. Chugley's beady eyes narrowed further and he appeared deep in thought. "Sarah Bertram. No, I've not seen hide nor hair of any such, and that's a fact, Your Grace."

Reginald described Scotty but Mr. Chugley, eyes narrowing even further, disclaimed knowledge of her. Reginald then asked about Miss Sarah Beacham, former governess.

"Sarah Beacham, did you say? Well now, that I do know. Lives just southeast of here. Little cottage. Forget its name. 'Twill come to me in a day or two. Such things often do, you know." Mr. Chugley straightened the sofa cushions as he spoke and tested the table top for dust. "Oh dear, oh dear," he murmured, obviously finding two specks. Then he looked back up at the duke. "But now, if Your Grace was to be asking me about a Miss *Rose* Beacham, well then, I might be able to help."

"Rose Beacham!" Reginald exclaimed, fairly pouncing on the hapless innkeeper. "Have you seen Miss Rose Beacham?"

"Oh dear. No, Your Grace. Never did set eyes on the lady, you must know. But there is a gentleman e'en now

382

n the private parlor, a Mr. Edward Weatherby, by
name. And he's waitin' for her. Expectin' her near to
luncheon, I should say."

"Expecting..." Reginald's eyes narrowed. "What
does he want with Miss Beacham?" he demanded
ominously.

"Oh dear, oh dear." Mr. Chugley took two steps
back. "He says she is a... a governess, you must
know. And him a merchant with a parcel of children,
and right beforehand with the world he is, too. Well, he
means to hire her and take her back to Northumberland. Hails from there, he does."

Reginald fought for control. He was here in time. He
managed to smile and dispatch Mr. Chugley with a
gentle reminder about his breakfast. And then, once the
innkeeper's footsteps had died away, Reginald made
his way down the corridor and tapped at the door of the
private parlor. He was about to be ruthless. It was not
his way, but then, as Martinez was fond of saying,
sometimes one had got to put aside one's scruples.

A blustering, jovial-sounding voice bade him enter.
Reginald did so and shut the door behind him. He
found himself facing a short, barrel-chested man with a
friendly, unhandsome face. The man was dressed in the
manner of the prosperous merchant he obviously was.

Reginald introduced himself, and Mr. Weatherby
returned the courtesy, quite pleased and impressed but
not at all intimidated at making the acquaintance of a
person of rank.

"I collect from Mr. Chugley that you are here to meet
a Miss Rose Beacham, governess," Reginald said
without preamble.

"Why, yes," responded Mr. Weatherby, gesturing
Reginald to be seated on the faded pink sofa. "Lucky I

383

am to have found her, make no mistake. 'Tain't easy to find one willin' to live so far north, nor to take on six gels, but Miss Beacham is. I've been here two days, not knowin' when she'd arrive, you must know. But she sent a message she'd be here afore nuncheon. So I've only to wait. Mrs. Weatherby will be vastly relieved, Your Grace, and that's a fact."

Reginald hated to do this. He rather liked the man. But it couldn't be helped. "I, er, understand how you feel, Mr. Weatherby. Indeed, I've a parcel of children—siblings—myself. But, er, Miss Beacham is not really a. governess." Mr. Weatherby's bushy brows rose. "That is, she used to be, but she isn't any longer. And, well, she isn't Rose Beacham any longer either." Reginald told himself that thus far, at the least, he'd told the truth.

"Whatever do you mean?" Mr. Weatherby asked, astonished. "She's not—"

"She's my wife," Reginald said simply, thinking Martinez would approve."

"Your *wife!*" Mr. Weatherby jumped up and began to pace the room. "How could—"

"'Tis a somewhat long story," Reginald said, rising as well. "And I'm terribly sorry you've rather landed in the middle of it. But you see, we are not long married, and we've had a little spat, and she . . . she ran away. I've trailed her here. And, well, you can see that I cannot allow her to go with you."

Mr. Weatherby agreed that of course the duke could not, nor would he himself ever dream of coming between a man and his wife. The merchant refused any offer of recompense for his time and trouble, merely saying that Mrs. Weatherby would be sorely disappointed and they'd have to advertise in the papers

384

again. Reginald insisted on paying Weatherby's shot at the inn and then asked his help in a bit of subterfuge. Weatherby looked doubtful, and Reginald smiled engagingly. "I truly do not relish explaining all this to Mr. Chugley, you must know," he began, clapping the man on the shoulder. Ruthless, he thought, as Weatherby's chest expanded under all this friendly condescension on the part of a duke of the realm. Reginald reminded himself it couldn't be helped. And then he proceeded to convince Weatherby to remain in his room through luncheon whilst, unbeknownst to Mr. Chugley, the duke would take over the private parlor. When Miss Beacham came looking for Mr. Weatherby, she would find the duke.

It remained only for Reginald, when his breakfast was served, to bespeak a room—or rather, a suite—upstairs and request not to be disturbed till he called. And to warn Mr. Chugley not to mention to Miss Beacham that a second gentleman was asking after her. Mr. Chugley, after a few "oh dears" and the exchange of several coins, agreed. Once shown to what Mr. Chugley assured him was the only suite the inn had to offer, Reginald spared only a cursory glance at the plain oak furnishings before tiptoeing down the stairs and letting himself into the private parlor. Good Lord, he thought, shutting the door behind him and heaving a sigh of relief, what would Martinez say about his scruples now?

He turned to survey the room. It was smaller than the sitting room, but quite adequate. Besides the pale pink sofa there was a wing chair in a faded blue damask, and a small round table flanked by two ladder-back chairs. The morning sun had receded behind the clouds and the room, which boasted only one picture window fairly obscured by trailing vines, was cast in shadows. So much the better, Reginald thought. He did not care to have Scotty recognize him until she was well into the room. He pulled the wing chair to the other side of the hearth, farther away from the window, and turned it to face the door. Satisfied that the chair was deeply shadowed, Reginald sat down to begin his vigil.

Susanna gave Beachie a hug and went slowly down the steps of the cottage to the waiting gig. Old Clem would drive her to the Hawk's Nest Inn, where her new employer awaited. She tried not to think and forced down the lump in her throat. This was the only way; she must go on. She had arrived here yesterday afternoon and Beachie, bless her, already had a prospective employer at the ready. Northumberland, just about as far away from Devon as possible, without going back to Scotland, that is. Resolutely, Susanna climbed aboard the gig.

A short, balding man who bore the aspect of an officious little mouse bustled forward and met her in the vestibule of the inn. When she introduced herself and stated her purpose, he looked at her most oddly out of his beady eyes. "Oh dear, oh dear," he muttered. "I suppose it'll be Mr. Weatherby you're wantin'." He cocked his head. "Leastways I hope so. Come this way, miss."

Susanna followed him somewhat reluctantly down the dank corridor. He paused at a closed door and rapped. At a muffled "Come in," he opened the door and announced her. Susanna peered into the room. It was bathed in shadows. She took several steps forward, still unable to see the owner of the voice. "That will be all, Mr. Chugley," the voice commanded hoarsely.

She heard the innkeeper retreat and click the door shut, murmuring, "Oh dear, oh dear," as he did so.

And then the voice bade her come forward. Perhaps he is elderly, she thought, given his voice and the fact that he had not risen at her entrance. She walked confidently to the center of the room. There is naught, she told herself, of which to be frightened.

"Turn around, gel, and let me have a look at you," the voice rasped.

She considered it a rather strange request, as she was certain he sat near the chimneypiece, and she was already facing him! Suppressing a tinge of alarm, she turned her back to him.

She heard movement, a quick rustling, and a moment later she felt hands at her shoulders. She gasped, but in that split second before he spoke she was aware that she was not afraid. Something about those hands . . .

"God, I was so afraid I'd never find you," he whispered, and, of course, she knew. She felt herself stiffen and whirled round to face him.

"R-Reginald!" she managed in a tremulous whisper. "How did ye . . . what are ye . . ." she sputtered in surprise, and then her eyes met his. Those clear gray eyes were regarding her intently, and suddenly she realized that she wasn't surprised at all.

She turned back round, unable to face him, needing to collect herself. No, she wasn't surprised. Not that he'd come after her at first stop, nor that he'd succeeded in finding her despite her attempts to gammon him. And neither was she overset, though, heaven knew, she should have been. But God help her, what she felt was relief. Relief and that surge of joy she had no right to feel.

His hands came down on her shoulders again. "Reginald," she breathed, and this time she spoke his name in a long, contented sigh.

He tightened his hold and rested his cheek against her hair. "Do not ever leave me again, Scotty. I couldn't bear it."

She turned then, in his arms, and put her hand to his cheek. "Oh, Reginald. I love ye so. But I *had* to leave. Do ye not see?"

He inhaled her scent and pulled her hard against him, wrapping his hands around her back. It felt so good to hold her again. Her head rested at his shoulder, and he wondered if she could feel the fast pace of his heart. "No, I do not see. How could I? You've told me naught but one great faradiddle after another," he said without heat. "And then that last cryptic, ludicrous statement of yours—that you do not know if you are indeed wed. Truly, Scotty, I do not see anything at all. I only know that—"

"Reginald." She picked her head up. "Ye are the duke of Milburne. How could ye offer for a woman ye dinna even ken?"

He smiled down at her. "But I know a great deal about you, love." At her raised brow he went on. "I know that you are Scottish. Tut, do not attempt to gammon me again. We are long past that, my dear. And let me see, what else do I know?" He kissed her brow and went on, his voice growing softer. "I know that you have brought light and joy to my life, with your laughter and song and even your flowers. I know that I cannot keep my hands off you. And I know that I love you, and that I felt absolute terror when I'd realized

388

you were gone and I didn't know where to look."

"How . . . how *did* ye find me, Reginald?"

"Martinez— Never mind, love. A story for another time." He bent his head to hers. "For now there are more important things—"

Suddenly she pushed out of his arms and turned her back to him. "But, Reginald, surely ye can see that naught has changed. Ye need a duchess of . . . of impeccable lineage and . . ." She whirled back round. "Why, look at what they were saying at the ball. A Russian princess, an Irish parson's daughter. I—"

"Scotty." He grinned and took her hands. "I was responsible for part of that. Oh, and Peter too. I, er, wanted to cloud the waters, since I hadn't the truth to promulgate."

"But—"

"And, my love, you've made a conquest of Lady Garnsworth, as I make no doubt you'll do of all the patronesses at Almack's and most of the ton. 'Tis all a matter of how one pulls it off, you must know. And as I am quite certain you are neither an actress nor a member of the muslin company, nor the daughter of some vulgar mushroom, I cannot suppose—"

"But ye see, Reginald," she interrupted, pulling her hands away, "what I am—what I have done is—is equally unforgivable."

He let her go and regarded her gravely. "Scotty, I think 'tis time you told me the whole," he said softly.

She met his gaze with tremulous eyes and bit her lip. She knew she would have to tell him. She did not want to, but there was no help for it. Not now.

He found that he was holding his breath. If she didn't tell him, he knew she would only be awaiting another opportunity to run away. Slowly she nodded and he

389

expelled a breath.

Susanna stepped back jerkily and moved toward the window. She stared out at the innyard and deliberately did not look at him. "'Tis not a pretty story, Reginald," she said softly, and knew her Scots burr was more pronounced than usual. It no longer signified. In fact, there was a curious comfort in it.

"Go on, my dear," he prompted gently.

Sighing, she rested her head against the window pane. "My father's land is in Sterlingshire. He . . . he is rather addicted to his gaming and his women and his whisky. Over the years, since my mother's death, he's bled the estate dry. I didna realize how badly sunk he was until . . . until he arranged a marriage for me. He betrothed me, without my consent, to our nearest neighbor, Duncan Mortimer."

Reginald inhaled sharply.

"Aye, the very same," she said wearily and still did not look at him. "A widower he was, some fifty years old. Duncan agreed to pay all my father's debts, and a healthy sum besides. He had his eye on the land, ye see, and . . . and"—her voice grew lower, for the words were difficult—"he wanted me as well, ye ken."

Reginald went to her then; he could not help himself. Lightly, he placed his hands on her shoulders. "Nae, Reginald, I must finish now I've started." She shook him off and he stepped back but stayed close. "I never could abide Duncan Mortimer, with his foul breath and the leering way he had of looking at me, ever since I was little more than fourteen years. And every time he'd touch me, even in passing, I cringed. I kenned I couldna wed him. And if that were not enough, 'twas said he'd tossed the skirts of near to every servant girl in Sterlingshire."

Reginald winced at the crudity, knew it was born of her fear and bitterness. "But my . . . my father insisted I wed with him. When I refused he locked me in my room for days, once even beat me in a drunken rage. He had never done that before." Suddenly she turned jerkily round to face him. "I began to be afraid, Reginald, for the first time. I didna ken what he would do next. And then"—she took a deep breath and plunged on—"one night he invited Duncan to dine. My father insisted I be present, of course. And when dinner was over and I rose to leave them to their whisky and cigars, a look passed between them. I didna understand it then. 'Twas a look of assent, and satisfaction, perhaps. Only Duncan came to rejoin me. He said my . . . my father had gone out. I tried to excuse myself but he merely laughed and grabbed my arm. He dragged me upstairs. There were two maids in the corridor, quite gaping at us. And Duncan surprised me by saying to them, very clearly, 'This is my wife.' I didna realize then what he was doing." Reginald frowned, but she went on, the words coming in a rush now that she had started.

"He dragged me to my own bedchamber and slammed the door, locking it and pocketing the key. I remember that he grinned at me then—'twas an ugly, evil grin—and reminded me of Scots law and the 'marriage by consent.' He had only to declare before two witnesses that I was his wife and . . . and"—she stammered and her eyes filled with tears—"and so I was. Now that we were legally wed, he said, he meant to assert his rights. He threw off his jacket and he . . . he kissed me and started . . . touching me, and I . . . I couldna bear it." She put her face in her hands, and her body began to shake. "I couldna bear it, Reginald," she cried softly, and he gathered her into his arms.

She went unprotestingly. "'Tis enough for now, Scotty," he murmured soothingly. "The rest will keep. I—"

"Nae, Reginald." She sniffed back her tears and looked up at him. "I must finish. And then . . . and then I shall never speak of it again." He nodded. This time she did not attempt to pull out of his arms. "He began tearing at my clothes and—oh, God, I thought I was going to be ill. Then he started to pull me to the bed. I wanted to die. He . . . he dragged me past my writing table and I . . . I . . ."

Now she did pull away and turned her back again. She took a deep breath, swallowed her tears. This was the hardest part, but somehow it must be said.

When she finally spoke, her voice sounded strange and remote to her own ears.

"I grabbed my letter opener. I hardly knew what I was about. Only that I could not let him . . . take me. I stabbed wildly, blindly at him, and caught him in the throat. The blood began to spout straightaway, all over. He made some horrible sound, like a gurgling, ye ken, and collapsed against me, then slid to the floor. I didna ken if he was alive or dead. I only kenned that I had to escape. My father had betrayed me. There would be no mercy there. I fished for the key in Duncan's pocket and threw what clothes I could into my portmanteau and a bandbox. I took the few pound notes that were lying about my father's desk drawer and fled into the night. I walked until dawn and then, finally, found a stage to take me south to . . . to . . ."

"To Beachie?" he prompted gently.

"Aye, to Beachie."

Finally, she turned back to him, but she could not

meet his eyes. "Now ye ken it all, Reginald," she said listlessly. "I am either a murderess or a runaway wife. I dinna ken which, but ye can wed with neither one. I will not bring dishonor down upon ye."

He took her face in his hands and forced her to look up at him. "Scotty, my dearest love, attend me. If ye— you—killed the blackguard, then 'tis self-defense and not a punishable crime. And of a certain it is no dishonor to defend oneself. As to being his wife, why, do you not know that 'marriage by consent' implies the consent of both parties? And since that was clearly not the case—"

"But—"

"And furthermore, my love, even if 'twere, as the supposed marriage was not yet, er, consummated, it could be annulled."

"But—"

"Surely you dinna, ah, do not doubt that my consequence is sufficient to accomplish such, do you?"

"No, of course not, but I—that is, you cannot wish to ally yerself to—"

"Scotty. Just who *is* your father?" His hands rested lightly on her shoulders. She tensed for a moment, and then relaxed. It was all right to tell him now.

"He . . . he is Laird of Ballincraig, Reginald," she said softly.

Reginald spluttered. "The Laird of—of— Devil take it, Scotty, Fergusson of Ballincraig? Why, he is one of the largest Scottish landowners south of the Highland line!"

"*Was,* Reginald," she corrected. "Much has been sold off. And all the rest is highly mortgaged. Every blade of grass," she said bitterly.

"That is much beside the point, love. Here I have

393

been cudgeling my brain as to exactly how to present you to the ton—No, do not get on your high ropes! I would wed you if you were indeed the daughter of that obscure country parson living in the North Sea, as you would have had me believe. Or anyone else for that matter. But you must own that matters are a good deal simpler this way."

"No, Reginald." She backed away. "There is naught—"

"Scotty," he said gently, taking two steps toward her and causing her to retreat further, "it is time you learned to trust me."

She smiled tremulously. "That is what Martinez said."

"A very clever fellow, Martinez. I've always thought so. He also said that most things are rather more simple than we think they are." He stalked her as he spoke and looked amused as she backed herself into the wall next to the window. "For instance," he murmured, putting his hands upon the wall on either side of her face, "our course from here is very simple." He ran one finger down the side of her cheek. "We shall take a drive after luncheon to visit one Miss Sarah Beacham, to—"

"How . . . how did you know her name?"

Reginald ignored her question. He was more interested in the rapid pulse beating at her throat as his fingers traced the curve of her ear. "To inform her of your change of plans," he continued. "And then tomorrow we shall leave for Scotland."

"Scotland?" Her eyes widened in shock. How could she possiby go back there?

"Yes, you know, that rather large region north of Hadrian's Wall?" He shifted his body close to hers and brushed her lips with his fingertip.

She felt her breathing become more and more shallow. His sounded none too even.

"I have some unfinished business there," he muttered.

She squirmed, putting her hands to his chest in what she knew to be a feeble protest. "No, Reginald. We—"

"But for now," he interrupted, feeling the heat rise within him as he pressed her further into the wall, "I have some unfinished business right here."

He gave her no chance to cavil, but finally kissed her, long and hard and deeply. His thrusting tongue, his frenzied hands, allowed no protest, demanded a response. She was stiff and unsure in the first moment, but then he felt her sweet and soft surrender as she molded her body to his and matched his passion. He was tasting her, caressing her breasts, her hips, her soft nape, reveling in the delicious feel of her. Only hours ago he'd not really been certain he'd find her. And now . . . Lord, he couldn't get enough. He wanted her, all of her.

He knew he had got to let her go, though. He could not afford to frighten her, knowing what he now did of Duncan Mortimer. Somehow, he must find the strength. . . .

First a distant knock at the door and then a clearing of the throat. Abruptly, he let her go. She stumbled, and he caught her with an arm about her waist.

"Oh dear, oh dear." Mr. Chugley had taken two steps forward and then stopped short, as if reluctant to go further, lest he contract some dread disease. "Mr. Weatherby, I . . . oh dear! You're *not* Mr. Weatherby! Beggin' your pardon, Your Grace, ah, and miss, but, ah, where *is* Mr. Weatherby? And whatever did happen to Miss Rose Beacham?"

Scotty tried to take a step forward, but Reginald

held her firmly. "Why I—"

Reginald hurriedly interrupted. "Ah, Mr. Chugley, allow me to present—"

"There you are, Your Grace," came the blustering voice of Mr. Weatherby. He advanced quite unabashedly into the room, one portmanteau in hand. "Well now, I see you've made it up all right and tight with Her Grace. Glad I could be of service. Day to you, Your Graces," he said jovially, tipping his hat to them before turning to Mr. Chugley. "I'll be off then, Mr. Chugley."

"B-but what about Miss Beacham?" Mr. Chugley asked in great consternation.

Reginald gave a warning squeeze to Scotty's waist. "I do not think she'll be coming, Mr. Chugley," Reginald said mildly, at which point Mr. Weatherby actually winked at him and took his leave.

Mr. Chugley shook his small head. "Oh dear, oh dear. Will you and, ah, the duchess be wanting your nuncheon, then?"

Reginald replied that they would, straightaway, and that they would, of course, be stopping the night. As soon as the innkeeper had departed, Scotty rounded on Reginald, as he'd known she would.

"Yer Grace!" she exclaimed, hands on those lovely hips. "I am not the duchess and ye had no—"

"Forgive me," he said, smiling and pulling her hands from her hips to enclose them in his own. "'Twas the only way I knew of to extricate you from the good Mr. Weatherby. And in truth, I am only anticipating matters a very little bit."

"Ye forget Scotland, Reginald. 'Tis—"

"I do not forget. You must trust me, love, or have *you* forgotten?"

She lowered her eyes. "Reginald, I . . . I cannot stop

the night here with ye. I shall stay with Beachie."

He lifted her chin with his finger. "Worried about your reputation, Scotty? Surely not the lady with the courage to hightail it the length and breadth of Britain masquerading as a governess!"

"'Tis not—"

"There is no need to trouble yourself, Scotty. You are traveling as my wife and—"

"'Tis not my reputation, Reginald, that troubles me." She colored and looked down again and he finally understood.

"Scotty," he said with firm gentleness, placing his hands on her slender shoulders. "Attend me." He waited until her eyes met his. "I want you very much. But until you are my wife, I—we—have a suite, Scotty. Two rooms. I shall respect the door in between."

"Thank ye, Reginald. Ye must see that if . . . if Duncan is still alive, I may be his wife, or at the very least, I am betrothed to him and I—"

"I understand, Scotty," he said, and meant it. It was all that and more. Much more. She was afraid, and knowing what he now did about Mortimer, Reginald could not blame her. He kissed her brow and told himself that he was going to have to be patient.

Susanna realized, as she took a bite of the cold glazed duck Mr. Chugley had served for luncheon, that she and Reginald had never before dined alone. She found that she liked doing so very well, indeed.

They sat across from each other at a small round table under the window. The sun kept going behind the clouds, as if it might rain. But at the moment a sunbeam streaked through the window and illumined Reginald's wavy, silver blond hair. His gray eyes were clear, his handsome face relaxed. She willed herself to relax as well, but fear had become a habit and she found it difficult to let go of it. Mentally, she shook herself. Martinez was right; it was all a matter of trust.

Reginald spoke of London, and of his work, and for the first time she was able to tell him of her home. She spoke of Ballincraig in happier times, of the beautiful rolling hills and deep green lochs. She spoke of her long-dead mother, of her Cousin Jamie, of the way she had loved to ride over the mist-shrouded moors.

When they had finished their trifle, Reginald leaned forward and took her hand. "Scotty, my love, may I know your given name?"

She smiled. It suddenly seemed implausible that they might know each other so well, and yet ... "'Tis Susanna.'"

"Susanna," he repeated. "A very beautiful name. It suits you. But, of course, you will always be 'Scotty' to me."

"I've rather grown to like ... 'Scotty,' you must know," she said softly and he squeezed her hand.

"How did you get from 'Susanna' to 'Rose'?"

Susanna chuckled. "Oh, well, Beachie's father was a vicar, and—"

"Ah, yes. I knew there would be a parson's daughter in this tale somewhere," he said mildly.

She could not keep the gleam from her eye. "Yes, well, he was something of a Hebraic scholar. Beachie told me, when I was a young girl, that 'Susanna' was from the Hebrew meaning 'a rose.'"

He rubbed the top of her hand with his thumb, back and forth in a slow, sensual motion. His eyes were half-shuttered and she noticed, for perhaps the first time, that his lashes were very long and very dark. He touched only her hand, and yet she felt her whole body begin to tingle. "Ah," he murmured. "And may I ask, my Scottish rose, how old you are?" The tone was casual, but she had the feeling she was being interrogated.

"I am two and twenty, Reginald."

He nodded, as if satisfied. "And I am *nine* and twenty. We are well matched, indeed, my love." The smile he gave her was subtle and full of promises. And then he rose and came round to help her out of her chair. He bent low, his lips grazing her ear. "There will be no more secrets between us, Susanna Fergusson," he said quietly, but she recognized the steel in his voice. And slowly, ever so slightly, she felt the knot of fear, lodged so long in the pit of her stomach, begin to dissolve.

Chapter 21

Miss Sarah Beacham was a pleasantly plump woman of some fifty summers. Her steel gray hair framed a face that smiled readily. She rushed out to the veranda of her cottage as Reginald drew his carriage to a halt.

As soon as he and Scotty had alighted, an elderly man came round from the back to see to the horses. Scotty pulled the duke forward. "Beachie, this is—"

"Obviously not Mr. Weatherby," Beachie interrupted, her hazel eyes dancing. "I'd know you anywhere, I think, Your Grace, from Susanna's description."

Reginald laughed. "And I am most pleased to meet the real Miss Beacham at last."

He saw Scotty blush and suggested she go upstairs to pack her things. She went, with only one rather uncertain glance at her former governess. That lady now took Reginald inside, where she put up the kettle and then bade him be seated in the cozy parlor.

"You do not seem unduly overset to see me," Reginald began.

Beachie's eyes twinkled. "Indeed I am most relieved, Your Grace. And not, if I may be so bold, particularly surprised."

"And yet you arranged for Mr. Weatherby."

"Yes, well, Susanna is very determined and then, of course, there was always the possibility that you would *not* come."

"That, I assure you, Miss Beacham, was no possibility at all," Reginald said sternly.

At that she chuckled delightedly. "Oh, I do like you, Your Grace. I think perhaps Susanna has finally met her match, in more ways than one. And what, may I ask, do you plan to do about Susanna's, er, difficulty?"

At that Reginald smiled, leaning back in his chair and crossing one leg over the other knee. "You needn't dissemble, Miss Beacham. I have finally wrung the entire tale from her, and we are off to Scotland in the morning. We travel, you must know, as man and wife. And that I mean to turn into reality as soon as may be."

Beachie grinned, lighting her face. "Oh, yes. I *do* like you! I rather knew I would."

"I'm so very glad, Miss Beacham," Reginald said dryly.

"You must call me Beachie. Everyone does, you know," she said genially. He was reminded of Scotty.

The kettle whistled, and she went in to make the tea, returning in moments with a tray.

"Tell me, Beachie, do you live alone?" he asked, lifting his teacup.

She eyed him shrewdly. "Since my sister passed on, yes. Why do you ask?"

"Do you not ever consider returning to work?"

"On occasion." Her eyes danced.

More and more like Scotty, he thought. "There is

poor Mr. Weatherby. A good-natured fellow, with undoubtedly amiable children."

"I daresay," she replied and sipped at her tea. "But I do not fancy the Northumbrian winters, you must know." She kept her eyes on the cup.

"I know of a position in the south. Rather vast estate, I'm told, with a large and boisterous brood of children."

"Do tell," she murmured, busying herself buttering a scone.

"Yes. Sad to say a rather ramshackle household, what with Cook and Mrs. Longbotham always ready to brangle, and then Horatio and Cleopatra—"

"That would be the milk cow," she interjected, meeting his eyes at last.

"Just so," Reginald said gravely. "And their mother being rather endearingly hen-witted, the children are much in need of a governess. Straightaway."

"I thought you'd never ask," she retorted, grinning.

When Scotty joined them minutes later, she was delighted with the news. Reginald convinced Beachie to leave on the morrow for Milburne, and gave her ample funds for the journey. Then he sat down to compose a letter of explanation to his mama. The matter would have been difficult enough to explain to a logical minded person, but to his mama, it was nearly impossible.

In the end, he made no attempt to explicate anything, merely laid before the duchess the basic facts. That is, he told his mama that a new Beachie was coming to be governess and that he would shortly return with the original Beachie, who was really named Susanna and who was soon to become the new duchess. His mama would be well occupied trying to unravel this little muddle. In the meanwhile, Beachie could explain the situation to Letty, who would undoubtedly explain it to the children and Martinez. And Martinez would take care of the staff. With a bit of luck, all would be running smoothly by the time Reginald and Scotty returned.

To that end Scotty bombarded Beachie with various instructions about the children's proclivities and lessons, not to mention Phoebe and Oswald. Reginald realized with chagrin that until that moment he had effectively forgotten about Phoebe. He recounted it all now, and Scotty was as relieved as he that Phoebe finally knew the truth, however painful, about Oswald Hastings.

Beachie assured them that she would have a care for Phoebe and, satisfied, Reginald strolled to the window. He saw the first droplets of rain begin to fall.

"Scotty, we needs must return to the inn. I do not fancy a drive in a downpour," he said, at which point Scotty began rather nervously elucidating on the subject of black cats, white milk cows, and very superstitious cooks. Obviously for Beachie's benefit.

Recognizing the tactic, Reginald smiled inwardly. Scotty was seated on the sofa next to Beachie. Reginald went to stand behind her and put his hand to Scotty's soft nape.

He quietly interrupted her. "Scotty, I believe Beachie has a great deal to do if she is to leave on the morrow."

Scotty jumped up, out of his reach. "Yes, of course. And . . . and I could help her. I really think I should stop the night here, Reginald."

"No, Scotty." His voice was soft but full of steel. "I mean to leave at first light and this is out of our way." Beachie had risen, and for some reason Reginald's eyes caught hers. Shrewd lady, he thought. She knows perfectly well the reason I want Scotty with me is that I'm afraid she'll run away again.

It was all a matter of trust, as a very wise valet had once said. And just whom did Scotty not trust, so that she feared stopping at the inn with him? Was it Reginald or Scotty herself?

The stableyard of the Hawk's Nest Inn was a sea of mud, the rain falling in sheets by the time Reginald's traveling coach lumbered its way in. Throwing the reins to an ostler and giving instructions for the horses and Scotty's luggage, Reginald helped her alight. He threw a traveling rug over them both as they dashed to the door. They were both laughing as they stumbled inside. It relieved some of the tension of the ride.

Mr. Chugley met them in the corridor. "Oh dear. Your Grace, you are, er, drippin'."

"Obviously," Reginald said dryly, handing the innkeeper the wet rug and keeping an arm on Scotty's shoulders. She was beginning to shiver; the dark corridor was colder than the air outside. He began walking toward the stairs, Mr. Chugley taking little running steps at his side to keep up. "Some brandy for me and a hot bath for Her Grace in our rooms, straightaway," Reginald requested in clipped tones. "We'll take dinner in the private parlor in one hour's time."

"Yes, of course, Your Grace. That is . . . oh dear, oh dear."

Reginald stopped in his tracks. "What is it now, Mr. Chugley?" he asked in exasperation. He pulled Scotty closer to warm her; she did not protest.

"Well, the, er, private parlor is, er, occupied, you must know."

"Surely Mr. Weatherby has not returned?"

"Oh no. No, it's—"

"I own 'tis a great deal too bad, Damon! A broken axle of all things!" The woman's animated voice floated to them as a rear door slammed shut.

"Come now, Pen, look at the bright side," came a male voice that Reginald thought he recognized. "'Tis raining and here we are again at the Hawk's Nest Inn."

The pair moved closer. Reginald could see them down the corridor but could not discern their faces. He heard the woman giggle. "Ah, and I collect that's put certain notions into your head, my lord marquis?"

The marquis chuckled and bent his dark head toward the petite red-headed lady at his side. "Let us just say I would not cavil if it rained all afternoon and night," he said devilishly, drawing his lady close. Reginald watched Scotty blush and thought resignedly that it was going to be a very long night, indeed.

"Oh dear, oh dear," Mr. Chugley blurted nervously, bustling forward. Reginald, bemused, stayed back in the shadows with Scotty.

The marquis took his time about releasing his wife, and turned with a gleam in his eye to the innkeeper. "Ah, Mr. Chugley. You do seem to get about this place, don't you? We were just now coming to seek you out. It seems we will be stopping the night, after all."

"Oh, yes, of course, your lordship. That is, oh dear. Beggin' your pardon, but the one suite, well, it's occupied, you must know, by the duke and duchess of—"

405

"Reggie!" Damon exclaimed, for Reginald had stepped forward, keeping Scotty close to him.

"Damon! 'Tis good to see you!" Reginald responded, taking Damon's hand. "And will you make me known to your lovely wife?" Damon performed the introduction and then Reginald turned to Scotty. He did not like the look in her eye, but with Mr. Chugley standing by had no choice save to introduce her as Susanna, Duchess of Milburne.

"My, you do work fast, Reggie," Damon said, grinning. He took Susanna's hand and kissed it. "Your Grace, 'tis a pleasure. I'd have known you anywhere from Reggie's description."

"Description?" Susanna turned puzzled eyes to the duke.

"Ah, Scotty, you're freezing. We really must get you into that bath," Reginald said quickly.

The marchioness's eyes gleamed impishly and Damon, after shooting Reginald a look that said, Sorry, old chap, invited them to dine in an hour's time. That agreed upon, Reginald ushered Scotty to the stairs, hearing Damon's chuckle and Mr. Chugley's "Oh, dear," float up behind them.

"Take off those wet clothes, first stop, Scotty. You'll catch a chill," Reginald said when they stood inside Scotty's room.

Scotty merely rubbed her arms with her hands. "When, or shall I ask *why* did you write to the marquis, Reginald?" she asked stiffly.

Reginald sighed and went to her, but the look in her eyes kept him from touching her. "'Twas when I'd first come home. I . . . suspected that you were not, er, what you said you were. And, well, Damon being from Lancashire, I—"

"Ye were checking up on me!" she exclaimed, eyes flashing.

He took her hands. "As would any man of responsibility. And might I remind you that I had good reason—"

"And what did ye learn from yer friend?" Her voice was a trifle less sharp, for he had moved his hands to her upper arms. It felt so good to be held.

"That Lady Darnley claims more than eighty summers and several great-grandchildren. I already knew that east of Winestead was the North Sea, you must know."

At that she broke into a reluctant smile. "Geography was never my strong suit." Reginald smiled in return and very gently enveloped her in his arms. For a moment she snuggled against him, but then lifted her head. "Reginald, why did you not confront me when—"

"That, my Scottish lass, is a very foolish question," he whispered, then added, "I burned the letter." He took her face in his hands and gazed at her intently. "I was afraid that you'd run away," he said rather hoarsely. And then he bent his head and began to kiss her, deeply, tenderly. She knew he was feeding the fire between them while all the time trying to keep it under control.

It was just as well, Reginald reflected sometime later, that the knock at the door, heralding Scotty's bath, had interrupted them. Now he could hear the gentle splash of her bathwater on the other side of the connecting door separating their rooms. He groaned aloud and began pacing the floor. How the devil was he to get through this night, or any other until they reached Scotland? It would be worse than at Milburne. Damn!

He should have ordered an ice cold bath for himself!

The rain had brought a chill to Mr. Chugley's one private parlor, and a cheerful fire burned in the grate. Damon rose to greet them and poured sherry all round. They chatted amiably for several minutes seated by the fire, and were very shortly, all four, using given names and speaking as old friends. Yet Reginald sensed a constraint in Scotty and thought he knew why.

His suspicion was confirmed when Pen quite innocently asked when they were married. Scotty stiffened and nearly spilled her drink.

"Yes, do tell us the whole, Reggie," Damon put in. "And you were quite right. *Nothing* like a governess."

Scotty, seated next to the duke on the sofa, shot a look of dagger points at him. He put her drink on the sofa table and took her hand. "Shall I tell them, love?" he asked softly.

She nodded and Reginald said, "The truth is that . . . well, it is all rather complicated, I'm afraid."

"You see," Scotty put in, "I was to meet Mr. Weatherby about a position, you must know. And Reginald thought the best way to, well, divert him was to say I was his wife, but then Mr. Chugley overheard and—"

"Why, you're *not* married, are you?" Pen asked, her eyes alight as if she had just uncovered some delicious secret.

"Not, er, yet," Reginald said, then hurriedly added, "but we plan to be, straightaway. There is a little matter that we must clear up in Scotland first." He found himself inching closer to Scotty.

"Something that is preventing you from marrying?"

Pen asked eagerly.

"Pen, I do not think we need to know all the details," Damon interrupted. Reginald sent him a grateful look.

"No. Of course not," Pen rejoined. "Forgive me. I did not mean to pry, though I own I am curious. 'Tis my nature, you must know." A handful, Reginald thought. The on dits was right. "So, you are traveling as husband and wife." She clasped her hands together delightedly. "Most clever of you, I should say."

"Clever?" Scotty asked doubtfully.

"Of course. I am persuaded it will save so much bother!"

"Bother?" Reginald asked, even more doubtfully.

"Oh, yes," Pen replied, eyes alight. "Why, imagine poor Mr. Chugley's face if he were to tumble to the truth. No, do not trouble yourself, Susanna." She held up a hand and smiled, then clapped that same hand to her breast. "We certainly would not tell him! Oh, but I wish you could have seen his face when Damon and I were forced to stop the night here. *We* weren't wed yet either. There was a rainstorm then too, but 'twas far worse than this, wasn't it, Damon?"

"Yes, Damon, do tell," Reginald said, beginning to enjoy himself.

Damon sighed, rolled his eyes heavenward and rose from his seat. He sauntered to the fireplace. "'Twas wintertime, you must know, and the rain was fierce. All the bridges were washed out and, well, here we were."

"Poor Mr. Chugley was most overset at the circumstance," Pen continued, "Especially since he kept interrupting us when we—"

"Pen!" Damon blurted, and his wife stifled a giggle.

"Yes, well, never mind that," Pen went on. "Truth to tell, Mr. Chugley might have survived the assault to his delicate sensibilities had it not been for Mrs. Biddleby."

"Mrs. Biddleby?" Scotty inquired, and for the first time all day, Reginald saw a twinkle in her eye.

"The rector's wife, you must know. One of the Evangelical types, poor dear. And there Damon and I were in our stockinged feet, rather wet, and my hair—"

"Pen, my love, I hardly think it—"

"Necessary to go into all the details," Pen finished for him with an impish gleam in her eyes. She rose and walked to him and patted his cheek. "Yes, I know, love." She turned to Reginald and Susanna. "Damon, I'm afraid, is nearly always right. 'Tis a great trial to me." She sighed and leaned close to her husband.

Scotty nearly choked on a giggle, and Damon put his hand to his wife's nape. "Sufficed to say," he went on mildly, "that we were wed here at the Hawk's Nest Inn, by the rector, that very night."

Reginald felt slightly scandalized and most definitely envious at the same time. If there were a rector here now . . . But there was that damned betrothal of hers to be nullified.

"Of course," Pen went on, "we had a proper church wedding several weeks afterward, for the sake of Damon's grandmama and my uncle. But my fondest memories will always be right here." She snuggled against her husband, whose fingers, Reginald noted, were subtly stroking the nape of her neck. Reginald had never seen such an open display of affection between husband and wife. Not among his acquaintances, certainly not between his parents. And he was suddenly seized with an impatience to be able to claim Scotty so publicly as his own.

"You two, however," Pen was saying genially, her blue gray eyes gleaming, "are in no danger of being embroiled in a scandal and so—"

"Pen!" Damon interjected warningly, and appeared most relieved to hear a knock on the door followed by Mr. Chugley's voice announcing dinner.

As a pink-cheeked serving maid began to lay the table by the window. Mr. Chugley, wringing his hands in some agitation, came toward the fireplace.

"Your Graces," he said, nodding toward Reginald and Scotty, then turned to the mantel. Reginald noted that Damon had not released his gentle hold on his wife's neck. "My lord, my lady," Mr. Chugley proceeded. "About your rooms. As I was sayin', there bein' only one suite, and Their Graces here already—"

"Oh, that's quite all right, Mr. Chugley," Pen said blithely, "we have no need of it."

"Pen!" Damon groaned and finally dropped his hand. Pen cast an unabashed look of wide-eyed innocence at her husband.

Mr. Chugley turned a strange shade of purple and Reginald realized that Scotty was shaking with repressed merriment. Good God, he thought, if Scotty ever said such a thing in company he'd strangle her!

But Damon's expression had changed from chagrin to a rather bemused affection, and his hand drifted back to his wife's nape. Besotted, Reginald realized. The on dits was correct. His gaze shifted to Scotty, whose soft red lips twitched as her eyes met his. Yes, besotted, he thought, and understood completely.

Mr. Chugley began to pace the floor, mumbling a few "Oh dears" under his breath.

"No need to overset yourself, Mr. Chugley," Damon said soothingly. "Our, er, former room will be fine. A duke and duchess take precedence over a marquis and marchioness, after all."

411

Penelope and Scotty, thankfully, waited until the only slightly mollified innkeeper had departed before bursting into a paroxysm of laughter. And Damon and Reginald exchanged a look of exasperation and complete understanding.

"Damon," Pen said as she carelessly tossed aside her wrapper and climbed into bed with him. He pulled the blankets over them. The rain fell in a gentle, relentless pitter-patter that reminded Damon of that other night, just months ago. But then Pen had huddled on the opposite side of the bed, and it had taken all of his skill . . . Ah, but it had all been worth waiting for.

And now she cuddled close to him, her naked body entwined with his, her head on his bare chest. His darling Pen had come a very long way in a very short time.

"What is it, love?" He kissed the top of her brow.

"He is quite besotted, is he not?" She began absently to stroke his chest. As always, his blood began to pound.

"I would say so, yes." His hand went to her hip, soft and smooth and warm. He felt her body curl in response. "But Pen, I really do not wish—"

"Damon?" She lifted her head up and regarded him earnestly.

Resignedly, he stopped massaging that inviting hip. "Yes, love?"

"Do you really think he's going to stay on *his* side of the connecting door? I mean to say—"

"Penelope!" Damon fairly shouted, and in one smooth movement rolled over and had her beneath him on the bed. "I refuse to discuss such a thing! Can

412

they not have a bit of privacy?"

"Of course, Damon. No need to fly into the boughs. And 'tisn't as though I would ask *them* such a thing." She wound her arms about his neck. "'Tis only that, knowing what I now do, I cannot imagine how they could resist."

He threw back his head and laughed. "Pen, you are incorrigible!" Then he smiled tenderly, threading his fingers through her unruly, luxurious hair. Hair that had driven him crazy from the first. And then there was no more talk as gently, and then not so gently, he took them both to that wondrous, fiery, secret place they had discovered together in this very room, all those months ago.

Reginald paced the floor of his room, oblivious to the rain, the furnishings, everything but the sounds coming from the other side of the connecting door. He had promised to respect that door, and he knew he had got to do just that. But he also knew it would be the most difficult thing he'd ever done. He'd heard her dress fall to the floor moments ago and had tortured himself with images of Scotty in her petticoat. Now he heard the rustle of bedclothes and knew she was settling into the big fourposter in her room.

He should not go to her. Not even for a moment. He had no right. Swiftly, he crossed the room and knocked on the connecting door.

"Come in," she called in a small voice.

He retied the sash of his burgundy silk dressing gown and walked into her room. A brace of candles burned on the mantel, a single taper at the bedside. She lay back against the pillows, her beautiful eyes luminous in

413

the candlelight, her slender body nearly dwarfed by the large bed. It was, he reflected wryly, a bed made for two. He swallowed hard and walked forward.

She looked more beautiful all the time! Her rich auburn hair spilled out over the pillows, tempting him to gather it in his hands. The coverlet came up to her chest, but the curve of her breasts was just visible above the scooped neck of her nightdress. He balled his fingers into fists and forced his eyes to her face.

"Reginald," she said and extended her hand to him.

"Scotty." His voice was hoarse. He stood by the bedside now and took her hand. It felt cold.

"You knew, didn't you?" she asked softly. He quirked a brow in question. "Knew that I would not be able to sleep."

Reginald sat down beside her before he thought better of it. "Scotty," he began, and raised his free hand to touch her hair.

"Thank you," she murmured. Her eyes looked trusting and all too vulnerable. "I . . . I keep thinking about the morrow, about setting out at first light. Oh, Reginald, I am so afraid." She clutched at him and leaned toward him.

"Afraid?" he managed to get out, realization beginning to dawn.

"Of Ballincraig," she whispered, and he felt a cad. "Of what I will find there. Of what . . . what they will do to me."

A complete and utter bounder, he thought, and cursed himself fluently. She was the woman he loved. She needed his comfort and protection. And all he could think of was . . . "Reginald, hold me," she rasped, and he had no choice but to comply. He could not even tell her he feared that if he did he would not be able to let her go. How could he tell her that when her eyes held such trust? Hadn't he wanted all along for her to trust him?

Very gently, he took her in his arms, steeling himself against the feel of her firm breasts and her soft, warm skin, against the faint but heady scent of jasmine that teased him from hidden parts of her. "Scotty, you needn't fear," he murmured. "I shall be with you every moment. You are the future duchess of Milburne. No one will harm you."

"You . . . you do not know—"

"Scotty. You are to be my wife. Trust me to protect you." She nodded against his shoulder, trying to sniff back tears.

"I . . . I keep seeing all the blood," she said after a moment. "If I killed him, I—

"No one will harm you, Scotty. You have done nothing wrong," he said firmly, his arm holding her close. He felt fiercely protective. "Do you understand, love?"

She did not answer, but he felt her body relax, and thought the tears ceased. And then she lifted her head and smiled tremulously. "I love you, Reginald," she said simply.

"I love you too, Scotty," he rasped. He slid his hand up to cradle her face and resolutely planted a soft, almost chaste kiss on her warm lips. He did not dare ought else, not here in her chamber, where he knew he would not be able to stop himself.

Susanna watched Reginald as he rose from the bed. She felt bereft of his warmth.

"Good night, my love," he whispered, before padding from the room.

She knew it was best that he leave, and yet she would

415

not have minded at all if he had really kissed her. . . . Susanna smiled to herself as she felt fatigue overtake her. She would sleep well this night, for the first time in many days.

"Good night, my love," she echoed in the silent room, and promptly fell asleep.

For Reginald, however, it was not a good night; sleep was very long in coming.

Chapter 22

In later years he would remember two things about the journey to Scotland. One was the rain. Indeed, it rained every day, drenching the Pennines as the carriage lumbered relentlessly on and forcing Reginald to ride inside the coach rather than on the box with his groom. Inside the coach with Scotty, watching her, wanting her, aching for her. And the other was the nights. The long, interminable nights when he tossed and turned and burned for the woman he loved but could not touch.

That first day he sat across from her in the coach, trying not to inhale her scent, nor let his eyes linger too long on her soft lips. In the late afternoon Scotty fell asleep. Her head kept bumping the leather-padded side of the coach and she frowned when it did so. Unable to help himself, Reginald went to her and gathered her close against his shoulder. She murmured unintelligible sounds of contentment. He kissed the top of her auburn head and saw that she was smiling in her sleep.

"I love you, Scotty," he breathed into her ear.

"I love you too, Reginald," she mumbled, and

promptly fell asleep again. Reginald did not sleep a wink.

That night he said good night to her outside the corridor door to her chamber and did not go near the adjoining door. He wondered if she slept any better than he did.

The next day was worse. The rain pounded harder and the coach, its windows closed, was stuffier. Scotty tried to make conversation. Yes, he responded curtly to one of her queries, he *had* been this far north, but not along this eastern route. No, he had previously taken the Great North Road, London to Edinburgh, and yes, the inns along that well-traversed route *were* more commodious and the journey faster. She finally subsided into silence, looking a bit wounded. He resolutely turned to stare out the window.

They stopped for lunch just outside Carlisle and from there took a post road north. England became Scotland, but the rain continued relentlessly, pounding the green meadows, lightly wooded moors, and bleak rock formations with equal fervor.

They spent the night just north of Glasgow in a tiny inn perched rather precariously at the edge of a stark moor. The rain had tapered to a light drizzle, and the Devil's Claw Inn was shrouded in mist.

As soon as Reginald had assisted her to alight, Susanna took a deep breath of mist-filled air. Dear God, it smelled like home. The home that was no longer hers. "I'd forgotten what the air smelled like in Scotland," she said wistfully. She thought she saw sympathy in Reginald's eyes, but he did not offer a word of comfort, nor did he touch her.

The ancient proprietor shuffled into the taproom just as they entered. "Well, an' ye come in good time,

Yer Graces," Auld Murdoch said in his gravelly voice once Reginald had introduced them. His hair was a white thatch, his light blue eyes friendly. "'Tis the gloamin' the noo an' the mist come richt heavy. 'Tis near full up I am, wi' every mon wantin' tae come in oot o' the rain, ye ken."

Reginald asked Susanna for a translation. "He says we've come just at the right time—just at twilight before the mist comes in heavily. And that he's nearly full."

Reginald requested two rooms. "Ye and the duchess be wantin' *twa* chambers is't?" the innkeeper asked rather incredulously, scratching his head. "Och, well, ye be Sassenach, after all," he added to Reginald, as if his being English explained the request for *two* rooms. Susanna felt her color rise. "Well, 'tis only one chamber I've left, yer grace an' that be fact." He grinned. Susanna's eyes flew to Reginald's. "But dinna fash yersel'. 'Tis a verra big bed." And with that Auld Murdoch chuckled and took himself off, leaving Susanna and Reginald, rather stunned, to follow in his wake.

The bed *was* large, just as the old man had said. Indeed, it dominated the rather small room. Scotty's eyes flew to it and back to Reginald, and he cursed inwardly, quite profusely. He ordered a bath for her and took himself to the taproom to drown himself in brandy.

The denizens of the taproom appeared to have already drunk themselves insensible. The only one standing was Auld Murdoch himself. Reginald bespoke a glass of brandy and sank down at an isolated corner table. As he watched the innkeeper fiddle with glasses and bottles, it occurred to him that he had not been thinking clearly. Tomorrow he would go into battle, as it were, yet he'd made not the slightest preparation. What had happened to all his soldier's instincts? All he'd done was concern himself with Scotty. Of course, he did have his pistol, but he sincerely hoped it would not come to that.

Auld Murdoch brought his drink and asked if His Grace might not prefer the private parlor. Reginald demurred, saying this was fine, and then realized that here was as good a place as any to start. He invited Auld Murdoch to take a drink and join him. Amazingly, the Scot assented, seemed rather pleased, in fact. In England, Reginald mused, an innkeeper would never do such. Often the lower orders had a more rigid sense of the propriety of such things than did the ton.

Reginald waited until two glasses of good Scotch whisky had loosened Murdoch's tongue, and then asked casually if he'd ever heard of Fergusson of Ballincraig.

"Ay, an' who hasna? I've ne'er met the blackguard, ye ken, but I heard tell. Ye're no a friend of his, be ye?"

"No, just, er, curious. He, ah, has a reputation even in England," Reginald prevaricated. "Is he truly a blackguard?"

"Aye. His auld father'd be turnin' in his grave did he ken the goin's on aboot Ballincraig these last years. Gambled away half the land, mortgaged the rest. Och, an' his women, wee lassies some of 'em. I tell ye, Yer Grace, there be many a father be wantin' to put a bullet through him, but of course, he's the laird," Murdoch said with a grimace of distaste. He did not have to add that no one could touch the laird. Not, at the least, for leaving by-blows about the countryside.

"I take it then, that he is feared rather than liked?" Reginald prodded gently.

"'Tis the lassies fear him most, ye ken. The men, well, 'tis more the magistrate they're afeared of. 'Ye dinna want to go doon for murderin' the laird,' he'll tell them."

"The magistrate, then, he's a friend of the laird?"

"Och, nae! Canna abide him. Been here a few times, has Dermot MacLeod. Got a daughter hisself, and he doesna like the way Ballincraig looks at her. Nae, Ballincraig's greatest friend be Duncan Mortimer. Another one with his eye for the lassies, but a coward in his heart, so they tell. Bit havey-cavey, the business with Mortimer, I'll tell ye that." Murdoch downed his whisky and Reginald poured more. Murdoch nodded his thanks. Reginald prompted him to continue.

"Ballincraig betrothed his daughter to Mortimer. MacLeod didna like it; she be a friend to MacLeod's daughter, and such a bonnie lass, and Mortimer of an age with Ballincraig hisself! Well, an' then one day the lass up and disappeared. Just like that! I ne'er did hear tell what come of her. Me sister, noo, she'll be proper overset to hear aboot it. She'll be comin' any day noo, for a visit. Bides in the Highlands these days, but once she lived in Ballincraig. Kenned the lassie when she were a bairnie. Me sister could tell ye all about Ballincraig, like as not, but I dinna ken what day she come."

Sister or no, Reginald had learned a good deal more than he'd hoped for. He next asked where the magistrate, Dermot MacLeod, could be found, and resolved to pay him a little visit on the morrow.

They drank in companionable silence for a time, and then Reginald bade Murdoch good night, hoping the man would be bosky enough to forget the entire conversation. Indeed, he imagined that, when sober, Auld Murdoch would not be too pleased with himself for having been so forthcoming with a stranger, and an Englishman, a Sassenach, at that.

Finally, Reginald rose, knowing he'd given Scotty enough time to bathe, undress, and, he devoutly hoped, to fall asleep. But by the time he returned, still quite steady on his feet, she hadn't. She was, instead, bending over two spindly, uncushioned chairs which she had obviously pushed together and was now attempting to pad with a quilt from the bed. He hardly noticed the bedding, however, for his eyes focused unerringly on that lovely, tempting derriere, twitching in the air as she patted the quilt and fluffed a pillow atop it.

He groaned and she jumped. "Och! Reginald! Ye— ye frightened me." Her Scots was more pronounced than usual. He loved the sound of it on her tongue. Did she realize that she seemed to switch from English to Scots at will, especially now since she'd finally told him the truth?

"I'm sorry. I did not mean to," he replied, and came into the room, closing the door behind him. He tried to ignore the way her light wrapper parted above her knees, revealing her flimsy nightdress, and the way her figure beneath it was so clearly silhouetted in the candlelight. "What on earth are you doing?" he asked, wondering how the devil he was going to get through the night.

"Why, 'tis plain as a pikestaff, I am persuaded. I'm fixing my bed." Susanna fluffed the pillow for emphasis.

"Fustain! You cannot possibly sleep there," he said

irritably. "'Tis much too small and deuced un-comfortable."

She straightened up and, with her hand, brushed her long mane of hair behind her shoulders. She saw Reginald shove his hands into his pockets. "Nonetheless," she said, "I mean to—"

"Dammit, Scotty," he snapped, "I made you a promise, and with or without the adjoining door I mean to keep it. We can sleep on opposite sides of the bed and—"

"Reginald," she interrupted, and sighed. She really did not want to discuss it. "It doesna signify. That is not the reason I . . . I wish to sleep on the chairs."

She gripped one chair back very tightly. He advanced toward her. "What then?"

Her chin came up. There was no help for it. "Ye've made it very plain ye dinna fancy my company, Reginald. Perhaps ye're regretting having come, and indeed ye needna continue. But I'll not disturb yer sleep and—"

"Dammit, Scotty, cease your prattling!" he fairly shouted, grabbing her upper arms. "For God's sake, woman, do you not understand anything?" He shook her lightly. "You sound as addled as my mother! Not fancy your company? Christ, Scotty! I want you so badly that just the sight of you, the sound of your voice, is sheer torture for me!"

"Oh," she said slowly, her eyes widening in dawning comprehension. Then her lips curled ever so slightly in feminine satisfaction.

"Hellfire!" he growled, and pulled her to him, seizing her mouth with his and forcing her lips apart. He kissed her deeply, without tenderness, as if all his pent-up

423

passion were rising up for just a moment. She swayed to him, feeling her knees buckle as her tongue met his. And then, as abruptly as he'd seized her, he thrust her away. "Now," he rasped, trying to catch his breath, *"now* do you understand?"

"Aye, Reginald," she replied, taking a deep breath, trying to steady herself. "I will sleep on the chairs."

"No, dammit! I am not a monster. I—we will contrive. Now get into bed and go to sleep, Scotty," he barked. Susanna walked shakily to the bed.

Reginald doused the candles and heard her remove her wrapper and slip into bed. Clenching his jaw, he removed his shirt and boots, splashed cold water onto his face, and climbed into bed. He would sleep in his britches; it seemed the better part of valor.

Scotty was curled up on the left side of the bed. Reginald settled himself on the right and pulled the down comforter over the two of them. There was utter silence in the room. First she turned. The mattress rocked and the comforter moved. Then Reginald twisted from his side to his back. Then back to his side, facing away from her.

"Reginald?" she ventured after many minutes had undoubtedly lumbered by.

"What?" he grunted.

"'Tis not easy for me either, ye ken," she whispered.

"Scotty, go to sleep," he muttered, and pounded his pillow. He would keep his word if it killed him.

It killed him. He could smell her lying there so close to him. He could see her in his mind's eye, her figure outlined in her flimsy nightclothes. . . . There was naught he could do but endure.

* * *

Susanna became more and more tense as they neared Ballincraig. Her hand gripped the leather strap at the side of her seat until her knuckles were white. She prayed the outcome of this day would be as Reginald had assured her.

The sky was rather gray, matching the bleak rock and stark moors surrounding them, but at the least the rain had stopped. "Reginald! The coach has taken a wrong turn," she said suddenly.

"I know, Scotty. Do not trouble yourself. My groom knows where he's going. There is a little matter to which I must first attend," he said cryptically.

A short while later she recognized MacLeod's cottage. "I'll only be a few moments, Scotty. I, ah, need to review a few fine points of Scots law with the magistrate," he said quickly, and before she could say a word, left her in the care of his groom and walked up the path to the cottage.

She fidgeted in the carriage until he returned, and they were on their way again. But Reginald was extremely reticent on the specifics of his conversation with MacLeod. Perhaps he thought to protect her in some way by keeping her in the dark. She sighed nervously and lapsed into the same tense silence as before.

Scotty's tension became more pronounced as the black moors became lightly wooded ones and finally gave way to a valley of rolling green meadows. At the center stood an ancient stone manor house. Ballincraig. If he'd not known by the directions she'd given the groom, he'd have known by the excessively strained look on her face and the way her hand shook as it clutched the leather strap.

He shifted across to sit next to her and took that very

same hand, warming it and trying to massage away the stiffness. "Scotty. I know how difficult this is for you. But please remember that I will be with you every second."

"Thank you, Reginald. I confess I *am* feeling rather . . . cowardly just now. I am glad you are here."

He drew her close to him. "A coward would have given in to Mortimer that night. A coward would have accepted my offer without ever telling me the truth. You are a soldier worth your mettle, love. But every good soldier knows when to obey orders. There will be no confrontation between you and your father. Nor Mortimer, if he is there."

She sucked in her breath and he nodded slowly. "You know well that he might be alive, love, and 'tis possible, after all, that he is there. It would be just as well, for he, too, must hear what I have to say."

She swallowed hard, bereft of speech, and he held her in silence the rest of the way.

It was only when they had passed through the crumbling gates to Ballincraig that she sat up straight, her face set resolutely. She held Reginald's hand tightly as the carriage drew up before an ancient manor house that had obviously seen better days.

Two footmen, one red-nosed and weaving unsteadily on his feet, gaped at the coach in astonishment. Reginald was at that moment very glad he'd sent no word of their arrival. The element of surprise would, he was certain, work to their advantage.

He helped Scotty to alight. Her face was completely composed. Good girl, he thought, and gave her hand a reassuring squeeze.

"Why, Miss Susanna!" yelped one of the footmen. The sober one.

"So 'tis," agreed his rather inebriated companion.

"An' a fine nib cove what come w' her."

"Good morning, Struan, Robbie," she said. And then she swept past them and up the stone stairs, her feet steady, her head high.

Susanna took a deep breath as she reached the front door. She was here, at Ballincraig. Somehow she must summon her courage. Before she could lift the knocker, the door flew open. Marta, the housekeeper, reeking of spirits as usual, stared at her out of dull, hardened eyes. She said not a word, but stepped back to let Susanna and Reginald enter.

"So, ye've come back, have ye? An' brought a Sassenach with ye," the woman commented coldly, looking them both up and down. "Well, we'll be seein' aboot that, will we no, miss?" And with that she turned on her heel and shuffled away, no doubt to inform Susanna's father. It was no more than Susanna had expected. Marta had been under her father's thumb, and under more than that, for as long as Susanna could remember.

"And just who was that pleasant creature?" Reginald whispered. As Susanna was explaining, they heard the sound of hurried footsteps.

A tall, slightly stooped figure rounded the bend and came forward.

"Is't truly ye, Miss Susanna?" he shouted.

She launched herself into his arms. "MacFarlane!" she exclaimed and felt him grasp her tightly.

A moment later he let her go, holding her at arm's length. Reginald came up behind her. "Ye've come home, lass. 'Tis right glad I am to see ye. I've worrited somethin' terrible."

"I'm sorry, MacFarlane. I . . . I couldna . . . I had to

427

leave, ye ken?"

MacFarlane frowned. "Ay, lass, I ken," he said heavily. He dropped his hands and lifted his eyes to Reginald, "And ye've found yerself a real man, lassie. I am happy for ye."

"Thank ye, MacFarlane," Susanna said, smiling. It was so good to know she had at least one friend here. She introduced the butler to Reginald.

"I'd best tak' ye both into the drawing room noo. Marta will have told him already," MacFarlane said. "An' I should warn ye, lass, the laird is no alone. The other one is with him. Seems he allas is, these days," he added with distaste.

Susanna gasped and Reginald took her hand. "'Tis for the best, Scotty," he murmured, and she tried to take reassurance from the warm pressure of his grip.

Reginald whispered something to MacFarlane as they turned to leave the entry lobby. The butler stopped, gazed a moment at Susanna, and his face lit into a smile.

"'Twill be my pleasure, Yer Grace," MacFarlane said, and the three marched down the stark stone corridor.

"The duke and future duchess of Milburne!" MacFarlane intoned after pushing the drawing-room door open.

Reginald strode into the room, and Susanna, her hand locked with his, had no choice but to follow. Her father rose from his threadbare wing chair, his blazing eyes directed straight at her. She froze, and out of the corner of her eye saw Duncan Mortimer uncoil himself from the sofa and saunter forward. A jagged scar, still red, was visible at his throat. Susanna swallowed hard, a mass of conflicting emotions assailing her. Terror, as

428

she remembered that dreadful night. Relief that she had, after all, not killed Mortimer, she was not a murderess. And then finally, as Reginald squeezed her hand reassuringly, she felt courage. He had asked her not to speak, and so she wouldn't. But she would not cower. Susanna lifted her chin.

"Nae! It canna be! I thought Marta was too bosky to ken what she said. Come back, have ye? And with a Sassenach duke! I'll not credit it!" her father thundered.

"Nonetheless, here you see us, Ballincraig," Reginald stated firmly.

Her father's eyes, bloodshot as always, narrowed and slid insolently from her to Reginald and back. "Future duchess, hah!" he spat. "He'll not wed with ye, slut that ye are. Did ye not discover that she's damaged goods, Yer Grace?" Susanna saw Reginald wince, felt him go rigid. She knew he was holding himself back with difficulty. She now squeezed *his* hand.

"Susanna will be the duchess of Milburne as soon as her betrothal to Duncan Mortimer is nullified," Reginald said frostily, his face set like stone.

"I'm afraid 'tisna possible," Duncan said, stepping close to her. With great effort, Susanna held her ground. His breath reeked of whisky. "'Tis very pleased I am ye've finally come to yer senses, Susanna." He lifted a hand toward her face.

"Touch her and I'll kill you," Reginald breathed between clenched teeth. The words were softly spoken but the deadly steel beneath them was evident. Mortimer paled and dropped his hand.

"And did ye not tell yer fine duke here that ye are already wed, in *every* sense?" Mortimer drawled, his eyes sweeping her frame lecherously.

"You lie," Reginald seethed. "Even Scottish marriage law requires *mutual* consent. As to the other, you will not speak so in front of my future wife." Reginald did not doubt her word for a moment, Susanna marveled. As long as she lived she would never forget that. How could she not have trusted him when he trusted her so implicitly?

"I see," Mortimer countered, "ye must have reason for being so certain."

Susanna knew Reginald wanted to smash his face. Instead he gritted his teeth, his entire body stiff. Few men, she thought, would have such control. He moved his hand to the nape of her neck in a gesture of pure possession.

Her father's eyes followed that hand. "'Tis difficult to come between a man and his whore, Duncan," he sneered. Susanna felt the color leave her face. Reginald took a nearly imperceptible step closer to her.

"You are not fit to clean her boots. Either of you," Reginald hissed, and her father blanched. "I want the betrothal papers. Now!" Reginald demanded. Susanna knew he was reaching the end of his tether.

"I'll no do yer bidding, Sassenach," Ballincraig said. "If ye—"

"Mr. Dermot MacLeod, magistrate," came MacFarlane's voice from the doorway. Reginald watched MacLeod, a tall, husky man with muscular arms and fiery red hair, stroll into the room.

"Mornin' to ye, Ballincraig, Mortimer, Yer Grace." He nodded to each of them, then turned to Scotty. "Susanna, lass, 'tis good to see ye again," he added quietly.

She smiled and greeted him warmly, then turned curious eyes to Reginald. He nodded to let her know all

430

was well.

MacLeod proceeded to make himself comfortable in a chair beside the chimney grate. "Dinna be troublin' aboot me, Ballincraig. I'll just bide here a wee bit. Ye carry on yer business."

Ballincraig frowned and drew himself up. "Yer Grace, just what is the meaning of this?"

"The betrothal papers," Reginald repeated quietly, firmly, dangerously.

Ballincraig darted a look at MacLeod, who merely smiled back, unnerving the laird, just as Reginald had hoped. His chin jutting out defiantly, his gray head high, Ballincraig strode to the bell pull. He requested the papers of MacFarlane and then went to pour himself another drink. Mortimer sauntered to the mantel. Reginald and Scotty stayed where they were. MacFarlane brought the papers straightaway and left with a reassuring smile to Scotty.

Ballincraig handed the papers to Reginald. He snorted derisively and tore them into shreds. Mortimer gasped and stormed forward. They stood but three feet apart. Reginald had not let go Scotty.

"Your betrothal is at an end, Mortimer. If you ever attempt to see Susanna, or come near her, or any of my family, I will haul you before the magistrates on charges of attempted rape. Is that clear?" Reginald said menacingly.

Mortimer's thin, angular face reddened and the veins at his temples throbbed. "How dare ye, Yer Grace! That was a legal betrothal. As to the other, Susanna and I are legally wed, by declaration, according to—"

"According to Scots law, 'tis a marriage by consent that is legal," said MacLeod from his chair. "Was there consent, lassie?" he asked gently.

Gripping tightly to Reginald's arm, Scotty shook her head. MacLeod merely cocked his head at Mortimer, but the latter refused to be cowed. "Nonetheless, ye have no right to tear up the betrothal papers. They were drawn up legally and—"

"Assault and attempted rape," Reginald interrupted angrily.

"Och, 'tis all talk," Mortimer said derisively. "I ken ye'd never—"

"Try me," Reginald warned. "You will have no further contact with Susanna from this time forth. If you—"

"This is an outrage!" Mortimer interrupted, his fists clenched, the jagged scar at his throat growing redder and more prominent. His foul breath assailed Reginald. "You may name your seconds, Milburne!" he declared, obviously forgetting the presence of MacLeod.

Scotty clutched at Reginald's arm. "Dueling is for gentlemen, Mortimer," he replied in frigid tones, "and you don't qualify."

Mortimer's face turned a mottled purple and he lunged for Reginald, grabbing the lapels of his coat. "I issued ye a challenge, damn ye!" Mortimer ranted. Scotty gasped and Reginald thrust her behind him. The magistrate rose but Reginald remained calm.

"I would like naught better than to put paid to your miserable existence this very day, Mortimer," Reginald said in a voice of quiet, deadly menace. "My aim is still as it was in my Peninsula days. But *I* am not a murderer, and *you* are stinking drunk. I suggest you remove your hands. Now!"

Mortimer swallowed and unclamped his hands, taking several steps back. His face had turned pale.

Reginald drew Scotty to his side again. "You tempt me, Mortimer, you really do," he continued. He did not add that it was only for Scotty's sake that he restrained himself. She had been sick over the thought that she herself might have killed Mortimer, even in self-defense. And she was not one of those women who would feel a thrill seeing men fight to the death for her. She would, he thought, be repulsed. He would not make her live with the knowledge that he had killed for her sake, especially now when she was no longer in danger.

"You will stay away from Susanna. And lest you take any foolish notions, know that I have agents the length and breadth of England. If you so much as cross the border I shall know about it. And I shall come after you."

Mortimer drew himself up. "And what does Dermot MacLeod have to say to such threats, I'm wondering?"

"Attempted rape, Duncan. 'Tis a rather serious crime, I'm thinkin'," MacLeod murmured, and Mortimer made a growl of disgust.

"She isna worth it, I assure ye. Not even for the land. I've other fish to fry. Ye can have her, cold as she is."

"Get out, Mortimer," Reginald spat. "And you'd do well to forget the land as well."

"Noo, see here!" blustered Ballincraig, but Reginald waved him to silence as Mortimer, with one last sneer of distaste, stormed out.

Reginald felt a great deal of tension ease from Susanna's body. But he knew they were a long way from home.

"Send for your solicitor," Reginald ordered and when Ballincraig began to protest, Reginald said, "For the settlements." And suddenly the laird puffed himself up, apparently deciding that perhaps it would do to cozy up to the duke after all. Reginald added ominously, "And for your will."

Ballincraig went white, but he rang again for MacFarlane. And then they settled down to wait, a tense, silent tableau. Only MacLeod seemed at his ease. He poured himself a drink and settled back to enjoy it. Reginald took Scotty to the sofa and the laird sank down into his wing chair. His hands were shaking. Good, Reginald thought. As far as he was concerned, Ballincraig was the real villain in this piece. How could a man do such a thing to his own daughter?

Reginald entwined his fingers with Susanna's. Marta shuffled in with a tray of tea and oatcakes, which she slammed down on the sofa table. "Get ye gone, ye drunken sot," Ballincraig snarled with a swipe to her rear. Marta mumbled something unsavory and left them.

No one touched the tray. The minutes ticked away, then an hour and more. Susanna felt her tension mounting again. Finally MacFarlane announced the arrival of the solicitor, Mr. Donald Drummond.

The little man strode in, briefcase in hand, and introductions were made. He greeted MacLeod, evincing some surprise, but his eyes truly widened at the sight of Susanna, and then he smiled. "Welcome home, lass," he said, and took his seat in a chair next to her father. He looked nervous, and Susanna instinctively knew he was aware of all that had gone on months ago.

"I mean to marry Miss Fergusson straightaway, and I wish the settlements taken care of now," Reginald said without preamble.

Drummond nodded uneasily, and Ballincraig said,

"Surely the lass oughtna to be here. She should rest—"

"She stays," Reginald cut in, and Susanna inched closer to him. He did not look at her but instead asked the extent of her father's debts. He agreed to pay them, so that Ballincraig was no longer mortgaged, and to give over a healthy sum besides. Her father looked pleased until Reginald went on. "There are conditions, however. If ever again you decide to mortgage Ballincraig, you will come to me and only me. I will hold the notes. And if necessary, I shall foreclose. I want that written into the settlement and all banks informed."

"What?" exclaimed the laird. "Ye canna—"

"He can," MacLeod put in quietly.

"I take it Ballincraig is not entailed, since you were prepared to give part of it to Mortimer," Reginald interrupted. Drummond nodded slowly. "Good. You will draw up a new will, Drummond, in which Ballincraig leaves the entire estate to Susanna and names one of her sons as the next laird." Susanna turned to Reginald, amazed and grateful that he had thought of all this.

"Nae!" Ballincraig exploded, jumping up. Susanna clutched Reginald's arm. "I'll never agree to such. She is no daughter of mine. She—"

"Sit down, Ballincraig!" shouted Drummond.

"Drummond! He canna do this. 'Tis unheard of! 'Tis—"

"Collusion in the forced marriage and attempted rape of one's daughter is also unheard of, at the least where I come from," Reginald barked, and her father subsided into his chair, casting a nervous glance at MacLeod and looking a bit green about the gills.

"I think ye'd best do as the duke says, Ballincraig,"

Drummond advised. "The estate will be yers for yer lifetime." He looked to Reginald for confirmation.

Reginald nodded. "Yes. Even if I foreclose, he may live here."

"I've known ye many years," Drummond said to the laird. "'Tis fair what the duke asks, considering . . . all things. And 'tis yer own flesh and blood ye'll be leaving it to. A grandson, Ballincraig. To carry on yer name. Ye have no sons, not by yer wife, after all."

"God's blood, Drummond! What kind of friend—or solicitor—are ye? He willna really bring these charges. It would cause a scandal, I make no doubt, and the Sassenach will do aught to avoid such," Ballincraig said derisively.

"Try me," Reginald said for the second time that day.

"The scandal would hurt ye too, Ballincraig," Drummond said quietly. "There are any number of fathers who've come to me aboot—"

"Enough!" Ballincraig thundered. "Ye forget, *all* of ye, that *I* am laird here! I've lived through scandal afore."

"'Tis more than scandal, this time, Ballincraig," MacLeod said ominously, rising for the first time.

"Ye, MacLeod!" He lurched from his seat and rounded on the magistrate, veins throbbing fiercely at his temples. "I'll have ye unseated for this! I'll—"

"I have many friends, Ballincraig," MacLeod said calmly. "I always kenned that someday ye'd cross the line. This time ye did."

The laird glanced at Drummond, who simply said, "Sign. He'll pay yer debts, after all."

Susanna's father cursed vilely under his breath, then sank back in his seat. "Well, get on with it, Sassenach.

436

I'll sign yer damned papers."

"Well, then, I'll be off," MacLeod said easily. "Thank ye fer the fine whisky, Ballincraig." he bade good day to Susanna and Drummond as well, but asked to speak to His Grace outside for a moment.

Reginald rose to follow him, taking Susanna with him. MacLeod thanked him profusely. "Ye've taken the wind from his sails, Yer Grace, and aboot time," he said.

But Reginald stopped him to return the thanks and bid the magistrate write periodically with any 'news.' They parted amicably, and Reginald and Susanna returned to the drawing room.

Their return had obviously interrupted another angry tirade, but the laird went silent at their entrance. A rather technical discussion of the settlement details followed; then Drummond finally rose, rather wearily. "I will have my solicitors contact you to draw up the final papers," Reginald said, and Drummond moments later took his leave.

The laird got to his feet, and Reginald and Susanna followed suit. She had kept silent the whole time; indeed, she had not wished to say a word to Mortimer. But to her father, surely she must try.

"Papa," she began, putting her hand out tentatively.

He drew himself up and regarded her with frigid, remote eyes. "Ye will have all this when I die," he said icily, "but while I live ye are not welcome here. Ye are not my daughter."

Susanna swayed and Reginald caught her about the waist. "And you, Ballincraig, are not welcome in England," Reginald countered menacingly. "You are no sort of a father." The two men glared at each other. Ballincraig looked away first.

Reginald led Scotty, shaking slightly, out of the drawing room.

MacFarlane met them in the entry lobby. "I kenned ye wouldna wish to bide here, so I had Cook pack ye a bit of luncheon. Cold meat and oatcakes and suchlike."

"Oh, MacFarlane, thank ye," she said brokenly, and Reginald watched as the butler wrapped her in his arms.

"Will ye write to me, lass? An' let me ken when the bairns come?"

Scotty nodded, her eyes welling up. "You write as well, MacFarlane," Reginald put in, "and keep us apprised of . . . things."

MacFarlane glanced down the corridor and back again. "Aye, that I will, Yer Grace. Ye take care of my wee lassie, ye ken?"

"I ken, MacFarlane," Reginald replied, smiling for the first time that day. "And thank you." Both men understood the thanks was as much for the past as for anything in the future. Reginald shook the butler's hand and then led Scotty out.

He sat next to her in the carriage. They did not speak until they had cleared the gates of Ballincraig. "Is there anyone here you wish to see before we leave, Scotty?" he asked softly.

"I should have liked to visit Aunt MacLaughlin. But not now. I wish . . . I wish to be gone from this place," she whispered. "I want to go home. Home to Devon. To our family."

"Oh, Scotty," he said unsteadily, and pulled her close into the curve of his shoulder. He held her tightly, as if he would never let her go. And finally the flood gates opened and she wept. Long, hard, bitter, cleansing tears.

Chapter 23

They had hoped to travel as far south and away from Ballincraig as possible that day. But it began raining again, harder and harder, and the coach moved slowly.

When Susanna had cried herself out, Reginald pressed some of MacFarlane's luncheon on her and afterwards she fell into a deep sleep. His arm was numb from holding her, but he would not for all the world have let her go. Now it was late afternoon, and they were just north of Glasgow.

Gently he shook her awake. "My love, it is pouring. We are near the Devil's Claw again, and I think we should stop."

She nodded sleepily. "That is fine, Reginald," she murmured, and clasping him about the waist, fell back asleep.

He was about to disentangle himself from her when she awoke again and sat up, pushing the hair from her eyes. She leaned back against the squabs and sighed heavily. It was a sigh of profound relief, and release. "I have been afraid for so long."

He brought her hand to his lips. "You need be afraid

no longer."

She closed her eyes. "Ye are right. I am no longer afraid."

Auld Murdoch came to greet them in the taproom, very happy to oblige them with accommodation. "I've a suite for ye this time, Yer Grace," he said.

Once they had settled in their rooms and refreshed themselves, they went down to dinner in the small private parlor. Auld Murdoch brought the barley soup, and in his wake came a spry elderly woman carrying a plate of what looked like scones and biscuits. Auld Murdoch introduced her as his sister, Mrs. Gowrie, "come doon from the Highlands for a good long visit." Reginald knew there was no love lost between the Highlanders and the English, and wondered what the woman's reaction would be when Murdoch introduced them as the duke and duchess of Milburne.

Her reaction was nothing like what he'd expected, however. For her eyes widened and her hand went to her ample bosom. Scotty inhaled sharply, and Reginald saw that she looked frozen in her seat. "Why, she canna be the duchess!" Mrs. Gowrie exclaimed. "This is Susanna Fergusson. I've kent her since she were a bairn."

"Elspeth," Susanna breathed, her expression one of a child being caught out in a prank.

Auld Murdoch looked rather taken aback, and Reginald suddenly decided Mrs. Gowrie was sent from Heaven. Very determinedly he took Scotty's hand from across the little table at which they sat. "The former Susanna Fergusson, Mrs. Gowrie. All grown up now,

440

as you see. And she is my wife, the duchess of Milburne."

Mrs. Gowrie turned to Scotty. "Is't true, lass? Have ye wed with a Sassenach?" She sounded incredulous but not at all unfriendly and suddenly Scotty smiled.

"Yes, Elspeth, 'tis true. I am indeed his wife." Reginald sent up a silent prayer of thanks to Heaven and released Scotty's hand as Mrs. Gowrie threw her arms about her.

"Well, an' a right handsome man ye've got, lass, even if he is a Sassenach," she declared, releasing Scotty and actually winking at Reginald. "Ye tak' care of her, Yer Grace. Bonniest wee bairn in all of Ballincraig, she were. 'Course, I havena been there nigh on ten years, since I married Angus Gowrie. How is yer father, lass? An' MacFarlane? Once upon time, I thought MacFarlane and I . . ." Her voice trailed off.

"MacFarlane is just fine, Elspeth. And . . . and . . ." Reginald finished for her. "And the laird goes on well, Mrs. Gowrie."

"Well, then, right glad I am to hear it. I willna be gettin' to visit there this year, more's the pity. Got to tak' care of Murdoch here and his plaguey rheumatism. Needs a wife, he does." Murdoch blushed, and Mrs. Gowrie went on in that vein for some time.

Mrs. Gowrie's prattle, and her offhand comment about not going to Ballincraig, seemed to relax Scotty. So that when the elderly couple finally took their leave, Reginald and Scotty enjoyed a most pleasant repast.

That night he shrugged out of his clothes and into his dressing gown then began pacing the floor. He could hear Scotty through the connecting door getting ready for bed.

At length her room grew silent. Reginald sat, he

paced, he threw himself on the bed. And finally he rose, sashed his dressing gown, and strode to the connecting door. Sometimes, as Martinez was fond of saying, it was necessary to put aside one's scruples.

At her response to his knock, he opened the door.

"I'm sorry to disturb you, Scotty." Tonight she wore a shimmering, peach satin nightdress with only the filmiest of coverings. A brace of candles burned at the bedside, clearly silhouetting her figure as she stood in the middle of the room. "'Tis the megrim, I fear. I suppose it's been building all day, but with one thing and another, I hardly took notice."

"Oh, Reginald. Come here," she said, rushing toward him, all concern. She took his hand and brought him to her bed and bade him lie down on the coverlet, his head at the side.

It was like that first time, and yet not like it at all. Her hands were just as magical, just as soothing. But he loved her now, and there were no conflicting emotions. There was only desire, hot, burning desire as she sat in a chair by the bed, his head nearly in her lap.

Her wonderful hands were on his neck now, and his shoulders. Her voice was like warm honey as she murmured softly to him. He would never tire of hearing that Scottish lilt in her sweet, musical voice. Her scent enveloped him.

"Scotty."

"Yes, Reginald."

"This, ah, isn't putting me to sleep."

"Oh," she said, and stilled her hands, raising herself up. "Shall we try something else then?" she asked ingenuously.

"Yes," he managed. "Why don't we?" He swiveled and put his hands to her sides, just under her breasts,

442

and he felt a tremor run through her.

"Scotty, do you recall when Auld Murdoch and Mrs. Gowrie came into the parlor?"

"Aye."

"We made a declaration, Scotty," he said softly.

"A . . . declaration?" He could see a pulse begin to beat at her throat. She put a hand to his chest to brace herself, then withdrew it. He put it back, resting her palm on his bare skin. Her hand burned him, making him want her unbearably.

"Yes, love," he rasped, and placing his hands on her shoulders, he drew her close. "Before two witnesses."

"Before two—" She stopped and her eyes widened. "Ye canna mean . . ."

"I said, 'She is my wife, the duchess of Milburne,' and you said—"

"Aye, I ken what I said." She straightened up. He let his hands slide down to her waist. "But can it really be true?"

"You did make the statement of your own free will, did you not?"

"Aye, but—"

"And you do want to be my wife, do you not?"

"Aye, but—"

"Well, then, my love, according to Scots law, we are legally wed." He drew her down so that she lay across his chest. Her heart beat wildly. His own heartbeat was none too steady. "Of course, we can do it up all right and tight in proper Sassenach style once we reach Devon. Mama will be in raptures planning the event, and the Reverend Mr. Honeyworth will feel most honored, I make no doubt."

"Reginald, I—"

"But none of that will change the fact that you are

443

already the duchess of Milburne. Even in England such a marriage is recognized."

He caressed her breasts for just a moment, then moved to her hips. The barrier of her nightdress was too great; he wanted to touch her bare skin. "Scotty, let me love you. Now. You are my wife, and I want you. You must know that I will be gentle."

"Och, Reginald. I love ye so. And I—I want ye, too," she said ever so softly. "B-But I am afraid of . . . of—"

"I know, love. But he cannot hurt you now. I will show you what loving really is. I will never hurt you, Scotty. I would give my life before I hurt you."

Slowly she lowered her head and brushed her lips to his. "Love me, then, Reginald," she whispered.

He grasped the nape of her neck and pressed her close, his mouth crushing hers. He kissed her, long and deeply, his tongue tasting and teasing and then, at her eager response, dancing with hers. He caressed her, felt her body take on the sweet languor of passion, until she lay stretched atop him, her entire body pressed into his.

He kissed her eyes, her throat, and again her mouth. Her eyes were smoky, almost black with passion. He felt the fires flare up within him as finally he lifted her gown and cupped that enticing derriere, naked at last under his hands. The skin was smooth, soft and rounded and perfect. He caressed her, gently and then harder. Suddenly she stiffened in alarm.

"Scotty," he rasped, amazed that he could speak at all, "did you know that this particular part of your anatomy was the very first part of you that I saw?" She looked puzzled, and he smiled. "You were under the sofa in the drawing room, trying, I believe, to retrieve Desdemona."

At that she let out a peal of laughter. Her hands were propped comfortably on his chest. "Goodness! What a way to meet one's employer! What must ye have thought?" Her eyes were dancing; the alarm was gone. Very gently, he began to caress her bare skin again.

"I thought, my love, that you had the most lovely bottom I'd ever seen, that you were like no governess I'd ever met, and that I couldn't wait to get my hands on you."

She laughed again. "In more ways than one, I own. Ye wanted to throttle me."

He chuckled. "Yes. But that was only to distract myself from the fact that I wanted to do . . . something quite different." His voice had grown husky; his hands slid up her sides, pushing the gown still higher.

"Oh," she said.

The levity was gone. The fire between them began to flare again. In one fluid motion Reginald rolled over, holding her gently, pinning her beneath him. "Scotty," he said huskily, "I am going to make love to you now. Do not be frightened, love."

She nodded slowly, and took his face in her hands. He bent to kiss her, and this time he knew he would not stop.

Susanna felt a strange, pulsing warmth building in her. He was kissing her, but this was different from his other kisses. He was touching her, caressing her breasts, her hips, and that, too, was different from the other times. There was a heat in his hands that was causing her skin to burn. There was an urgency in his kiss that she could not help but answer. She wrapped her arms about him and felt that pulsing warmth intensify, become hot ripples of pleasure, building,

taking her higher and higher to a place she did no
know.

She became aware suddenly that they were bot
naked and all she could think was how beautiful h
was, his powerful thighs pressed to hers, the golde
hairs of his broad, masculine body glistening in th
candlelight. Her hands, of their own volition, began t
explore the contours of his back. It was hard an
muscular, so different from her own. He was strokin
her body to a feverish peak she did not understand
Now his mouth was at her breast. She heard someon
moan his name and realized it was she. She writhe
beneath him, feeling his need, that hot, pulsing mal
need she had only had hints of before. She pulled hin
closer, wanting to give him everything a woman coul
give a man.

Reginald felt her begin to shudder violently. Sh
cried out, and he knew he could wait no longer. H
held her face in his hands as he took her, pouring hi
need and his desire into her. Her eyes flashed open in
astonishment, perhaps pain, but there was no fear. H
stilled himself, murmuring soft words of love in her ear
until her eyes became smoky again. And then he began
to move and she clutched blindly at him. He took them
higher and higher, the blood pounding in his temples
until at last they plunged over the edge, smothering
their mutual cries in one last, desperate kiss.

When finally his breathing had calmed, and hers, he
rolled to the side and held her tightly against him as a
sweet heavy languor overtook them both. She is truly
my wife, he thought, at long last.

"Ye are my husband," she murmured, echoing his
thought. There was joy, and wonder, in her voice as he
pulled the blanket over them and they drifted together

into that most peaceful of sleeps.

Reginald awoke, to find himself wrapped about Scotty's sweet body. He remembered with delicious clarity the night before. He pulled her closer against him, his arm just under her soft breasts, his face nuzzled in her luxurious hair.

He was going to find it nigh impossible to take himself out of bed in the mornings. He knew that already. Clearly Martinez would no longer be able to come in with hot water and towels at daybreak. But then, perhaps Martinez would be otherwise occupied as well.

And that thought set him to wondering about how his ramshackle household had fared in their absence. Had Thomas and Timothy managed not to destroy any chandeliers? Had Sarah Beacham arrived? Had she and his mama, and perhaps Letty, contrived to comfort Phoebe? He supposed now he *would* have to take Phoebe to London for the Little Season, after all, but he decided that he did not mind so very much. Not when he'd have Scotty with him.

She sighed in her sleep and snuggled closer to him, and his body's response was a sweet kind of torture.

"Reginald?" Her voice was full of sleep, and love.

"Good morning, sweetheart." She turned in his arms, and her hands began to play idly, softly, with the hairs on his chest. "We had better get an early start and—"

"Oh, Reginald. I . . . I have never felt so right, never slept so deeply."

"Neither have I," he responded, his free hand beginning to stroke her.

447

She pillowed her head on his shoulder, not looking at him as she murmured, "Does yer, ah, head still hurt?"

He grinned, his chin resting on her head. "Well, sweetheart, let us just say that you have quite perfected the cure."

And then the new duchess of Milburne wrapped her arms about his neck and looked up at him with that special twinkle in her midnight blue eyes. "Nae, Reginald. 'Tisna quite perfect yet. I should like to work on some . . . refinements, ye ken?"

"Oh, I ken, Scotty, I ken," he replied.

And His Grace, the duke of Milburne, fairly shook with warm, loving laughter as his mouth came down over hers.